RETURN
to
EDEN

Harry Harrison

ILLUSTRATIONS BY
Bill Sanderson

*Book Three
in the* WEST OF EDEN *Trilogy*

BANTAM BOOKS
NEW YORK • TORONTO • LONDON • SYDNEY • AUCKLAND

RETURN TO EDEN

A Bantam Spectra Book
Bantam hardcover edition / August 1988
Bantam paperback edition / July 1989

Library of Congress Cataloging-in-Publication Data

Harrison, Harry.
  Return to Eden.

  (A Bantam spectra book)
  "Book three in the West of Eden trilogy."
  I. Title.
PS3558.A667R48 1988   813'.54   88-10436
ISBN 0-553-27700-6

Published simultaneously in the United States and Canada

Bantam Books are published by Bantam Books, a division of Bantam
Doubleday Dell Publishing Group, Inc. Its trademark, consisting of the
words "Bantam Books" and the portrayal of a rooster, is Registered in
U.S. Patent and Trademark Office and in other countries. Marca Registrada.
Bantam Books, 666 Fifth Avenue, New York, New York 10103.

PRINTED IN THE UNITED STATES OF AMERICA

O   0 9 8 7 6 5 4 3 2 1

CRITICAL ACCLAIM FOR HARRY HARRISON'S *WEST OF EDEN* SAGA

WEST OF EDEN

"An epic in the tradition of *The Clan of the Cave Bear* . . . great escape reading."
—*Playboy*

"An absorbing, poignant portrait . . . his best novel in years."
—*New York Daily News*

WINTER IN EDEN

"Don't wait for the paperback. This is one of the finest adventure stories of the year."
—*Science Fiction Chronicle*

"Exquisitely researched . . . a detailed exploration of an intriguing alternative."
—*San Francisco Examiner*

RETURN TO EDEN

"The concepts are original, imaginative, worked out in intricate detail, and the storytelling is superb."
—*The Denver Post*

"Harry Harrison has retained more vigor and vision than most of his contemporaries. . . . The *Eden* series is handsomely produced and altogether enjoyable."
—*The Washington Post Book World*

CONTENTS

PROLOGUE

ix

RETURN TO EDEN

1

THE WORLD WEST OF EDEN

345

GENDASI

PAUKARUTS

SASKU

ALPÈASAK · DEIFOBEN

ALAKAS-AKRENENT

MANINLÈ

AMBALLASOK

TESKETS

ULARUAQ

IKHALMENETS

ENTOBAN

DYEBÉISK

This is a story of the world today.

This is our world as it would be if a meteor had not struck the Earth 65 million years ago.

The world at that time was populated by the great reptiles. They were the most successful life form that the Earth had ever seen. For over 140 million years they had ruled the land, filled the sky, swarmed in the seas. Scuttling beneath their feet were the mammals. These mammals were the ancestors of mankind. Tiny, shrew-like animals that were preyed on by the larger, faster, more intelligent saurians.

Then, 65 million years ago, this all changed. A meteor six miles in diameter struck the Earth and caused disastrous atmospheric upheavals. Within a brief span of time over seventy-five percent of the species then existent were wiped out. The age of the dinosaurs was over; the evolution of the mammals that they had suppressed for 100 million years began. The world as we know it was born.

But what would our world be like today if that meteor had not fallen?

This is the story of that world.

Today.

PROLOGUE: KERRICK

Life is no longer easy. Too much has changed, too many
are dead, the winters are too long. It was not always this
way. I remember clearly the encampment where I grew
up, remember the three families there, the long days,
friends, good food. During the warm seasons we stayed on
the shore of a great lake filled with fish. My first memories
are of that lake, looking across its still water at the high
mountains beyond, seeing their peaks grow white with the
first snows of winter. When the snow whitened our tents
and the grass around as well, that would be the time when
the hunters went to the mountains. I was in a hurry to
grow up, eager to hunt the deer, and the greatdeer, at the
hunters' side.

That simple world of simple pleasures is gone forever.
Everything has changed, and it must be said, not for the
better. At times I wake up at night and wish that what
happened had never happened. But these are foolish
thoughts and the world is as it is, changed now in every
way. What I thought was the entirety of existence has
proved to be only a tiny corner of reality. My lake and my
mountains are only the smallest part of this great continent that borders an immense ocean to the east.

I also know about the others, the creatures we call
murgu, and I learned to hate them even before I saw
them. I will tell you about them.

As our flesh is warm, theirs is chill. When you look at
us you see that we have hair upon our heads. A hunter
will grow a proud beard, while the animals that we hunt
have warm flesh and fur or hair. But this is not true of the
murgu. They are cold and smooth and scaled, have claws
and teeth to rend and tear, are large and terrible, to be
feared. And hated. When I was very young I learned

about them, knew that they lived in the warm waters of the ocean to the south and on the warm lands to the south. They cannot abide the cold so although I grew up fearing them I also knew they could not trouble us.

All that has changed so terribly that nothing will be the same ever again. That is because there are murgu called Yilanè who are intelligent, just as we Tanu are intelligent. It has become my frightening knowledge that our world is only a tiny part of the Yilanè world. I know now that we live in the far northern part of a great continent. Know as well that to the south of us, over all the land, swarm only murgu and Yilanè.

And there is even worse. Across the ocean an even larger continent exists—and in this distant land are no hunters at all. None. Yilanè, only Yilanè. The entire world is theirs except for our small part.

Now I will tell you the worst thing about the Yilanè. They hate us as we hate them. This would not matter if they were only great, insensate beasts. We would stay in the cold north and avoid them in this manner.

But there are those among them who may be as intelligent as hunters, as fierce as hunters. And although their number cannot be counted it would be truthful to say that they fill all of the lands of this great world.

I know these things because I was captured by the Yilanè, grew up among them, learned from them. The first horror I felt when my father and all the others were killed has been dimmed by the years. When I learned to speak as the Yilanè do I became as one of them, forgot that I was a hunter, even learned to call my people ustuzou, creatures of filth. Because all order and rule among the Yilanè comes down from the top I thought very well of myself. Since I was close to Vaintè, the eistaa of the city, its ruler, I was looked upon as a ruler myself.

The living city of Alpèasak was newly grown on these shores, settled by Yilanè from across the ocean. They had been driven from their own distant city by the winters that grow colder every year. The same cold that had driven my father and the other Tanu south in the search for food sent the Yilanè questing across the sea. They came here and they grew their city on our shores. When they found the Tanu who were here before them they killed them. Just as the Tanu killed Yilanè on sight. It is a shared hatred.

For many years I had no knowledge of this. I grew up among the Yilanè and I thought as they did. When they made war I looked upon the enemy as filthy ustuzou, not Tanu, my brothers. This changed only when I met the prisoner, Herilak. A sammadar, a leader of the Tanu, who understood me far better than I understood myself. When I spoke to him as enemy, alien, he spoke to me as flesh of his flesh. As the language of my childhood returned so did my memories of that warm earlier life. Memories of my mother, family, friends. There are no families among the Yilanè, no suckling babies among egg-laying lizards, no possible friendships where these cold females rule, where the males are locked away from the sight of all the others for their entire lifetime.

Herilak showed me that I was Tanu, not Yilanè. Because of this I freed him and we fled. At first I regretted it—but there was no going back. For in escaping I had attacked and almost killed Vaintè, she who rules. I joined the sammads, the family groups of the Tanu, joined them in flight from the onslaught of those who had once been my companions. But I had other companions now, and friendship of a kind I could never know among the Yilanè. I had Armun, she who came to me and showed me that which I had never even known, awoke the feelings I could never have felt while I was living among that alien race. Armun who bore our son.

But we still led our lives under the constant threat of death. Vaintè and her warriors followed the sammads without mercy. We fought back—and sometimes won, even capturing some of their living weapons, the death-sticks that kill creatures of any size. With these we could penetrate far to the south, eating well of the teeming murgu, killing the vicious ones when they attacked. Only to flee again when Vaintè and her endless supply of killers from across the sea found us and fought to kill us.

This time the survivors went where we could not be followed, across the frozen mountain ranges to the land beyond. Yilanè cannot live in the snows; we thought we would be safe.

And we were, for a long time we were. Beyond the mountains we found Tanu who did not live by hunting alone, but who grew crops in their hidden valley and could make pots, weave cloth and do many other wondrous things. They are the Sasku and they are our friends, for they worship the god of the mastodon. We brought our mastodons to them and we have been as one people ever since. Life was good in the Sasku valley.

Until Vaintè found us once again.

When this happened I realized that we could run no more. Like cornered animals we must turn and fight. At first none would listen to me for they did not know the enemy as I did. But they came to understand that the Yilanè had no knowledge of fire. They would learn of it when we brought the torch to their city.

And this is what we did. Burnt their city of Alpèasak and sent the few survivors fleeing back to their own world and to their own cities across the sea. Among those who lived was Enge who had been my teacher and my friend. She did not believe in killing as all the others did, and was the leader of a group who called themselves the Daughters of Life, believers in the sanctity of life. Would that they had been the only survivors.

But Vaintè lived as well. This creature of hatred survived the destruction of her city, fled on the uruketo, the great living vessel of the Yilanè, vanished into the trackless ocean.

I put her from my mind because of more urgent matters. Although all the murgu in the city were dead, most of the burned city had survived. The Sasku wished to stay with me in the city, but the Tanu hunters returned to their sammads. I could not go back with them for the part of me that thinks like a Yilanè kept me in this Yilanè city.

That and the fact that two of their males had survived the destruction. I was drawn to this half-ruined city, and to them, and forgot my responsibility to Armun and my son. It must be truthfully said that this selfishness nearly led to their destruction.

We labored to make this murgu city one in which we could live, and we succeeded. But in vain. Vaintè had found new allies across the ocean and returned once again. Armed with the invincible Yilanè science. No attacks with weapons this time, but poison plants and animals instead. And even as the attacks began the sammads returned from the north. Their death-sticks had died in the winter and they could not survive without them. Here in the city we had these deadly creatures, so here the sammads must remain despite the slow approach of Yilanè destruction.

The sammads brought me even crueler news. Since I had not returned to her, Armun had tried to return to me. She and our son were lost in the deadly winter.

I would have ended my life then were it not for one tiny spark of hope. A hunter who traded far to the north, with the Paramutan who live in that frozen wasteland, had heard that a Tanu woman and child had been seen among them. Could it be them? Could they still be alive? The fate of the city and the Tanu and Sasku living in it meant nothing to me now. I had to go north and search for them. Ortnar, my friend and strong right arm, understood this and went with me.

Instead of Armun we almost found death. Had the Paramutan not discovered us it would have ended there. We survived, although Ortnar is still crippled by his frozen feet. The hunters of the ice saved us, and to my great joy Armun was with them. Then, in the spring, they brought us safely back to the city in the south.

Which was Yilanè once again. The sammads and the Sasku had retreated to the distant Sasku valley and were being followed closely by Vaintè and her forces, dark portents of certain death. And I could do nothing. My little sammad and the two Yilanè males were safe enough for the moment at our hidden lake. But the others would die and I could not save them.

It would be difficult enough to save ourselves for it was a certainty that one day our hiding place would be found. I knew that the Paramutan who had brought us here would soon be crossing the ocean to hunt upon the far shore. Perhaps there might be safety there. Armun and I joined them and crossed the sea—only to discover that the Yilanè were there ahead of us. But from death came life. We destroyed them, and in doing so I discovered where Ikhalmenets was, the city on the island which was aiding Vaintè in her war of destruction.

What I did was either very brave or very foolhardy. Perhaps both. I forced the eistaa of Ikhalmenets to stop the attack, to stop Vaintè at the very brink of her victory. In this I succeeded and the world is again at peace. My sammad is once more joined and complete at our hidden lake. The battle is ended.

Yet there were other things that had happened that I did not discover for a long, long time. Enge, my teacher and my friend, was still alive. She and her followers, the Daughters of Life, had found refuge in a new land far to the south. They had grown a city there far from the other Yilanè who wished to see their destruction. Another place of peace, another end to strife.

But there was yet another thing that I did not know. That creature of hatred and death, Vaintè, was still alive.

That is what has happened in the past. Now I stand by our hidden lake squinting into the sunset, trying to see what will happen in the years to come.

Uveigil as lok at mennet, homennet
thorpar ey wat marta ok etin.

MARBAK PROVERB

No matter how clear the river,
there is always some darkness
upstream drifting down towards you.

ONE

There was silence and peace.

It had been a hot day, for the days were always warm here. But the evening air was a little cooler with the light breeze blowing over the water. Kerrick squinted into the sun, wiped some of the perspiration from his face. It was easy to forget the slow changing of the seasons of the year this far to the south. The sun, as always, was setting behind the lake, the last glint of it shining on the unruffled waters, with the red sky reflected there as well. A fish stirred the surface and waves of color moved out in all directions. This was the way it always was, unchanging. Sometimes there would be clouds, or rain, but no really cold weather, no slow cycle of seasons. The rain and fog were an indication of winter. Then the air was cooler at night' as well. But there was never the fresh green of spring grass, the russet of leaves in the autumn.

Never the deep snow of winter; there were some things that Kerrick did not miss at all. In damp weather his fingers still ached where they had been frozen. Far better the heat than the snow. He squinted at the vanishing sun, a tall, erect man. His long, pale hair reached to his shoulders, was bound about his forehead by a thin band of leather. In recent years wrinkles had formed at the corners of his eyes; there were pale scars of old wounds on his tanned skin as well. He turned to look as the water moved in larger waves as something dark broke the surface just offshore. There was a familiar rumbling snort that Kerrick recognized. Schools of hardalt came close to the surface at dusk and Imehei had grown adept at netting them in the failing light. He came ashore now, puffing and blowing, with a netful of the creatures. Red reflections glinted on their shells, their tentacles trailed down his back. He dropped them before the shelter where the two Yilanè males slept and called out attention to speaking, firm authority in his voice. Nadaske emerged and expressed sounds of approval as they opened the net. There was peace in sammad Kerrick—but still peace at a distance. The Yilanè stayed on their side of the grass clearing, the Tanu on theirs. Only Kerrick and Arnwheet were at home in both.

Kerrick frowned at the thought and rubbed his fingers through his beard, ran them along the metal ring about his neck. He knew that Armun was not pleased that Arnwheet visited the Yilanè. To her the males were just murgu, creatures that would be better off dead and forgotten rather than waddling about, repulsive companions to their son. But she was wise enough not to speak of it. On the surface at least there was peace in the sammad. Now she emerged from the tent that was sheltered under the trees, saw Kerrick sitting there, came and joined him at the water's edge.

"You must stay under the leaves, not out here in the open," she said. "Are you not the one who tells us always to remember the bird who watches by day, the owl by night?"

"I said that. But I think we are safe from them now. It has been two years since I first came here with Ortnar and those two on the shore there. We have not been disturbed in all that time. Lanefenuu ended the war as I told her to. She said she would do that so it was done. The murgu cannot lie. The attackers have returned to the city, have never left it since."

"But their hunting parties must still go out."

"We are far from them and remain watchful."

"There is still fear."

He rose and put his arms about her, sniffed the sweet smell of her long hair, held her close, but not too tightly because of the rounded swell of her body. "It would not be easy for you to travel now," he said. "After the baby is born I will scout to the north with Harl. He is old enough now to be a hunter and Ortnar has trained him well. He is no longer a child, this is his sixteenth summer. He has a good spear. We will search to the north. I know that there are more lakes there, that is what Ortnar says."

"I don't want to be left here. When you go I must go as well."

"That we will talk about when the time comes."

"It is already decided. I would like to go to another lake. And when we leave the two murgu will remain here?"

Kerrick did not answer but instead turned and with his arm still about her started back towards the tent. The baby was due now, was perhaps late, and he knew that she was in pain although she did not tell him. This was no time to discuss the Yilanè males. The sides of the tent were rolled up, it had been a very warm day, and he could see Arnwheet already asleep on the skins. Six years old now and growing fast, a strong and happy boy. The girl Darras was still awake, for she was much older, lying there and watching them in silence. She was still very quiet and only spoke when talked to. If she thought of her dead parents she never mentioned it. She was very much like a daughter to them now.

The night was so still that the murmur of voices from the hunters' tent could be clearly heard. One of them laughed and this pleased Kerrick. Ortnar, crippled as he was, still had a place here. As long as his skills could be taught to the two boys there was no more talk of walking into the forest and not returning.

A night bird called in the distance, the lonely sound emphasizing the silence. There was peace, food for them all, the family and the sammad. Kerrick wanted no more. He smiled into the darkness until Armun's whispered words disturbed him.

"I wish the baby would come. It has been a long time."

"Soon. Don't worry. Everything will be fine."

"No! You should not say that—it brings bad luck to speak well of things that have not happened yet. That is what my mother said. No matter how clear the water in the river is, there is always something dark upstream drifting down towards you."

"Rest now," he said, reaching out to find her mouth in the darkness, placing his finger gently against the cleft in her lip. She murmured something but was close to sleep and he could not make out what it was.

When Kerrick awoke it was to the grayness of a misty dawn. The haze would soon burn away under the searing touch of the summer sun. Armun sighed in her sleep when he gently took his arm from beneath her head. He stood and yawned and made his way from the tent as silently as he could. Arnwheet must have slipped out at first light for he was returning now from the direction of the lake, chewing on a rich lump of raw fish.

"Nadaske and Imehei go far around the lake today," he said. "To a place where fish live/grow/swarm richly."

He shook his hips with this, for he had no tail to express the modifier of expansiveness. As always when he had been with the males he spoke Yilanè to Kerrick. In the time his mother and father had been away, the best part of a year, he had grown proficient in speaking. Kerrick glanced back at the silent tent before he answered. They were careful to talk only in Marbak when Armun was present.

"A good exercise/walk for male/fat/Yilanè. But a young ustuzou hunts in the forest with me today."

"Yes, yes!" Arnwheet said, clapping his hands and falling into Marbak. "Harl too?"

"And Ortnar. They have found a tree where there is a

bansemnilla den and will need help driving them out. Go get your spear. Ortnar wants to leave while it is still cool."

Armun heard them speaking and emerged from the tent. "Will it be a long hunt?" she asked, worried, her hands unknowingly resting on her rounded midriff. He shook his head *no*.

"The den is very close by. I won't leave you alone until after the baby comes, not for longer than the smallest part of the day. Don't be afraid."

She shook her head and sat down heavily. "Return swiftly. Darras will be with me," she added as the silent girl joined them. "It might happen today."

"I don't have to go . . ."

"It won't happen that soon. There are no signs."

"Tonight we will eat bansemnilla. Baked in mud in the coals."

"I would like that very much."

Before they set out Kerrick walked along the lake to the vine-covered shelter that the males had grown at the water's edge. One of them emerged and Kerrick called his name in greeting.

"Imehei."

Kerrick smiled to himself as he realized the name meant soft-to-touch. Nothing could be less appropriate for this squat, grim Yilanè who now shaped his arms in respectful acknowledgment of welcome. His round eyes, both looking towards Kerrick, were empty of emotion. But his great jaw opened slightly in the gape of pleasure, to reveal a white row of conical teeth.

"Eat with us/join with us," Imehei said.

"I have already eaten, regretful thankfulness. Arnwheet tells me you explore the world today?"

"Little wet-from-the-sea sees our small journey as a great adventure/exploration. Along the lake shore is water of some depth/ springs of fresh water. Fish of great size abound. Desire to catch/ eat. Will small/soft go with us?"

"Not this time. Bansemnilla have been found in the forest and we mean to hunt them."

"Lack of knowledge of creature/name unknown."

"Small furry, long-tailed, pouched; good to eat."

"Pleasure of contemplation of a portion! We will bring back fine fish in exchange."

"May your nets be full, your hooks sink deep."

Nadaske emerged in time to hear this and signed pleased gratitude. Kerrick watched as they shouldered their rolled nets, secured their hèsotsan so that it rode high, then eased themselves into the water, to swim off easily along the reed-covered shore. They had come a long way from their protected existence in the hanalè of the city. They were now strong and secure individuals in their own right. A shrill ululation sounded behind him and he turned to see Arnwheet calling out and waving to him.

"We are here, Atta," he said.

Kerrick walked over and saw Ortnar standing in the shadows. As always the wooden crutch was tucked under his left arm, supporting his weight. The falling sickness had not killed him, but the strength had never truly returned to his left side. His leg dragged and his arm had just enough strength to hold to the wooden support. With its aid he could limp along, slowly but steadily. There must have been pain, though he never mentioned it, because sharp grooves were cut in the skin below his eyes; he never smiled. But the strength of his right arm had not been affected and the spear he held was as deadly as ever. He tipped it towards Kerrick now in silent greeting.

"Shall we have good hunting?" Kerrick asked.

"That—and good eating. There are many of them there, but one fat one that lives in the tree, that is the one we must try to get. I have watched it."

"Then show us the way."

The two boys had bows as well as spears, but Kerrick brought only his hèsotsan. The cool length of the living weapon stirred in his hands as he walked last in the column. The darts that it spat forth were instant death for any creature, no matter how large. Without this Yilanè weapon, death-stick the Tanu called it, life would have been impossible in the forest. Their spears and arrows could not kill the large murgu that roamed here. Only the

Yilanè poison could do that. They had only three of the
weapons now, one had died, drowned by accident. It was
irreplaceable. When the other three died—then what?
But they were not dead yet, it was too early to worry.
Kerrick shrugged off the dark thought. Better to think of
the hunt and the sweet flesh cooking in the fire.

They walked in silence along the forest track—even
more silently when Ortnar touched the spear shaft to his
lips. It was hot in the still air under the trees and they
were quickly drenched in perspiration. Ortnar pointed to
a large-boled tree, at the thick branches high above.

"There," he whispered, "you can see the opening of
the lair." A squat dark form scurried along the branch and
Arnwheet giggled with excitement until hushed by Ortnar's
sharp gesture.

But killing any of the animals was not that easy. They
sped along the branches and vanished among the leaves,
aided by their clutching claws and agile tails. Arrows were
fired, missed and retrieved. Ortnar had sharp words to say
about their accuracy. Kerrick stood aside, watching the
hunt when he could, but keeping more aware of the
surrounding forest and any dangers that might be hidden
there. In the end both boys had to climb the tree and
hammer on the trunk with their bows. When a dark form
scurried out along a branch Ortnar's deadly spear made
quick work of it. The impaled bansemnilla squealed
once as it fell into the shrubs below, to be retrieved by the
happily shouting boys. Kerrick admired the fatness of
the still form while Ortnar muttered about the excess noise.
In single file, the boys carrying the creature on a pole
between them, they returned to the camp by the lake.

As they emerged from the trees, Ortnar stabbed his
spear skywards in sharp warning. They stopped, frozen in
their tracks. Moving air rustled the leaves above their
heads and through this sound they heard a muffled cry.

"Armun!" Kerrick called out, brushing past Ortnar, running forward. She emerged from the tent, spear in one hand,
her free arm wrapped protectively about the sobbing girl.

"What happened?"

"That thing, the marag, it came here, screaming and twisting, attacked us, I used my spear. Made it leave."

"A marag? Where did it go?"

"Yours!" she shouted, anger pulling her face into a livid mask. "There by the shore. The things you allow to live close to us, that will kill us all . . ."

"Be silent. The males are no threat. Something is wrong. Stay here."

When Kerrick ran across the grass to the shore Nadaske emerged from hiding, his arms clasped about his body, stumbling and swaying. There was foam on his lips and the tip of his tongue protruded from between his teeth.

"What is wrong?" Kerrick called out, then took him by the thick, hard flesh of his arms and shook him when there was no answer. "Where is Imehei? Imehei. Tell me."

Kerrick felt the shudder pass through Nadaske's body when he heard the name. The nictitating membrane slid away as he rolled a reddened eye towards Kerrick.

"Dead, worse, not known/end of life . . ."

His words were muttered, the motion of his limbs hesitant and slow. His crest flamed red and twisted in agony. It was a long time before Kerrick could understand what had happened. Only then did he let the distraught Yilanè slip down to the grass, turn away and walk back to face the others.

"Imehei may be dead, he doesn't know for sure."

"They murder each other, then attack me!" Armun screamed. "Now kill that thing, finish it."

Kerrick fought to control his temper; he knew she had reason to feel like this. He handed his weapon to Harl and put his arms about her.

"It is nothing like that. He was trying to tell you something that is all, speak to you, trying to find me. They were on the other side of the lake, fishing, when they were attacked."

"Murgu?" Ortnar asked.

"Yes, murgu." Kerrick's voice was cold as death. "Their kind of murgu. Yilanè, females. Hunters."

"Then they have found us?"

"I don't know." He pushed Armun gently away from him, saw the fear still in her eyes. "He was just trying to talk to you. His friend is captured, perhaps dead. He fled, escaped, did not see what happened after that."

"Then we must find out what these others were doing at the lake, what they know about us," Ortnar said, shaking his spear in impotent rage. "Kill them." He dragged his foot towards the lake, stumbled and almost fell.

"Stay here and guard," Kerrick said. "I leave the sammad in your trust. I will go back with Nadaske and find out what has happened. We will be very careful. Remember, the hunters saw only their own kind, they can not know of our existence."

Unless Imehei is still alive, tells them about us, he thought to himself, keeping his fears silent. "We're leaving now." He hesitated a moment, then took a second hèsotsan. Ortnar watched grimly.

"The death-sticks are ours, we need them to survive."

"I will bring it back."

Nadaske sat slumped back on his tail in exhausted silence and only stirred slightly when Kerrick came close. "I lost all control," he said with sharp motions of self-deprecation. "Stupid as a fargi on the shore. I even dropped the hèsotsan, left it there. It was their voices, what they said as they seized Imehei. All intelligence fled. I fled. I should have stayed."

"You did the right thing. You came to me. Now you have a weapon. You won't drop it this time." He held out the hèsotsan and Nadaske took it without thinking. Seized it incorrectly, a thumb near the creature's mouth. He scarcely noticed when it chewed his flesh with its sharp teeth. Then he slowly drew his thumb away and looked at the drops of blood.

"Now I have a weapon," he said. Then heaved to his feet. "We have weapons, we will go."

"I cannot swim as you do."

"No need. There is a track along the shore. I came back that way." Resolutely he waddled forward and Kerrick stayed close behind him.

It was a long walk in the noon sun. They had to stop often while Nadaske slipped into the lake to cool; Kerrick seeking shade under a tree while he waited. The sun was halfway to the horizon before Nadaske signed alertness/silence, then pointed.

"Beyond those tall reeds, that is the place. Move/water/silence/unseen."

He led the way, knee-deep in the swamp, parting the reeds as they went forward, slowly and carefully so they would not be seen. Kerrick was close behind him, wading just as silently through the murky water. The reeds thinned and they went slower, looked out from the spare cover. Despite the need for silence a strained moan came from deep in Nadaske's throat.

It took Kerrick long moments to understand what was occurring. A Yilanè was sitting on her tail, her back turned to them and very close, a hèsotsan clasped in her hands. Carrying packs lay on the ground beside her, as well as two more weapons. Beyond her was a locked immobile group of Yilanè that she was staring at intently. There were two, no there were three of them, clutching to one another in strange embrace. Then Kerrick realized what was happening.

It was Imehei who was stretched out on his back on the ground. There was a female sitting on him, holding him down with outstretched, immobile arms. The other female was sitting on top of Imehei as well, locked in the same immobility. While they watched Imehei writhed slightly and moaned. The two females were as motionless as though carved of stone.

Unbidden the memory seared across Kerrick's eyes, obscuring the scene before him. Vaintè holding him that way when he was a boy, pressing him to the ground, forcing herself upon him. Pain and pleasure, something new then, terrible, strange.

No longer new. In Armun's arms he had found there could be warmth in this embrace, happiness. Forgetfulness.

But now at this entwined sight he remembered clearly what had happened to him and hatred overwhelmed all thought. He pushed forward through the reeds, splashing noisily through the shallow water. Nadaske cried a warning as the watching hunter heard him, stood and turned, raised her hèsotsan.

Fell forward as Kerrick's own weapon cracked out a dart of death. He stepped over the body, heard Nadaske running after him, strode towards the fierce, silent coupling.

The females did not stir, seemed unaware. Not so Imehei. He gasped beneath their joined weight, writhed, rolled pained eyes towards Kerrick. Tried to speak but could not.

It was Nadaske who killed them. Fired and fired again then ran forward to push at the collapsing bodies. They fell, hitting the ground heavily, already dead.

As they fell their muscles relaxed in death, releasing Imehei. One, then the other of his organs withdrew, and his sac closed. But he was too exhausted to move. Kerrick had no idea what to do next.

Nadaske did. Death by silent dart was too simple a fate for these two. They could not feel his attack now, but he could, could release his hatred upon them. He fell on the first one, worried her throat with his teeth until he tore it open, did the same to the other. Blood flowed and spattered. Only when this had been done did Nadaske stumble to the lake and push his head under the surface and wash himself clean in the clear water.

When he returned Imehei was sitting up wearily, unspeaking. Nadaske sat down slowly next to him, supported his weight, also in silence.

Something terrible had taken place.

efenenot okolsetankènin anatirènè
efeneleiaa teseset.

UGUNENAPSA'S FIRST
PRINCIPLE

_We live between the thumbs of
Efeneleiaa, the Spirit of Life._

TWO

"Good foot. Fine foot. New foot," Ambalasei said slowly, her open palms moving with color, speaking the simple Sorogetso language.

Ichikchee lay before her on the thick grass, shivering, her eyes wide with fear-of-unknown. She looked down at her foot, then quickly away. The pink skin that covered it was so different from the green skin of her leg above. This troubled her very much. In an attempt to comfort her, Ambalasei reached down and lightly touched her ankle, but she only shivered the more.

"They are simple creatures," Ambalasei said, signing her assistant Setèssei to her side. "As simple as their language. Give her something to eat, that always has a calming effect. Good, see she eats and registers pleasure. We leave now—follow me."

Ambalasei had become a familiar sight to the Sorogetso, by design and not by accident of course. She had the patience of the true scientist so did not hurry her contact with these wild creatures. They had always been hesitant in the presence of the larger Yilanè, so she was careful not to rush forward to issue orders or question them. Enge had done her work well in learning their language and had taught Ambalasei, who had become a fluent speaker, her vocabulary much larger than Enge's since Enge was so occupied with the city. Now, when the Sorogetso were unwell or injured, they looked to Ambalasei for help. She was always there, asking them only about their symptoms, with perhaps a few other small questions that seemed relevant. Her knowledge grew.

"They are completely lacking in fact/knowledge, Setèssei —look on and be amazed. You might be peering back through time at our own ancestors, as they existed soon after the egg of time cracked open. Poisonous spiders thrust forward as a defense, as we used crabs, lobsters. And there, see how they have assembled bundles of reeds? Wrapped and tied they have excellent insulating properties, not to mention being a haven for insects. With what care they assemble these into walls of small structures, spread them above to keep out the rain. We are so accustomed to having our sleeping chambers grown to order that we forget that we once lived just as they do."

"Preference of city comforts: dislike of sleeping on bare ground."

"Naturally. But forget comfort and think as a scientist. Watch, consider—and learn. They have no water-fruit so again artifice comes to their aid. Hollowed-out gourds to hold water from the river. And something of even greater relevance which I discovered on my previous visit, when I came alone."

"Apologies amplified for absence at that time—importance of fungal procedures needed for plant infection."

"Apologies unneeded: I ordered those procedures. Now through here . . ."

"Back, back, don't come here!" Easassiwi shouted at them, springing forward from his hiding place in the brush, his palms flaming red. Setèssei stopped, stepped back. Ambalasei stopped as well, but reacted sternly.

"You are Easassiwi. I am Ambalasei. We talk little."

"Back!"

"Why should I? Give reason? Easassiwi is strong/male not afraid of weak/female."

Easassiwi signed negative, looking warily at Ambalasei. He still made a face of rejection but the color faded from his palms.

"Here is good food," Ambalasei said, waving Setèssei to her side with the container. "Eat it. Ambalasei has plenty food. You think I take your food? That food in hole there."

Easassiwi hesitated, then accepted the gift, muttered to himself as he chewed on the piece of eel, watching the strangers closely all the while. He expressed relief when Ambalasei turned and moved away. He signed a protest but did not move aggressively when Ambalasei reached up and pulled an orange-colored fruit from the tree that arched over his head.

When they were out of sight Ambalasei stopped and handed it to her assistant. "Do you know this fruit?"

Setèssei looked at it, then broke it open and bit a mouthful from the pulp inside. Spat it out and signed positive knowledge. "It is the same as the one you gave me to test."

"It is. And what did you find?"

"Glucose, sucrose . . ."

"Yes, of course," Ambalasei snapped. "To be expected in a fruit. But what did you find that you did not expect?"

"A simple enzyme very close to collagenase."

"Good. And what does this lead you to conclude?"

"Nothing. I simply did the analysis."

"Asleep in daylight/brain ossified to stone! Am I the only one in this world who possesses rational processes of thought? If I tell you that I found meat in that hole in the ground beneath that tree, the freshly killed carcass of an alligator, what would you think then?"

Setèssei stopped and gaped, accepted the momentous thought. "But, great Ambalasei, this is a discovery of impossible magnitude. The connecting tissue in the meat would be dissolved by the enzyme, the tough meat rendered edible. Just as we do in our enzyme vats. This is, could be, we are watching . . ."

"Exactly. The first step up from brutish manipulation of mechanical artifacts, the beginnings of control of chemical and biological processes. The first step on the path that will lead to true Yilanè science. Do you understand now why I ordered that the Sorogetso be barred from the city and be allowed to remain in their normal state?"

"Understanding achieved—with great appreciation. Your studies here knowledge/expanding value/incredible."

"Of course. At least you have some little comprehension of my great work." Ambalasei, who had been sitting, comfortably slumped back on her tail, straightened up now, groaning as she did.

"Intellectual pleasures marred by age of body/dampness eternal." She clashed her jaws angrily and signed Setèssei to her. Her assistant held out the carrying creature with both hands. Muttering to herself, Ambalasei dug through the contents of the container. Anticipating her wants, Setèssei reached in as well and extracted the tiny basket.

"Killer of pain," she said.

Ambalasei snatched it from her angrily—were her needs this obvious?—opened it and took out the tiny snake, holding it by the tail. It writhed unhappily as she seized it behind the head by her thumbs, forcing the jaws open, then pierced her skin over a vein with its single fang. The modified toxin brought instant relief. She slumped back comfortably on her tail and sighed.

"Ambalasei has not eaten this day," Setèssei said, restoring the snake to its basket and digging deeper into the container. "There is preserved eel here, still cool from the vats."

Ambalasei stared grumpily into the distance but allowed one eye to look down at the jellied flesh as her assistant unwrapped it. It was true, she had not eaten this day. She chewed slowly and let the juice trickle down her throat; reached for a second piece. "How does the city grow?" she asked, some of the modifiers muffled by her full mouth. From long experience Setèssei understood the old scientist well enough.

"Fertilizer is needed for the inland water-fruit groves. Nothing more, all else grows well."

"And the inhabitants of this city, do they also grow well?"

Setèssei moved in a quick indication of ambiguity as she sealed the container and straightened up. "Pleasure in knowledge continual in the service of Ambalasei. To see a city grow, to discover this new species of Yilanè, is pleasure overriding labors. To live among the Daughters of Life is labor overriding pleasure."

"Excellent observation: more eel. Then you are not tempted to join them in their heady philosophizing, to become a Daughter yourself?"

"I grow in strength and pleasure in your service; I need serve no other."

"Yet if the eistaa were to order you to die—would you not die?"

"Which eistaa? We have dwelt in many cities. Your service is my city, therefore you are my eistaa."

"If I am—then you live forever for I order no one's death. Though with these Daughters . . . I am sorely tempted. Now, amplify earlier statement. Groves in need of fertilization, qualifier of incompleteness termination. The Daughters?"

"Ambalasei knows all, sees through solid stone. Twice aid has been requested, twice postponed."

"Not a third time," Ambalasei said with modifiers of destiny-certain. She struggled to a standing position and when she arched her body the bones in her spine crackled. "Slackness grows, work diminishes."

They walked back along the trail through the grove, aware of hidden Sorogetso eyes upon them. A figure moved halfseen along the track ahead of them, and when they came to the floating tree it had already been pushed into position by Ichikchee. She lowered her eyes and turned away when Ambalasei raised a green-to-red palm to sign her appreciation.

"She shows gratitude," Ambalasei said. "Labor given in return for service. They are simple creatures, yet complex in many ways. They will bear more study."

She led the way across the floating tree to the far bank, then pointed at the stream they had just crossed.

"Eel," she ordered and held out her hand. "Have you wondered, Setèssei, why we cross on this tree to their island instead of walking through these shallow waters?"

"I am without curiosity in these matters."

"I am curious in all matters, therefore cognizant of everything. I have applied my great intelligence and have solved this minor mystery."

She dropped the piece of meat into the stream and the waters roiled and seethed with movement.

"Tiny carnivorous fish in great numbers. A living barrier. This new continent abounds in wonders. I go to the ambesed for the afternoon warmth. Send Enge to me there."

Setèssei went ahead of her carrying the container, her head bobbing as she walked. Ambalasei saw that her crest was gray and ragged at the edge. So quickly? She remembered quite clearly the young fargi struggling to be Yilanè, listening and remembering, eventually to become an invaluable assistant. All those years of patient work while Ambalasei probed the secrets of the world. To end up here in this newgrown city with its fractious inhabitants. Perhaps it was time to leave; certainly it was time to make careful records of all that had been discovered. Yilanè of science, still unborn, would gasp in awe at the scope of knowledge revealed. Scientists alive this day might turn black in the face and die of envy. A pleasant thought.

The root of the sunwarmed tree was genial against Ambalasei's back, the sun even warmer along the length of her rib cage. Her eyes were shut, her jaw opened wide in the heat that soaked into her aching muscles. The search for knowledge was endless and pleasurable, but very tiring. Her thoughts were broken by the sounds of attention to presence. She opened one eye, slitted it against the light.

"It is you, Enge."

"It is spoken that you wished my presence."

"I am displeased. Something must be done. Your Daughters of Drudgery drudge even less every day. You know of this?"

"I do. It is my fault. Caused by my inability to find the correct solution to our problem. I labor but despair at attaining the needed grasp of knowledge of Ugunenapsa's principles. I know the answer to our difficulties is there before my eyes—but I do not have the vision to see it."

"You confuse theory with reality. One of them exists, the other might."

"Not for us, great Ambalasei, you of all people know that." Enge's eyes glowed with proselytizing fervor as she settled back comfortably on her tail; Ambalasei sighed. "The truth of Ugunenapsa's words is proven. When an eistaa orders one of her Yilanè to die—she dies. We do not."

"Easily explained. My researches on the subject are complete. You live because your hypothalamus is not triggered, nothing more."

"Absence of knowledge, desire for instruction."

"I just wish the rest of your Daughters of Dissipation were desirous of instruction as well. Listen then and remember. Just as we progress from egg to ocean, fargi to Yilanè, so has our species progressed from ancient to modern form. We know from our teeth that we were once eaters of shellfish for that is the function they are shaped for. Before we had cities, before we had assured food supplies and defenses against inclemencies of existence, hibernation played an important part in our survival."

"Humility at even greater ignorance. This hibernation, did we eat it?"

Ambalasei clacked her jaws together angrily. "Closer attention to speaking. Hibernation is a torpid state of the body, between sleep and death, where all of the vital functions slow down greatly. It is a hormonal reaction caused by prolactin. This normally regulates our metabolism and sexual behavior. But too much prolactin over-

loads the hypothalamus and causes an unbalanced physiological state that ends in death. This is a survival factor."

"Survival—that ends in death?"

"Yes. Death of an individual that aids survival of the
group. Another form of the altruistic gene that appears so
counterproductive for the individual, yet very positive for
the species. If the eistaa rules, the social order survives.
Errant individuals die when so ordered. Essentially they
kill themselves. They believe that they will die—so they
do. The terrified reaction to the imminence of death re-
leases the prolactin. The individual dies. A self-fulfilling
prediction."

Enge was horrified. "Wise Ambalasei—are you saying
that Ugunenapsa's great work is nothing more than the
ability to control a physiological reaction?"

"You said it—I didn't," Ambalasei responded with
great satisfaction. Enge was silent a long time, rigid with
deep thought. Then she stirred and made an approving-
appreciation gesture.

"Your wisdom is infinite, Ambalasei. You state a physical truth that makes me doubt, forces me to consider the
truths that I know, to find the answer that reinforces these
truths. It is there, the answer, clearly stated and only
waiting for interpretation. All of Ugunenapsa's wisdom is
stated in her Eight Principles."

"Spare me! Must I be threatened with all of them?"

"No threat, just revelation. Just one of them embodies
them all. The first and most important. This was Ugunenapsa's
greatest discovery and from it all the others flow. She said
it was her most significant insight. It came as a revelation,
something long hidden and suddenly revealed, a truth
once seen never forgotten. It is this—we live between the
thumbs of Efeneleiaa, the Spirit of Life."

"My mind grows numb! What nonsense are you
speaking?"

"Truth. When we recognize the existence of Efeneleiaa
we accept life and reject death. The eistaa does not control
us then since we are a part of Efeneleiaa as Efeneleiaa is a
part of us."

"Enough!" Ambalasei roared. "Abandon heady theorizing for more pedestrian activities. Each day your Daughters work less and less and the city suffers for it. What do you intend to do about this?"

"I intend to explore deeply in Ugunenapsa's Eight Principles, because you, great Ambalasei, have shown me that the answers to our problems lie there."

"Do they? I hope so. But you had better explore quickly, as well as deeply, because even my well-known patience has its limitations. Without me this city dies. And I grow weary of your endless differences. Solve them."

"We shall. Give us but a bit more of that patience for which you are so well known."

Ambalasei closed her eyes as Enge finished speaking, did not see the motions of the modifiers that indicated what was well known about her patience. Enge moved slowly away, seeking the solitude she needed to explore the insight revealed to her. Yet when she reached the shadow-dappled walkway under the trees she was confronted by she whom she wished least to see at this moment. But that was an ungracious thought and a selfish one. If this daughter was disputatious it was only because she was a seeker after truth.

"I greet you, Far<, and ask why you express desire to speak in my presence?"

Far< had become even thinner of late; her ribs projected in rounded rows. She ate little, thought much. Now she wound her thumbs together in a knot of suppressed emotion. She had difficulty in expressing herself and her large eyes grew even larger with the effort.

"I struggle . . . with your words, and my thoughts, and Ugunenapsa's teaching. And I find them in conflict. I seek guidance, instruction."

"And you shall have it. What disturbs you?"

"It is your orders for us to obey Ambalasei as though she were our eistaa. Now we do this, although we have rejected the rule of the eistaa when we accepted Ugunenapsa's principles."

"You forget we agreed to do this only until the city

was grown and complete. Because without a city we cannot exist and any other action would be against life."

"Yes—but look, the city is grown. It appears to be complete, and if this is so then the time of servitude is at an end. I, and many whom I have talked to, feel that we cannot proceed in this manner . . ."

Enge's raised palms stopped her; a command that demanded instant obedience. "Do not speak of this now. Soon, very very soon, I will reveal to you all of what has been revealed to me today. The secret to our continued existence is there in Ugunenapsa's Eight Principles. If we look carefully it will be found."

"I have looked, Enge, and have not found it."

Was there a slight modifier of rejection, even contempt, in her speech? Enge decided to ignore it. This was no time for a confrontation.

"You will work for the city, under Ambalasei's instruction, as will I and every one of our sisters. Our problems will be resolved, very very soon. You may go."

Enge looked at the thin, receding back, and not for the first time felt the burden of her beliefs and realized the freedoms of an eistaa. Who would have ended this problem simply by ordering the death of this one.

Still very much alive Far< walked away under the trees.

Also under the trees, on the distant shores of Entoban∗ across the sea, Vaintè walked at a plodding pace. Stopping often, her tracks in the mud wandering as haphazardly as her thoughts.

Sometimes, when she first awoke, she saw clearly what was happening to her. Abandoned, rejected, lost here on this inhospitable shore. At first her anger had sustained her and she had hurled threats after her betrayer, Lanefenuu, secure aboard the uruketo that was vanishing out to sea. Lanefenuu had done this to her and hatred of that eistaa possessed her. She had screamed her anger until her throat hurt and her limbs grew weary and foam flecked her jaws.

But this had accomplished nothing. If there had been

dangerous animals here she would have been killed and
devoured during this time of her madness. But there were
none. Beyond the strip of muddy beach there were shallow
rotting swamps, quicksand and decay. Birds flew among
the trees, a few creatures crawled in the mud, nothing
had value. That first day her violence had made her
thirsty and she had drunk from the scummed waters of
the swamp. Something in the water had made her ill and
retchingly weak. Later she had discovered where a
spring of fresh water bubbled up among the trees, ran
down the mud flats into the sea; now she drank only
there.

Nor had she eaten at first. Lying motionless in the
sun she had not needed to eat, not for many days. Only
when she had fallen down from weakness had she realized the stupidity of this. She might die—but she would
not die this way. Some spark of the anger that had
possessed her at her desertion and betrayal drove her
into the sea. There were fish there, not easy to catch,
the skills that had once enabled her to do this long
forgotten. But she caught enough to keep alive. Shellfish
in the muddy inlets were easier to find and soon formed
the main part of her diet.

Many, many days passed in this manner and Vaintè
felt no need for any change. Very rarely now, when she
awoke at dawn, she would look down in puzzlement at
her muddy legs, her stained skin bare of any decoration,
then out at the empty sea and sky. And wonder briefly at
her circumstance. Was this the totality of existence? What
was happening to her? These flitting moments of concern
never lasted long. The sun shone warmly and the numbness
in her skull was far better than the screaming agonies she
had felt when first she came here.

There was water to drink, always something to eat
when she grew hungry, nothing to disturb her in this place.
Nor were there any of the dark thoughts that had so
obsessed her when she had been abandoned on this inhospitable shore.

No thoughts at all. She dragged one foot slowly after another along the shore and her path in the mud was twisted and scuffed. The marks of her passage soon filled with stagnant water.

Bruka assi stakkiz tina faralda—
den ey gestarmal faralda markiz.

TANU PROVERB

---

*Enjoy this summer of your life—for
life's winter always follows.*

THREE

Nadaske stood waist deep in the lake, splashing water on his body, scrubbing away the blood that streaked his skin. Bending to plunge his head under the surface to suck water in and out of his mouth. When he had spat out the last of the blood and flesh and cleansed himself completely, he waded ashore and pointed all four thumbs at Imehei who sat in slumped despair. It was a gesture of darkness, of loss of hope.

"What do you mean?" Kerrick asked, stunned by the terrible events he had just witnessed.

Nadaske writhed but did not speak. Nor did Imehei, not for a long while. Then he stirred and rubbed at the bruises on his arms and thighs, finally climbed slowly to his feet and turned wide and vacant eyes to Nadaske.

"How long?" Nadaske asked.

"With the two of them, I think long enough."

"You could be wrong."

"We will know soon enough. We must return at once to place of resting."

"We leave."

27

Imehei swayed but did not move. Nadaske went to him at once and put a strong arm across his shoulders. Helped him forward, one shuffling step after another. Together they went along the lakeside and vanished among the trees. They did not look back nor speak to Kerrick and seemed oblivious of his presence.

There were questions he wanted to ask but he did not. He sensed that he was in the presence of a great tragedy, yet one that he could not quite understand. He remembered the songs the males used to sing in the hanalè, songs filled with grim references to their great fear of the beaches.

"Enough!"

He said it aloud, looking about him at the torn, dead bodies. He wanted to know what would happen to Imehei— but it would have to wait. There would be time enough later to find out the meaning of the horrifying events that he had witnessed. For the moment they would have to take care of themselves. Right now he had the rest of his sammad to consider. What of the future? What of these corpses and the supplies?

Three Yilanè in this hunting party. Now all dead. How long before they were missed? There was no way of telling, no way to know if others would come looking for them. Yet he had to act as though this was a certainty. He must see to it that there were no traces of the crimes committed here. The corpses first. Should he bury them? Unwise. The carrion eaters would smell them out, dig them up, leave the bones as witness. They had to disappear without trace. The lake, that was the only answer.

One by one he dragged the dead Yilanè through the reeds and shallows to the edge of the deeper part of the lake. They floated there, the water pink about them. Not good enough. Disgustedly he splashed ashore and looked through their packs. They contained some newly skinned furs, a few other items, but mostly bladders of meat. With his knife he slashed open the tough coverings and threw the meat far out into the lake: the fish would take care of that. Then he filled the packs with gravel and pebbles from the lakeshore. It was hard, disgusting work but in

the end it was done. When the packs were strapped to the
bodies he pushed out into deep water, sunk them there
out of sight. Insects and rain would take care of the blood
that had soaked into the ground. If searchers should ever
pass this way there would be nothing at all for them to
see. Let the disappearance of the hunters remain a mystery.

Kerrick shook his head in disbelief when he saw that
Nadaske had forgotten his hèsotsan. The weapons were
essential for survival—and he had forgotten his, simply
walked away from it. A surer measure of his grief than
anything that he might have said. Kerrick used twisted
grass to lash it into a loose bundle with the three other
weapons that the hunters had brought. The extra hèsotsan
would be needed: at least this much good had come out of
this terrible encounter. He seized up his own weapon,
took a slow look around in case he had missed anything,
then started back along the shore.

Now that he had time to think one fact became painfully clear. They must get away from this lake, all of them.
If Yilanè hunters could come here, as these indeed had,
then the sammad was too close to the city. Others might
come looking for these three. Even if they did not come
the camp was still too close. One day it would be discovered and then it would be too late. They must go north.
But they would have to wait until the baby was born.
Armun was in no state to travel now. After the birth,
when Armun had recovered, then they would leave. It
would not be easy. He had been right to kill the mastodon
that had brought them here; it would have been impossible to hide and would have been seen by the flying
creatures that sought them out. But he missed it now.
Never mind. They would take only what they could carry.
He would make a travois and pull it himself. Harl was big
enough and strong enough now to pull one as well. All
Ortnar had to do was move himself along. He did it, not
well, but at least he did it.

Something dark moved under the trees ahead. Kerrick
bent double and ran quickly to shelter among the shrubs.

There were murgu concealed there, silent killers. He slipped forward with his weapon raised and ready.

Until he realized that he was looking at the two male Yilanè. One of them stretched out and resting, the other sitting up at his side.

"Attention to presence," he called out, stood and strode forward.

Nadaske just turned one eye enough to look at Kerrick, then slowly away again. Otherwise he did not speak or move. Imehei lay at his side, eyes closed, immobile.

"What is it?" Kerrick asked.

Nadaske replied with an effort, and when he did his meaning was muffled with palpable sadness.

"He has gone to the beach. The eggs are in his pouch."

"I do not understand."

"That is because although you are male you are not Yilanè male. You ustuzou order things differently. You have told me that your females carry the eggs, though I do not really understand how this can be possible. But you saw what happened to him this day. They did it to him. Now the eggs are in his pouch and his eyes are closed in the sleep that is not sleep. He will be like that until the eggs hatch and the young go into the water."

"Is there anything we can do to stop this?"

"Nothing. Once it begins it must go to the end. He will remain like this until the hatching."

"Will he . . . die?"

"Probably yes, probably no. Some die, some live. We can only wait. He must be taken back and cared for, fed and watched over. I must do that for him."

"Do we carry him?"

"No. The water. He must be in the water, the warm water of the birth beach. That is so the eggs will mature and hatch. If they die now he dies as well. This thing must run its course. Help me take him into the lake."

Imehei was unconscious, heavy, hard to move. Working together they struggled with his torpid body to the shore and dragged it through the reeds. Once in the water he would be easier to pull along.

Kerrick helped until the lake deepened enough so that Nadaske was able to swim. He grasped Imehei under the shoulders and kicked with his stout legs, making slow but steady progress. Kerrick waded ashore, seized up the hèsotsan and moved quickly off. It was late and he wanted to get back to their camp before dark.

They were waiting for his return. Armun looked down the path behind him and saw it empty. She nodded approval.

"Good. You have killed the murgu. It was time."

"No, they are still alive. At least for the present." How could he explain to them what had happened—when he was not sure about it himself? "There were murgu hunters from the city out there, three of them. I killed one, Nadaske killed the other two. Imehei is—hurt, unconscious. Nadaske is bringing him back."

"No!" Armun screamed. "I hate them, hate them here, don't want them here again."

"There are more important things for us to talk of and we need not concern ourselves with them now. What is important is that we are no longer safe in this place. If hunters from the city could come this far they are sure to be followed by others. One day they will come."

"They came because of those two, their own kind, you must kill them quickly . . ."

Kerrick's temper rose to meet hers, but he controlled it because he knew why she was so disturbed. The baby was late, she was sick, worried. He had to understand. She needed reassuring.

"It will be all right. We must wait until the baby is born, until you feel better. Then we will all leave here, go north, we cannot stay if the hunters are this close."

"And what of these two murgu you care so much for?"

"They stay here. We go without them. That is enough now. I am hungry and want food. And look at this—we have three more death-sticks. It will be all right."

All right for them, he thought as he chewed the cold meat. But what about the males? They must stay here. With Imehei immobile in the lake it would be impossible for them to leave. Yet the rest of his sammad must go as soon as possible. That was all there was to it. There was no choice.

It was late in the afternoon of the next day before Nadaske finally appeared with Imehei in tow. He was exhausted and moved one slow stroke at a time, floating and resting often. Kerrick took up Nadaske's hèsotsan and went to help him, stopping Arnwheet when he tried to follow. The boy did as he had been ordered, stood and gnawed his knuckles, worried and insecure, knowing only that something bad had happened to his friends. He watched in unhappy silence as the unconscious Imehei was dragged up onto the shore, until his head rested on the sand with the lower part of his body still in the water.

Kerrick thought that he was unconscious until his lips moved and he said something with languid motions of his arms. It was as though he were talking in his sleep for his eyes never opened.

"Food . . . desire to eat . . . hunger."

Nadaske went to fetch fresh fish from the little holding pond that they had dug with such great effort. He tore pieces from the fish and pressed them into Imehei's gaping mouth. Who slowly closed his jaws and chewed placidly.

"How long will he be like this?" Kerrick asked.

"A long time. There is no count to the days that I know. Others may know, it is no knowledge that I have."

"And at the end of that time?"

Nadaske made a shrugging motion of hope/fear, knowledge/ignorance. "The eggs break, the elininyil feed, they enter the lake. Imehei lives or dies. Only then will we know."

"I am going to have to leave with the others, as soon as Armun can travel, to go north. It will be dangerous to remain here."

Nadaske rolled one eye in his direction and signed suspected knowledge. "It was my consideration you would do that. Others are sure to follow those who were killed. They may hunt in this direction. I cannot come with you."

"I know that. But I will come back for you, for both of you, as soon as we have found a safe place."

"I believe you Kerrick Yilanè/ustuzou. I have learned how you feel about these things and I know that you must consider your own ustuzou efenburu first. Take them to safety."

"We will talk of this again. It will be some days yet before we can leave."

When Kerrick started back he found that Ortnar had stumbled down to the beach and was waiting for him.

"The baby is coming soon. She told me to tell you that. I know nothing of these things and cannot help you."

"Guard us from harm, Ortnar, that is what a strong hunter can do. I know as little as you do of these matters, but I must try to help her."

He turned and hurried away. This was a day of many events. One who was perhaps moving towards death, one surely coming into life.

Darras looked up when he came in but never let go of Armun's hand. Armun smiled wearily, her hair soaked and perspiration beading her face.

"Do not look so worried, my hunter. It is a late baby but a strong one. Do not worry."

He was the one who should be comforting her, he realized, not the other way around. But this matter was beyond his knowledge. It was the women who always took care of it themselves.

"We should never have left the other sammads," he said. "You should not be here on your own."

"I do what many women have done before. My own mother, our sammad was small, no other women. This is the way things are, have always been. You must go, eat and rest. I will send Darras for you when it is time."

Kerrick could say nothing, do nothing. He went out to the fire where Ortnar was cooking meat. He looked up, then hacked off a piece and gave it to Kerrick who chewed it in silence. Harl and Arnwheet, their faces well smeared with grease, sat across from him finishing their meal. Ortnar stared out at the gathering darkness, then signalled to Harl who rose and kicked sand over the fire. They must stay on their guard, particularly now.

The moon was out, the night warm, marsh birds calling quietly to each other as they settled down. Kerrick could just make out the dark form of Imehei where he rested half in and half out of the water at the lake's edge. He knew that there was nothing he could do now for the males, nothing.

He heard a murmur of voices behind him in the tent and turned to look. But there was darkness, only darkness. Kerrick threw the unfinished meat away; he suddenly had no appetite. He blamed himself for what was happening now. The baby might die, worse, he dared not think about it, Armun might die, because of him. If he had returned to the sammads with the others they would all still be together. The other women knew how to take care of things like this. It was all his fault.

He climbed to his feet, unable to sit still, torn by fear and worry, walked under the tree to stare out at the lake in the moonlight. He looked but did not see it, saw only his inner fears. They should not be here. They should have been with the sammads now, safe in the valley of the Sasku, all safe.

FOUR

The poisonous murgu vines rimming the Sasku valley had turned brown, then died and fallen to the valley floor. They had been pushed into the river and washed away, vanished from sight along with the memories of the last murgu attack.

Herilak sat by the fire turning the shining knife over and over in his hands. Kerrick's knife of skymetal. He had worn it always about his neck, hanging from the solid metal band the murgu had put there. Across the fire from him Sanone nodded and smiled.

"In my ignorance I thought it meant his death," Sanone said.

"His life and our life, that is what it means."

"At first I could not believe you, lived with the fear that Kadair had deserted us, that we had strayed from the path he prescribed for us."

"I care nothing for your Kadair, Sanone, only for Kerrick who saved us. I hold this knife so I will not forget what he did . . ."

"I am not pleased when you talk of Kadair that way."

Herilak stared across the fire at the old man, spoke his mind because the two of them were alone and had come to understand each other.

"I care as little for your Kadair as you do for Ermanpadar who guides the Tanu. That is the truth. Now we put aside this talk of the invisible powers that control our lives and talk instead of what we ourselves must do. I talk instead of two of my hunters . . ."

"I will not hear their names, do not speak them aloud for their offense was great. The porro sacred to Kadair, they stole it and drank it."

"To you sacred, to them a very interesting thing to do. The other hunters envy them and have asked me to ask you for more of this drink."

"You cannot mean this!"

"I do, and there is something else, still more important, that we must talk about. The hunters who drank your porro have been banished from this valley. They now have their tent far up the river. It comes to me that the sammads will join them there."

Sanone looked back down at the flames, stirred them with a stick before he spoke. His voice was quiet again, the anger gone. "I have been waiting for you to say that, my friend. We will talk of that, not of the porro, never again must you speak of it. Has the time come for you to leave?"

"It has. When we fought together we lived in peace together. In the city by the ocean, then here in the valley. In the war against the murgu all else was forgotten. Now the battle is over, the murgu are gone, and my hunters grow restless. Drinking the porro was just a sign. To you this valley is a home. For them it is a trap that keeps them away from the plains and the forests, the freedom to move, stay, do as they will. And there is another reason for me."

Sanone saw Herilak's eyes drop to the knife again and he understood.

"It is Kerrick. You have spoken to me of the differences that grew between you. Do they still exist?"

Herilak shook his head slowly. "I don't know. And that, I think, is what I must find out. He is alive, that I believe, or the murgu would have pressed their attack and we would all now be dead. But is Armun alive—and his son? If they are dead then it is my doing. I must tell him that. I no longer see him as my enemy, I wonder why I ever did. But he may still think of me as one who has wronged him greatly. That must be ended. It should never have happened at all. Now I have come to believe that it was all my doing. My hatred of the murgu filled me full, welled out and embraced any who thought different from me."

"Do you still hold those hatreds within you?"

"No." He held up the knife. "This is the difference. Despite what I have done to him, despite my treatment of his sammad, he did this. Stopped the murgu and made them send this to us to let us know that he had stopped the attacks."

Herilak lowered the knife and looked across the fire. "Tell me, Sanone, have we done all that we promised to do? When our death-sticks died and we came to that city on the shore, Kerrick told us what must be done and all the sammadars agreed to do as he asked. We received new death-sticks only when we agreed that we would stay with you in the city and defend it. Have we done that?"

"It is finished. The city was well defended until we were forced out. The murgu who followed us you attacked with all the skills of the hunters of the Tanu. Now we are safe, for I believe as you do that this was the message of the knife. If yours is the wish to leave, and the wish of the hunters of the sammads as well, then you must leave."

"And the death-sticks?"

"Yours by right. How do the other sammadars feel of this matter?"

"In agreement, all in agreement. It takes but your word to release us."

"And where will you go?"

"North!" Herilak's nostrils flared as he smelled the

forests and the snow. "This warm land is not for us, not to spend all of the days of our lives."

"Then go now to the others. Tell them what we both now know. That Kerrick released us from the murgu. So there is no more need for you to remain."

Herilak sprang to his feet, held the knife high and shouted his pleasure, his voice echoing from the valley walls. Sanone nodded with understanding. This valley was the Sasku home, their refuge, their existence. But for the hunters of the north it was only a trap.

He knew that before the sun had set again they would be gone. Knew also that when the other sammads went to the forests to hunt as they always had, that Herilak would not go their way. He would go east to the ocean, then south again to the murgu city. His life would not be his own, not until he had offered it to Kerrick to take or refuse.

It was almost dawn before fatigue closed Kerrick's eyes. Sleep would not come earlier. He had sat by the dead fire and looked out across the lake. At the calm water and the stars that marched slowly across the sky, tharms of dead warriors in their nightly progression. They moved overhead steadily until they vanished from sight in the waters of the lake. When the moon had set as well and the night darkened, that must have been when he fell asleep.

He awoke with a start, the grayness of dawn around him, aware of a touch on his shoulder. He rolled over to see the girl, Darras, there.

"What is it?" He choked out the words, filled with fear.

"You must come now." She turned and hurried away and he rose and ran after her, passed her and threw open the skin entrance to their tent.

"Armun!"

"It is all right," her voice spoke from the darkness. "Nothing is wrong. Come see your daughter."

He pulled the flap wide and in the faint light saw that she was smiling up at him.

"I was so worried," she said. "I had the great fear that the baby would be like me, with my lip, but now that fear is gone."

He dropped down beside her, weak with relief, and turned back the skins from the baby's face. It was wrinkled and red, eyes shut, mewling faintly.

"It is sick—something is wrong!"

"No. That is the way babies always look when they are born. Now we will sleep, but only after you put a name to her. It is known that a baby without a name is in very great danger."

"What will her name be then?"

"That is not for me to decide," she said with firm disapproval. "She is your daughter. You must name her. A girl's name, one that is important to you."

"Armun, that is a name of great importance to me."

"That is not done, two of the same name. The best name is of someone who died who was of importance."

"Ysel." The name came to his lips without his bidding; he had not thought of her for years. "She died, I lived. Vaintè killed her."

"Then that is a very good name. That she died so that you might live is the most important name I have ever heard. Ysel and I will sleep now."

The sunshine was warm, the air fresh, the day new, all of existence as it should be. Kerrick strode with happiness to the shore to wash and plan for the day. There was much to be done before they left. But leave they would, just as soon as Armun was ready. She would decide. He must get everything ready for that day. He splashed water over his face, spluttered and rubbed. Wiped his eyes with his forearm and saw the first rays of sun shining between the trees, striking warmly across the sand.

To Imehei's still form stretched out in the water. Nadaske was already at his side, sitting in frozen Yilanè immobility.

The day was no longer bright. Kerrick walked over slowly, in silence, stood in silence and looked down at the immobile Imehei. He was breathing slowly through his half-opened mouth. A bubble of saliva formed, then vanished. Nadaske moved one eye to look at Kerrick, then away again.

"Attention to speaking," Kerrick voiced and waited until Nadaske was looking at him again before he spoke.

"In some few days we will be leaving. We will hunt, leave you meat."

"Do not. It will turn green and stink. I will fish, there will be enough for both of us. Why do you not leave now?"

Armun and the baby, the unconscious Imehei here with his unwelcome burden of eggs: there was an unwelcome similarity here that Kerrick did not wish to point out.

"The time is not appropriate, preparations to be made. Meat will be brought."

Nadaske was silent again and there was nothing more that Kerrick could do here, nothing more to say. He went slowly back to his own encampment. Ortnar was awake and supervising Harl, who was fixing arrowheads to their shafts.

"More arrows will be needed," Ortnar said. "When we hunt and travel arrows that miss cannot always be searched for. Now that the baby is born we can leave."

"Only when Armun is ready. But we must make the preparations so we can go as soon as she says. And this we must consider as well—where shall we go?"

"Tighter, the thong tighter or the arrowhead will be lost. Use your teeth." Ortnar shuffled about until he was facing north, then pointed with his chin. "That is the only way to go. I know the path well. And I think I know of a place where we can stay as long as we have the death-sticks. With them we cannot go to the snows for they die in the cold. Nor do we want to stay close to the city of the murgu. Now I will show you what I have been thinking of."

He used his speartip to scratch a line in the sand, then stabbed the lower end of it. "This is the shore of the ocean and at the bottom the city of the murgu. Now we are here."

He circled the lake into the sand. Then drew the spear up along the line and pushed it down again on the shore-line. "Here is a place I know of. We hunted there once. It is as far north from this lake as this lake is north of the city. Is that far enough?"

"It will have to be. Close or far they can find us if they want to. If they seek us out we can run to the snows and they will be right behind us every step of the way. What did you find when you hunted there?"

"A river of sweet water, then a shallow lagoon filled with flying birds. Then, beyond the water, there is an island. On the other side of it there is more water and narrow islands again along the ocean. I thought this. If we go to the large island we can kill the dangerous murgu there. The hunting and fishing is very good. But the large island is not on the ocean. If the murgu sailing creatures go along the shore, even if they land, they will not know we are there. It is the best I can think of now."

"It is a far better plan than I could have made. We will go there—as soon as Armun is ready. Until then we must hunt and smoke meat, make ekkotaz. The less time we take to hunt when we are on the move the faster we will get to this place."

From the tent behind him there came the sudden loud cry of a baby. Arnwheet came running over and took his hand, looked up with worried eyes. Kerrick smiled down at him and rubbed the tangle of his hair.

"Do not worry. All babies sound like that. You now have a sister and she must be very strong to cry like that."

Arnwheet looked doubtful, but relieved. "I wish to talk with my friends."

When he said "friends" he moved his arms to say the same thing in Yilanè. It was obvious that they were of far greater interest to him than any little sister.

"Yes, go to them, Nadaske will like that. But you will

not be able to talk to Imehei. He sleeps in the water. It is a thing that only Yilanè do and it is hard to explain."

"I will ask Nadaske, he will be able to tell me."

Perhaps he will, Kerrick thought, then turned and shrugged off his worries. There was much to be done here.

enotankè ninenot efendasiaskaa
gaaselu.

UGUNENAPSA'S
SECOND PRINCIPLE

_____

We all dwell in the City of Life.

FIVE

When Ambalasei woke this morning she was not rested, still felt as tired as she had when she had closed her eyes at dusk the evening before. She was not at all pleased with this for she knew that she was no longer a fargi fresh from the sea. Or even a young Yilanè, for that matter, filled with the fresh juices of life. She was old, and for the first time that she could remember she felt old. What was the Yilanè lifespan? She did not know. Once she had attempted to do research on this topic but eventually had been forced to admit failure. No records were ever kept about major occurrences: no individual Yilanè would even hazard a guess as to how old she was. Ambalasei had recorded events for ten years, using the constellations in the night sky to mark the passage of each year. But some of the Yilanè she was recording had left the city, some had died—and eventually she had lost her records. How long ago had this been? She did not know—for she had not even kept a record of this.

"It is not in the nature of the Yilanè to take note of the passage of time," she said, then pulled a water-fruit to her and drank deep.

44

Nevertheless she was old. Her claws were yellow with age, the skin on her forearms hung in wrinkled wattles. It must be faced. Tomorrow's tomorrow would continue to be like yesterday's yesterday, but on one of those tomorrows she was not going to be around to appreciate it. There would be one Yilanè less in this world. Not that anyone would care, other than herself, and she would be past caring. She champed her jaw with disgust at this morbid thought so early on a sun-drenched day, reached out and pressed hard on the gulawatsan where it clung to the wall. The creature made a highly satisfactory blare of deafening sound and very soon after that Ambalasei heard Setèssei's claws on the flooring, hurrying close.

"Ambalasei begins her labors early. Do we visit the Sorogetso again today?"

"We do not. Nor do I labor. I shall indulge myself in a day of contemplation, enjoying warmth-of-sun, pleasures of mentation."

"Ambalasei is wisest of the wise. Fargi work with their bodies, only Ambalasei has uniqueness of mentality to labor with thoughts alone. Shall I paint your arms with designs of delicacy to show all that that labor of limbs is beneath you?"

"Excellence of thought: appropriateness of suggestion."

When Setèssei hurried off for her pots and brushes she looked back with pleasure to see that Ambalasei had found a spot in the sun, had sat back on her tail and was relaxing in the warmth. This was very good. But when she turned around again she found her path blocked by a thin Yilanè whom she knew far too well.

"I heard a great sound from the place where Ambalasei works/sleeps. I wish to speak with her," Far< said.

"Forbidden/wrong/disastrous," Setèssei said with added modifiers of firmness of commands.

"It is a matter of some importance."

"It is a matter of greater importance that Ambalasei be not spoken to by anyone this day. This is an order spoken by me for Ambalasei. Do you wish to ignore this order?"

Far< began to speak, remembered the wrath of
Ambalasei, changed her mind and signed negation.

"Very wise," Setèssei said. "Now go through the city
and tell the others you meet to make clear to all that none
shall approach or speak to great Ambalasei while the sun is
in the sky this day."

The sun was very comforting; Ambalasei relaxed and
enjoyed it to the utmost. A period of time passed before
she was aware of the light touches on her arms and opened
her eyes to look with approval upon the designs being
traced there.

"This is a day of great importance, Setèssei. Already
cessation of physical labors, inauguration of cerebration
has produced important results. I must now look upon this
city I have grown and take note of its fecundity."

"I have ordered with some firmness that you are to
pass through the city undisturbed."

"You are the perfect assistant Setèssei. You recognize
my desires even before I do."

Setèssei lowered her head in humble acceptance, her
crest flaring with color. This day must be remembered for
never before had Ambalasei spoken in this manner to her.
Approval of labors/acceptance of assistance was all she
required.

Her thirst slaked, her arms painted, Ambalasei strode
forth into the city of Ambalasokei that she had created on
this hostile shore. As she passed through it she observed
and took note of its growth and none spoke nor approached
her.

From the thick trunk of the spreading central tree the
city stretched out in all directions. Within the embrace of
its branches and roots hundreds of other life forms grew,
interacted, proliferated. Water was drawn up from the
roots to the protective canopy of leaves above, was tapped
by the water-fruits, fed to commensal plants, drunk by
symbiotic animals. Ambalasei walked on the living mat of
the floor kept clean by the hungry insects below. Saw the
fruit groves that fed the small flock of elinou in their
fenced enclosure. Her slow progress took her to the river-

bank and the strong dock where the uruketo lay, looking
at her blankly with a large bone-ringed eye. On she went
to the wall of thorns, now flourishing and high, a thick
protection against any intruders.

Here she turned away from the water and followed the
living wall across the isthmus to the other shore. The nets
were being brought in and a gigantic eel was just being
dragged ashore. It moved its body in slow coils, but represented no danger since it had been stunned with the toxin
Ambalasei had provided. Into the city again and past a
sealed doorway. Seeing this she stopped, immobile, resting on her tail for a long while. When she looked at the
door that had never been opened its significance became
immediate and her thoughts went far beyond it. The sun
moved in its slow arc across the sky until the shadow of a
tree enveloped her and she became aware of the chill.
With this she stirred to life, went into the sunlight again.
When the heat had warmed her she walked on. She
passed a grove where wild flowers grew between the
trees, stopped and thought about their significance, their
novelty. Of course—there were no other groves of decorative flowers as one found in other Yilanè cities. Perhaps
flowers were like arm-painting, too frivolous and unim-
portant for the very serious Daughters. She walked on and
made her slow way to the ambesed. Here, where the
heart of the city should have pulsed with life, she found
only emptiness. There, on the warmest part of the sun-
facing wall, where the eistaa should have sat, there was
only rough bark. With even slower tread she crossed over
and leaned her back against the bark in this, the chosen
spot. Stood wrapped in thought until a flicker of motion
penetrated her concentration. She turned one eye towards
the Yilanè who was passing through the ambesed.

"Attention to speaking!" she roared in her cracked
voice. The Yilanè stopped, startled, turned to face her.

"To disturb you is forbidden . . ."

"Your talking-not-listening is all that disturbs me. Silence and attention to orders given. Find Enge instantly.
Tell her presence required imperative. Go."

The Daughter of Life began to speak of Ugunenapsa's principles concerning the giving of orders, saw the grim shaping of Ambalasei's body, thought better, closed her mouth and hurried away.

Ambalasei relaxed and enjoyed pleasure of cogitation, lack of physical labors, until a movement penetrated her thoughts. Enge stood before her, arms curved in expectancy of orders.

"You shall have them, Enge. A time of decision has come. I wish to meet with those few Daughters of some intelligence to discuss the future of this city. I shall tell you the names of those whom I wish to be present."

"Difficulty of ordering, great Ambalasei. The Daughters of Life see equality in all. Decisions must be made by all."

"That is for you to do if you wish. After I have talked to those whom I wish to talk to. Do you find difficulty in arranging this?"

"There is difficulty, but it shall be done as you have commanded."

"Why difficulty?"

"Each day the Daughters grow restive in following your orders as though you were an eistaa. They say the city is now fully grown . . ."

"Spare me their thoughts. I am well aware of what they think and that is why I want this meeting with those of my own choosing. You will be there, as well as my assistant Setèssei, and Elem who commands the uruketo and respects knowledge. And Far< who represents the thoughts of Ugunenapsa at their most simplistic and argumentative. Are there others of intelligence you wish to be present?"

"With gratitude, there are. Efen, who is closest to me. Omal and Satsat as well for we are the only survivors of those who were sent to Alpèasak."

"Let it be done. Order them to attend now."

"I shall request their presence with suggestions of urgency," Enge said then turned and left.

Ambalasei's quick anger was replaced by appreciation.

A Yilanè of some intelligence. If only she could rise above
thoughts of Ugunenapsa she could be a scientist of note,
an eistaa of a great city. It was an incredible waste.

They arrived, one by one, the last two hurrying up
with mouths agape since they had come the greatest distance. Ambalasei looked at them in silence, then twitched
her tail in the quick motion that signified attention.

"And silence as well, particularly you, Far<, for you
are a born interrupter, until I have finished speaking. I
will tell you of matters of some importance. And then you
will speak to me in response. Then, as Enge has informed
me, all of the sisters will talk to each other at once and at
great length but I will not be there. Now listen in silence,
interruption forbidden. Like all great thinkers and speakers I go from the general to the specific, from observation
to conclusion.

"Observation. Look around you. Do you know where
you are at this present moment? Of course you do for you
are Yilanè, and every Yilanè knows of the ambesed for
every city has an ambesed. The chromosomes for its growth
were there in the city's seed, as were those of the hanalè.
I went there today and looked at the door that has never
been opened for there are no males here to be locked
away behind that door."

She paused for a moment so they could think about
these facts and saw that Far< was poised for speech. Until
Setèssei, who had anticipated this, trod hard on her foot.
Ambalasei registered silent approval; a perfect assistant,
then moved in disapproval as she saw only blankness in
their bodies.

"You have minds and do not use them. I give you
facts, but you do not draw conclusions. So I will have to
do your thinking for you as I have done in the past, as I
will undoubtedly have to do in the future.

"The conclusion inescapably reached is that this is an
incomplete city—just as you Daughters of Disability are
an incomplete society. Ahh, you stir with disapproval and
lack of understanding. At least you are listening. Expla-
nation/definition of a society. This is a technical term of

which you will be ignorant, as you are ignorant of most things. A society is a closely integrated grouping of organisms of the same species, held together by mutual dependence and showing division of labor. Examples follow.

"Insects. The anthill is a society with workers, soldiers, larval attendants, an eistaa to produce eggs, a group working in harmony. Observe as well the ustuzou deer where a large horned male keeps predators at bay so the females can bear young. Think of an efenburu in the ocean where all the elininyil work together in the pursuit of food. That is a sufficiency of examples. Now think of the city where you went as fargi, grew and became Yilanè. It was shaped as all cities, like this city, with an ambesed where the eistaa ruled and ordered. A hanalè to contain the males that would guarantee the continuation of the city when the time came for them to go to the beaches. That is what a living city is—a viable society. I still see blankness of knowledge. A viable society is one that lives and grows and never dies."

Ambalasei looked around and registered disgust at her silent audience. "And what do you have here? You have a dead society. A city that lives only when I order it, that will die when I leave it. And a system of dying beliefs because Ugunenapsa's words will die when you die. Perhaps it is correct to call you Daughters of Death. Because you will die and the words of Ugunenapsa will die with you. Which I, for one, am beginning to think is not a bad idea at all."

She nodded approval at her gasping audience, the inadvertent body movements of disapproval and disagreement. "Now," she said with certain overtones of appreciation of entertainment to come, "now that I have drawn your attention to matters imperative, it is your turn to talk."

There were churning limbs then, and cries of attention to speaking. Only when Enge signed urgency of speech did the others cease their protests. She indicated Ambalasei with movements of appreciation as she spoke.

"You must replace anger with gratitude to wise Ambalasei

who sees all, knows all. Do you kill the messenger who brings the bad news? Is this what Ugunenapsa has taught you? We thank Ambalasei for pointing out the truth of our existence, the realities of our lives. A problem can be solved only when one is aware of the problem. Now we can turn all of our intelligence to its solution. We must search for the meaning in Ugunenapsa's words for I know the answer must be there. For if it does not lie there we die—just as Ambalasei has said." She raised a thumb, held it high.

"One problem with two sides. Both sides are blank, empty, and we must fill them. We stand in one emptiness, the ambesed. We will not have an eistaa—but we must have a system of order to this city, order as represented by the ambesed. This problem we must solve first. Only when this has been done can we address ourselves to the empty hanalè. When we order our thoughts we will order our lives. When we order our lives we will order the city. Then, and only then, can we consider the continuity of this city. Again Ambalasei is terribly right. What do we have here? A city of perfect harmony—and perfect death. We will grow old and die, one by one, and only emptiness will remain. Think on it."

A shiver of pain moved through the listening Yilanè, sparing only Ambalasei who nodded with grim approval. The Daughters of Life were now as silent as death. Except for Far< of course. Her voice was shrill with emotion, the movements of her limbs erratic with stress. This did not stop her from speaking.

"I hear what you say, Enge, but you are misled. Ambalasei may be a scientist of knowledge, but she is not a follower of Ugunenapsa. That is her fault and her failing. Now she misleads us with talks of an eistaa and of the eistaa's rule. This we have rejected, and our rejection has led us to this place. We listen to Ambalasei corrupting thoughts and we forget Ugunenapsa. We forget Ugunenapsa's third principle. The Efeneleiaa, the spirit of life, which is the great eistaa of the city of life and we are dwellers in

this city. We must think of that and reject Ambalasei's
crude city with its ambesed and primitive hanalè. She
misleads us when she speaks to us of these things. We
must turn our backs on her and turn our faces to Ugunenapsa
and follow where she leads. We must go forth from this
ambesed and seal its entrance, just as we must grow vines
over the door to the hanalè for we have no need of either
of them. If this city is wrong for us then we must leave
this city. Go to the beaches and the forests and live free as
do the Sorogetso. We need no eistaa, we need no captive
males. We will go to the shore when the young efenburu
emerge from the waves. Speak with the fargi while they
are still wet from the sea, lead them into the light and the
life that is ours under the guidance of Ugunenapsa . . ."

She stopped speaking, shocked, as Ambalasei made
the rudest sound known, spoke the coarsest phrase ever
heard, moved her limbs in the most gross insult ever
conceived.

"Your thoughts are like the excrement of a thousand
giant nenitesk, a single turd of which would fill this
ambesed," Ambalasei thundered. "I ordered you to think—
not proclaim your world-filling stupidity. Leave the city?
Please do that—to be eaten by the first carnivore to pass
this way. Greet the emerging fargi at the ocean's shore?
Do that—but you will have a very long wait since the
nearest birth beach is an ocean away."

She moved slowly about to face every one of the Daughters in turn, her body arched with contempt, her claws
tearing great grooves in the ground as she moved in
uncontrollable anger.

"I leave you now since I will hear no more of this
stupidity. Speak it to each other after I have gone. This
city is yours, your lives are yours. Decide what to do with
them. You will have all the time you need for I go now to
sail with the uruketo up the great river on a voyage of
exploration. It is also for my health's sake for it is being
destroyed by you Daughters of Desperation. Now, you,
Elem, do you guide the uruketo for me or must I also do
this myself?"

In the shocked silence that followed every eye was on
the commander of the uruketo. She stood, head lowered
in thought for some time. Then she spoke.

"I follow Ugunenapsa wherever she may lead me. I am
also a follower of science and follow where that leads as
well. Ugunenapsa and science led us here, both embodied
in Ambalasei who has made this city and our life possible.
Enge, and others here, are wise in the interpretation of
Ugunenapsa's words. I will follow where they lead, so I
need not be here while you decide. Therefore I will guide
and protect Ambalasei while you consider our future. I think
Far< is wrong because Ambalasei speaks only the truth.
I say do not listen to her. Find a path into tomorrow
that both Ambalasei and Ugunenapsa may tread. That is
what I have to say and now I will go."

She turned and left the ambesed. Setèssei hurried
away as well for many preparations must be made for the
voyage. Ambalasei followed at a more leisurely pace, turning before she left since she always had the last word.

"You hold your future between your thumbs, Daughters of Despair. I think you will all die because you are too
stupid to live. So—prove me wrong. If you can."

Lanefenuu, Eistaa of Ikhalmenets, sat in her place of
honor in the ambesed, the great carving of uruketo and
waves rising up behind her, and was not happy. Not at all.
This was her ambesed, her city, her island. Everything
that stretched before her or around her was hers. Cause
for pleasure once, cause for blackness of humor now. She
looked past the walls of the ambesed to the trees beyond,
where they climbed up the slopes of the long-dead vol-
cano. Up to the snowcapped summit, hideously white all
of the way through the heat of summer. Her body arched
and writhed with movements of hatred, so much so that
Elilep who was painting her arms had to move aside
quickly or be struck. The other male, who had carried the
tray of pigments, shivered delicately at Lanefenuu's strong
emotions.

She saw the movement, looked at him with one eye,

then back to the mountain peak. An attractive male, delicate. Perhaps she should take him now? No, not this day, not the day when it all ended.

Elilep was trembling now as well, so much so that the brush in his hands was unsteady and he could not control it.

"Finish the painting," Lanefenuu ordered. "I wish the mountain and the ocean there on my chest, in the greatest of detail."

"Great Eistaa, it was said that we leave this island today."

"We do. Most are gone. When we board the uruketo we will be the last."

"I have never been in a uruketo. I am afraid."

Lanefenuu fingered his crest and signed abandonment of fear/reasonless. "That is only because you are a simple male, plucked from the sea, raised in the hanalè, which is the right and proper thing. You have never left this island—but you shall now. All of us. We will cross the ocean and I command you to abandon fear. We go to the city of Alpèasak which is larger than Ikhalmenets, is rich in new/delicious animals, has a hanalè of pleasurable size."

Elilep, who was sensitive to others' feelings, as were most males, was still not calmed. "If this distant city is so fine why does the Eistaa show anger and grief?"

"Anger at the whiteness of winter that drives me from my city. Grief that I must leave. But enough. What is done is done. Our new city awaits us on the shores of distant Gendasi∗, a city of golden beaches. Far superior to this rock in the ocean. Come."

She stood and stamped across the ambesed with the males scurrying after her. Head lifted, filled with pride and strength. Perhaps it was best to leave this ambesed forever, leave this place where the ustuzou had humiliated her, ordered her obedience. She snapped her thumbs at the memory, but remembered as well that there had been no choice. Two of her uruketo dead. She had had no choice. Better the conflict to end. Enough had died. If she had not listened to Vaintè's counsel none of this would have happened. Her body writhed as strong emotions seized her. It was part of the past and could be forgotten along with this city and this island.

Her uruketo waited, the others had already left as she had commanded. She ordered the males aboard, started to follow them, turned back to look despite herself. The green below, the white above.

Her jaw gaped with powerful emotions—until she snapped it shut. Enough. It was over. Her city was now warm Alpèasak. Winter could come to Ikhalmenets. It was no longer her concern.

Yet she stayed on top of the fin, alone, until Ikhalmenets finally sank into the sea and was gone.

Es alithan hella, man fauka
naudinzan. Tigil hammar ensi
tharp i theisi darrami thurla.

TANU PROVERB

---

*If the deer go, the hunters follow.
An arrow cannot kill a beast in the
next valley.*

SIX

Sanone did not approve of this kind of meeting. Among the Sasku they ordered things differently. It was the manduktos who labored with their minds and not their hands, who studied Kadair and his effect on this world, as well as other important things, it was they who met and considered and decided. When consideration and decision were needed. Not in this disorganized manner where anyone at all could give an opinion. Even women!

None of these thoughts showed on Sanone's lined, dark face; his features were calm and unrevealing. He sat crosslegged by the fire, listened and observed but did not speak. Not yet. He had good reason to be here, though he was Sasku and not Tanu, and he could see the reason for his presence there behind the seated hunters, among the women. Malagen felt his eyes upon her and moved unhappily back into the darkness. Sanone's expression did not change at the sight of her—though his nostrils did flare with annoyance when a horde of screaming children ran by and kicked sand upon him. He brushed it off and turned his attention to Herilak who rose to speak.

"Much has been done. Fresh poles have been cut for the travois, leather harnesses have been repaired. Meat has been smoked and is ready. I think all has been done that needs to be done. Speak if anything has been left unfinished."

Merrith climbed to her feet, made insulting gestures at the hunters who tried to shout her down. As big as a hunter—as strong as one too—she had been on her own since Ulfadan's death.

"You speak of leaving this valley of the Sasku. I speak of staying."

The women behind her were silent, the hunters noisy in their disagreement. She waited until the shouts had died down, then spoke again. "Hunters you have mouths at the wrong end—when you talk it sounds like farts. We have good food here and there is good hunting in the hills. Why should we leave?"

Some of the women called out in agreement with this and the discussion became heated and confused. Sanone listened, expressionless, guarding his thoughts. Herilak waited until he saw that it would not end easily, then shouted them into silence. They obeyed since he had led them in war against the murgu and they had survived.

"This is not the place to discuss these things. Tanu does not kill Tanu. It is also true that Tanu cannot command Tanu. The hunters who wish to come when we leave will come. Those who wish to stay will stay."

"Hunters only?" Merrith called out brazenly. "Is it that women no longer have a voice?"

Herilak controlled his temper and wished that one woman at least had lost hers. "A woman will talk to her hunter, they will decide what they must do. We are here now because those of us who wish to leave this valley must get all in readiness . . ."

"Well here is one who does not wish to leave," Merrith said, standing and pushing her way through the crowd, then stopped to look back. "Unless I am not welcome to remain here. What do you say, Sanone, mandukto of the Sasku?"

They turned to Sanone now, with great interest. He raised his hands as high as his shoulders, palms outward, and spoke in accented but good Marbak. "Sasku and Tanu fought as one in the city on the shore, came to this valley and fought side by side again. The Tanu are welcome to stay, free to go. We are as brothers."

"And sisters," Merrith added brusquely. "This one is staying." She turned her back and left.

If any of the other women felt as she did they kept their silence. They were free, as all Tanu are free, to live their lives just as they wished. If a sammadar displeased them they would go to a new sammad. But the bonds to a hunter who had fathered their children were not as easily broken. And the hunters yearned for the forests; they could not be prevented from leaving.

The discussion went on for a long time. The fires died down and children fell asleep. Sanone waited patiently and when it was time he rose to his feet.

"I am here because of two matters—may I speak?"

"Do not ask," Herilak said firmly. "The bonds of battle tie us close."

"Then I have a request. The mastodon who was born here, that is named Arnwheet and through which Kadair speaks to us. Is it clear that this mastodon will stay when you leave?"

"This was never in doubt."

"Then we are grateful. Now, the other matter. There is one here who is not Tanu but Sasku. Malagen the woman of the brave warrior called Simamacho . . ."

"Who is now dead," Newasfar called out angrily. Sanone nodded solemn agreement.

"Who now is dead, killed in the battle against the murgu. But his woman Malagen lives and she is Sasku."

"She is my woman now and that is all there is to it," Newasfar said, striding forward, fists clenched. "She goes with me."

"I thought that among the Tanu each decided for one-self. Yet you speak for Malagen?" Sanone looked up at the tall hunter out of slitted eyes, did not move. Newasfar trembled with anger. Herilak took him by the arm, spoke quietly.

"A hunter has respect for age. Sit with the others." He waited until Newasfar had turned grumbling away before he pointed at the Sasku woman. "Do you wish to speak, Malagen?"

She gave him one horrified glance, then hid her face in her arms. Herilak did not want this to go any further and cause trouble. The woman would not say anything for that was the Sasku way. But he knew that she wanted to leave with Newasfar. He also knew that Sanone was watching him, waiting for an answer to his question. There could be only one.

"I see no problem here. For is it not just as Sanone said, that the Sasku and Tanu fought as one in the city on the shore, then came to this valley where they fought side by side again? He has said, in his generosity, that the Tanu are welcome to stay here, free to go. We are as brothers—and sisters too—of course. We Tanu can say no less. Malagen may come with us if she so wishes."

If Sanone felt that he had been defeated by his own words he gave no sign, merely lifted his hand in acceptance, stood and left. Herilak looked at his retreating back and hoped that there would be no unhappiness, no difficulties now. They had fought together in war: they must part in peace. He turned to the sammads again.

"We will leave in the morning. Do we agree upon the way we go? It is too cold to the north and no need to retrace the snow route across the mountains. I say we go east, the way we came, until we reach the great sea. Other decisions can be made then."

"There is the great river that must be crossed," Fraken complained. He was old and frail now and felt that his knowledge was not respected any more. Few even cared what he said when he explored the owl pellets for a glimpse of the future.

"We have crossed the river before, alladjex. Rafts will be made, the mastodon swim it easily at the place where it is narrow. It will not be a problem. Do others wish to speak? Let it be that way then. We leave in the morning."

As always when the sammads trekked the mastodons, screeching in protest at the restriction of their freedom, were loaded and harnessed before dawn. When the sun rose all was in readiness. Herilak stood aside to watch the first of them leave, the trail was a familiar one and there was no precedence or command among the sammadars. He felt a great relief when he saw that Sanone was among the watching Sasku. He went to him and took him by the shoulder.

"We will meet again, my friend."

Sanone shook his head in a solemn no. "I do not think so, my friend. I am no longer young and I do not wish to leave this valley again. I have obeyed Kadair's commands, have seen things that I never dreamed existed. And now I am tired. And you? I think that you will not come this way again either."

Herilak nodded solemn agreement. "There is no need. I shall look for you in the stars."

"We all follow in Kadair's path. If Kerrick is alive, and you find him, tell him that Sanone of the Sasku thanks him for our lives."

"I shall," Herilak said, turned and left without another word, nor did he look back at the valley or the Sasku with whom so much had been shared.

He trotted along the path beside the river, caught up with the slow-moving sammads, passed them. The sammadar Kellimans had only one mastodon and his sammad was small. But it was larger now by one Herilak saw as he started by. There was Merrith leading her mastodon, striding out as strongly as any warrior.

"I see here among the Tanu someone who chose to stay in the valley of the Sasku," Herilak said.

Merrith marched on, chewing strongly on a mouthful of smoked meat. She extracted all of the nourishment and spat out the gristle before she spoke.

"Does the sammadar Herilak say I am not welcome here?"

"You are Tanu."

"Of course I am. Which is the reason why I could not stay in that cave of a valley and work in the fields and talk nonsense with the women. A Tanu cannot live without the forest, without the freedom to go anywhere."

Herilak was puzzled. "Then why all the talk of staying? I see no reason . . ." He hesitated and saw that she was looking at him out of the corners of her eyes, smiling. His eyes opened wide, then he began laughing. And struck her on the shoulder with appreciation.

"You act like a hunter but think like a woman. You knew that Sanone did not want that Sasku woman, Malagen, to leave the valley. So you took away his arguments even before he made them. You never intended to stay in that valley!"

"You said that, brave Herilak, not I. A weak woman must use her mind to survive in this world of strong men."

As she said that she struck him on the back such a blow that he staggered forward. But did not stop laughing.

Herilak wondered if Sanone knew that he had been bested in argument. He may have suspected it last night— would surely know it today when he discovered that Merrith had not stayed behind after all. It was good to be on the trail again. He touched Kerrick's skymetal knife where it hung about his neck, wondered if he were out there somewhere, still alive. If he were—he would find him.

Their path took them north along the riverbank to the place where the mastodons could cross. Hanath and Morgil, banished from the valley for their theft of the holy porro, had put up their tent here, close to the water. Hanath waved and called out as they passed, but Morgil lay stretched out on the ground and did not move. Herilak was concerned. Had there been an accident—or murgu about? He carried both death-stick and spear when he ran down the bank.

Hanath waved again when he saw him coming then sat down heavily next to his companion.

"What is wrong?" Herilak asked, looking for wounds or blood and seeing none.

"Porro," Hanath said hoarsely, pointing to the clay pot standing inside the opening of their tent. "Not too good."

"You should have thought of that before you stole it."

"Stolen porro was very good," he said, smacking his lips dryly. "It is when we make it that something happens. It tastes right, but makes a hunter feel very sick next day."

"You have been making it? How?" Herilak looked into the pot and twitched his nose at the smell.

"Easy enough to do. We watched how they did it, many times at night. They aren't good hunters, we crawled right on top of them. It is easy to make, you just take the ground up things they grow, the tagaso. Put it in water, put it in the sun, put in the moss, that is all there is to it."

Morgil stirred and opened one bloodshot eye and groaned. "It must have been the moss. I think we used too much moss."

Herilak had enough of their foolishness. "The sammads are leaving."

"We'll follow. Maybe tomorrow. We will be all right."

"Not if you drink any more of this," Herilak said and kicked over the pot so the porro poured out and soaked into the ground. It smelled awful.

"It could only have been the moss," Morgil said weakly.

Kerrick looked at the baby and was worried.

"Has she a sickness? Her eyes are open at last but they roll around and around and I don't think that she can see."

Armun laughed loudly at that, a clear and happy sound. "You do not remember when Arnwheet's eyes were just like this? It is the same for all babies. Ysel will see very well. It just takes time."

"And you, are you ready to walk?"

"I have been telling you for days now that I am strong. And I want to leave this lake." She did not look across at the other encampment but he knew what she was thinking. He knew that he had been putting off their departure, but could do so no longer. Everything that they were taking was rolled into bundles and secured to the two travois. It was a small portion of a mastodon's load—

but they had no mastodon. What they took was limited to
the amount he and Harl could pull. Armun and Darras
would take care of the baby. Arnwheet would carry spear
and bow. If Ortnar carried himself that was burden enough.
The time had come to leave.

Flies swarmed on the hindquarters of a freshly butch-
ered deer that was too much for them to take. The males
would appreciate it. He brushed off the flies, seized it up
and swung it onto his shoulder.

"We won't leave this to rot. As soon as I get back we
will go."

When he started across the clearing Arnwheet called
out and ran after him, walked at his side.

"I don't want to leave our friends," he said in Yilanè
when he knew that his mother could not hear him. He
had never been told to do this, but instructions can be
delivered in many ways. Armun made no secret of her
hatred of the two Yilanè males.

"Neither do I. But many times in life we take actions
that we don't want to do."

"Why?"

"Because sometimes things just have to be done. We
must leave here before more of the hunters come and find
us. We must do that as soon as possible. Imehei cannot
come now—and Nadaske will not leave him alone."

"Is Imehei sick? Nadaske will not tell me."

"It is a sickness of a kind. When it is over, then I hope
he will be able to travel."

"They will both come and find us. Then we can talk
again."

"Then we will talk again," Kerrick said, concealing any
reservations that he might have had.

Nadaske sat at the water's edge, at his unconscious
friend's side. He looked up but did not move when they
approached. He grew more alert when Arnwheet went
into great detail about their preparations for the trip, how
well he could shoot his new bow, and here, feel at the
sharpness of his speartip. Kerrick looked on with pleasure
for the boy was Yilanè indeed. But would he remember all

this when they left the lake and his Yilanè friends were not there to talk to?

"Wet-from-sea is a mighty hunter," Nadaske said. "After he has gone we will miss all the meat that he has killed/brought."

Arnwheet arched his back proudly, not catching the sophisticated overtones of size of meat and quantity brought. In truth he had only managed to impale one small lizard since he began shooting his bow. Kerrick appreciated the effort Nadaske was making, for there were also undertones of unhappiness and despair hidden behind his surface meanings.

"All will be well," Kerrick said, "With you, with us."

"All will be well," Nadaske repeated but there was only darkness in his modifiers. In the lake Imehei burbled in his perpetual sleep and his hand drifted slowly under the water in unconscious parody of farewell.

"When we find a safe place you will join us," Kerrick said, but Nadaske had looked away and did not hear him. Kerrick took Arnwheet's hand in his and went to join the others.

"It grows late," Ortnar said grumpily, dragging his bad leg forward, "and the trail is long."

Kerrick bent and picked up the poles as did Harl. They walked in silence into the forest and only Arnwheet looked back. But the trees were in the way and his two friends at the water's edge were already out of sight.

apsohesepaa anulonok elinepsuts
kakhaato>.

YILANÈ APOTHEGM

---

*There are more strands to the web
of life than there are drops of
water in the sea.*

SEVEN

Ambalasei sat on the stranded tree trunk on the shore, blinking happily into the sunlight that bathed her in warm waves. It was an unaccustomed pleasure to relax, take pleasure of sun/surroundings, and contemplate this admirable river. So wide that the far bank was scarcely visible, brown with the soil of the continent it drained. Grassy islands in the river drifted past. The sky was cloudless here, but there must have been heavy rain and flooding somewhere upstream for tree after great tree floated majestically past. One drifted into the shallows and stranded itself ponderously on the bank close by: small chattering ustuzou jumped from it to the safety of the shore. One of them passed close, turned to flee when Ambalasei moved, fell dead when the hèsotsan snapped. Brown fur, prehensile tail. She turned it over with her claws and saw movement in its midriff; a tiny head appeared. A marsupial with young. Excellent. Setèssei would preserve the specimen for study. Ambalasei sat down on the tree again and sighed with pleasure.

A verdant new land for her to explore. Pleasures of

ratiocination amplified many times by absence of disputatious Daughters. The harmony of her work was not disturbed by their continual interrupting existence: she only thought of them now to take pleasure from their absence. The commander of the uruketo, Elem, was different, a Yilanè of science. She knew how to monitor her speaking without being told. The hated name of Ugunenapsa had not passed over her teeth or colored her palms in all of the many days of this voyage.

Ambalasei's thoughts were interrupted by a crashing from the forest behind her: she turned her head slightly so she could watch both river and jungle at the same time. Her hèsotsan was ready, but she lowered it when one of the crewmembers appeared. She had a large stringknife which she was using to cut a path through the shrubs and vines. It was hard work and her mouth gaped wide; she staggered and almost fell.

"Cessation of labors!" Ambalasei commanded loudly. "Into the water before you perish from overheating."

The crewmember dropped the stringknife and stumbled to the riverbank and fell full length into the water. When she surfaced she raised one palm to Ambalasei and signed gratitude for aid.

"Gratitude indeed. Not only must I order and guide incompetents but I must think for them as well. Stay there until you can close your mouth."

She looked up at the river again, but the uruketo was still not in sight. It did not matter, it was only midafternoon and Ambalasei had given them the entire day to exercise the enteesenat and catch food for the uruketo. Now there was movement from the other direction as Setèssei and two heavily burdened crewmembers emerged from the forest. The crewmembers let fall their bundles and joined their companion in the water. Setèssei had her mouth open but did not appear to be as overheated as the others.

"Discovery exactly as Ambalasei predicted," she said.

"Excellent. From the contours of the land and the

configuration of the tributary I knew that there had to be a lake in there."

"A warm one, alive with fish, shored by sunny beaches."

"And uninhabited?"

"Creatures of all kinds. Except Sorogetso."

"Again as I predicted, the same as at the other sites. And of all the lakes we have examined this one is the nearest to the city. I am forced to the reluctant conclusion that the small group of Sorogetso that I discovered is the only one in existence. Certainly the only one on this river. Do you know what that means?"

"Ignorance of meaning/desire for enlightenment."

"It means, faithful Setèssei, that our Sorogetso are not native to these shores. They were brought here, planted here, left here, as I had supposed. A single colony, fruit of dark experiments by a scientist unknown. Did you find anything else of note on your expedition?"

"Specimens of interest, featherless/furless flying creatures, and another of possible value."

The crewmembers were emerging from the river now and Setèssei ordered that the discarded bundles be brought forward. She opened one and took out the body of a small, beaked lizard that was no longer than her forearm. Ambalasei examined it with interest, stretched out the lengthy tail.

"Agile, it is obvious that it grazes on all fours—yet can flee danger using its hindlegs alone. It can also feed anywhere with this sharp beak, eat woody stems, tough leaves."

"Tastes good too. They were sitting on nests in the undergrowth. Admission of dislike for repetitive diet. I have consumed a sufficiency of preserved meat. I killed two, ate one . . ."

"Solely in the interests of science."

"Solely. But it was my considered opinion that if the flesh was good I would collect the eggs."

"And of course you have. You are turning into a true scientist, Setèssei. A new food source is always appreciated. And I am a little tired of eel as well."

Ambalasei's lips unconsciously drew back from her teeth
as she examined the specimen. Her mouth opened. Then
snapped shut since, in the name of science, she needed
this specimen intact for dissection. "It shall be known as
naeb because of its beak. Now—show me what else you
have brought back."

Ambalasei never ceased to be amazed at the quantity
of new species that this continent held. It was to be
expected, but was still pleasure magnified many degrees.
A beetle bigger than her hand, tiny ustuzou, butterflies, a
bewildering array. "Most satisfactory. Into the preserving
containers—they have been exposed to the air long enough
now. We will have a feast of discovery when we return.
Which will be far too soon."

Setèssei caught the overtones of Daughters/depression
behind her statements and quickly went to get a water-
fruit that had been cooling in the river. Ambalasei drank
gratefully but would not be turned aside from her morbid
preoccupations.

"Exploration and pleasures at an end: depressing con-
frontations to come. I have refrained from thinking about
what we will find when we get back. I consider it now
since when the uruketo returns—so do we."

"Interests of science/explorations incomplete," Setèssei
said temptingly. Ambalasei signed a regretful negative.

"Nothing would give me greater pleasure than to continue our scientific investigations. But I fear for the city
that I have grown, that is now left in the hands of those total
incompetents. I forced realities upon them—then left to see
if they could solve the problems their own way in my
absence. Do you think they have done that? I agree,
highly unlikely. Now, are my eyes dimming with age or is
that the uruketo returning?"

"Great Ambalasei's eyesight is like that of a young
fargi. They return."

"Excellent. Prepare your samples at once so they can
be loaded aboard before darkness of night. I have kept
count of the days and the landmarks. We will be going

downstream now, moving with the current. If we leave at
dawn we will be at Ambalasokei during daylight tomorrow."

"We are that close?"

"No—but the river flows that swiftly."

As befitted her status, Ambalasei rested at ease while
the others labored to preserve the specimens. The enteesenat
surged towards the riverbank, leaping high in the water.
They were fine, intelligent beasts, a pleasure to watch.
The uruketo came steadily on behind them, slowing and
stopping with its beak resting on the shore. Elem herself
came down from the high fin to aid Ambalasei in boarding.
The creature's bill was slippery and gave little purchase to
her claws. Once safe on the wide back she rested before
beginning the climb to the top of the fin.

"The creature is fed?" she asked.

"More than adequate. The enteesenat found many large
eels, not as large as the ones we catch, but appreciable in
size. The uruketo seemed to take pleasure in consuming
them."

"You can actually understand responses from this brain-
less creature?"

"One learns by long association and observation. There
is great satisfaction and skill in doing this, satisfaction of
the kind I sometimes feel . . ."

Elem stopped in confusion, registered apologies, her
crest flaming orange then red. Ambalasei signed accepted/
understood.

"You were overwhelmed by the pleasures of command/
understanding. I do not take offense. I take note of the
fact that in the many days we have been away from the
city this is your first lapse, the first time you have even
considered mentioning the unmentionable in my presence. But now—speak the name aloud. Ugunenapsa!"

"Thank you, a pleasure to hear it . . ."

"Not to me. I only say it now to accustom my ear to its
coarse sound. Ugunenapsa. How it grates on the nerve
endings. We leave in the morning, reach the city the same
day. That is why I permit the lapse. A small abomination
compared to the ones that I will hear tomorrow."

Elem signed hopefulness. "Perhaps all is well."

Ambalasei answered with a rude sound. "Knowing your fellow Daughters as you do—do you really think that is what will have happened?"

Elem was too wise to answer a question like that, asked instead for permission to load cargo. Stirred by her righteous anger Ambalasei now found the strength to clamber up the fin and into the cool interior of the uruketo. She slept at once, knowing that she would need all of her strength in the days to come. Slept until Setèssei woke her with sounds of imperative attention.

"The city is in sight, great Ambalasei. It was my thought that you might wish to prepare yourself for arrival. Perhaps arm paintings of strength and victory?"

"I would not waste the pigment to impress those creatures. Bring meat instead so I will have the fortitude to listen to their stupidities."

The uruketo must have been seen because Enge was waiting alone on the dock. Ambalasei signed appreciation.

"She knows I can bear her presence, but she spares me the sight of her disputatious companions for as long as possible. Setèssei, take the specimens to the examining chamber. I will join you there as soon as I discover what has happened in our absence. I hope for the best, yet expect the worst."

Ambalasei was puffing and blowing from the exertion when she stepped onto the dock: Enge signed welcome greetings, with modifiers of happiness.

"Is it because of pleasure at my safe return that causes you to express such good cheer—or are you the bearer of good tidings?"

"Both, great Ambalasei. Long study of Ugunenapsa's Eight Principles has led me unerringly to the seventh principle. When I told you that answer to our problems lay in Ugunenapsa's words I truly believed it. But still there were doubts . . ."

"Spare me, Enge. Results will be sufficient, detailed explanation of route taken not needed. Are you sincerely informing me that all of your problems have been solved during my absence by application of philosophical principles? If that is so I enroll in the ranks of the Daughters instantly!"

"We would welcome you with gladness. While solutions are now possible there remains a problem . . ."

Ambalasei sighed dramatically. "Not totally unexpected. State the problem."

"It is Far< and those who listen and follow her way."

"Also not unexpected. What has the repulsive creature done now?"

"She has taken her companions and they have gone to join the Sorogetso."

"They have done *what*?"

Every pigmented area of Ambalasei's body flared scarlet, throbbing with color like a pulsating heart about to burst. Enge stepped back in alarm, weakly signing danger-to-health. Ambalasei snapped her jaws shut with a loud crack.

"My instructions given, strongest orders issued. Sorogetso to leave this city and not to return. And not to be contacted by anyone. Promise of my instant withdrawal from city and destruction of same if not obeyed. And now this!"

Enge swayed before the storm of emotion, fought to speak, finally was signed permission by Ambalasei who was so enraged she could no longer talk coherently.

"This we all understood and appreciated and obeyed. But Far< refused to accept your orders, said that since we had rejected the rule of eistaa we must reject you as well. If having the city was the price of obedience, she said, then the city must be abandoned. She took her followers with her. They have gone to the Sorogetso. They intended to live with them, live like them, and convert them to the true belief in Ugunenapsa and to build the true city of Ugunenapsa in the jungle there."

"And has this happened?" Ambalasei asked, regaining some of her control, positive that she knew the answer in advance.

"No. Far< has been injured, but will not return. Some stay with her, the rest have come back."

"Put these disobedient creatures to work at once butchering/cleaning/preserving eel until I give permission for their labors to end. Which, if I have my way, they never will. I go to the Sorogetso."

"There is danger now."

"I fear nothing!"

"But I wish to tell you of our successes."

"Only when this appalling matter is concluded. Order Setèssei to join me, bringing the healing-container with her. Instantly."

One of the young boats had grown large enough now to carry two passengers. This would have made the journey easier, except for the fact that the boat's training had barely begun. It thrashed its tentacles and spurted water, rolled its eyes back toward Setèssei who was thumping the creature's nerve endings mercilessly. They made their way erratically down the isthmus and past the protective wall. Ambalasei's anger slowly faded and she was appreciative of this interval that would permit her to restore her composure. Cold thinking was needed now, not hot anger. Yet she held the hèsotsan so tightly that the creature writhed in her grip. This was protection against marauding animals—but how she longed to use it on Far<. Disobedience of strict orders, disruption of scientific observations. The creature had really gone too far this time. And she was injured, that is what Enge had said. Mortally, Ambalasei hoped. Perhaps a little toxin injected into the bloodstream instead of painkiller, just to help the process along.

There was ominous silence in the forest. After securing the still-disturbed boat to the bank, Setèssei led the way along the track, weapon ready. Before they reached the floating tree that gave access to the Sorogetso, on a bit of shaded beach by the lake, they came upon a small group of Yilanè. Three of them were bent over something on the ground and reacted with fear when Ambalasei called loudly for attention to speaking. They looked at her, shivering, eyes wide with fright.

"You deserve death, destruction, dismemberment for disobeying my orders and coming here. You are creatures of wicked stupidity and you will now tell me where the wickedest and stupidest of you is, she known as Far< but who should be known as Ninperedapsa, the great disobeyer/destroyer."

They trembled as they moved aside to disclose Far<'s body on the ground beside them. There was a soiled nefmakel about one arm and her eyes were closed. Ambalasei felt a great burst of pleasure in the thought that perhaps she was dead.

It was not to be. Far< stirred and her large eyes quivered and opened, stared up at Ambalasei. Who bent close and spoke with the most venomous overtones she could manage.

"I was hoping that you were dead."

"You speak as an eistaa would speak. In the name of Ugunenapsa I reject you as I do all other eistaa."

"Is that why you disobeyed my orders?"

"Only the spirit of Ugunenapsa orders my life."

Ambalasei pulled off the nefmakel slowly and painfully and took pleasure from Far<'s uncontrollable moan. "And for what reason did Ugunenapsa send you here to the Sorogetso?"

"To speak of her truths to these simple creatures. To lead them to Ugunenapsa and to ensure the future. For when their young fargi come from the water they will learn of Ugunenapsa as well and thus it will be."

"Will it? Some creature with dirty teeth has bitten you and the wound is infected. So you intend to talk to them of Ugunenapsa. That means you speak their language?"

"A few words. I will learn more."

"Not if I have any say in the matter. What bit you?"

At this question Far< turned away, hesitated before she spoke. "It was the male, whose name I think is Asiwassi—"

"Easassiwi, you Daughter of Dumbness!" Ambalasei roared, greatly enjoying herself. "You cannot even get his name right—and you are going to preach to him of Ugunenapsa. Stringknife, nefmakel, antiseptic," she ordered Setèssei. "And I see by this reaction that he was not too impressed by your preaching. Sensible creature: my estimation of their intelligence has risen. I will heal and bandage this wound, treat you with antibiotics—then remove you from this place before you cause irreversible damage."

"I will remain. You can not force me . . ."

"Can't I?" Ambalasei bent so close that her angry breath washed over Far<'s face. "Watch. Your followers are going to pick you up and carry you back to the city. If they refuse I will take my hèsotsan and kill them. Then I will kill you. Do you have any slightest doubt that I will do that?"

If Far< had any doubts her companions certainly did not. They gave her no time to answer but seized her up as gently as they could and carried her, protesting feebly, back down the path and out of sight.

"This is turning out to be a very good day after all," Ambalasei said happily, holding out her hands so that the admiring Setèssei could clean them with a large nefmakel.

The boat was a bit more obedient when they returned to the city so Setèssei fed it some fish as a reward. As before, Enge was awaiting their arrival.

"Far< has returned and has spoken to me of your threat of violence. Would you really have killed her?" Enge was upset by the incident and Ambalasei mistook her concern.

"You put survival of your dismal Daughters ahead of racial survival of the Sorogetso?"

"That is not my concern, neither they nor Far<. I am just concerned that a scientist of note, a Yilanè of great accomplishments, should consider murder of an inferior."

"My anger was so great I might very well have bitten her head off. But as anger wanes good sense returns. Science instead of violence. Perhaps I would not have injured any of them. But prospect of death was very close. Now permit me to forget that Daughter of Destruction and listen now to item of importance and happiness you were to tell me."

"Mine is the pleasure to disclose. You must first understand Ugunenapsa's Eight Principles . . ."

"Must I?"

"Of course. You would not attempt to understand the science of the body before you had understanding of the science of the cells?"

"Reprimand accepted," Ambalasei sighed, settling back onto her tail and sniffing the breeze from the river. "I listen/learn."

"The first principle derives from Ugunenapsa's insight and understanding of a truth that has always existed. This truth is that we exist between the thumbs of the spirit of life, Efeneleiaa."

"Ugunenapsa's eyes must have been superior to mine. In all my biological research I have never seen this Efeneleiaa."

"That is because you searched in the wrong places," Enge said with great enthusiasm. "The spirit of life is within you, for you are alive. Within all Yilanè as well. Most creatures do not have the capacity to comprehend the reality of their own existence. But once the truth of Efeneleiaa has been grasped all else follows. Thus the second principle . . ."

"Just stay with the first one now. I still have no idea of what you are talking about. Definition required of new concept introduced, new term never heard before. Spirit?"

"Ugunenapsa created the term spirit to describe something inherent to Yilanè, describable yet unseen. She gives the example of twenty fargi, ten yiliebe and unable to speak, ten yilanè. If they do not attempt to communicate they are indistinguishable. If they were all dead no amount of physical dissection could tell one group from the other. Therefore all-understanding Ugunenapsa used the new term spirit to describe the difference, in this case the spirit of communication. In the case of life she used Efeneleiaa, life-eternity-indwelling. Is this clear now?"

"Yes and no. Yes, I hear what you are saying and follow your arguments. And no, I reject the concept of spirit as being artificial, nonexistent and deleterious to clear thinking. But I put that aside for the moment and go back to the yes. Though rejecting the basic concept I will now allow it for discussion's sake in order to see what follows from the concept."

"Your reservations are noted and perhaps some other time I might attempt to clarify the concept of spirit. I admit that it is difficult . . ."

"Not difficult. Wrong and unacceptable. But, yes, to finish this tiresome discussion before darkness descends. For the moment I will not grasp the truth that your Efeneleiaa exists, but will entertain it as a theory. Continue. You were about to discuss the second principle."

Enge signed acceptance of terms-of-discussion. "It shall be as you have said. When we recognize Efeneleiaa we understand that we all dwell in the city of life, which is greater than any Yilanè city. Do you not see the truth and simplicity of this?"

"No. But it is your argument. Carry on to the end."

"Next is the third principle—that the spirit of life, Efeneleiaa, is the supreme eistaa of the city of life and we are citizens and beings in this city."

Ambalasei opened her nictitating membranes which had slipped down over her eyes beneath the barrage of theorizing. "And your Daughters believe these arguments?"

"Not believe—live! For they make life possible for us."

"Then continue. You at least agree that you are citizens of a city and that is something."

Enge made signs of acknowledgment of great intelligence. "Your mind detects my arguments before I make them!"

"Naturally."

"Then hear then the fourth principle. When we know the Greater Truth we are possessed of a new strength, for we then have a greater and higher center of identity and loyalty."

"No wonder you are hated by the eistaa of every city. Next."

"The fifth principle teaches us that the power of truth requires a new vision of the mind. This vision enables the viewer to look at those things seen by all living things, but to look beyond the surface to the unseen but present true order of existence."

"Arguable. But my brain reels with fatigue. Did you not say that the solution lies with your seventh principle? Could you not leap forward to that?"

"It derives from the sixth principle."

"Then by all means let us have that next and be done." Ambalasei shifted position because her tail was getting numb. Enge had the light of conversion in her eyes as she raised joyous thumbs.

"In her sixth principle Ugunenapsa teaches us that there is an order of interdependence within and sustaining all living things, an Order that is more than those living things themselves, but also an Order in which all living things participate, knowing or unknowingly—an Order that has existed since the Egg of Time!"

Ambalasei signed lack of necessity. "We did not need your Ugunenapsa to tell us that. It is a simple description of ecology—"

"Seven!" Enge said with enthusiasm so great that she did not even realize that Ambalasei had spoken. "Daughters of Life are enabled and obligated, by the recognition and understanding of that Order and in loyalty to the Spirit of Life, to live for peace and the affirmation of life. Therein lies the solution to the problem of the city."

"It certainly does and it took you long enough to get around to it. Are you telling me that your Daughters who agree with Ugunenapsa's arguments and words will now feel that they must work peacefully together in cooperative harmony to affirm life?"

"That is what we believe, what we know—what we will do! Just as we follow the eighth and last principle . . ."

"Spare me that at least. Save it as a pleasure for me to enjoy some day when I am jaded and in need of inspiration. Better for you to explain to me how obedience to the seventh commandment will save this city."

"I will take you and show you. When we understood how Ugunenapsa was guiding us we sought ways to show

our appreciation. All now wish to work in the city of life
and hurry to volunteer. Those with the most talents, such
as fishing or horticulture, lead the way. They seek your
guidance in matters they are not sure of and celebrate
your safe return."

Ambalasei straightened up and walked the length of
the dock, then back. The evening breeze was cooler and it
would soon be time to sleep. She turned to Enge and held
up her clasped thumbs to indicate that an important question was held between them.

"All of this pleases me, as you correctly said. Though I
will be pleased even more when I see the system in
operation. But has Ugunenapsa in her wisdom revealed to
you the answer to the other vital question that I asked
you?"

It was Enge's turn to sign a worried negative. "If she
only could. The pleasure I have gained in the salvation of
the city is lost in the reality that I see no salvation
for the Daughters of Life. We will remain here, studying
Ugunenapsa's wisdom, and grow old in our studies."

"Grow old and die and that will be the end of
everything."

"Everything," Enge echoed in tones and overtones
dark as death itself. She shook herself as though a cold
wind had brushed her, held out her hands and willed
them to turn from the dark green of grief to a roseate color
of hope. "Yet I will not stop searching for an answer to
this. One must exist. It is my own inferior inability to
recognize it that is the problem. You do think that there is
an answer, don't you, great Ambalasei?"

Ambalasei did not speak. That was kindest. She turned
away and directed her attention to the water and sky. But
the failing light made her think of death.

Death was something that Vaintè never considered. Nor
life either. She just existed. Catching fish when she grew
hungry, drinking at the spring when thirsty. It was a
mindless and empty existence which suited her now. Oc-
casionally when she did think of the things that had hap-

pened she grew restless and uncomfortable and clashed her teeth together in the grip of strong emotions. She did not like that.

It was better not to dwell on such disturbing matters, best not to think at all.

Fanasso to tundri hugalatta, ensi
to tharmanni—foa er suas tharm, so
et hola likiz modia.

TANU SAYING

———————

*Keep your gaze on the forest and
not on the stars—or you may catch
sight of your own tharm up there.*

EIGHT

Kerrick called a halt when the heat under the trees became oppressive.

"It is too early to stop," Harl said, making no attempt
to conceal his disagreement with the decision. This was
his sixteenth summer and he was more of a hunter now,
less of a boy.

"For you, perhaps. But the rest of us will stay here
during the heat of the day, go on when it is cooler. If the
strong hunter does not wish to rest he can scout the track
ahead. Perhaps his spear can find fresh meat."

Harl happily dropped the poles of his travois and
stretched his tired back. As he seized up his spear again
Kerrick stopped him.

"Take the death-stick as well."

"It is not good for hunting."

"It is good for killing murgu. Take it."

Harl loped off silently down the trail and Kerrick turned
to Armun who was seated, wearily, with her back to a
tree.

"I should have stopped earlier," he said.

"No, this is good. Unless I walk I will not get my strength back." Darras, who had been carrying the baby, passed her down to her mother. Armun wore only a loose skin around her waist because of the heat, held the baby now to her breast. Arnwheet was not pleased by all this domesticity and lack of attention and he pulled at Kerrick's arm.

"I want to go hunt with Harl. My spear thirsts to drink an animal's blood."

Kerrick smiled. "Big talk for small boy. You have been hearing too many of Ortnar's hunting stories." He glanced up as he said this, looked back under the trees and along the trail they had taken. It was empty. The lame hunter would be some time catching up with them for he moved very slowly. This march was going to be a long one. Kerrick took the smoked meat that Darras handed him, sat down beside her and began to eat. Arnwheet, hunting forgotten at the sight of food, sat next to him as well. They had almost finished when there was movement under the trees. Kerrick reached for his hèsotsan and Arnwheet laughed.

"It is only Ortnar. Do not shoot him."

"I won't. But my eyesight is not as keen as that of the mighty small hunter."

Ortnar limped up slowly, dragging his dead leg, streaming with perspiration. Darras hurried to him with the water gourd and he drained it, then let himself slide down the bole of a tree until he sat on the ground. "You stop too early," he said.

"Armun tires quickly. We will go on when it is cooler."

"Keep your death-stick pointed towards me," he said quietly. "There is something out there, it has been stalking me for some time now."

"Come to me, Arnwheet," Armun said quietly. "You too, Darras. Leave those things, move slowly."

The girl trembled but did as she was told. Kerrick stepped to one side so he could see the forest wall without Ortnar being in the way.

There was a sudden crashing and the large dappled,

green and white form hurtled through the undergrowth towards him.

When he raised his weapon the beast screamed fiercely through widespread jaws. Kerrick squeezed the hèsotsan but the marag did not stop. Squeezed again as it loomed over him, stepped back as it fell heavily, almost at his feet.

There was a quick movement in the air and Arnwheet's little spear thudded into the carcass.

"Well done, great hunter," Ortnar said, an unaccustomed smile on his lips. "You have killed it."

Arnwheet came forward, more than a little afraid of the large creature, then bent and pulled his spear free. "What is it?"

"A marag." Ortnar spat on the corpse. "See the teeth, a meat eater."

"Then we will eat it, instead of it eating us!"

"They are no good, the flesh is poison."

"Then I will cut off its tail."

Ortnar smiled. "The tail alone is bigger than you. But take one of the claws from the hind foot. You can hang it around your neck next to your knife for all to see."

"Will there be more of them?" Armun asked, taking up the baby and moving along the trail away from the corpse. It stank.

"I don't think so," Ortnar said. "This kind, I've seen them before, they hunt alone. Its smell will keep any other murgu away."

"Myself as well," Kerrick said, going to join Armun and the others. Ortnar stayed where he was, spear ready, to watch over the boy. Harl returned soon after that and admired the kill.

"There is no game. I think this marag has frightened off everything else in the forest. We are not far from a large trail. There are the marks of travois poles on it."

"New marks?" Armun asked, hopefully.

"Very old, grown over. Hard to see." He took his flint knife and went to help the blood-splattered boy cut off the claw.

It was not a long trek, but they moved even more

slowly now. Ortnar protested but Kerrick insisted that
Harl stay with him, armed with a hèsotsan. Kerrick would
go ahead with the others and guard them against the
deadly creatures of the forest.

They were eight nights more on this trail, the main
one leading north that the sammads had used, before Harl
came running up from behind them, calling out.

"What is wrong?" Kerrick said, raising his weapon.

"Nothing. But Ortnar says that you have passed the
track we must take. Not far back."

Ortnar was leaning on his spear when they came up.
He pointed with satisfaction to a broken branch that was
almost completely concealed by the undergrowth. "I marked
it, when I was here last. This is the way."

Ortnar went first and they were forced to go as slowly
as he. But it was not far, along a ridge and across a shallow
stream. From the top of the next ridge they could see the
shore of the ocean. The waveless shore of a slow-moving
river, tall reeds and birds, and across the narrow stretch of
water the bulk of an island.

"Beyond the island there is an inlet, much wider than
this river, before you reach the small islands along the
coast," Ortnar said.

"Then we will make our camp on this side of the
island, among the trees over there, where we cannot be
seen from the sea. We must get wood for a raft. If we do
that now we can cross before dark."

"I like it better than Round Lake," Armun said. "I
think we will be safe here. Far away from murgu. Of all
kinds."

Kerrick ignored what she said, knowing perfectly well
who she was talking about. But she was right, she would
be happier here away from the Yilanè males. But would
he? Already he missed the richness of their talk, the
subtle references and gestures, implications of a kind he
could not express in Marbak. They were a part of his
sammad and he was the lesser for their absence.

"Is the hunting good here?" Arnwheet asked.

"Very good," Ortnar said. "Now help Harl gather the wood for the raft."

It had been a hot and dry summer. Because of this the great river was very low. The water meadows, flooded during the winter and spring, now stretched verdantly along the river's edge and were carpeted with lush green grass. The deer moved through it, thigh deep, grazing. When the sammads had arrived and reached the edge of the bluff above the meadows there had been only happiness at this sight.

They had spread out and made camp in the cool shadows under the trees. After dark, after they had all eaten, the sammadars drifted up one by one to sit by Herilak's fire. He was no longer their war leader for they were no longer at war. But it was a natural thing to do as long as the sammads marched together.

"The mastodons grow lean," Har-Havola said. "We could stop in this place, the grazing is good. That is what I am going to do."

"It is not the mastodons I care for—it is the hunting," Herilak called out and there were many shouts of agreement. "And I am tired of killing murgu. Some of them are good for eating, but nothing tastes like deer. You saw the fields below. We need skins too—most of you look like Sasku with woven charadis tied about you instead of warm furs."

"Fur is too hot in the summer," said Kellimans, humorless and unimaginative as always.

"Of course," Herilak said. "But the hunting is good here, winter will come, it might be that we will hunt north in the cold. Many things can happen. I am stopping here with my sammad to hunt. Then we will go on."

There were shouts of agreement, not a dissenting voice. The women who were listening agreed as well. Here they could find familiar things to eat that they had almost forgotten about, roots and berries, mushrooms, tubers in the ground if you knew which were the right plants to dig up. There were already young girls who had never done this: they must learn. A stop here would be a very good thing.

Merrith wanted to stay here just as much as the others. But she found one who was unhappy.

"You have been beaten, that is why you cry," she said to the girl. "No hunter should do that to you. Take a piece of wood and hit him back. If he is stronger than you are, then you hit him when he is asleep."

"No, it is nothing like that," Malagen said, the tears glistening in her dark eyes. Like all Sasku she was far thinner and shorter than the Tanu, her olive skin and black eyes a contrast to their blond hair and pale skin. "Newasfar to me is good, that is why I come with him along. I am foolish to act like this."

"Nothing foolish. You miss your friends, your sammad, even the way we speak is different."

"I learn."

"You do. Me, I never learned a word of your Sasku."

"It is called Sesek, what we speak. And what you say is not true. I have heard you say tagaso, that is Sesek."

"That is because I like to eat it, easy to remember."

"I have some of it dried that I can cook for you."

"Save it. You will want it for yourself. And tomorrow we will have many new things for you to try. We will take the berries and make ekkotaz. You are going to like that."

The Sasku girl was small, no bigger than her children were when they were little. Merrith wanted to reach out and touch her hair. But that was not right, not with a grown woman. The girl was better now. Merrith walked on along the fires, just wanting to be alone. Or maybe she did not want to be alone and that was the trouble. Her daughters grown, gone. Soled dead in the murgu city. Melde now with her hunter, with sammad Sorli. No one knew where they were for they had gone north when the others had fled to the west. Perhaps she was still alive somewhere. But Merrith's own hunter, Ulfadan, wasn't. She knew that the Tanu do not mourn the dead, knew that every hunter found his rightful place when his tharm was there in the stars. She looked up at the star-filled sky, then back at the fires and sighed. Better a hunter alive than a tharm in the sky. She was a strong woman. But she was also alone.

"Don't walk too far from the fires," a voice called out. "There are murgu out there."

She squinted in the firelight to see who the guard was. "Ilgeth, I have killed more murgu than you have ever seen. Just keep your death-stick pointed out there and I will take care of myself."

The sammads slept but the fires burned brightly. Guards watched the forest. Something crashed about in the darkness and there were shrill squeals of pain. It was always like this. Without the death-sticks they could not stay this far to the south. Only the tiny but deadly darts could kill the large murgu that hunted here.

The noises of death in the forest woke Herilak who had only been lightly asleep. He looked up at the starlit sky through the open tent flap. Something buzzed in his ear and he slapped the flying insect. The hunting would be good tomorrow. But he did not want to stay here too long. Kerrick was out there somewhere and he was going to find him. That meant searching carefully along the track as he went, to see if other tracks went off of it. There should be other sammads out here, perhaps Kerrick was with one of them. As soon as they had hunted and the mastodons had eaten their fill they must go on.

A bright line of fire struck across the sky, then died away. A new tharm perhaps. Not Kerrick's, he hoped that it was not Kerrick's.

Enge hantèhei, atè embokèka
iirubushei kaksheisè, hèawahei;
hèvai'ihei, kaksheintè, enpeleiuu
asahen enge.
YILANÈ APOTHEGM

---

*To leave father's love and enter
the embrace of the sea is the
first pain of life—the first joy
is the comrades who join you
there.*

NINE

Here, just beyond the breaking waves, was a very satisfying place to be. Vaintè floated with her body submerged, her head above the water. The waves rose and fell under her with an easy rolling motion, marching in from the ocean in steady rows. Lifting her, passing on, curling and crashing onto the sand in a surge of white foam. When the waves rose the highest she looked towards the shore and could see beyond the green wall of the jungle to a row of gray mountains far inland. Had she seen them before? She could not remember; it did not matter. She opened her nose flaps and blew them clear of water, inhaled again and again. The transparent membranes slid over her eyes as she slipped under the water, dived deep.

Deeper and deeper until the water darkened and the surface was a distant glitter high above her. She was a strong swimmer now, almost a part of the underwater world. The seaweed beds were just below her, bowing and swaying in the undercurrents from the shore. Small fish sheltered here, darting for safety as she moved towards them. They were not worth pursuing. Ahead she

saw something better, a large school of flat, multicolored
fish moving like an underwater rainbow. Vaintè rolled
over and kicked in their direction, arms extended, her tail
and legs moving together to drive her forward.

Dark forms arrowed down before her, she twisted
aside; she was not the only one to see the fish. More than
once she had been pursued by large predators and had to
escape by swimming ashore. Were these the same? No,
they were smaller and more numerous and somehow familiar. For too long now she had existed in a timeless
state, seeing but not thinking, making no effort to ration-
ally analyze what was before her eyes, so that at first she
did not recognize them. Hanging motionless in the water,
a thin stream of bubbles rising from her nostrils, she
watched as they approached. Only when they were very
close did she realize that she was looking at other Yilanè.

The pain in her chest and a growing darkness before
her eyes forced her to realize that she had been down too
long, drove her to the surface to gasp in air. The shock of
seeing Yilanè in this empty place tore at the fog that had
clouded her mind, idle so long. An efenburu of young in
the sea, come here from some distant city, that is what
they must be. But the young elininyil never ventured far
from their birth beaches. And there was something else,
something different. These creatures were too large, far
too large to be an unemerged efenburu. They were fully
grown. If so—what were they doing here?

A head surfaced nearby, then another and another. As
she had seen them, so had they seen her. Unthinkingly
Vaintè turned in the water, swam towards shore, away
from their presence. Into the breaking surf, riding it up
onto the sand, then struggling through the surge to the
familiar beach beyond. When her feet left the sand and
slapped through the mud she halted, looking at the trees
and swamp ahead of her. What was she doing? What did
she want to do? Was she fleeing from them?

Unaccustomed questions, unaccustomed thought. She
felt restive, disturbed at the idea of trying to escape. She
had never before retreated, had never sought to flee from

difficulties. Then why was she doing it now? Although she had been standing with arms hanging limply, head lowered, when she turned about to face the ocean her head was high, her back straight. Dark figures were emerging from the surf and she walked slowly towards them and stopped at the edge of the sand.

Those closest to her halted, knee-deep in the surf, staring with expressions of doubt on their partly opened mouths. She stared back assessing them. Fully grown fargi. But they stood with a blankness of movement that communicated very little.

"Who are you? What are you doing here?" she said.

The one she addressed, the nearest, moved back a few steps in the water. As she did this she raised the palms of her hands. The colors moved in the simplest of patterns, unaccompanied by sounds of any kind.

Together, she said. *Together*.

Vaintè signed back the same, scarcely realizing she was doing it. Had not done this since she had first emerged from the sea a timeless time ago. It took an effort to recall exactly what it meant. Yes, of course, it was the simple recognition between efenselè in the sea. Together.

The speaker was shouldered roughly aside, staggered and fell. A larger fargi strode forward onto the sand but stopped at the water's edge.

"Do . . . what I say . . . you do that."

Her expressions were clumsy, her vocalizations crude and hard to understand. Who was this creature? What were they all doing here?

These considerations were driven away by a spurt of anger, an emotion unfelt since she had come to this beach, to this place. Her nostrils flared wide and her crest flowed with color.

"Who is this fargi, an upright worm that stands before me and issues orders?"

It came out imperiously, automatically. The fargi gaped with incomprehension, understanding nothing of her quick communication. She saw this and began to understand a little. She spoke again, slowly and simply.

"Silence. You are inferiority before superiority. I command you. Speak name." She had to repeat this, in simpler form, mostly arm movements and color changes before it was understood.

"Velikrei," she said. Vaintè noted with approval that the fargi shoulders had slumped and her body was now bent in a curve of inferiority. As it should be.

"On sand. Sit. Talk," Vaintè commanded, sitting uprightly on her tail as she did so. The fargi stumbled up onto the beach and sat, arms shaped in gratitude. This creature who had tried to bully her was now thanking her for issuing orders. Seeing this the others emerged slowly from the sea, huddled before her in a half-circle of staring eyes and gaping mouths. It was a familiar grouping and she was beginning to understand who they were and just what they were doing here.

It was a good thing that she did for Velikrei could explain very little. Vaintè had to speak with her for she was the only one who was even slightly Yilanè. The others were little more than large elininyil, immature young. None of them appeared to even have names. They communicated only with the simplest movements and colors that they had learned in the sea, with an occasional harsh sound for emphasis.

They fished during the day, she discovered that much. Slept on the shore at night. Where had they come from? A place, a city, she knew that without asking. Where was it? When Velikrei finally understood the questions she gaped out at the empty ocean and finally pointed north. She could add little more. Further questioning accomplished nothing. Vaintè realized that this was the limit of the intelligence she could abstract from Velikrei. It was enough. She knew now who they were.

They were the rejected ones. From the birth beaches they had gone into the ocean. Lived there, grew there, until they had emerged from the sea at maturity, physically able at last to dwell on land, free to walk across the beaches for the first time to the city beyond. To be accepted by the city, fed by the city, absorbed by the city.

Perhaps. In every Yilanè city existence was always the same. She had observed it for herself in all the cities that she had ever visited. There would be the Yilanè busy about the manifold tasks, the fargi hurrying to their assistance. The eistaa above and the countless fargi below. These were everpresent, indistinguishable one from the other. Shuffling in crowds through the streets, stopping to look at anything of interest, faceless, nameless, identical.

But not always identical. Those of intelligence and ability learned to speak, improved their speech until they became Yilanè. Once they possessed the power of communication they moved gradually from the mass of inchoate fargi to attain the status of Yilanè, the speaking ones. To become a vital part of the city's function. Those of even greater ability would rise even higher, to apprenticeship to the Yilanè of science where they would learn skills and advance in work ability and status. Every eistaa was once a fargi on the beach; there was no limit to the heights a fargi might rise to.

But what of those of limited ability, who could not understand the fast speech and commands of the Yilanè who spoke to them? Who remained yiliebe, incapable of speech. These were the silent ones who stayed always on the fringes of the crowds, moving continually away from the intercommunication of intelligence instead of towards it. Identical, indistinguishable, doomed to remain forever at the outer edge of Yilanè existence. Eating and drinking and living, for the city gave life to all.

But just as the city accepted those of ability it must also reject those who lacked it. It was inevitable. There would always be those who stayed forever on the fringes of the crowds, who were the last to eat and got the smallest, castoff pieces of food. Who spent their days in gaping incomprehension. Their status was the lowest and they had just enough ability to understand that. Day by day they would be pushed aside, would stay further away from the crowds, would spend more and more time on the empty beaches where they would not be troubled by any feelings of rejection, returning to the city only to eat.

Perhaps they would begin catching fish in the sea again, something they knew how to do, their only real ability. And whenever they went back to the city they would again face the humiliation of not even knowing why they were being humiliated. Going less and less often until one day they just did not return. It could not be called cruel. It was merely the ongoing process of natural selection. It could not be condemned or praised. It just was.

Vaintè looked around at the uneven ranks of uncomprehending bodies and faces. Eager to understand: fated never to know. The city had not rejected them because the city could not do that. They had rejected themselves. Many, most undoubtedly, had died once they had moved away from the protected shores of the city. Taken in their sleep by the creatures of the night. So these were not the lowest of the low; those were already dead. These were the rejected ones who were still alive. Vaintè felt a sudden kinship with them for she was also rejected and alive. She looked around at their simple faces and signed warmth and peace. Then, the simplest of simple signs.

"Together."

"Have your Daughters finally learned to work together in harmony and peace as prescribed by Ugunenapsa?" Ambalasei asked suspiciously. Enge signed modified confirmation.

"Ugunenapsa did not express it in exactly that manner but, yes, we are learning to understand Ugunenapsa's directives and have applied them to our daily lives."

"Desire for observation of outcome."

"Instantly available. I think that the preparation of food will be most suitable. Necessary for life, equally necessary cooperation."

"You are not employing the Sorogetso again at this task?" Overtones of dark suspicion. Enge's quick reaction was a sharp negative.

"The Sorogetso no longer enter the city."

"Half of the problem. Does anyone visit them from the city?"

"Your orders were clear."

"My orders were always clear—yet the vile Ninperedapsa, who you still insist on calling Far<, went there with her minions and her proselytizing enthusiasms."

"And was badly bitten, as you know since you were the one who dressed her wound. She rests and still has not recovered; her followers stay close to her."

"May her recovery be a slow one," Ambalasei said with enthusiastic malice, then pointed to the giant eel thrashing feebly on the riverbank. "No shortage of these creatures yet?"

"None. The river teems with them. Now look, there, you will see a perfect example of the spirit of Ugunenapsa at work."

"I see Daughters of Dilatoriness actually hard at labor. I am struck dumb."

"You will notice that the one who directs the operation is Satsat who was my companion in Alpèasak. The workers chose her because of the punishment she received there for her beliefs, and for her survival in the face of every adversity."

"Not exactly what I would call prime qualifications for leading fish-butcher."

"As wise Ambalasei knows this is a fairly mindless occupation that any Yilanè of intelligence could do. Since all of us labor equally in the cooperative spirit of Ugunenapsa, it is a great honor to be chosen to supervise the work of others. Satsat is doubly appreciated because she has organized the work so well that if all labor equally and enthusiastically, if that is done, then there is always the possibility that the work will be finished early and she will be able to speak to them in detail of the principles of Ugunenapsa. Today she will tell them of the eighth principle—which I know that you have not heard. See, they stop now to listen. You are very lucky."

Ambalasei rolled her eyes towards the sky in appreciation of the opportunity. "Was my luck arranged by you?"

"Ambalasei sees everything, knows everything. I did

speak of the fact you would be here and grateful for enlightenment concerning the eighth principle. Which I lacked the opportunity to reveal to you."

Ambalasei saw no escape from the well-baited trap. She settled back on her tail with a grunt. "Time for brief listening since I am fatigued. Brief."

Satsat spoke as soon as Enge signed to her, climbing onto one of the enzyme vats so all could see her clearly.

"The eighth, the last, and the principle that clearly guides our lives once we have accepted the words of Ugunenapsa ourselves. This principle states that the Daughters of Life bear the responsibility to help all others to know the spirit of life, and therefore discover the truth of the way of life. Think of the significance of this all-too-brief yet all-too-clear statement. We who know the Way must help others to learn and understand, to consciously follow the spirit of life. However as soon as this truth is perceived two immensely important questions arise. Firstly—how can we attempt to do this in the face of those who seek our deaths for speaking out? Secondly—how can we maintain the peace and harmony that affirms, while we continue to live by causing death? Must we cease to eat to avoid killing that which nourishes us?"

She stopped when Ambalasei struggled to her feet, waddled forward and dug a piece of fish from the enzyme bath and popped it into her mouth. "Have this one emptied by dark. Gratitude for information on eighth principle, necessity for departure now."

"My thanks to you for presence, Ambalasei. You might like to hear my amplifications . . ."

"To respond with a succinct answer. No. All Eight Principles now understood, application of seventh appreciated, departure now." She turned and signed Enge after her.

"I am pleased. Your Daughters are actually capable of doing the work of fargi despite their disputatious intelligence. I must go upriver for a few days so I take much pleasure from the fact that the city will function well during my absence."

"This is Ambalasokei, the city of Ambalasei. You have given it—and us—life. It is a pleasure to widen/enhance this gift."

"Well spoken. And there is my assistant Setèssei waiting by the uruketo. We leave now. I look forward to witnessing other wonders of organization upon my return."

Setèssei put down the large container she was carrying to help Ambalasei onto the broad back of the uruketo, then signalled to Elem in the fin above.

"You have instructed her?" Ambalasei asked.

"As you ordered. We go first to the beach above the lake where one of the crew already waits in a boat."

"The boat is better trained than the last one?"

"The same creature, but very much under control now."

The voyage was a short one, transferring to shore by boat far easier than Ambalasei had expected. She grunted as she climbed down to the beach, waving Setèssei after her.

"Bring the case, follow me. You, crewmember, stay with the boat until we return."

They trod the familiar paths towards the island in the tributary, where the Sorogetso lived. As they approached the tree bridge they saw someone crossing it, coming towards them.

"We begin here," Ambalasei said. "Open container."

There was worry as well as obedience in Setèssei's body as she placed the container on the ground and opened it. She took out the hèsotsan and handed it to Ambalasei.

"Unsureness and fear," she signed.

"The responsibility is mine," Ambalasei said with grim certainty. "It will be done. There is no other way."

The small Sorogetso, Morawees, came trustingly forward; she had never seen a weapon before.

She stopped and made a sign of greeting.

Ambalasei raised the weapon, aimed carefully. And fired.

The Sorogetso crumpled and fell, lay unmoving on the ground.

TEN

"Behind you!" Setèssei warned. "Attacking!"

Ambalasei shuffled about to face the male who was rushing towards her, screaming with rage. The hèsotsan was accurate only at short range so she waited calmly until he was almost on top of her. The weapon snapped and he dropped into the brush.

"Is it Easassiwi?" she asked. Setèssei hurried forward and turned the body so she could see the face.

"It is."

"Good. Let us find the rest. It is important that none should escape."

"I have great fear—"

"Well I don't. Are you speaking now as strong/scientist or weak/fargi?"

"The effects on the metabolism. There is no surety."

"There is. You saw the foot that one of them grew from a Yilanè bud. Genetic similarity proven. Efficacy and safety of drug proven as well. Did I not inject you with it when you volunteered?"

"Reluctant volunteer—to stop you from giving it to yourself."

"No sacrifice too great to forward science. You recovered, they will recover. The modified gland in this weapon secretes unconsciousness, not death. They will regain consciousness when the drug is neutralized, just as you did. Now, seize up the container and forward, the task to be accomplished with alacrity."

Two other of the Sorogetso were found, and anesthetized, before they came to the island. They crossed the tree-bridge and penetrated further among the trees than they had ever done before. Those they met were shot. When they tried to flee the weapon still reached out and felled them. Ambalasei had to stop to reload the creature with darts, then they went on. For the first time now they entered the area that had been forbidden them by the Sorogetso. They reached another tree-bridge that they had never seen before, crossed it and followed a well-marked track. From the shelter of the screen of trees they looked out upon the sandy beach and a most interesting scene.

A male was lying torpidly in the warm water, his head on the sand. A smaller female sat close by holding a cupped green leaf filled with tiny silver fish. A birth beach obviously, with an attendant caring for an unconscious and egg-carrying male. With a single difference. When the male had finished his slow mastication of a mouthful of fish he opened his eyes and raised one arm from the water.

"More," he said.

Setèssei signed surprise/confusion. Not so Ambalasei who reared back in heart-stopping shock. This could not be—yet it was. Setèssei looked at her, terrified.

"Something of great consequence!" she said. "Does Ambalasei require aid/assistance?"

Ambalasei recovered quickly. "Quiet, you fool. Use your intelligence and not your eyes. Do you not realize the importance of what you are watching? All biological questions about the Sorogetso now explained. The strength of the males and apparent equality with the females. It is there, before your eyes. A natural development? I doubt it greatly. Suspicion of scientist working in secret now appears correct. A natural mutation could not have done this and exactly this."

"Humble request for clarification."

"Look for yourself. The male is conscious, not torpid. Which means extended lifespans for all males. You will remember, if you ever knew, that due to inability to return from the torpid state one out of three males on the average dies after the young are born. Now this need not be, need not be . . ."

Ambalasei sank into an unmoving torpor of concentration herself, considering all the ramifications and possibilities of this new state of affairs. She roused only when movement disturbed her, to see that all of the fish had been eaten and the attendant was leaving. When she had crossed the beach and made her way through the trees, Ambalasei fired and she fell. There were sounds of interrogation from the water that soon died away.

"Attention for instructions," Ambalasei said. "Leave the container here, you can return for it. It is imperative that as soon as I shoot the male you must hurry forward to keep his head from slipping under the water. We do not want him to drown. Now—forward."

They crossed the beach as silently as they could and the male, eyes closed, only grunted an interrogative when they were close. Ambalasei aimed the dart at his crest, rich in blood and circulation, and his head fell. Setèssei was at his side, hauling him by the shoulders. He was so heavy that she was unable to move him so she sat beside him instead, cradling his head above the water.

"Hold him until I return," Ambalasei ordered, then went back to the container. She opened it and drew out one of the living cloaks. It was a large one and warm to the touch. Returning with it to the beach she aided Setèssei in dragging the male up onto the sand, then carefully wrapped him in the cloak.

"It is done," she said, standing and rubbing her weary
back. "The young are safe. Variation of body temperature
contraindicated. Therefore the cloak in place of constant-
temperature water. Now you will take the hèsotsan and
search carefully for any of the Sorogetso that we may not
have seen. When this has been done return to me here.
Leave."

Ambalasei waited until her assistant was well out of
sight before she bent and unwrapped the cloak from about
the male's legs. With a light touch she probed his swollen
pouch, then carefully opened the loose lips of the sac and
peered within.

"So!" she said, dropping back onto her tail with amaze-
ment. "Explanation by observation. Four young there,
possibly five at the most. Normally fifteen to thirty eggs.
Much thought required for explanation of significance."
There was a sudden splashing from the lake and she
looked up to see tiny heads breathing at the surface,
quickly sinking back below. "And that will require thought
as well. There is an efenburu of young already in the
water. What is to be done with them?"

She was still sitting frozen in thought when Setèssei
returned, was hard to rouse so intense was her concentration. Eventually she blinked in awareness of sound and
motion and turned to her assistant.

"Five eggs, not thirty, that is the difference. Numbers,
numbers."

"Communication received, understanding/comprehension
missing."

"Survival of the species, that is what it is. Our males
may not appreciate it, but once to the beaches suffices as
far as the species is concerned. What matters if they
die—if thirty eggs hatch out? It matters not at all. But
these Sorogetso carry only four or five eggs. They must go
to the beaches six or seven times to equal our once. No
wonder they are conscious and not torpid! They have to
live to return again and again. Which gives them social
equality, perhaps even superiority. This will bear much
more consideration and thought." Her attention returned

to the present and she realized that Setèssei was standing patiently before her. "You have searched well? There are none in hiding?"

"None. I will look again, go over the same ground, but I am sure that we have rendered them all unconscious."

"Excellent. Return at once to the boat. I follow at a more leisurely pace. You and the crewmember there will start carrying the Sorogetso to the beach. I shall go to the uruketo and send others to help you. After I tell the commander what must be done. She will be pleased to cooperate in important labors once I have explained matters to her."

Elem was not only less than pleased, she was shocked into immobility. "Lack of comprehension," she said, her meaning muffled by her rigidity. "Sorogetso to be moved from this place? Why do they want to do that?"

"It is not their desire but mine. At present all lie unconscious so permission for move not needed."

"Unconscious . . ."

"Elem! Your confusion of thought, inability to comprehend is annoying me. Explanation in detail. All of the Sorogetso now await removal from here. Instruct your crewmembers to go to the beach, to place them into the boat, to bring them to this uruketo and then to place them securely inside. Understand? Good. When they are all aboard we will take them upriver to a place I have chosen where they can live without disturbance of culture, interference with natural system."

"But, great Ambalasei, more clarification desired. Is not the removal of them from their natural habitat a disturbance of major importance?"

"No. Firstly I do not believe this is their natural habitat. What was done once can be done again. More important—they will be safely out of reach of interference by Daughters of Disruption. Your companions have brought nothing but ill to the Sorogetso. It shall not happen again. Any more questions?"

"Many . . ."

"Then frame them in your mind while the Sorogetso are being brought aboard. That is my order. Do you obey it?"

Elem hesitated only an instant before she joined her thumbs in the sign of obedience to authority, then turned to call orders up to the crewmember on the fin.

The crewmembers, disciplined by their long service in the uruketo, now reinforced by obedience to Ugunenapsa's seventh principle, did as they were ordered. While the loading took place Ambalasei and Setèssei once more quartered the island, and the surrounding area frequented by the Sorogetso, but found no one. Their sweep had been complete. When the last of the limp bodies had been loaded aboard Ambalasei ordered that the area be searched carefully, that all artifacts and objects of any nature that belonged to the Sorogetso be taken as well. There were gourds for water, cages containing deadly spiders, bright stones in woven bags, as well as other objects of uncertain usage. All were brought. Only the dried grass nests they slept in were left; they could be replaced easily enough. By late afternoon the uruketo had struggled back out of the shallows and was following the leaping enteesenat upstream. Ambalasei stood at the top of the fin, enjoying her ease after the labors of the day. It had been hard work, but well worth it. She turned at the sound of attention to speaking to see that the commander had joined her.

"Well done, Elem," she said. "A notable contribution to the future welfare of these simple creatures."

"How long will they stay like this?"

"Until they are injected and awakened. You need have no fear of violence or aggression. Now—information required. You will do as always this night? That is you will let the uruketo drift in the shallows until dawn?"

"As always in the river."

"Excellent. At dawn then I will be awakened and with Setèssei's assistance will direct the creature's progress. None will join me, none will climb this fin."

"I do not understand."

Ambalasei signed weakness of intelligence. "I thought that my meaning was obvious. Under my instruction Setèssei shall direct this creature to the beach where we will land. Since one stretch of river looks very much like another, particularly to the inattentive Daughters of your crew, none but my assistant and I shall know where the Sorogetso were brought ashore. Will you be able to recognize the landing site?"

"I am sure I will, but . . ."

"Then you will remain below. I know that you are a treetrunk of strength, commander, and a good scientist. But some day I will be gone from this part of the world and I force myself to remember that you are a firm follower of Ugunenapsa. If asked for information in her name I am sure that you would give it. I cannot take that chance. The Sorogetso must remain undisturbed by any future incursions into their well-being. Now, tell me, will my instructions be followed?"

Elem signed confusion of desires. "I am a follower of science, just as you are, great Ambalasei. Thinking as you do I agree that matters must be arranged just as you have ordered. Yet I am also a believer in the wisdom of Ugunenapsa and I must reconcile these two."

"Easily done. Think only of Ugunenapsa's third principle and your thoughts will be clear, your commands obvious. Did Ugunenapsa not say that the spirit of life, Efeneleiaa, is the great eistaa of the city of life, that we are citizens and beings in this city? This must include the Sorogetso. So while they will be going to a new and physical city on this river they will still be residing in the greater city of life. As Ugunenapsa said. Is that not right?"

Elem still hesitated. "I think that it sounds right, certainly that is what Ugunenapsa said and I thank you for reminding me of it. And I am humbled that even though you are not a Daughter of Life you know so much of Ugunenapsa's thoughts that you correct me in my misjudgment. You are right, of course, and your orders will be obeyed."

*   *   *

It was not that Vaintè wished to issue commands to the
fargi, it just seemed to have become part of the natural
order. If Velikrei had any resentment that her place had
been taken by Vaintè she gave no indication of it. Quite
the opposite in fact. She stayed at Vaintè's side, stretching
her limited comprehension to understand Vaintè's instructions. She brought the tastiest of the freshly caught fish to
her, watched with pleasure while she ate, did not eat
herself until Vaintè had finished. It was the natural order
of things. Some are destined to give orders, others to
obey.

Not that any real thought was needed to command this
elderly efenburu. Fishing was the only thing that they
did in common; they were all certainly skilled enough
in that. When they entered the sea they moved apart,
swimming slowly. If a school of fish were seen this fact
was remarked upon with the simplest of signals, passed
from one to the other and eventually to Vaintè. She
would swim in the indicated direction, decide if the school
were big enough, the fish of edible interest. If they were
she signed attack and they moved in a familiar and
reassuring fashion.

When not fishing they did not communicate. When
thirsty they drank. When chilled they sought the sun.
Like basking lizards they littered the beach and Vaintè
found the sight a reassuring one, in no way a disturbance
to her mindless peace.

There is a pleasure in companionship, no matter how
inarticulate. Day followed day in a repeated pattern that
did not require either intelligence or attention. Here,
close to the equator, one day was very much like another.
At times it rained, usually it didn't. The sea was filled with
fish, the freshwater stream always ran. It was existence,
simple and unthinking existence.

This was all that the fargi were capable of. If they
thought at all, which was doubtful, they must surely have
preferred this to the pressures and confusions of the city.

If Vaintè thought, and she twisted away from it when cogitation came close, she merely took pleasure from her surroundings and her companions.

Dawn followed dusk, dusk followed dawn in stately, unending progression.

Alitha hammar ensi igo vezilin
gedda. Sammad geddar o sammadar
oapri.

TANU SAYING

---

*A deer cannot have two heads. A
sammad has only one sammadar.*

ELEVEN

It was raining. A heavy tropical downpour that cascaded ceaselessly from the leaden sky. It drummed so loudly on the stretched skins that they had to raise their voices to be heard.

"Is it ever going to stop?" Armun asked. The baby wailed as the sky split with lightning; thunder rumbled through the trees. Armun opened her clothing and nursed the infant into silence.

"This is the third day now," Kerrick said. "I don't think it has ever rained for more than three days at a time. It should stop today, perhaps tonight. The cloud seems to be thinner."

He looked at Harl who was drying a thin slab of deer meat over the fire. The smoke spread out along the ground; a gust of wind blew it swirling around him and he coughed and rubbed his eyes with his forearm. Arnwheet, squatting across the fire from him, laughed—until he breathed in some smoke as well. Ortnar sat as he always did, his swollen and useless leg stretched out before him, staring sightlessly into the rain. He had become too silent and sat like this too much of the time since they had come to the island. Kerrick was worried. It was his only concern now, for the island was far superior to their encampment at Round Lake. There were ducks in the reeds that could be taken with nets, game to be hunted, deer and small murgu with sweet flesh. They had killed the large murgu carnivores as they found them. More of them had crossed over the shallow river since then from the mainland, but not many. This was a good place to be. Armun, as she did often when they were together, seemed to be sharing his thoughts.

"This is a good camp. I don't think that I would ever like to leave it."

"Nor I. Though sometimes I think about the sammads. I wonder if they are still with the Sasku in the valley?"

"I worry that they are all dead, killed and eaten by the murgu with the death-sticks."

"I've told you many times—they are alive and well." He reached over and moved aside the strands of hair that had fallen across her face when she looked down at the baby. Tucked them aside, then ran his fingers over her sweetly cleft lip until she smiled. This was not a thing a hunter was supposed to do, not with others looking, and for this reason she appreciated it all the more.

"You can't be sure," she said, still worried.

"I am sure. I've explained, these murgu cannot tell lies. It's the way they talk, think really. It's as if you spoke aloud every thought that went through your head."

"I wouldn't do that. Some people might be very unhappy." She laughed. "And some of them happy too."

"Then you understand. The murgu have to say what they think when they speak. The one I talked with, the sammadar of their city, the one I gave the skymetal knife to, she said she would stop the fighting and return to the city and stay there. She said it—so it happened."

The rain was slowly dying away, although water still dripped down from the sodden trees. Before dark the skies cleared a little and the late afternoon sun slanted between the boughs. Kerrick rose and stretched and sniffed the air. "Tomorrow will be clear, a good day."

Happy to finally be out of the confining tent he took his spear and hèsotsan and started up the hill behind the encampment. Arnwheet called after him and he waved the boy forward. It was good to be moving about again. Arnwheet trotted at his side with his small spear ready. He was learning woodcraft from Harl and Ortnar so already, at the age of seven, he moved far more quietly than his father. There was a rustle in the undergrowth and they both stopped. Something small hurried away and Arnwheet hurled his spear after it.

"An elinou," he said. "I saw the colors on its back, I almost had it!"

He ran to retrieve his spear. Elinou, a small and agile dinosaur, very good eating. Arnwheet had learned its correct name from one of the males by the lake, so he spoke in Yilanè when he talked about it. But he used the language less and less now, had little opportunity to.

They reached the ridge and looked across the lagoon to the little islands of the coast. White surf broke on their far sides, a heavy sea from the storm. The ocean was empty—as it always was. The Yilanè in the city never seemed to venture north along this coast. He wondered if their hunters had gone to Round Lake again. And if so—what had happened to the males there?

"Can we go for a swim?" Arnwheet asked. In Marbak, Yilanè forgotten already.

"Too late, almost dark. We can go in the morning—and see if we can catch some fish."

"Don't want to eat fish."

"You will—if that is what we are having."

They had not eaten fish very often since they had left the lake. Perhaps there had been too much of it. The lake, it stayed on his mind and he knew why. What had happened there since they had left? Had the eggs hatched, or whatever they did? And if this had happened was Imehei still alive? The thoughts occupied his mind, as they had increasingly more and more these days. If Imehei were dead then Nadaske would be alone, with no one there to talk to. Both of them liked to speak all of the time—even if no one was listening. But it was better with an audience. What had happened to them?

They went back to the camp before dark, ate and talked about what they would do the next day. Harl agreed that fishing and swimming would be a good idea. Darras, who rarely spoke, asked to go with them.

"Take her," Ortnar said. "Armun knows how to use the death-stick, my spear arm is strong. There is nothing to fear in this place now."

What Ortnar had said decided Kerrick. He knew now what he must do. When he and Armun were alone, ready for sleep, he spoke his thoughts to her in the darkness.

"Do you know how the Sasku mark the passage of time? They don't count the days at all."

She made an interested sound, on the border of sleep.

"Sanone used to do it for me when I asked. It was a secret knowledge of the manduktos he said, but it was easy enough to understand. I can't make the drawings on the ground the way he did. But I can count by the moons. From one full moon to the next full moon is the time you count. It is many days. The moon has been three times full since we left the lake."

It was not his words but something in his voice, the meaning behind the words that drew her attention. He felt her body stiffen beside him.

"We are gone from there," she said. "So there is no need to talk about it. It is time for sleep."

"Since we left—I wonder what has happened at the lake?"

She was wide awake now and staring into the darkness, her thoughts rushing ahead of his.

"The lake is of no importance, there may be murgu there. You must forget about those two. You won't see them again."

"I am concerned about them—can you understand that? To you, I know, they are just two more murgu, better off dead."

"I am sorry I ever said that. I am trying harder now to understand how you feel about them. I try to think of you living among murgu. I don't know how it would feel, but I think I can understand how you might like some of them, those two."

Kerrick held her to him. She had never before talked like this. "If you understand—then you know that I have to find out what has happened." He felt her stir in his arms, then push him away.

"Don't go back there. Don't. I know how you feel about this, but for them I feel nothing. Stay here."

"We will talk another time."

"We talk now. You will return to them?"

"Just to see what has happened. I'll be careful, just a few days away. You'll be safe here."

Armun turned her back and rolled away from him, ceased to listen. It was a long time before either of them fell asleep.

She had been right; his mind was made up. There was continued silence next morning as he made up a light pack of smoked meat, added some of the roots that had been parched in the ashes. Ortnar thought it was all a great mistake.

"The lake is nothing. We are gone, no reason to return. There may be more murgu there now. It is a trap."

"You know my reasons, Ortnar. I am going. I will only be a few days. Guard the sammad while I am away."

"I am only half a hunter . . ."

"Your spear arm is as good as it ever was, your spearhead just as sharp. Harl is more of a hunter than I am, Armun uses the death-stick as well as I do. You will survive very well in my absence. Will you do this for me?"

Kerrick took the grunted response as a *yes* and he tied the strong skins about his feet for the trail ahead. Armun spoke to him only when he asked her a direct question, otherwise she was silent. She had been like this ever since he had decided to return to the lake. He did not wish to leave when she was angry at him—but he had no choice. Once again she surprised him by calling out as he left.

"Go carefully, return safely."

"You know why I must do this?"

"No. I only know that you must. I would go with you but I could not take the baby. Be quick."

"I will. You must not worry."

Harl went with him across the river on the raft that they had made, thick poles tied together with vines. He would return with it and hide it among the trees. Harl had nothing to say, just lifted his hand in farewell. Kerrick strode off between the trees, the hèsotsan held ready.

When he reached the wider trail, still scored deep by the passing of the sammads, he turned south, then stopped and looked about. His woodcraft was no match for any of the Tanu who had grown up in the forest. He could not even see the broken branch that Ortnar had marked the path with. He put the hèsotsan aside and took out his flint knife. With it he peeled away a patch of bark on the nearest tree. After that he looked carefully at the land and the forest and tried to remember just what this place looked like so he could find the path when he returned. Seizing up the hèsotsan he turned and started down the trail.

When the sammad had come north from the lake they had taken many days, able to go no faster than Ortnar could hobble. Now that he was alone he made much better time. On the third day he left the rutted track for the familiar path that led to Round Lake. He had hunted these woods often, knew them well. He circled when he came close to the encampment, approached the lake close to the spot where they had had their tents. Slower and slower, lying flat and crawling the last part under the cover of the bushes. Their campsite was empty and already overgrown, the black traces of their cooking fire the only indication that anyone had ever been here. When he stood behind a large tree he could see across the water to the other camp.

Something moved near the shore and he raised the hèsotsan. A Yilanè was there, back turned. He waited until the figure straightened up and turned towards him.

It was Nadaske, without a doubt. He started to call out, then thought again. Was he here alone? Or were there others in hiding? It appeared to be safe enough. He saw Nadaske go to the shore and bend over a dark figure in the water. It could only be Imehei—still alive! He felt a sudden great pleasure, stepped forward and called out attention to communication.

Nadaske spun about, ran to the shelter, came out a moment later with his hèsotsan raised and ready to fire. Kerrick stepped out where he could be seen.

"Greatings great hunter, killer of all that dares move in the forest."

Nadaske stood as though carved of stone, the hèsotsan still ready, and did not move until Kerrick had come close. Only then did he lower the weapon and speak.

"Pleasure multiplied. Presence unexpected/unbelieved. Lack of talking has made me yiliebe. You did come back."

"Of course." Kerrick pointed a thumb of query at Imehei.

"He is as he was. The eggs have broken."

"I don't understand. The eggs are gone?"

"In my ignorance I forgot your ustuzou failure of knowledge in these matters. After the eggs are laid in the pouch some time passes. Then the eggs crack and the elininyil emerge and grow within the same pouch, taking nourishment from certain glands. When they are large enough they will come out of the pouch and swim into the lake and then we will know about Imehei."

"Doubt of complete meaning."

Nadaske turned to look at the water, at his unmoving and silent friend. He made the sign of life and death, equal and opposite. "He remains as you see him until the young emerge. Then he lives—or dies. We can only wait. It should be soon now. They move about a lot, look you can see."

Kerrick looked at the stirring beneath the skin, then turned away from the unconscious figure in the lake. "How long before it happens?"

"I don't know. Today, tomorrow, more days. When it

happened to me I had no memory of it." He saw Kerrick's movements of interrogation. "Yes, I have been to the beaches. Once. They say in the hanalè that once you may live, twice you may die, thrice you are dead. This is Imehei's first. We have good reason to hope."

There was no real reason to make a fire that evening, other than to drive the biting insects away. The air was warm as always—and Kerrick had eaten raw fish before. And Nadaske detested the smell of smoke, sniffed and withdrew from the traces on Kerrick's garments. They ate and talked until it was too dark even for twilight talk. Then slept close to each other under the shelter that the two males had grown and shaped in place. It was more like a Yilanè sleeping chamber than a Tanu tent and, for some inexplicable reason, Kerrick slept very, very soundly.

The raw fish did not look that appetizing in the morning. Kerrick took his hèsotsan and walked along the lake to a grove of fruit trees, ate some of that instead. When he returned Nadaske was feeding Imehei, then, when he stirred uncomfortably rolled him over in the water to a better position.

"Will it happen today?" Kerrick asked.

"Today, some day. But it will happen."

This was the only answer he could get to his question and it was highly unsatisfactory. If he stayed here—how long would it be? He had promised to return quickly—but how quickly? He still felt that Nadaske and Imehei were part of his sammad, just as much as the Tanu, and he owed them equal loyalty. The others would be safe on the island. If he had a responsibility now it was here by the lake.

Easy enough to say. But one day became two, then three. On the fourth day without change Kerrick knew that the time had come to return to the island. He had told Armun it would only be a few days: that time had long since run out. One day more, then he would have to leave, perhaps come back later. But that would mean another long trip, mean being away from the island for an even longer time.

"There is no change," Nadaske said next morning in response to his unspoken question.

"I think we could use some fresh meat. I am sure that you, like me, have had enough fish." Nadaske signed modifiers of magnification of statement many times. "I thought so. I saw deer far down the lake. I'll bring one back."

It wasn't only the fresh meat that he wanted. He needed an opportunity to be away from the beach for a time. The sight of Imehei, neither alive nor dead, was one that he found very difficult to bear. This had to be the last day. If nothing happened he would start back in the morning.

After this decision he became engrossed in the hunt. He had not brought his bow, had never attained the skill with it for successful hunting, but used the hèsotsan instead. While this required more skill at stalking, since it was not as accurate as the bow, it also insured that no creature wounded by a badly aimed arrow would escape from him. By circling under cover of the forest he put himself downwind from the small herd. His first stalk failed when he was seen and the deer quickly bounded out of sight. He had better luck with the next herd and managed to bring down a small buck.

Nadaske could not bear fire, hated the smell of the smoke. If he cooked any of the meat for himself it would have to be done far from the shore. It would be better to build a fire here and eat some of the meat, bring back the rest for the males.

Finding dry wood, then coaxing a spark from the flint took some time, as did roasting a hind leg over the fire. The meat was tough but good and he ate it right down to the bone. It was late in the afternoon before he kicked dirt over the remains of the fire, threw the carcass over his shoulder and started back to the lake.

As he came along the shore he called out sounds of attention to speaking. He did it again when Nadaske did not respond. This was not like him. Was something wrong? He let the deer slide to the ground and sank down in the

brush. Carefully and silently, the hèsotsan pointed before
him, he moved among the trees to approach from the
sheltered side. If Yilanè hunters had found the camp he
wanted to be able to fire first. There was a large conifer
that overhung the shore and he wriggled up behind it,
carefully looked out.

Something terrible had happened. Nadaske sat on the
sand, slumped forward, arms hanging limply. He had
pulled Imehei up on the shore where he lay on his back
with his mouth open, motionless. Dead. There was much
blood and small bodies littering the sand.

When Kerrick stumbled forward making sounds of in-
quiry Nadaske turned empty eyes to him. It took a great
effort but he finally spoke.

"They emerged. He died. It is over. My friend is
dead. He is dead."

When Kerrick went closer he saw that the bodies were
of tiny Yilanè. Nadaske saw where he was looking and
sprang to his feet. His jaw clacked shut, hard, again and
again until saliva ran down his neck. There was pain in
every movement, every expression.

"They lived, Imehei died. They killed him. I watched
them being born in the water even when he was dead.
The females, they are there on the shore, every one. I
killed them. They, the females, they killed him. Now
others of their kind are dead here." He gestured towards
the lake and snapped his thumbs together loudly. "Not
the males. They are out there. If they live they will live
free of these others. That is a chance they will have—that
Imehei never had."

There was nothing that Kerrick could say that would
lessen Nadaske's pain, that could change the terrible events
of this day. He went back and found the deer where he
had left it, brought it back.

In the city Imehei's body would have been put to rest
in one of the burial pits, where the roots of specialized
plants would dissolve it, flesh and bones as well, restoring
the nutrients to the city that had nurtured him. Here all
that they could do was dig a grave in the soft sand beneath

the conifer that stood behind camp, lay his body within it. Kerrick dragged up stones to cover the loose earth, to keep the animals from digging it up.

There was nothing here now for Nadaske. When Kerrick rolled his sleeping covers in the morning Nadaske came over to him and held out a small, leaf-wrapped bundle.

"Will you carry this for me? Exercise of care in transport/prevention injury."

He opened the wrapping to disclose the wire sculpture of a horned nenitesk. Kerrick signed agreement/gratitude for trust, rewrapped it and put it carefully inside the skins.

"I will carry it safely, return it when we reach our destination."

"Then let us leave."

The sun was just over the trees when they started down the trail. Neither of them looked back at the empty beach.

TWELVE

"The fishing is good here," the sammadar Kellimans said, stirring the fire with a stick.

"And the fishing is good in the ocean everywhere—because there are fish everywhere." Herilak spoke sharply, trying to control his anger. "And will you still be able to fish here in the winter when it is so cold that the death-sticks die? You will have to leave then. So you could leave now."

"When the cold comes, then we will leave," Har-Havola said. "In this I agree with Kellimans. And fishing is good in the river also, not only in the sea."

"If you like fish that much—you should live in the ocean with them!" Herilak snapped. "We are hunters, that is what we are, not fish eaters . . ."

"But the hunting is good here as well."

"I think we can hunt better to the south," Hanath called out. "Kerrick has done something important for us."

"Like keeping us alive," Morgil said. "We go with Herilak if he seeks to find him."

"Go! Who needs you," Kellimans said with indignation. "You stole the porro from the manduktos, caused us all trouble. There are those of us who will take pleasure in seeing your backs. Leave with Herilak. But I am one who is going to stay. There is no reason to leave now."

"There is." Herilak jumped to his feet and pointed south into the darkness. "Will anyone here deny that Kerrick, somewhere out there, saved our lives, all of our lives?" He pulled hard at the knife he wore about his neck and the thong snapped: he hurled it down at their feet. "The murgu returned this to us. The skymetal knife that Kerrick always wore. It is a message to us. It tells us that he made them stop the war. He made them send this to us to show that we had won. The attack ended and they went away. He made them do all that. Will anyone here say that I am not speaking the truth?" He glared across the fire at the sammadars who nodded agreement. He looked up at the hunters and women behind them who were listening in silence. "All of us know that this is true. I say we must go south to see if Kerrick is there, if he is still alive, if we can help him."

"If he is alive he will not need help," Kellimans said and there was a murmur of agreement. "Herilak, he is of your sammad and if you want to seek him out you must do that. But we will do as we wish."

"And we wish to stay here," Har-Havola added.

"You all have spines like jellyfish, minds of wet mud."

Herilak seized up the skymetal knife as Merrith walked over to the fire. She faced them with her hands on her hips, the fire reflected in her eyes. "You are all little boys that talk big—then piss yourselves with fright. Why not say what you really think? You are afraid to go near the murgu. So you will forget about Kerrick and eat your fish. May your tharms drown in the ocean and never see the stars!"

There were even angrier shouts at this.

"You should not speak like that. Not about the tharms," Herilak said.

"I said it and I will not take back my words. Since you hunters believe that we stupid women do not have tharms—I see no reason to worry about yours. Do you leave in the morning?"

"Yes."

"Does your sammad march with you?"

"They do. We have talked about it and they will go south."

"Even your mastodons are wiser than these sammadars. I will travel with you."

Herilak nodded in gratitude. "You will leave with us." He smiled. "I can always use another strong hunter at my side."

"Hunter and woman both, sammadar. Don't ever forget that."

Everything that could be said around the fire had been said. Merrith left them and went past the dark mounds of the tents, to the meadow where the mastodons were tethered. Her old cow, Dooha, lifted her trunk and smelled the air, rumbled a greeting to her and reached out her trunk to touch her with the delicate tip. Merrith patted its hairy surface.

"I know you don't like to walk after dark, but it's not far. Now—stand still."

Merrith had her mind made up long before the meeting around the fire had begun. She had struck her tent, tied it and all of her bundles to the carrying poles which she now secured to the mastodon. Dooha rumbled complaints but permitted herself to be led away. As soon as Merrith knew that Herilak was leaving she had made preparations. The rest of the sammads could stay here by the river and get fat and oily eating fish. She would go south with Herilak's sammad. It would be good to move on—and she was fond of Malagen. There was no one else here who she cared about—or who cared about her. When she dropped the travois behind the tents and tied Dooha to a tree she went to Herilak's fire. Malagen looked up at her, smiling with pleasure. "You will come with us!"

"I will. This place stinks too much of fish."

Malagen leaned over and whispered. "It is not only

you—but Fraken, the alladjex is coming too. That will be very good."

Merrith sniffed loudly. "Old Fraken is a burden. He eats his fill of others' food." Malagen was shocked.

"But he is the alladjex. We need him."

"Not that old windbag. I have forgotten more healing poultices than he ever knew how to make. Don't confuse him with your Sasku manduktos. They are at least possessed of some wisdom and leadership. This one is too old and foolish. He will be dead soon and boy-without-a-name will take his place."

"It is not true that Fraken can see the future with the owl packets?"

"Some say so. I have little faith in the skins and bones of regurgitated mice. I can tell the future without their help."

"You can?"

"I'll show you. He did not say it yet—but Nivoth will be leaving this sammad before morning."

"May Kadair always guide you!" Malagen's eyes were wide in the firelight. "You were not here, could not have seen, but Nivoth just dragged his tent away."

Merrith laughed out loud and slapped her thigh. "I knew it. But it took little intelligence to predict that. If we go to search for Kerrick and find him, why then we may find Armun who went to join him. Once she knocked Nivoth to the ground with her fist, broke his nose, that is why it is twisted so. He has no desire to meet her again. It is very good to see his back."

"You know everything about the sammads. You must tell me."

"Not everything, but enough."

"You will put your tent here?"

"Not tonight. It is rolled and on the poles, ready to leave in the morning."

"Then you sleep in my tent."

"No, it is the tent of your hunter, Newasfar. There can only be one woman in a tent. I will lie by the fire. It won't be the first time."

The fire was cold ashes by morning, but the night had
been warm. Merrith lay, still wrapped in her robes, as the
morning star faded over the ocean in the first red touch of
dawn. She rose and had tied the poles of the travois into
place long before the others emerged.

"If you sleep until noon you won't get far today,
Herilak," she said as he emerged and sniffed the air. He
scowled.

"Your tongue first thing in the morning is no pleasure."

"My tongue only speaks the truth, great sammadar. Is
it true, old Fraken joins us? His love for Kerrick was
never that great."

"His love of warmth is. He fears the winter here."

"That I can understand. How far do we march?"

"Today, until we camp by a small river we have stopped
at before. If you mean how far do we march to seek
Kerrick, we march as far as is needed."

"To the murgu city?"

"If we must. I know he is out there somewhere."

"I have not gone there for many days," Kerrick said,
keeping his voice calm so his anger would not show.

"That is of no importance," Armun said. "You are a
hunter. A hunter goes where he wants. You can go there
every day. But Arnwheet stays here with me."

From where he sat in the shade of the large oak tree
Kerrick could see across the clearing to the water. This
island was a very good place to be. Both of the tents were
hidden under the trees. The hunting was good, fresh
water close by. There were duck, fish for the taking,
berries carpeted the island. Armun and Darras had brought
back baskets of roots and mushrooms. And they were all
well, the baby growing. Even Ortnar, though he grumbled, was as good as could be expected. Only Nadaske's
presence caused Armun's unhappiness; she would not let
it rest. He was unseen—yet always seen by her. He was
like a scab that she picked at constantly and made to bleed
again and again.

"It does the boy no harm," Kerrick explained patiently—

and not for the first time. "And he wants to go." He
looked over to Arnwheet who was sitting with Harl, had
fled there when his parents seized up the argument one
more time. Armun followed his gaze, tried to be reasonable.

"Think of how I feel, not how he feels. He will grow
up something different, half murgu, half Tanu. Like . . ."

"Like me?" There was bitterness in his voice. "Half of
something, all of nothing."

"That is not what I meant—or perhaps I did. You have
said you are not a good murgu or a good hunter. Let him
be a good hunter, that is all I ask."

"He will grow to be a great hunter because he is not
being raised by the murgu—as I was. You must not fear
that. But to be able to talk with them, to know about their
ways, is something of great importance. We share our
world with them and I am the only one who knows anything at all about them. When he grows up, able to speak
with them, then there will be two of us."

Kerrick felt that argument was useless. This was not
the first time that he had tried to explain to her, to make
her understand his feelings, so this trouble would not be
between them always. But she would not understand,
perhaps could not. He seized his hèsotsan and stood up.

"I am going to see Nadaske. I will be back before
dark." She looked up at him, her face as set as his.
"Arnwheet will be coming with me. There is nothing more
to talk about." He turned and walked quickly away, not
wanting to hear anything more that she might say now.

"Can Harl come," Arnwheet said happily, shaking his
spear with excitement.

"What do you say, Harl?"

"Will you fish or hunt?"

"Perhaps. But first we go to talk with Nadaske."

"You do not talk, you shake and gurgle," the boy said
with pentup anger. "I will hunt by myself."

Kerrick watched him stamp away. He was less of a
boy, more of a hunter every day. And he listened too
much to Ortnar who filled him with his own bitterness.
He should have others to talk to, not Ortnar alone. This

was a good camp, there was little danger and all the food they needed. Yet there was unhappiness too. It was his fault—but there was nothing he could do about it. "Let's go see Nadaske. It has been a long time since we talked with him."

The sky was beginning to cloud over and there was the smell of rain in the air. The leaves would be falling soon in the north, the first snows were on their way. Here the nights might be cooler, little else changed. The path led down to the swamp. It was deep in places so Kerrick carried Arnwheet on his shoulders through the green water. They swam the inlet to the island on the other side. Arnwheet called out attention to speaking shrilly and Nadaske emerged from his shelter to greet them. There was pleasure of talking in his movements.

"To one who hears only the waves, voices of friends are like songs."

"What are songs?" Arnwheet asked, imitating Nadaske's movements and sounds for the new word. Kerrick started to explain, then stopped. Arnwheet was here to listen and learn; he was not going to interfere.

"You have never heard a song? Perhaps because I have never sung one for you. I remember one that Esetta* used to sing."

He sang hoarsely, disturbed by memories.

> Young I go, once to the beach,
>   and I return.
> Twice I go, no longer young,
>   will I return?
> But not a third . . .

Nadaske broke off suddenly, sat staring sightlessly across the water, seeing only memories.

Kerrick had heard the song before, in the hanalè where the males had been imprisoned. He had not understood it then. He did now, knew all there was to know about death on the beaches.

"Did someone swim on the beach and drown?" Arnwheet

asked, aware of the unhappiness in the song, but not understanding it. Nadaske turned an eye in his direction, but did not speak.

"Do you eat well?" Kerrick asked. "If you are tired of fish I can bring meat . . ." He grew silent when he realized that Nadaske was not listening.

Arnwheet ran over and took Nadaske by one of his thumbs and shook it. "Aren't you going to finish the song?"

Nadaske looked down at the boy, then signed inability. "It is a very sad song and one I should not have sung." He carefully pulled his thumb free and looked towards Kerrick. "But this feeling has been growing since I have been here. What is to become of me? Why am I here?" The weariness with which he spoke muffled his motions, but his meaning was clear.

"You are here because we are efenselè and I brought you here," Kerrick said, worried. "I could not leave you alone back there."

"Perhaps you should have. Perhaps I should have died when Imehei died. For two there was something. For one there is nothing."

"We are here, Nadaske. We are your efenburu now. Arnwheet has many things to learn that only you can teach him."

Nadaske stirred and thought about this, and when he answered some of the great sadness was gone.

"What you say is true. This is a very small efenburu of only three, but that is superior/magnified to being alone. I will think hard and I will remember a better song. There must be one." His body moved as he thought of the songs he knew, searching for an appropriate one.

efendasi'esekeistaa
belekefeneleiaa, deenkè deedasorog
beleksorop eedeninsu∗.

UGUNENAPSA'S THIRD
PRINCIPLE

———————

*The spirit of life, Efeneleiaa, is
the supreme Eistaa of the City of
Life and we are citizens and
beings in this city.*

THIRTEEN

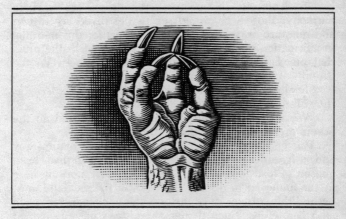

As she walked the sunny pathway between the tall trees, Enge felt very much at peace with her surroundings. The trials of her life were part of the past, remote memories of cruelty and death. The present was warm and bright, the future hopefully so as well. When she entered the ambesed these emotions were in her walk and the movements of her body. The others already there saw this and were pleased.

"Share your thoughts, Enge," Satsat asked, "for we can see they are the finest."

"Not fine—just simple. As the sun warmed me my memories warm you. As I looked at our city I realized how far we have come. Think about it and join my pleasure. First there was Ugunenapsa and she was alone. She was the creator and her Eight Principles changed the world. Then came the time when a few of us believed what she taught, and for our beliefs we were condemned. Many of our sisters died, and there were the days when death seemed to be the fate awaiting all of us. But we kept our belief in Ugunenapsa always before us and it has now

come to pass that we live in the world created by our
beliefs. This city of beauty surrounds us, we work in
harmony, those who would see us destroyed are distant
and unaware of our existence. As we gather this morning
in affirmation of our beliefs we can see about us the proof
that our faith was not misplaced. We are between the
thumbs of Ugunenapsa and find peace there."

She looked in the direction of the eistaa's place, as
they all did, and raised her clamped thumbs.

"We are between her thumbs," she said and all the
others present repeated the gesture.

This ceremony had come about in a most natural way
and it greatly pleased them all. Those who had been
chosen to lead in the city's labors met each morning here
in the ambesed to discuss the work of the day, the most
natural thing to do, since this was the unchanging ritual of
all Yilanè cities. Even though the eistaa's place remained
empty they still gathered before it. Someone had remarked upon the bare and sunwarmed wood and, with
sudden insight, Enge had observed that it was not empty
for it was Ugunenapsa's place. Efeneleiaa, the spirit of life,
was the eistaa of this new city and ruled invisibly from
within this ambesed. Now when they gathered they took
strength from the empty wood knowing that it was not
empty at all.

The quiet of this satisfying yet simple ceremony was
fractured by Far<'s sound of attention to speaking. Before
she could say any more Elem broke in.

"Matter of urgency, necessity to speak first. The uruketo
hungers. I must take it into the ocean for some days so
that it may feed."

"Do it today, when you leave here," Enge said.

"Matters of equal urgency," Far< said, "to be discussed before departure of uruketo."

"No," Elem said with great firmness. "The safety and
health of the creature comes first, priority ahead of any
discussions."

"Perfectly phrased, content of wisdom," Ambalasei said
as she walked slowly across the ambesed towards them. "I

have noted often before that the predilection here for talking far outweighed the physical realities of life."

She passed by and settled down comfortably in the eistaa's place against the warm wood. If she was aware of the murmur of consternation that swept the Daughters she ignored it. She knew of the current superstition, therefore enjoyed sitting metaphorically in the invisible Ugunenapsa's lap.

"It was of this unbeliever that I wished to speak," Far< said with modifiers of distaste.

Shocked silence followed these bold words and Ambalasei's crest stirred and flared with color. But before she could reply Enge broke in quickly, hoping to forestall another battle of wills.

"Ambalasei grew this city and it is named for her. You have no cause to speak of her in this insulting manner."

"Cause enough," Far< said, still speaking in the rudest possible way. "I have given this very much thought so you must all understand that I do not speak out impetuously. As we do not enjoy yesterday's sun during this day's rain, so do we not praise yesterday's victories in the face of tomorrow's failures."

"If there is a point of any intelligence behind these ambiguities—make it," Ambalasei said with modifiers of even greater insult. "Though I doubt it greatly."

"You speak truth when you speak of your doubt," Far< said, her large eyes glowing with the intensity of her feelings. "For you are the great doubter. You sit now in Ugunenapsa's place and would have us think that you are superior to her. You are not. You block her will. You have removed the Sorogetso from this place and they were our future which is her future."

"The Sorogetso, Daughter of Dissension, are no part of your sisterhood nor will they ever be."

"Not now—but they were our hope. From their future efenburu of elininyil would have come the daughters of our future. You have interfered . . ."

"The first true statement you have made!"

"This shall not be. They must be returned. I have

spoken with the crewmembers of the uruketo and none know the place where the Sorogetso were abandoned. You must tell us."

"Never!"

"Then you condemn us to death."

Shocked silence followed this cry of pain and only Ambalasei was unmoved by the strength of her feelings, feeling only distaste, then shaping her body so this would be clear to them all.

"I think we have had enough of your insolence and insults, Ninperedapsa. Leave us."

"No, for you cannot command me. You shall not evade the results of your evil actions that easily. I said death and I meant it. All here will die one day as all creatures must die. But when the last of us dies this city will also die— and with it Ugunenapsa's words and her memory. You destroy us all. You take away our future."

"Strong words from one so frail." Ambalasei's anger had faded. She was beginning to enjoy this contest of wills; life had been too peaceful of late. "It was Ugunenapsa who insured the end of the Daughters of Life by not supplying them with any Brothers of Life as well. I am not to blame for the frailties of your philosophy. Show me which of the Eight Principles describes breeding Sorogetso for your own purposes and I will be pleased to acknowledge that I am in the wrong."

Even as Far< was starting her retort Enge stepped forward and stood between them.

"I will speak. Although I feel great pain at Far<'s manner of address I thank her for reminding us of this great problem. I thank great Ambalasei as well for reminding us that the solution must lie in Ugunenapsa's words— for it is as she has said. If the answer does not lie there, then the problem is indeed insoluble. I do not believe that this can be so. The wisdom and insight that shaped the Eight Principles must also have considered the future of these principles. If we search we will find the answer."

"I have sought and I have found," Far< said. "I asked Ambalasei for aid only to save lives. But Ambalasei is the harbinger of death and aids us not. Therefore we turn our eyes from her and to Ugunenapsa as is only right. We turn our thoughts to the eighth principle. Daughters of Life, we bear the responsibility to help all others to know the Spirit of Life and the truth of the way of life. We must do as we have done in the past, go to the cities of the Yilanè and speak of the truths we know—"

"And die the death you so richly deserve," Ambalasei broke in, her movements as cold as her words. "You called me the salvationer because I brought you from bondage and gave you a city where you could live without being killed for your beliefs. If you wish to reject this, then that is your choice. I ask only that Ninperedapsa, she who disrupts, formerly called Far<, be the first to go."

Far< stood, slim and straight, and signed acceptance of all adversities. "I will do that." She turned to Elem with a motion of query. "Will you take me to the shores of a Yilanè city so I can speak there of Ugunenapsa's truths? Will you take me and those who believe as I do?"

Elem hesitated, confused and uncertain, then turned to Enge and signed for guidance. Enge accepted the burden of responsibility as she always had.

"This request cannot be ignored—nor can it be answered in an instant. Thought and consideration and consultation are required . . ."

"Why?" Far< broke in, rudely. "We are all free, all equal. If you stop me from doing what must be done you are restoring the rule of the eistaa who orders all things. This is unacceptable . . ."

"No!" Enge said loudly with signs of obedience and attention. "What is unacceptable is your coarseness of manner and degree of insult to she who made everything we now possess possible. We will give consideration to what you have said because it is of the gravest importance. But I order you into silence now for the manner of its presentation."

"I will not be silenced, I will not be ordered. You have said you will consider this—then do so. I withdraw from your presence because that is my wish. But I will return to this place tomorrow at this time to hear your conclusions."

Having said this Far< turned and left, followed by her acolytes. The silence that followed was filled with distaste and despair. Ambalasei spoke out quietly but with great intensity.

"Had I been there I would have stepped upon that one when she was still in the egg."

Enge signed weary unhappiness. "Ambalasei, do not speak so, for you stir a response within me that shames me greatly."

"You wish her disposed of just as I do. Natural enough."

"She spoke only the truth."

"And brought night to us in the sunlight of the day," Satsat said. There were motions of agreement. "If she wishes to leave, perhaps to her death, is there reason to stop her?" The signs of agreement were stronger, perhaps even vehement.

"That should not be done," Ambalasei said, to their astonishment. "I would be pleased beyond belief to see that one's crest vanishing in the distance—but it would be a deadly mistake. Think twice before you inform the world of Yilanè of this city's existence. What we have grown, they can take."

"I understand your concern on our behalf," Enge said, "and thank you for it. But it was never our thought to hide from others. We are here and here we shall remain. We have nothing to fear. It is not the way of the Yilanè, the thought itself is unacceptable, to go to another city except in peace."

"Under what might be termed normal circumstances I agree. But the Daughters of Life are a threat to the rule of any eistaa. Has your presence or your teaching been tolerated anywhere, by any eistaa? I see the answer in your limbs. Never. There are cities to the north that are now threatened by the increasing cold of winter. If one of these cities should learn of your presence here—would they not want to take this empty city for their own?"

"But this city is not empty."

"To an eistaa it is empty, for no eistaa rules here. Were I an eistaa who found this place I would consider it not as a possibility but as a necessity to bring rightful rule to disorganized chaos." Ambalasei raised her voice to be heard over the loud cries of disapproval. "I say this from the point of view of an eistaa and it is the truth as she would see it. So beware of this expedition of doubtful value. Instead of bringing back converts it may bring extinction. You have been warned."

"And you have our gratitude, Ambalasei," Enge said. "But if Far< and her followers wish to leave they must be allowed to do so. We cannot stop them or order them. We must consider their suggestions as equal to any other suggestion. How are we to insure that Ugunenapsa's words do not die with us? Search the Eight Principles, I beg you, just as I shall. The solution must be found."

"And found before the uruketo returns," Ambalasei said. She looked at Elem. "Suggestion strongly given to leave at once and not return until the creature has eaten its fill."

Elem signed complete agreement and turned to go. Ambalasei left with her and did not speak until they were well away from the ambesed. "How many days will this take?"

"Three, possibly four, depending upon the fishing."

"Take seven. If they have not come up with a solution to this problem in six days they never will. Far< is not going to do us the service of lying down and dying."

Nor did she. Every morning she and her followers appeared in the ambesed. They asked the same two questions always. Have the Eight Principles revealed the answer? For five days they were answered only with silence, after which they asked the second question; has the uruketo returned? Then they left. Ambalasei did not attend these unhappy sessions: if there were solutions of any kind she would hear of them soon enough. She spent peaceful days examining and cataloging the specimens they had brought back. Only on the sixth day did she go to the ambesed soon after the sun rose, taking the eistaa's place with some

satisfaction. She was the first to arrive and acknowledged
the greetings of the others as they approached, waited to
speak until they were all there.

"Have you found the solution?" she asked. There was a
great unhappiness behind Enge's negative response.

"It eludes us."

"Undoubtedly because it does not exist. Then you will
permit Far< to leave?"

"We cannot stop her."

"That is to be seen."

There were movements at the ambesed entrance as
Far< and her loyal followers entered. There were more of
them now for her intent-of-purpose had inspired many.
Ambalasei writhed in obvious distaste as Far< came and
stood before them, then spoke.

"Has the answer been found among the Eight Principles?" There was superiority in her attitude as she looked
at each of the silent Yilanè in turn. As she started to speak
again Ambalasei interrupted.

"The answer is yes and no."

"I do not speak to you or listen to you because you do
not believe."

"Your not speaking is too wonderful to even consider.
But you will listen because what you do depends on my
permission."

Far< turned her back with motions of dismissal, would
hear no more. It was Enge who spoke.

"Sorrow and apologies for lack of grace/rude behavior
of a companion. What permission is it you speak of,
Ambalasei?"

"The uruketo returns tomorrow."

"We will leave then," Far< said firmly; she had been
listening with one eye.

"You will not!" Ambalasei spoke the command loudly
and harshly. "I will remind you that the uruketo is mine,
taken by me and controlled by me. Do you have any
doubt about that?"

As always they turned to Enge for guidance. She stood
in silent, unmoving thought, then gestured compliance.

"In this matter we must do as Ambalasei says. Freely she had herself imprisoned with us, escaped with us—and did indeed see that we left that city of unhappiness in this uruketo. She guided us here and grew our city of life. We have used the uruketo, but we use it only as she wills . . ."

"Wrong!" Far< said loudly. "If she does that then she is our eistaa and we have no eistaa."

"Nor do you have an uruketo," Ambalasei said with pleasurable malice. "You will do as I say or you will stay in the city. You are very young, hotheaded, vain and foolish Far<, though others might not agree. But you will do as I say, accept my instructions or try to swim back to Gendasi*. And it is a very long swim, even to one of your great strength of will."

Ambalasei leaned back against the warm wood and basked in the intensity of Far<'s hatred.

FOURTEEN

It was Enge, as always, who labored to bring peace to the warring factions

"Ugunenapsa teaches us that we all dwell in the city of life. Ambalasei is equal to you in this city, Far<. And she is superior to you in all other ways, in her knowledge and skills, and particularly in her labors for the Daughters of Life. In this she is far ahead of me and second only to Ugunenapsa who revealed the truths. We are here, our city is here—and you are here Far<—because she brought you here. Any future labors that you may do will be done because she freed you. I do not ask for gratitude, but I do request acknowledgment of this fact from you."

Far< was still angry. "Am I to take your orders, too, Enge? Are you my eistaa now?"

Enge stayed calm in the face of her wrath. "I command you only to state a fact. Is Ambalasei responsible for your freedom?"

After a reluctant silence Far< signed a stiff positive motion. Enge acknowledged it.

"That is good. Never forget it. As Ambalasei has helped

us in the past, so will she help us in the future. Therefore when she wishes to speak to you of conditions of use of the uruketo you owe her the courtesy of at least listening. You may reject the conditions, but you must listen. Do you agree?"

Far< lowered her eyes in deep thought and when she raised them again her anger had faded and she signed supplication. "In my zeal to spread the teachings of Ugunenapsa and to insure the continuation of those teachings, I have permitted myself to be moved to anger. For this I apologize to you and the other Daughters of Life." She directed a gesture of dismissal in Ambalasei's direction. "I do not and will not apologize to this unbeliever."

"Nor do I wish it, obnoxious one. I have heard that the stature of a Yilanè is measured by her enemies. I hope that I can number you among them because I am lost if I call you friend. Now—will you follow my instructions?"

"I will listen to them," she hissed in answer.

"For you, a reasonable statement." With signs of dismissal of unimportance she turned away and addressed the others. "We will now discuss facts historical and their bearing on events to come. All of you here were at one time unbelievers. Then you were spoken to by such as Enge, saw the light, so to speak, and became believers. Is that not what happened?" She nodded at the motions of agreement. "So that is the way Daughters are recruited. Where did this take place? I ask you Enge."

"For me it was in the city of Inegban* where I spoke with a Yilanè of great learning by the name of Essokel."

"In the city?"

"Yes, of course."

"And you others," Ambalasei said with a gesture that embraced their totality. "All of you learned of Ugunenapsa's inspiring philosophy in a city?"

Each signed agreement, even Far< with great reluctance. "Of course it would have to be that way. You were all Yilanè or you would not have been able to understand the arguments. But do these conversions really conform to

Ugunenapsa's exhortations in her eighth principle? Do I not sense strong discrimination here?"

There were movements and signs of puzzlement on all sides—and a flare of colored rejection from Far< who would not even consider Ugunenapsa's principles when voiced by this unbeliever. Only Enge stood silent and thoughtful, her limbs and tail writhing slightly in echo of cogitation. Now Ambalasei watched her alone as her movements quickened and coalesced and she threw her arms wide with joy of discovery.

"As always, great Ambalasei brightens us with the clarity of her thought and we must give her praise, highest praise."

Far< signed refusal, the others query, Ambalasei a pleased acknowledgment of credit where credit was due. Enge's body moved uncontrollably with the intensity of her emotions.

"Ambalasei has the breadth of intelligence and understanding to show us where to look in Ugunenapsa's teachings. The answer was always there, it was just our ineptitude that prevented us from seeing it. Does not the eighth principle state that we bear the responsibility to help all others to know the spirit of life and the way of life? Yet why do we limit ourselves so?"

She ended with a query and desire for answer. There was still puzzlement and contempt from Far<.

"Will you have us explain the principles of Ugunenapsa to the fishes in the sea?"

"Silence, Far<," Satsat said, anger sharpening her movements. "You dishonor us as well as yourself with the darkness of your thoughts. Ambalasei has indeed led us to the truth—and in that she is more loyal to Ugunenapsa's teachings than you are with your rejections. We were all Yilanè when we learned of Ugunenapsa. Because of this we think only of Yilanè. But we forget the fargi. All of them wanting only to learn from us, their minds empty vessels ready to be filled with Ugunenapsa's truth."

"It takes one of great intelligence to see things hidden from those of lesser ability," Ambalasei said with her usual

modesty. "Here is what you must do. Go to the fargi and
teach them. In their urge to communicate they will believe anything. Go to them when they leave the beaches
and before they enter the city. Give them food, that will
certainly draw their attention, then speak to them of
Ugunenapsa and tell them how they will live forever. Do
that and you will get all the recruits you need. And by
staying away from the city you won't get seized and imprisoned as you have in the past. The fargi are number-
less; your converts will never be missed. Agree to do this
and the uruketo will take you to a city, to the beaches
beyond the city."

Ambalasei accepted their gratitude as her due, listened
to the animated discussion. But she kept one eye on Far<
always and Enge soon became aware of this. She signed
for attention, then turned to Far<.

"And what do you say to this? Will you take Ugunenapsa's
truth to the fargi?"

They were all silent and watching now, interested in
what their argumentative sister would answer. They saw
her lift her head, sign firmness of resolve, then speak.

"I have not been wrong—but I have perhaps been
overzealous. Ambalasei has led us to the truth and for this
I thank her. I will go to the fargi and speak to them so that
this city may live. I thank her again for helping us."

There were overtones of dislike behind what she said,
but she still spoke with sincerity. Enge, filled with the joy
of revelation, seeing the answer to this vexatious problem
before her, ignored these small signs. Peace had been
restored. Ugunenapsa's great work would proceed.

"What are your commands, great Ambalasei?" Enge
asked, speaking as a supplicant and not an equal. Ambalasei
acknowledged this with easy acceptance.

"I will grow containers for preserved meat. When these
are ready and filled we will leave. I suggest a limited
number be allowed to preach so there will be room in the
uruketo when it returns for those whom you have con-
verted. When the meat is gone and the conversions made

the uruketo will come back here. This city will grow, particularly with young and strong fargi to do the labors."

"When you spoke of leaving you said when *we* leave," Enge observed. "Then you intend to go in the uruketo?"

"Naturally. Who else is able to organize this better than I? And I yearn for discussions where a certain name is never mentioned. Now agree among yourselves who is to go. I suggest five as a maximum number."

"Suggest?" Far< said, an edge of apprehension and distaste behind the question.

"Order, if you prefer that. But I am magnanimous and do not bear grudges. You and four others if that is what you want. Will you come, Enge?"

"My place must be here in the city now, readying it for the newcomers, though my strongest wish is to join you. Satsat, closest to me, will you go in my place?"

"Gladly!"

"Three more then," Ambalasei said and stretched her stiff muscles and walked away. "I will inform you when it is time to leave," she called back, then left the ambesed. At an easy pace went through the city that she had grown, that was named in her honor. But she walked slowly now and she knew that this was more than fatigue. She was old and often, in moments of quiet thought, she felt that she was reaching the limits of her physical powers. The end would come, not tomorrow but perhaps tomorrow's tomorrow was waiting with its void of emptiness. There were things that must be done before that inevitable moment arrived. Setèssei was mounting specimens when she entered but instantly ceased and signed readiness for instruction.

"Containers to be grown," Ambalasei said as she rooted through a store of dried eggs and pods. She found what she wanted and gave them to her assistant. "Nutrient fluid needed for growth, then preserved meat to be sealed in them. But first bring me the ugunkshaa and a memory creature."

"Which memory do you seek?"

"One of no real importance for I need to make a record."

"There are early reminders of ocean currents and winds of the south, now supplanted by observations of discovery."

"Perfectly correct. I do not keep partial records of vagueness—only historically important successes."

The ugunkshaa, a severely mutated creature of no intelligence, squatted before Ambalasei, its great organic molecule lens staring sightlessly up at her. Setèssei placed the memory creature beside it and delicately inserted one of the tendrils above its withered eyes into a fold of flesh on the memory-speaker. As she made subtle adjustments a black and white image flickered across the lens and there were muted sounds of a voice. These stopped when the other, smaller eye, slowly opened and stared at Ambalasei.

"As you speak now, so shall it listen and remember," Setèssei said stepping back.

Ambalasei dismissed her, gathered her thoughts, then began to talk. Every motion, every sound she made was registered indelibly in the memory creature's brain.

"I will tell you first of the rivers in the sea that led me to this new land . . ."

"My greatly-trusted Setèssei will stay with you while I am away," Ambalasei said. "While of course not my equal, she is skilled in the matters of the city, having helped to grow it, and is skilled also in the treatment of wounds that your clumsy sisters seem to acquire with such ease."

"Gratitude-magnified-multifold," Enge signed. "All is in readiness for departure?"

"Almost all. The last of the preserved meat should be ready today. As soon as it is aboard we will leave. The morning will be best since I want to make observations of the ocean currents as they flow north and diminish. The connections between my new charts and the old must be made. After that I wish to see this city you spoke to me of, Alpèasak."

"Death and destruction by fire! All Yilanè dead and ustuzou with killing stone-teeth in the streets and groves."

"Yet you lived, Enge, and others."

"The few surviving Daughters of Life fled in the uruketo and are here now with me. There was also the uruketo's commander and the crewmembers. And one whose name I will not speak. There was also a male, name unknown, and the scientist Akotolp."

"Akotolp! She who was fat and round as a river eel?"

"The same."

"Where is she now?"

"Unknown. We left the uruketo, as I have told you, to escape persecution at the thumbs of the nameless one."

"I must see this city. Perhaps the ustuzou have gone. In any case the currents flow in that direction and past and on to the shores of Entoban∗. Observations to be made, charts to be rationalized."

They departed soon after dawn, slipping out into the river and down to the open sea. Ambalasei had enlisted the aid of two crewmembers to trail the neskhak in the sea as they went. The neskhak swam strongly, seeking safety, but were pulled back aboard by their grossly extended tails. Since their skin color varied with the water temperature, Ambalasei would make notes on her charts and have them thrown overboard again. Freed of any labors, the missionary Daughters of course spent their waking hours in discussion of the Eight Principles—deep within the uruketo where Ambalasei could not hear them.

It was a pleasant and warm journey to be greatly enjoyed. All too soon they were passing the island of Maninlè, then the jewel-like islands of Alakas-aksehent. By this time Ambalasei was fatigued by her labors and sleeping below. The charts, new and old, were joined and complete. The known world was that much bigger thanks to her genius. Having accomplished this she slept very well, wakening only at the touch on her arm. It was Elem, the commander, signing attention and obedience to commands.

"You ordered me to waken you when the mainland of Gendasi∗ was in sight."

"Is it?"

"Obscured by rainclouds at the moment, but it is there certainly enough."

"I come. Assistance in rising needed. Muscles stiffen from damp and sleep."

Elem's strong arms helped her to her feet and she walked slowly to the fin, climbed it laboriously, complaining continuously. The two crewmembers there came tumbling down pursued by her wrath, though she signed Elem to join her.

"Have you been here before?" Ambalasei asked.

"No, but the charts are clearly marked. We have but to follow the chain of golden islands to this swampy coastline. Alpèasak lies to the north."

The rain had blown out to sea and the low coastline was clearly visible now. A sandy shore with forests behind. Elem glanced up at the sun. "We should be there before dark."

"If there is any doubt, stand out to sea. Remember the ustuzou Enge told us of."

"Horrible, beyond understanding, deadly."

"But nevertheless there. Precautions manifold."

"Perhaps not needed," Elem said, shielding her eyes against the sun. "Movement near coastline, uruketo, boats."

Ambalasei muttered and blinked but could not see them clearly at first. Only when they were closer could she make out the details.

"Observations of great interest. The city is obviously Yilanè once again. Docks there, other uruketo. But do not approach it yet. Go close to shore, there, by those beaches. And have the missionaries come up here now. Bring up the meat containers as well."

When the five Daughters had joined them, Ambalasei indicated the shore and the clump of towering trees beyond. "Note this place and note as well the number ten. The count of two hands. The uruketo will return to this place after that number of days. To pick you up—and those as well to whom you may have shown the way. The surf is light, your swim to the shore an easy one."

"What of this meat?" Far< asked.

"It will be pushed into the sea, the waves will carry it ashore, you will retrieve it. Be back at this place in ten days."

"And if we have not finished our work?" Far< said, always finding something to query.

"Conclusions will be reached then. I call you missionaries because you go on a mission to speak to the fargi of those truths which seem to be all you care about. Make them believe and return with them. But, please, see if you can't return with intelligent and strong ones. There is work that needs doing in Ambalasokei."

"You do not join us?" Far< asked suspiciously.

"No. I have far more important labors. Ten days." She waited until the last of them had slid into the ocean and was swimming towards shore before she spoke again. "Take me to the dock. As soon as I step ashore, leave. Talk to no one there. Return to get me in the early morning on the tenth day. Understood?"

"Understood, great Ambalasei. Ten days."

FIFTEEN

As Ambalasei stepped from the back of the uruketo to the worn wood of the dock she felt a great satisfaction. With one eye she watched the uruketo swim back towards the open sea, to be quickly lost in the bustle of the port. Before her was a vista of wide streets, hurrying fargi carrying fresh fish, pieces of meat, unknown bundles. The air carried a burden of odors, cries of command and issued orders.

"A great city, a busy city, a city where for ten days I shall eat well, talk intelligently—and not hear the name Ugunenapsa spoken at all. Almost unbelievable." She laid the small container down on the dock next to her feet and looked around at the gaping fargi. One stood quite close with her mouth almost closed and with what might be a flicker of intelligence in her eyes.

"Do you understand/comprehend?" Ambalasei said, slowly and clearly.

The fargi raised her hand and signed understanding with colors alone, then added verbal modifiers. "Comprehension and seeking of guidance."

"That you shall have. Pick this up. Follow me." She had to repeat this twice before the fargi signed colors of understanding and hurried forward.

Ambalasei, with the fargi trailing happily behind, strolled along the wide street, greatly enjoyed the bustle of the city. She came to a slow-moving line of fargi each carrying a bloody slab of fresh meat. She turned to follow them, clacking her jaws with pleasure, suddenly realizing how monotonous the constant diet of eel had become. Cool, jellied meat: fresh, stillwarm meat!

The street widened into a large eating area. She passed the interesting display of fish, later perhaps, and moved on to the shaded vats where the fresh meat was curing. She lifted the cover on the first and took out the leg of a small animal, admired it for a moment—then bit out a large and juicy mouthful.

"Attention to speaking," a harsh voice said, and Ambalasei looked up chewing contentedly. The Yilanè before her had fat wattles on her neck; the hanging flesh on her arms was painted in patterns of elaborate coils. "Put down that meat, I do not know you old one. This is reserved for the eistaa."

Beside Ambalasei the fargi with her container began to shake with fright at the threat-in-speaking that she heard. Ambalasei signed her to remain easy, protection of superior, nothing to fear. She chewed slowly, savoring the sweet meat, shaped her limbs into commands from highest to lowest, swallowed—then hissed with anger.

"Fat gilded-beetle to be crushed! Decayed worm from lowest dungpit! Before you stands Ambalasei highest of the high, eistaa of science, intelligence of the world, possessor of infinite powers. I should sentence you to death for your ill-speaking. I consider that now."

So powerful were her movements, so strong her will and her contempt that fargi screamed and fled on all sides, the fargi next to her stood with eyes closed, moaning and shaking. The pudgy Yilanè stepped back, gasping, the colors of her skin fading before the onslaught. She could not talk, could barely think. Ambalasei was very pleased with herself and took another bite of meat, chewed and swallowed before she spoke again.

"Approval of your fearful respect," she signed. "Magnanimity in greatness, insult forgotten. Your name?"

"Muruspe . . ." the terrified creature finally gasped.

"Tell me Muruspe, who is the eistaa of this great city that has such fine meat?"

"She is . . . Lanefenuu, Eistaa of Ikhalmenets before Ikhalmenets came to Alpèasak."

"Seagirt Ikhalmenets come here. I had not heard."

"Cold of winter, snows of cold whiteness descending."

"I can well believe that. Your city was too far to the north. Now, lead me to Lanefenuu for I have heard of her and desire the pleasure of her acquaintance."

The ambesed was large and sunfilled. The eistaa, arms gleaming with multicolored painting, sat at ease and issued orders to those gathered about her. It was a pleasant, civilized scene and filled Ambalasei with much pleasure as she approached and spoke.

"Powerful Lanefenuu, Eistaa of seagirt Ikhalmenets now come to Alpèasak, accept the salutations of Ambalasei knowledgeable of all things who now stands before you."

Lanefenuu curved her arms in warm greetings and admiration. "If you are the Ambalasei of whom I have heard ever since I was a wet-skinned fargi you are amplified/welcomed to my city."

"Could this world possibly contain two Yilanè of such achievements? Impossibility. I admit to being the Ambalasei of whom you speak."

"Ambalasei!" the name rang out, the tones echoing hers, and she turned to see a familiar figure pressing forward. "Ambalasei who instructed me in all the wisdom of science. Greatest pleasure in life to witness your presence here."

"Undoubtedly. Is that you lean Ukhereb, my student?"

"I am. And look, hurrying there, another of your
students."

"Figure of fatness—it can only be Akotolp. The greatness of your city increases, Lanefenuu, with scientists of
their knowledge, who learned from me of course, serving
you here."

They pressed thumbs in greetings and Lanefenuu ordered a chair of great comfort to be brought forward
for the old scientist. The Yilanè present moved with
pleasure for all had heard of Ambalasei, while the rings
of fargi behind them stirred with the knowledge of
great events occurring. There was silence as the Eistaa
spoke.

"By what unknown scientific means do you appear in
our city?"

"The science of the uruketo. The commander now
takes the beast north along the shore to continue my
oceanic researches, which are important beyond comprehension." She waved over the fargi with her container,
reached into it and held up the recording creature. "Facts
contained herein, Eistaa. Discoveries of note to change
complete knowledge of the world. None in any of the
cities of the Yilanè know of this yet. The pleasure is mine
to share this knowledge first with Lanefenuu. Even before
it is imparted to scientists/friends. For a great eistaa, who
can safely move her city across an entire ocean, is deserv-
ing of highest rewards."

Lanefenuu signed only magnification of pleasure in
return. This was becoming a day to be long remembered.
"All of you back," she ordered. "This greatest Yilanè of
science shall speak with me alone."

They pushed and stumbled over each other so forceful
was the command, so great the event. Moved back ten,
twenty, thirty paces until Lanefenuu and Ambalasei were
at the center of an immense ring of admiring Yilanè, they
in turn surrounded by fargi. The ambesed was now filled
to capacity as word spread and all in the city hurried to
witness what was occurring.

They saw Ambalasei hand the recording creature to the Eistaa, saw them bend close in conversation, their voices so low that the meaning of their movements could not be understood. But they all understood easily enough when the Eistaa climbed to her feet and held the recording creature over her head as she moved her body in arcs of triumph. A great rustle of sound came from their feet as they hurried close at her signed command.

"A day that will be talked about, remembered forever. This greatest Yilanè of knowledge has revealed it to me—and I reveal it to you. The world that we know now is incomplete. We Yilanè have come here to Gendasi∗, from Entoban∗, have seen the size of the known world doubled in our lifetime. We knew of but one continent and now we have voyaged to this second continent. Now listen and be amazed. Great Ambalasei, in her wisdom, has discovered yet a third immense, warm continent to the south of us." She turned to the scientist. "You have described this new land, Ambalasei, but you have not told us its name. Will you do that now?"

"I will, since it is the eistaa's request and must be obeyed, but modesty has prevented me up until now. One aboard the uruketo with me when first we saw this land said that since I had divined its existence and had led the uruketo there, since I had known of it when no other did, why it was suggested, and I hesitate to say it, it was suggested that this new land be called . . . Ambalasokei."

"And so it shall! I, Lanefenuu, so proclaim it and so it shall be known hereafter. Ambalasokei, the place that Ambalasei found. This is a wonder indeed."

An even greater wonder than they could possibly ever know was Ambalasei's silent thought as she watched their jubilation. She sat, unmoving, her body shaped in a silent curve of acceptance of honor, revealing nothing. If she chose not to speak of some matters, a new city grown, new Yilanè discovered, and they had not the knowledge to ask of these matters, then that knowledge would not be trans-

mitted. Enough to bring them an entire new continent.
Satisfaction sufficient for one day.

Akotolp waddled over and took the recording creature
from the Eistaa when she was summoned, cradled it gently
between her thumbs. When Lanefenuu granted permission she hurried off with Ukhereb to the laboratory.
Ambalasei watched them leave with a feeling of great
relief; her place in history was safe. Knowledge of her
discoveries would slowly spread from scientist to scientist,
city to city. Not quickly, for that was not the Yilanè way,
but surely. One day other scientists would come here,
hear the record, bring the word to still others in Entoban*.
Interest would be roused among those cities threatened
by the approach of winter and expeditions would be
mounted. Some day her city of Ambalasokei would be
contacted, but not in the foreseeable future, not in her
lifetime. She owed the disputatious Daughters at least
that much. This would give them some time to resolve
their problems and, if possible, insure the future of their
city.

The Sorogetso were another matter altogether. Their
future was between her thumbs and it was a grave responsibility. How lucky they were that she was the one to both
find them and secure their untroubled existence. Such
responsibilities she bore upon her broad shoulders! Ambalasei
smiled with happiness and signed to an attendant fargi for
a water-fruit.

Days of pleasure followed. The Eistaa saw to her comforts and regaled her with the story of their heroic move
from Ikhalmenets. She spoke very briefly of the battles to
displace the ustuzou from this city and the long war that
followed. When she made curt mention of the name Vaintè
Lanefenuu's anger was so great that Ambalasei was careful
to never speak the name again in her presence. But she
did question the two scientists about the matter, and
expressed approval at the successful biological warfare they
had waged against the enemy.

"What you did was perfectly correct. This is a Yilanè

city, therefore it was your duty to destroy the intruders who occupied it, to drive them back to their caves and dens. But as you were right, this Vaintè was in error to pursue and attempt to annihilate them. They sound a poisonous and deadly species, but still a species which, like all others, must be preserved. Like any trapped animal they fought back viciously. Two uruketo dead before the fighting ended, Vaintè sent away in disgrace! Terrible. But still a lesson taught, hopefully learned. The attempt to destroy another species is the seed of self-destruction."

The two scientists signed complete agreement, together with modifiers of great intensity. This matter was so distasteful that they were happy to turn their thoughts away from it to a more pleasurable discussion of Ambalasei's biological discoveries and how some of the species she described seemed related to others here in Gendasi∗. It was a delightful and fruitful discussion.

The days flew by swiftly after this. Fine food for the body, fine nourishment for the mind. Lanefenuu pressed her to stay, as did Ukhereb and Akotolp, but Ambalasei was firm. "Pleasures here greatly enjoyed. But my work is not complete. Each day that I grow older is one day less to finish my labors. They must go on. The uruketo is charting water temperatures and will return soon. I must leave on it when it arrives." She was becoming quite adept at vagueness that suggested lack of knowledge. This was the ninth day and the uruketo would be back in the morning and she would be gone. But it had been a very pleasant stay.

This pleasure was not to last. As the three scientists sat at their ease they became aware of shouts and a great disturbance from the ambesed. Before they could inquire a messenger arrived. Not a fargi, but Muruspe herself, Lanefenuu's efenselè, gasping for breath.

"Presence required . . . urgency of motion . . . strongest desire."

The fargi were pushed back to make way for them, until they reached the center of the ambesed and the group around the Eistaa. There was a tall Yilanè there clutching the arms of a smaller one. A thin figure that looked horribly familiar to Ambalasei.

"See this!" Lanefenuu called out. "Look what has been discovered on our beach."

Ambalasei was paralyzed with shock, speechless for the first time in her life.

It was Far<.

SIXTEEN

"Lack of understanding," Akotolp signed. "Confusion as to meaning of this presence."

"Speak, esekasak," the Eistaa ordered. "Tell all assembled what you have found."

The tall Yilanè who was esekasak, the birth-beach guardian, shook Far<'s thin body, then pushed her forward so all could see.

"It is my duty to guard the beaches, to guard the males who rest there. I guard and assure the safety of the beaches when the males are in the hanalè. I assure the safety of the elininyil when they emerge from the sea. They are weak and need protection. It is my duty also to look at each elininyil as it emerges from the sea because in the efenburu in the sea it is not as it is in the city . . ." Her speech stopped and she turned to the Eistaa for aid.

"I shall talk of this matter," Lanefenuu said, "for the esekasak is not permitted to do this. Her duty, in addition to protecting all, is to separate the males from the females when they leave the ocean, to take them at once to the hanalè. It was in the performance of her duty that she found this one she holds leaving the beach."

Lanefenuu paused because her fury was so great that her body writhed and she could not speak clearly. She fought for control and raised her thumbs and pointed to Far<, then spoke again with great difficulty.

"Found this one . . . leaving the beach . . . with an elininyil. A MALE!"

It was an unheard-of crime, an inconceivable crime. The order and organization of the city did not, could not permit this to happen. Males were confined to the hanalè and rarely seen; were never seen unguarded. What had happened? What could possibly have happened? Most of the spectators were so rigid with shock that Ambalasei's stunned silence drew no attention. It was Akotolp, ever the scientist, who stepped forward with signed queries.

"Where is the male?"

"Now, in the hanalè."

"Did it say anything?"

"It is yiliebe."

"Has this one spoken?"

"No."

Akotolp pushed her face close to Far<'s, shouted her command.

"I do not know you—tell me your name!"

Far< signed negative, then gasped with pain as the big guardian closed hard thumbs on her thin arms. Akotolp looked to the circle of Yilanè. "Does anyone recognize her? Who here knows her name?"

There was only silence, and it was Lanefenuu who spoke next.

"Her name—unknown. Then she is not of this city and is a stranger. Where are you from, stranger? Someone must know you if you came with us from Ikhalmenets."

Far<'s limbs moved as she listened and, with no intention of speaking, she still signed *not Ikhalmenets*. There was no way for her to avoid the truth for, like all Yilanè, she lacked the ability to lie. What she thought, she said, and it was clear for all to understand. Lanefenuu was relentless.

"You attempt to hide who you are and where you are from. But you cannot. You cannot hide from me. I will name a city and you will answer. I will ask you until you tell me. I will find out."

Far< looked about, writhing now with panic, not wanting to speak but knowing that she would be forced to. Her glance fell on Ambalasei's rigid body for a moment, hesitated, moved on. Understood.

For an instant, unnoticed by any of the others who had eyes only for the questioning Akotolp and the prisoner, Ambalasei had spoken. A single, simple nonverbal expression. Far< understood. She writhed in understanding and hatred, so strong that the Eistaa recoiled.

Death, Ambalasei had said. *Death.*

Far< knew that she would eventually have to convey information. And in doing so she would reveal the existence of the city and of the Daughters of Life. They would be found, captured, killed, their newfound freedom doomed. She would speak and everything she had lived for would die. The hatred was for Ambalasei who would live on. For her there could be only one thing.

Death.

Hers—or all the others'. At the thought of all the deaths she would cause Far< writhed with agony. Her eyes closed and her body sagged. Ambalasei watched, immobile and expressionless.

"Dead," Lanefenuu said with disgust, as the esekasak opened her thumbs and Far< dropped to the ground. "Now we will never know."

Akotolp waddled over and nudged the limp body with her foot, signalled to the nearest fargi. "We will do a dissection, Eistaa. Perhaps there is a disease, an infection of the brain, that may explain this unusual happening."

Lanefenuu signed termination of presence and the corpse was hurried from her sight. Most of the onlookers left as well since the Eistaa, still moving with anger and affront, was obviously in no humor for conversation. Forgotten for the moment, Ambalasei moved away with the others, determined not to be noticed again. The fargi milled about in the dusk, seeking sheltered sleeping places, and she stayed close to them. When darkness fell they took no notice of her presence in their midst. She slept, as well as she could on the hard ground, and was awake and on her way to the waterfront at first light. She walked past the tethered uruketo to the open space at the dock's end and waited there, forcing herself into stolid silence. Very soon after this an uruketo appeared from the sea haze and she saw, with great relief, that Elem was on the fin. Their presence was not noticed among the other uruketo: a crewmember helped her aboard and Ambalasei ordered instant departure.

"You sign great worry, great unhappiness," Elem said when she had climbed up to join her.

"I have good reason to. I will speak of it later. Because right now you and your crew have no time for listening since you will be working as hard as you can to get this creature to the beach just as quickly as possible."

They were waiting on the sand, the four Daughters of Life and a huddled group of frightened fargi. There was a great deal of milling about before the fargi could be urged into the surf, to swim out to the uruketo. But once started they came strenuously on, strong swimmers since they were but recently emerged from the sea. They swarmed aboard and were gaping about stupidly long before the Daughters arrived. Satsat was the first to pull herself out of the water, to face an enraged Ambalasei.

"What happened out there? What possessed that idiot Far<? Do you know what she has done?"

"I do. She could not be dissuaded. Our work here was finished, she said, for we had talked to the fargi and had given them food. Those who understood us stayed with us and listened, but the ones that were still yiliebe drifted away. Those who learned of Ugunenapsa are with us now. Our city shall grow and prosper . . ."

"Cease rambling? Speak of Far<."

Satsat looked with great unhappiness at the fargi and her companions now climbing into the uruketo, fought to order her thoughts. "She said that we had new Daughters of Life—but only daughters. For our city to grow and prosper in the natural way males were needed, as she has always said. We urged her not to go, spoke of the danger, but she would not listen to us . . ."

"I can well believe that."

"Although she risked death she took the risk gladly. She felt that if she could but bring a single male to the wisdom of Ugunenapsa no sacrifice would be too great. She left us, did not return. Not last night nor this morning."

"She did as she desired," Ambalasei said coarsely, "her greatest wish has been granted. She is dead. She died to stop herself from speaking. Probably the only intelligent thing that she ever did in her entire life."

Ambalasei turned away from the horrified Satsat and made her way into the interior of the uruketo and sought a dark and quiet spot to rest. She remained there for most of the return voyage, eating little but sleeping a great deal, ignoring the others. Although she did talk to some of the fargi, slowly and quietly with none of her usual brusqueness. Most of the time she slept. It was midday, warm and humid, when they returned. She was first ashore and left the unloading to the others. They had been seen upon the river and it seemed that the entire city was there.

"Looking instead of working. Typical of Daughters of Dissitude." She ignored Enge's respectful signed welcome and turned instead to her assistant, Setèssei. "I am sure many tragedies befell during my absence?"

"A few accidents—"

"Any fatal?"

"None."

"Too bad. Otherwise the city grows in order?"

"It does."

"That at least is appreciated." She turned to Enge and

signed for attention and obedience. "Walk with me along
the shore where I can avoid sight of the Daughters and all
thoughts of Ugunenapsa."

"With pleasure. I see fargi aboard, so all was successful."

"I would hardly say that. One has stayed behind in
Alpèasak. Far<."

"I do not understand. Why did she do that?"

"She had no choice. She was dead."

Ambalasei spoke with enjoyable malice, then walked in
silence until Enge had recovered some of her composure.
When she spoke again her explanation of events was brief
and unflattering.

"She died from applied stupidity, that is what I believe."

"You are too harsh on the dead, Ambalasei. She will
never trouble you again. She died in the hopes of seeing
this city live. We will long remember her death with our
sorrow."

"I would suggest that you remember it with joy—
because if she hadn't died that would have ended everything for you. Nor will you be happy with your new
converts. I have talked with them and find them barely
Yilanè and incredibly stupid. They are like trained animals. They know nothing of Ugunenapsa, care even less.
They learned to repeat certain phrases that they had
been taught. They did this so they would get food in
return."

"They will grow in understanding."

"If they don't they will still make good workers. But
this will be the last missionary attempt. It is too dangerous
to go near other cities. You must find another way to
ensure your survival. Try the Eight Principles again."

"I will, though not at the present time. I am too filled
with the despair of our lost sister. I know, Ambalasei, you
don't have to say it, she was foolish and headstrong. But
what she did she did for us all and we shall mourn her."

"That is your choice. Mine is to further my studies of
this new continent. I will be going up the river again as
soon as I have made my preparations."

Enge signed respectful farewell when Ambalasei left. It was difficult to think that she would not see Far< ever again. She regretted now the harshness with which she had treated her sister. There was an emptiness now that would be hard to fill. But she must not brood about it. There was one of the newcomers, staring about with wonder at this new city. Enge approached her and signed greetings. The fargi recoiled.

"Do not fear. All here are Daughters of Life and no harm will ever come to you. Do you have a name?"

The fargi merely stared at her, though her jaws worked uneasily.

"Do you understand what I am saying?" There was still no reaction. "Well, you will learn to speak. Then you will learn the truths as taught by Ugunenapsa . . ."

"First principle," the fargi said, slowly and crudely. "We resist between thumbs spirit life named Efeneleiaa."

"Then you are not yiliebe, and I can see that you have learned wisdom . . ."

"Second principle. All dwell city life. Third principle. Spirit life Efeneleiaa supreme eistaa city—"

She slowly stopped speaking and her jaws worked and she writhed in an attempt to remember what came next. She could not so she began over. "First principle . . ."

"That is enough, you can stop now."

"Food—food—food!" the fargi said and opened her jaws wide like a bird in a nest.

Enge took her arm and led her to the food vats. She was very depressed. Ambalasei had been correct. This fargi had learned to recite sounds and movements she could not possibly understand, to be rewarded with food for her efforts. Trained like an animal, not Yilanè at all. And Far< was dead.

Enge fought back despair. There was much to be done, very much.

Es mo tarril drepastar, er em so
man drija.

TANU SAYING

---

*If my brother is wounded, I will
bleed.*

SEVENTEEN

Herilak walked the track ahead of the sammads, his eyes never still. Not only looking into the forest on both sides but also up at the branches above. He stepped over the trunk of a tree that had fallen across the track: it had been a long time since a sammad had passed this way. Something rustled in the undergrowth and he stopped and stared but could see nothing. Bird cries sounded among the leaves—and the sudden, distant snap of a death-stick.

He turned about and listened, there were shouts and a mastodon screeched. With his own death-stick held ready he ran back along the track to the sammad. Nadris was prodding a large, still form with his foot, the marag that they called spike-back.

"What happened?" Herilak called out.

"This thing came out of the trees, started towards the mastodons. I had to kill it."

The tiny eyes were glazed in death. It was covered with armored plates and had rows of spikes down its sides and all along the length of its tail. It had been a good shot, the poisoned dart striking the creature on its mouth.

"They are good to eat," Nadris said.

"But hard to butcher," Herilak said. "If we turn it over we can take off the rear legs. But we will have to stop for the night soon so you don't have much time. Stay here and get started—I'll send Newasfar to help. Use his mastodon to carry the meat and be sure to leave before dark."

They started forward, the mastodons rolling their eyes and trumpeting with fear when they passed the immense corpse. Herilak went ahead again, looking for a clearing where they could stop and build their fire. They would need dry wood, a lot of it, to cook all of the meat. It would spoil in the heat if they didn't, a waste.

An animal trail crossed the larger track, angling off into the forest. He stopped to see if the trees were thinner here and something caught his attention; he bent and looked closer. It was a blaze on the treetrunk, a mark where a section of bark had been peeled away. Though it was partly grown over it had been done this season. And there, higher up, was a branch that had been broken and left to hang. This trail had been marked by Tanu.

Merrith was leading her mastodon, the others following in line behind it, when she saw Herilak waiting on the track ahead. When she came close she saw that he was smiling, pointing into the forest towards the east.

"I've found something, a marked path leading towards the shore. Marked more than once."

"Could it be Kerrick?"

"I don't know, but it is something, another sammad perhaps. If he is not there they may know of him. We'll stop here. You tell the others—I want to see where this trail goes."

It was almost dark when Herilak came to the water and looked across at the island. Too dark to go on. He sniffed the air. Was there a trace of woodsmoke? He could not be sure. He would find out in the morning.

They ate well that night, gorged themselves because there was far more meat here than they could possibly eat or preserve. Only old Fraken complained at the toughness of the meat, but this was because he had very few teeth

left. The boy-without-a-name had to cut Fraken's food into
small pieces for the old man, was ordered to do this before he ate himself. Though he did stick some of the
pieces into his mouth when Fraken looked away. Herilak
chewed the meat without thinking about it, wondering
what he would find on the island in the morning. He lay
awake a long time that night, slept restlessly, then awoke
while there were still stars in the sky. He took some cold
meat from the ashes of the fire and bit off a piece, went to
wake Hanath.

"I want you to come with me. I'll need help crossing to
the island."

Morgil awoke when Herilak spoke. "What about me?"
he asked.

"Stay with the sammad. Smoke as much of the meat as
you can. We'll be back as soon as we see if there are Tanu
out there. If there is a sammad Hanath will come and tell
you."

It was a cool morning and they moved swiftly down the
trail to the water's edge. Hanath lifted his head and sniffed
the air.

"Smoke," he said, pointing at the island. "Coming
from over there."

"I thought I smelled it last night—and look here, these
marks. A raft or a boat has been pulled up onto the mud.
There is someone on the island, there has to be."

"How do we get across?"

"The same way . . ."

"See—something is moving over there, under the trees."

Both hunters stood motionless and silent, peering at
the shadows under the distant trees. A bough was pushed
aside and someone emerged into the sunlight, then another.

"A hunter and a boy," Hanath said.

"Two boys, one big enough to be a hunter."

Herilak cupped his hands before his mouth and called
out an ululating cry. Both boys stopped and turned—then
waved when they saw the hunters. Then they turned and
disappeared back under the trees.

Kerrick looked at them when the boys came running

down the slope, shouting, so out of breath they could
barely gasp out the words.

"Hunters, two of them, over the water."

"Were they Tanu?" Ortnar asked, dragging himself up.

"They had hair just like ours, and spears," Harl said.
"They are Tanu hunters."

"I must see them," Kerrick said, taking up his hèsotsan.

"I'll show you where they are!" Arnwheet was bounc-
ing with excitement.

"All right."

Armun heard this as she came from the tent with the
baby in her arms.

"Let the boy stay here," she said.

"There is nothing to be afraid of. They're Tanu. Ortnar
will be here with you. Arnwheet saw them first, he de-
serves to meet them as well. Maybe they can tell us what
has happened at the valley."

"Bring them here."

She watched as they raced away, the boys shouting to
each other. Could it be another sammad? There would be
other women to talk to then, other children. She was just
as excited as the boys were. Darras came out of the tent,
silent and fearful as always. It would be good for her to be
with other girls. It would be wonderful if there really was
another sammad close by.

The boys ran ahead, shouting with excitement and
were already pulling the raft out of the brush when Kerrick
reached the shore. They were right, there was a hunter on
the other side. Just one though, large and somehow familiar. He waved a hèsotsan and called out.

It was Herilak, it could be no other. Kerrick waved
back in silence, remembering the last time they had met
in the city. The sammadar had been angry at him for
forcing the sammads to stay and help in the city's defense.
They had not spoken since then because Kerrick and
Ortnar had gone north the next morning. Their route
carefully chosen so they did not pass near any of the Tanu.
If they had, the two Yilanè males with them would have
been killed on sight. What was Herilak doing here—and

what would he say now? There had been many harsh words between them.

Kerrick stood silently on the raft while the boys poled it across. Looking at the big hunter who was silent as well now. When the raft grounded on the shore, Herilak placed his weapon on the grass and stepped forward.

"I greet you, Kerrick," he said. "Greet you." He touched the skymetal knife that hung around his neck, then pulled it free and held it out before him. Kerrick reached over slowly and took it. He could see that it had been polished with sand and glistened in the sunlight.

"They brought it," Herilak said. "The murgu. They had been attacking us, they were winning. Then they stopped. And left this for us."

"It was meant as a message for another. But it is good you saw it too. You understood its meaning?"

Herilak's grim face broke into a rare smile. "I understood not at all how it had happened. But knew that something had been done, the attack which was killing us had stopped, the murgu were gone. And it must have been your doing. I knew that it had to be you when I saw this." Herilak's face was grim again and he stopped and folded his arms. "When we met last I said many harsh things, Kerrick. You are of my sammad yet I said and did things that I should not have done. I did not do as I should have for your woman Armun. I have a great shame for that."

"It is the past, Herilak. We will not talk of it again. Here, greet my son Arnwheet. This is the sammadar, Herilak, first among sammadars and hunters."

"Not first, Arnwheet," Herilak said looking down at the boy. "Take pride of your father. He is first among all of us. And this one, I know him. The son of Nivoth. He left with Armun. She is here then as well?"

"She is here. And also Ortnar of your sammad."

"There was a darkness in my head then. I treated Ortnar as I treated you. Worse perhaps. I struck him. I can only say that the darkness is gone. I wish I had not done the things I did—but I cannot take them back now."

"There is no need to talk of this here. The boys said there were two hunters?"

"The other has returned to the sammad, to bring them here to the water. Will you join with us, you and your sammad?"

"Where do you trek to?"

"Why—to find you."

Kerrick burst out laughing at Herilak's baffled expression —and Herilak frowned at first, then laughed as well.

"You have found me, so the trek can end here. Join us. The island is safe, the hunting good. There are deer and small eating murgu. It is a very fine place to camp."

"Killer murgu?"

"Some, but not many cross the river from the mainland. We watch for their spoor in the mud here, track them down and kill them at once." Talking about murgu brought something important to mind.

"You and the sammads are welcome here," Kerrick said, then hesitated. "But I must tell you, one of the males from the city is close by, on an island by himself."

"One of those who lived through the fire in the city?" He frowned and unconsciously lifted his weapon.

"The same. There were two, the other . . . died. I know you think that every marag should be killed, you told me that. But this one is harmless."

"Are you saying that if we come to this place—the marag must not be disturbed? That is a hard thing to ask."

"Hard, perhaps, but that is the way it must be. I talk with him. And because I can talk with the murgu I did what had to be done to save the valley, to make them stop the war. To bring you this knife."

"I have not thought of these things before. To me, always after the death of my sammad, murgu were there to be hated and destroyed. All of them. You have said that some of them are different, but I cannot understand that."

"This one is harmless, a male, locked away with other males all his life. It is the females that make war. I want this one to live."

Herilak frowned, but finally nodded his head. "It will be as you say. I will not go near the beast."

"And the others?"

"They must each say the same thing—or they cannot stay here. The island where this marag is will be forbidden, that is the best way. Tell us which island it is so each Tanu will make an oath not to go there. The children as well. I do not like this. But it is you who we owe our lives to, we can at least do this thing for you. The creature will be safe."

There was a trumpeting from the forest and the first of the mastodons came into view. The sammads had come to the island.

EIGHTEEN

Armun heard the mastodons well before she saw them and clutched the baby to her with excitement. There they were, tearing at the leaves as they came, hunters leading them between the trees. Not only hunters, for the first one was a woman—and someone familiar.

"Merrith!" she cried, again and again until the older woman heard her, turned and saw her, waved and hurried over.

"Armun! You are here, you are safe. You have a family. You were only a girl, now a mother—such a baby of great beauty. I must hold her."

"Her name is Ysel," Armun said, smiling with happiness as she passed her over. "And her brother has grown, you must have seen him, he went to meet you."

"Look at her eyes, just like yours." Merrith glanced up when the tent flap moved aside and Darras looked out shyly. "And another daughter as well!"

"She is like a daughter to us now, but not our daughter." Darras clung to Armun's leg, reluctantly coming forward to meet this new woman she had never seen before. "This is Merrith, who I have known since I was only a little girl, when I was even younger than you are now, Darras."

Merrith smiled and touched the girl's hair, felt her shiver beneath her fingers. Then the girl twisted away and ran over to look at the mastodon who stood placidly chewing a great mouthful of leaves.

"She was alone when we found her," Armun said. "Just her and a mastodon. The rest of the sammad killed by the murgu. She has been with us ever since. She has dreams that wake her at night."

"Poor baby," Merrith said, then passed Ysel back to her mother. "Do you know what sammad it was?"

"Sorli, sammad Sorli."

Merrith gasped and clutched her hands to her breasts. "Then she is dead, my daughter is dead! She and her hunter, they went with sammad Sorli. Melde. Dead now, like her sister."

When she heard this Armun went rigid, holding the baby so tightly that she began to wail. She controlled herself, caressed the infant until it stopped crying, until she could talk. Yet her voice still trembled when she did.

"At first Darras would not speak when we found her, could only cry. She had watched them all being killed. Later I could talk to her, she told me about it, how she had been alone in the forest. Told me her name. Darras. Told me her mother's name as well." Armun hesitated, then forced herself to speak. "She spoke her mother's name. It was Melde."

The two women looked at each other in shocked silence and it was Merrith who managed to speak first.

"Then this child—my granddaughter?"

"She must be. I must talk to her. She never told me, but she must know her father's name."

At first Darras did not know what was happening, could not understand it. Only when the relationship had been explained over and over again, often enough to make it clear to her, only then did the long-hidden tears come as she clung to her grandmother and wept.

"You will live with me," Merrith said, "if that is what you want to do. If Armun says it will be all right."

"She is your daughter's daughter. She is yours now. You must put your tent close by so we can be together always."

Her tears changed to laughter and Armun joined in and, after a little while, even Darras managed to smile through her tears.

The days that followed the arrival of the sammads were the happiest that Armun had experienced in her entire life. The murgu who had fought against them fought no longer, they did not have to be considered or feared. The coming of the sammads had changed life completely on the island. The tents stretched away under the trees and smoke rose from many cooking fires. Children ran and screamed between them and their cries were echoed by the trumpet of the mastodons from the field. Game was abundant, their stomachs were full—while the dried meat hung heavy in the smoking huts. A large hardwood tree had been cut down, trimmed of its branches and floated to the shore near the tents. Here, under Herilak's direction, it was being hollowed out by fire. When it was finished they would have a boat to go into the marshes with, to trap the feeding birds that now had grown very wary of the hunters. Arnwheet and the other boys of the sammads had watched this being done and were now hard at work making a smaller version for themselves. There were some burned fingers and tears, but the work progressed.

In her newfound happiness Armun realized how much better off they all were for the joining of the sammads. Herilak had come and spoken to Ortnar, and while none had heard what was said it was clear that the rift between them was closed, the bond restored. Ortnar's tent was now beside the sammadar's and he sat next to the fire in the evenings with the other hunters, even managed to laugh with them. He no longer talked of going alone into the forest.

Now, when he wasn't working on the boat, which was a sporadic thing indeed, Arnwheet was playing with the other boys his own age: Harl went with the hunters. Life was as it should be and she was very happy. She sat in the sun before her tent, the baby kicking and crowing on a soft skin laid in the grass before her. Malagen knelt and watched her with wide-eyed pleasure.

"May I pick her up?" she asked, speaking Sesek. Armun could still remember the language; it was the greatest pleasure for Malagen to hear it and speak it again. She cradled Ysel in her arms, the baby's fair hair a contrast to her dark skin. She never ceased being amazed by it. "And her eyes, look, as blue as the sky! I have made something for her, it is here."

She reached inside her clothing and took out a length of dark ribbon which she passed to Armun. "When her hair grows longer you can use it to tie about her head, in the Sasku manner."

Armun ran her fingers along it with admiration. "It is so soft, but it is not the cloth you weave—what is it?"

"It is something very important and I will tell you about it. When we left the valley I brought my loom, you have seen it, and I have woven the charadis fibers into cloth. But none of the charadis is left, I have used it all up. Then I looked at your waliskis and when they permitted I touched them. This was very wonderful."

Armun nodded agreement. She knew that waliskis, the Sesek word for mastodon, were somehow very important to the beliefs of the Sasku. Malagen could sit happily for the entire day and admire them.

"I touched them and they let me brush them and they liked that. Then I discovered that when they were brushed some hair came off and I saved it for it is very precious. Then one day I twisted it, as we do with the charadis fibers, and discovered that it might be possible to weave into cloth. And I did! And this is it." She laughed and leaned close to whisper. "I made the headband to bring to the manduktos one day. But I can make another. And this is so small. I think it will be better now for Ysel."

The Sasku could do many things and Armun was very glad that Malagen was here. Malagen had searched the

island, then made Newasfar go with her to the mainland
before she found the right kind of clay she needed. The
hunters would not help the women with the work, but
they at least stood guard against wild creatures when they
went to dig the clay. The women had loaded Merrith's
mastodon and returned with baskets of it. Now a proper
oven was being built and soon they would have the hard-
as-stone pots to use, just like the Sasku.

So many things were happening that Armun no longer
minded when Kerrick went to see his marag. She noticed
that he went alone most times, that Arnwheet was busy
with the other boys, and that pleased her very much
although she did not say it out loud. Kerrick was her
hunter and he could do things that no other hunter—or
sammadar—could do. One thing he could do was talk with
the murgu. If he had not talked to that one on the island
when they killed the big sea beasts, none of this would be
taking place. All of the sammads would be dead. Everyone
now knew what he had done, and how he had done it, and
they never tired of hearing her tell about it. And about the
Paramutan, and crossing the entire ocean, and all of the
other things that had happened to them. They listened in
respectful silence when she spoke, and not only because
Kerrick was her hunter but because she had done these
things herself. She no longer hid her cleft lip from sight—
nor even thought about it. Life was full, the sun was
warm, the endless summer far better than the endless
winter had been. Some of the women talked about the
snow, and the berries you could find only in the north and
other things. She listened but did not speak herself for she
had no desire to see any of these things ever again.

Kerrick saw this change in Armun, did not question it
but accepted it with gratitude. It had not been a very
happy sammad before the others had arrived. A lame
hunter, a sad little girl, and two boys too different in age
to really enjoy each other's company. All this had changed.
Darras was with her grandmother now, smiling and talking for the first time; she seemed to have finally forgotten
the death of her own sammad. Kerrick just wished that

Arnwheet was not so busy with his friends, that he could find the time to talk with Nadaske. Not that he went that often himself. It had been many days now since his last visit, so many days that he had forgotten just how long. This was no way to treat a friend. He cut a leg from the freshly killed deer that hung from the tree behind the tents, took his hèsotsan and walked the well-trodden path towards the ocean. He saw no one when he crossed the channel and made his way across to the smaller island. On the crest he looked out to sea, empty as always. The Yilanè kept to their city as Lanefenuu had promised. If he had brought the sammad here sooner, left Round Lake earlier, they would never have met the Yilanè hunters. And Imehei might still be alive. He shook his head to dislodge the thought. It was not worth thinking about: the past could not be changed. As he came through the brush he called out attention-to-speaking.

The shelter was there but it was empty. The hèsotsan was missing so perhaps Nadaske had gone hunting. Kerrick found some freshly cut leaves inside and put the meat on them. When he came out he found Nadaske waiting there. Kerrick curved his hand in appreciation.

"Nadaske is the forest creature who moves as silently as the wind. Were you hunting?"

"No. Hearing sounds of walking I went to place of hiding." He put his hèsotsan inside and saw the meat. "Sweet flesh of dead animal magnified many times better than fish. Gratitude to efenselè."

"I will bring some more again soon—but many things have been happening, it has been very busy. But why were you hiding? Playing a game from the hanalè?"

Nadaske's mouth was too full of meat to answer at once; he chewed enthusiastically and finally was able to swallow. "Ten times ten times more pleasurable than fish. A hanalè game, yes we did play them. Boring/stupid. It is hard to think of that life now—or why we thought it had any pleasure. No, not a game. But small ustuzou have been here, threatening death-by-stone-tooth. Now I watch and hide."

"They were here? Who, hunters like me?"

"No, not large ustuzou, but small like little/soft, or perhaps larger."

"Some of the boys, that's who it must have been. Did they attack you with their spears, throw them?"

"Shout and wave weapons, run away into trees."

"I'll take care of that," Kerrick said grimly. "They know that they are forbidden to come here. They think they are very bold—but we will see about that. It won't happen again."

Nadaske worried the bone with his teeth, eating every fragment. He swallowed, gulped and signed sweetness of meat, sweetness of life. Kerrick was thinking about the boys, how to make sure the incident was not repeated, and it took a moment to understand what Nadaske was saying. With Tanu all about him now, the world of Yilanè was growing distant and alien. The great jaw and shining skin of Nadaske were so different from the Tanu. And the way he held the bone between opposed thumbs. A motion caught Kerrick's eye and he saw a lizard dart across the clearing. Nadaske dropped the bone and the lizard stopped when it saw the motion. Still as a carving, motionless— just like Nadaske. They were equally different, equally alien.

"Something else occurred," Nadaske said and the moment of strangeness was gone. This was Nadaske, his friend.

"What was that?"

"There was an uruketo."

It was as though a chill wind had passed over him. "No! Here? Did they come ashore?"

"Negative-negative. It was out in the ocean, not near shore. It went north, then the next day came back in the other direction."

"The same one?"

"Assumption positive, evidence negative."

The sudden fear was ebbing. The Yilanè had not come ashore, it had nothing to do with the sammads. Of course there were uruketo in the ocean. But as long as the sammads stayed away from the shore there was nothing to fear. Yet it was like an omen, the same as seeing two black birds at the same time which meant there would be bad luck that day, that is what Armun said. That and never putting a knife down with the point towards you, also bad luck. He did not believe in omens.

"Have you seen uruketo before?"

"Once far out to sea."

"I don't think that we have reason to be alarmed. Alpèasak is south of us, along the coast. Uruketo, boats for fishing, they all use the port. As long as they don't come ashore."

"They won't." Nadaske moved a thumb in the direction of his teeth in the expression that means once bitten, you avoid the creature that bites. "The eistaa who cares for uruketo will remember the two dead on the shore. They stay in the city, we stay here, plenty of food for all."

"You must be right. But it is hard to think that peace is ever possible between Yilanè and ustuzou."

"There is peace between us. Probably because we are males; females cause all ills in world. Beware your females."

Kerrick signed agreement and awareness. He had given up trying to explain the relationships of the Tanu sexes. Nadaske would never believe that he wasn't following Armun's instructions. "Time to return," he said, climbing to his feet.

"Query of interest, desire Kerrick to see hèsotsan."

Nadaske brought out the weapon and pointed to one of the curled and useless legs of the creature. "Smallness of change, occurrence of importance?"

Kerrick took the hèsotsan, the living weapon that was essential for their existence. Any change in the creature was a matter of concern. This one looked like all the others, shriveled eyes shut, atrophied limbs tight against its side. Once the creature had gone through its young and active stage, this permanent change took place. He looked at the leg, at the white dusting on the dark skin, brushed it with his fingertip.

"The skin is gray here, I see that. I don't think I have

ever noticed it before on one of these. Perhaps the creature is getting old. Do you know how long they live?"

"Knowledge lacking. Other than this mark, it functions as always."

Kerrick took one of his own darts and inserted it under the flap of skin, pointed the hèsotsan towards the ocean and squeezed. There was the familiar crack of sound and the dart flew out in an arc. When he rubbed its lips the mouth slowly opened. It ate the scrap of meat he fed it.

"Seems to be normal in every way. There is no need to worry."

"Every need to fear," Nadaske took back the weapon and examined it closely. "No hèsotsan, no life. Death by eating from predators."

"That is not a worry yet. Fears groundless, future filled with sun and meat."

Kerrick started back to the camp. When he was out of sight of the shore he stopped and looked carefully at his own hèsotsan. It was normal.

But the seed of worry had been planted. He trotted across the island, eager to return.

He wanted to look closely at the other hèsotsan that the hunters used.

NINETEEN

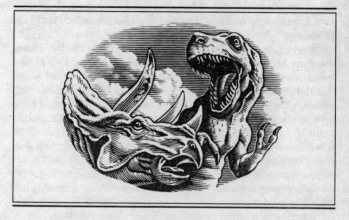

They never discovered what was causing the trouble; had no idea at all how they could stop it.

At first Kerrick's fears proved unfounded. All of the hèsotsan he looked at appeared normal, without any trace of the gray skin that had been on Nadaske's weapon. It must have been an accident, the creature had probably been injured. He put it from his mind because, like the other hunters, he was looking forward to the first bird hunt. There was more rain now, and fog some mornings. Old Fraken still had enough of his wits about him to observe that the days were indeed shorter; winter had returned to the north again. They could tell this even without Fraken's aid, because large flocks of birds were now landing in the channels and marshes. They would circle, making a great noise, then land in wave after wave. They would never stay more than a day or two, just long enough to rest and feed before they started on their way south again. The log had been hollowed out and shaped, the boat was finished and it was time to start eating some of those countless birds.

Many hunters had worked to feed the fires that shaped the boat and each of them wanted to be first to use it. Before the quarrels broke out Kerrick decided that the four who would go must be chosen by chance, using a game the boys played. Straws were cut, all the same length, one for each hunter, and stood up in one of the newly baked pots. Four of them had their lower ends dipped in the dyesack of a hardalt and were stained purple. In turn each hunter drew one of the straws. There was much shouting, complaints from the losers and insults from the winners. In the end they all went to the boat, to load the nets and spread reeds over the four hunters so they would not be seen. They paddled out in midafternoon, disturbing the flocks already there. The hunters made no attempt to net any of these as they rose, but moved the boat into the shelter of the reeds. They would be ready when the newcomers arrived before dark.

Herilak drew Kerrick aside and spoke in a low voice. "Come with me and see something." He led the way to his tent and brought out his hèsotsan. "You asked about the death-sticks. Was this what you meant?"

Kerrick turned it over in his hands, felt a jab of worry when he saw the creature's foot. It was gray and dangling limply. "How long has it been like this?"

"Some days, I don't know. What does it mean?"

"Maybe nothing. These creatures get old, they must die some time. It might be that."

It wasn't. The grayness on Herilak's weapon spread, slowly at first, but it did not stop. One day the creature would not fire the darts and began to stink. They buried it in the forest away from the tents.

"I know of two more like this," Herilak said.

"An illness of some sort," Kerrick said. "Perhaps it spreads from one to the other. We must keep them apart."

"What if more of them die. What then?"

"Then they die. We do not need them for hunting."

"No, but we need them to kill murgu." Herilak looked grimly across the water to the land beyond. "Another of the large murgu crossed over last night. The mastodons heard the thing, or smelled it. Hanath heard their noise and he killed it before it got among them. It is twice as big as a mastodon—with teeth as long as your arm. You cannot kill a marag like that with an arrow or a spear."

"One death-stick is dead. We have others."

"And others have the grayness already. If they all die . . ."

Kerrick could think of no easy words to say, was as worried as Herilak by this possibility. "We could trek north in the spring, go where the murgu cannot go, to the snow and the mountains."

"We could do that—but for how long? The winter that never ends still holds the valleys. Those Tanu who still hunt there will not welcome us. Tanu have killed Tanu before—and it will happen again if we go north. We can live well here, the hunting is good. But only if we have the death-sticks."

This fact was so obvious that they did not want to talk about it. Only when two more of the death-sticks sickened did Herilak send for the sammadars. They gathered about the fire, speaking quietly. There were few smiles, no laughter. They grew silent when Herilak rose and faced them.

"You all know of the trouble with the death-sticks. One is dead, two more have the grayness upon them."

"Three," Har-Havola called out. "It is upon mine today as well. If they all sicken, all die—what then?"

"All of them are not even sick yet," Kerrick said. "Do not kill them that quickly."

"But it could happen, what if it does happen? How will we then kill the murgu?"

There was much cross discussion with nothing of importance said. It was Merrith, standing with the others beyond the circle of sammadars, who grew impatient and called out.

"You cackle like birds on a nest—and do not even lay eggs. Where do the death-sticks come from? From the murgu, we know that. Can we get more if ours die?"

They all looked to Kerrick for an answer to that. "Not easily. If they even suspect we need more death-sticks they will be very pleased. They will not give us any, that is certain."

"Capture them then," a hunter called out.

"That would mean war again, because there would be a dead marag for every one we took. You all know that I stopped their attack on the valley with a threat. I don't think I could do that a second time. Whatever we do we must not kill any of the murgu—or let them know that we need more death-sticks."

There were more questions. They were curious as to how the death-sticks were made.

"Not made, grown. They look like ordinary lizards when they are young, though they have longer bodies than most lizards, are perhaps a little like snakes. They are raised in a place with a swampy pond, walled about so they cannot escape. As they grow older they move about less and less until one day they are as we see them."

"Could we breed them ourselves?" Merrith asked.

"I don't think so. When we were in the city I watched them often, tried to understand them, but it is still a secret from me. I don't even know whether they hatch from eggs or not. When they are young they move about. Then they stiffen and become as we know them as they grow older. They cannot possibly breed then. There may be a third state they pass through that I have never seen, although I looked carefully. It is a murgu secret."

"This place in the city where the death-sticks are kept," Herilak said. "You know where it is?"

"I know where it was. Whether it is still there I have no way of telling. When we were in the city much of it was burnt, other parts died. Now that the murgu have returned it will have grown, changed."

"Still, if we can find the young death-sticks, bring them back here, that will be what we need. We could do that."

"Not easily . . ."

But Kerrick's protests were lost in the rush of other voices. A hunting party could do it, find the place. Get more death-sticks, get enough to last them a long time. Kerrick shouted until he was heard.

"This may be a good plan, fine. But what if they are guarded, what if the murgu are there? What then?"

"We kill them!" a hunter cried and there were shouts of agreement.

"Hunters of great stupidity!" Herilak roared. "Do that and the war starts again. You have heard Kerrick. Do that and next time it will be our end. There must be another way."

Kerrick looked away from them, stared into the fire, yet knew from the silence that they were looking at him, waiting for him to find an answer. He was the one who knew all about murgu, he would find a way. He sighed, stood and turned to face them.

"If the worst happens, if all our death-sticks die, we will need new ones. They have death-sticks in the valley of the Sasku."

"That is a long distance to go," Herilak said. "And I do not think they will willingly part with many. They fear the return of the murgu. Ours die now, perhaps theirs are already dead. The city is closer."

"Close—and deadly. It will be very difficult to get there with a hunting party. That should not even be thought about now. Not until we are sure where the death-sticks are. They must be found first."

"You and I," Herilak said decisively. "You because you know the ways of murgu. I, because I know the forest. The two of us will go."

Kerrick glanced up and found he was looking into Armun's horrified face. She knew the risks, they all did. There were murmurs of agreement and they turned to Kerrick for an answer. He did not look at Armun as he nodded.

"Herilak and I will go. We will take only one death-stick. Herilak will carry it. If this is a sickness they have, and I was told about this by one who knew about sickness, it spreads from one animal to another. That is why you must keep the rest of them apart, keep them warm and feed them well. If we do find any in the city I will carry them, keep them far away from the one that Herilak will have. We cannot risk new ones getting the old sickness."

It was agreed that the remaining hèsotsan would be guarded and watched, and used only to kill any of the large marauders that came to the island. Up until this point the hunters had taken the weapons very much for granted: now they realized how vital to the existence of the sammads they were.

The visit to the city must be done quickly. They would carry only their weapons and smoked meat. Kerrick packed some of this into a bag for the morning: Armun looked on.

"I will go with you," Armun said.

"This will be a quick scouting trip, no more. You must stay and care for the baby."

"I said once that we would never be parted again."

"We will not be. I went on the hunt with the Paramutan. This is the same. We will move fast, find the place we are looking for, come right back. Herilak knows the forests, we will not be seen. And I know the murgu. You must not be afraid."

She was. They both were. He did not say it aloud but they shared the knowledge that the peace of the island had been broken. The future was once more doubtful and unclear.

It began to rain during the night, thundering onto the tent and creeping in under the flaps. In the gray, wet dawn the two hunters left the island and started south towards the city. They knew the track well and made good time. On the third day they turned off of the wide track that the sammads had used and moved instead among the trees on one of the animal trails. They had hunted here many times before and Herilak seemed to know every stand of forest and depth of stream. When they reached a dark and stagnant pond he stopped in the shelter of the trees.

"We are very close now. Beyond the water there was the swamp of the large murgu with three horns."

"Nenitesk. Are you sure? I don't think I ever entered the city from this direction before."

"I am sure."

"They were always in the most distant fields, the furthest out from the center of the city. If we can locate them I think I can find the place with the death-sticks from there."

There was a loud crashing from the forest ahead of them, followed by a hoarse bellow. Weapons ready they approached the outermost barrier of the city. The trees here were thickly grown and interlaced with vines, some of them growing poisonous thorns. This barrier stopped or turned away most animals—but not the one that had just passed. Branches were broken and undergrowth crushed; deep footsteps in the marshy ground were still filling with water. Stamped there by massive feet armed with sharp claws.

Herilak grunted in recognition. "The big killer marag."

"Epetruk. It must have smelled the nenitesk. We must follow it—this is the best way to get inside the city."

A great roaring and screeching ahead marked the encounter of the epetruk with its prey. But it was an evenly matched battle. As the epetruk circled about, the nenitesk turned always to face it with the large bony shield that protected its head. The epetruk was wary of the three long horns; smears of blood on one of them showed why. There was another bellow from the swamp as a second nenitesk lurched towards the battle. The epetruk, enraged though it was, had enough intelligence to see the danger. It turned its head back and forth and roared. Twisted about, lashing its tail as it backed away. The hunters, feeling very small and exposed, ran for the protection of the large trees beyond. Behind them the crashing died to silence as the epetruk retreated. Kerrick looked for a way out of the field, for any familiar landmark.

"That way," he said. "We'll have to circle about since we must stay away from the inner fields as long as possible."

Once he recognized where they were he realized that little or nothing had changed in the years since the city had grown. The trees were larger and there was different undergrowth, but everything was basically the same. His arms and legs moved as he thought of the familiar Yilanè expression—tomorrow's tomorrow will be like yesterday's yesterday. Grown to a plan and a model the city would stay that way as long as it existed. He should have remembered this. The areas that had died, or been destroyed by the fire, had been regrown exactly as the original. He had walked this same path as a boy. He tapped Herilak's shoulder and pointed, spoke in a whisper.

"There are groves just ahead. The murgu go there to gather fruit for their deer, other animals. Unarmed ones do the work, but there will be guards with death-sticks this far from the city center."

The field was still there, rotting fruit lying on the ground, but empty now of any Yilanè. Kerrick led the way through the scattered trees to the far side.

"It is not too distant from here now. See, that high bank there? It is just on the other side."

Herilak bent to examine the ground. "Tracks, very fresh."

"What kind of animal?"

"The murgu who live in the city now. Very recent, since the rain last night."

He led the way, silent as a shadow through the trees, with Kerrick following carefully, looking at the ground, trying to walk as quietly. They came around the bank just as the others were coming towards them. There was no way back.

Two fargi with burdens, eyes wide with astonishment.

The Yilanè with them raised her hèsotsan. Herilak was faster, fired first. She doubled over and fell.

Kerrick cried out, but he was too late. Herilak's weapon

cracked again sharply, twice, and the fargi were dead as well.

"You didn't have to kill them. They're harmless."

"Can they speak, those two?"

"They could have, I suppose. You're right. They saw us. They are workers so they can understand and speak well enough to take instructions. They could tell what they saw."

"Stay here—there may be more."

Herilak slipped under the trees, ran silently past the bodies. Kerrick looked at them, eyes wide with death, mouths dropped open. Each of the fargi had been carrying immature hèsotsan he saw, and these had been spilled on the ground. Their legs twitched feebly and they crawled off slowly through the grass. Kerrick remembered that he used to collect them as well at this stage, when they could not escape easily. He went and gathered them up, six of them: their tiny legs scratched at his arms but they could not escape.

"There were just the three murgu," Herilak said, then saw what Kerrick was carrying. "You have them! The death-sticks that we need. We must leave before more murgu come."

"Not until we have done something about these bodies. The murgu would not use the death-sticks on each other. If these three are found they will that know someone from outside the city killed them."

"Drag them into the swamp. Bury them."

"They might be found." Kerrick looked up at the mound beside them. "The death-sticks, the young are in there, very many of them. I remember we used to feed them meat from this wall."

"There is meat here," Herilak said crudely, pushing the dead Yilanè with his toe. "If these beasts eat fast the murgu who may come to look for them will find nothing."

"Make sure you drop the bodies into the water at the deep end, so their bones won't be seen. That's all we can do." He bent to pick up the guard's hèsotsan, had to pry it from the Yilanè's fingers. Herilak dragged the first body away.

Before they left Herilak searched the ground for any traces of what had happened, brushed away some tracks they had made. Moving quickly they left the city as they had entered it, past the nenitesk now peacefully grazing, to the safety of the forest beyond.

TWENTY

When they were once more back among the trees that surrounded the city Kerrick called out. "Wait."

Herilak looked around warily, listened to the forest noises. "We should go on. It is not safe to stop this close."

"We must take some time. Look."

Herilak now saw that Kerrick's arms and chest were scratched and bleeding where the death-sticks had dug at him with their claws. Kerrick dropped them into the grass and went to the water nearby to wash himself clean.

"You must find a better way to carry them," Herilak said. "Are they poisonous when they can still move like this?"

"I don't think so. One of them was chewing on my arm—so I hope they are not."

"Their teeth are sharp, but they are not poisonous when old. I know, I have had my fingers bitten more than once feeding them. Put the meat from your bag into mine. Cut up the leather to tie them with. But do it quickly."

Kerrick slashed his bag into ragged strips and tied them about the hèsotsan. Then he bound them into a

bundle with the shoulder strap, leaving a loop of strap to
carry them by. They went on again as soon as he was
done.

Just before dark Herilak killed one of the little running
murgu, but did not go near it, left it for Kerrick to butcher.
They stayed apart, keeping the weapon he was carrying
away from the ones they had captured. Kerrick cut up the
still-warm corpse and fed bits of it to the hèsotsan. He and
Herilak ate the dried meat, not wanting to light a fire so
close to the city.

"I don't want to go back to the city again," Kerrick said
as they settled down in the darkness.

"We won't have to—if these death-sticks live. But now
we know where to go if more of the creatures die."

"The risk is too great."

"No risk is too great—because without them we cannot
live."

In the morning they fed the immature hèsotsan more
of the fresh meat, then went north at a steady pace along
the track. The rains had ended and the sunlight filtered
down through the tall trees, spreading bars of light across
the ground.

The sunlight reflected off the crystal eye of the ugunkshaa,
clearly revealing Ambalasei's image as the memory-creature
had recorded it. The sounds it made were weak but audi-
ble, her meaning clear.

"The river has many tributaries, two at least almost as
large as the main stream. It obviously drains a major part
of this continent. I intend to go as far upstream as it
is navigable, taking water samples at measured daily
intervals . . ."

The sounds of attention-to-speaking drowned out the
small voice. Ukhereb turned one eye towards the entrance
to see her assistant, Anatempè, standing there.

"What is it?" Ukhereb asked.

"Pain at interrupting meeting of scientific importance,
but a fargi with message of singular gravity has arrived.
The Eistaa wishes your/both presence."

"Tell the creature to return with the communication that we attend."

Anatempè left, but the two scientists did not follow her until they had silenced the ugunkshaa and placed it, and the recording creature, safely away.

"These discoveries—wonderful! Ambalasei is the greatest of the great," Akotolp said, waddling towards the doorway. Ukhereb signed agreement.

"Even though she says it herself, often enough, I agree. There is none like her alive today. Should we paint our arms out of respect for the Eistaa?"

"Note of urgency obvious in message. Opinion that immediate presence takes priority over decoration."

Lanefenuu was locked in silent thought when the two scientists entered the ambesed. She turned an eye in their direction, so she was well aware of their presence, but it was some while before she spoke.

"Intelligence/aid desired from Yilanè of science."

"Command, we obey Eistaa."

"I do not enjoy the new, do not like the inexplicable. Now there is a new event that displeases me greatly. Yesterday a working party was sent to bring hèsotsan from the growing pit. They did not return. This morning I have sent others to the pit, and among them was Intèpelei who has some skill as a hunter. She is here. Listen to what she says."

Intèpelei, a grim and muscular Yilanè, her skin mud-streaked and covered with many small, bloody bite marks, stood close by with two wrapped bundles at her feet. She spoke in a crude but concise manner.

"There were signs of walking around the hèsotsan pit, bent grass, scuffed ground, clear prints of Yilanè feet in mud. Made yesterday. I searched and found nothing. Then I saw that many of the hèsotsan were feeding in the water and not at the spot where meat is left for them. I entered the water, drove them off, and found this. There are two others."

She bent and picked up the smaller bundle and shook out a Yilanè skull. The scientists signed dismay and shock.

It grew worse. She unwrapped the other bundle to reveal an even more gruesome mass of flesh and bone.

"It is a Yilanè rib cage," Akotolp said. "Flesh still adheres, tendons and muscle attachments are there." She poked it with her thumb. "Recently dead, not an ancient body."

"Could she have been alive yesterday?" Lanefenuu asked.

"Yes, certainly," she said with modifiers of horror of discovery.

"I feel as you do. Horror and curiosity of reason as well. What happened? Did they fall in? Were they alive or dead when they entered the water? And when I thought of this I remembered the number three. And three hunters who left this city once and never returned. They were searched for but never found. Three and three—and one. The one is the Yilanè who came to this city and seized a male from the sea and who died. Three and three and one. Now I speak to you, Akotolp, and you, Ukhereb, Yilanè of science. Three strange things have happened, three things without explanation and I am not pleased. Now I want you to tell me—are they related? Is there a common factor with three and three and one?"

Ukhereb hesitated, trying to make an evaluation. Akotolp shook the fat wattles of her neck and spoke with feeling. "Common factor. Death of three and one, possibility of death of three. Perhaps certainty, or three would have returned. Death outside our city, coming into our city. Not death from the inside. Facts needed. Birds to fly again."

"The birds that were used to watch the fleeing ustuzou?"

"Those, Eistaa. They have not been used for a long time. There was boredom of looking at pictures of trees and beach."

Lanefenuu snapped her jaw with anger. "End of boredom! Something out there is causing death in my city. I want you to find out what is happening. End of mystery— then end of deaths."

"It shall be as you order. Suggestion of increase in

armed guards at all times. More plants of poison to be sown about the walls."

"Do that. And report daily what you see on all sides."

The scientists signed obedience and loyalty and left. They walked slowly, deep in thought.

"There has been peace since we returned to the city," Ukhereb said. "Has killing started again? Have we not had enough? Is it possible that ustuzou of death caused this?"

"They will be searched for. If they are close they will be seen and watched. We would know better if Vaintè were here. She was the greatest killer of ustuzou."

Ukhereb signed acceptance/rejection. "You served her, I know. She saved your life, you have told me. But death was her only eistaa and that was whom she served. Enough new death now, favor requested, name of Vaintè to be put aside from thoughts."

For Vaintè all days were identical. They blended together and could not be told apart. The sun in the sky, the fish in the sea, the approach of night. Nothing ever changed.

Now there was a change and she did not like it. The fargi were upset. They came out of the ocean, looked back at the waves, came higher up on the beach and hurried past her. She queried them, she was disturbed herself now, but of course received no reply. Velikrei who was somewhat Yilanè was too distant to hear her, was moving with the others up the beach and under the trees into the swamp. This had never happened before. Vaintè turned from them to the ocean, looked out across the breaking waves to the dark object on the horizon.

Was there something there? Impossible. Nothing, other than the fish and other sea creatures, was ever in the sea. Larger fish, long-toothed and beaked predators came some times, but there was nothing so large that it could be seen emerging high above the water. She felt the fear the others felt now, turned and looked back to the refuge of the trees.

Felt a sudden spasm of anger. She was not one to be afraid. This was a disturbing thought, mostly disturbing in

that it made her think again. Something that she was not
used to doing. She was upset, hissed with anger and raked
the claws of her feet into the sand. Angry at the sea, at the
thing in the sea. She looked for it and found that it was
closer to the beach now.

And it was familiar. She knew what it was. That was
why she felt the surge of sudden hatred, for its presence
brought back the anger she had last felt here on this
beach.

Deserted.

Cast out.

Left for dead.

An uruketo.

Now she could stand and look at it coldly for the brief
spasm of anger was finished. It had really been the memory of an anger long gone. What was there to fear in an
uruketo?

She studied it calmly, seeing the black height of its fin,
noting the heads of Yilanè who were standing there on its
summit. A splash in the sea close by, then another. The
enteesenat of course. Lifetime companions of the great
living craft. Accompanying it, feeding it, always there.

The uruketo was so close to the shore now that waves
were breaking over it, rolling off in sheets of foam. A
Yilanè was climbing down to the fin, standing on the
creature's back, water surging about her legs. Something,
Vaintè could not tell what, was passed down to her. When
the next wave washed about her she dipped the object
into the water. That was all she did before climbing back
up the fin.

What had she been doing? What was the uruketo itself
doing here? The unaccustomed thoughts made Vaintè shake
her head in anger. Why was she thinking about these
things? Why was she angry?

The uruketo was standing out to sea now, getting
smaller. No, it was not heading out to sea but was moving
off along the coast. That was important.

But why important? This scratched at her thoughts,

made her irritable, so much so that one of the returning fargi fled when it saw the angry movements of her body.

The uruketo had gone north, that was what it had done. That direction was north, the other was south. But it had gone north. The importance of this escaped her for a long while. It was almost dark when she saw Velikrei coming from the sea with a fish, striding with long steps through the surf.

Velikrei had walked like that when she had first arrived with the other fargi. And they had come from that direction too. From the north.

There was a city out there. A city with beaches, where these fargi had been born. A city that they had gone to when they had emerged from the sea. Later they had deserted the city that had deserted them, turned their backs and swum away from it and had come to this beach.

Vaintè stood staring north until it was too dark to see at all any more.

TWENTY-ONE

It was like awakening after a long sleep, the sleep of an endless night. Or perhaps was even more like cracking out of the egg, of leaving the long first night of life and being born into the world. These were the thoughts that Vaintè had. First she puzzled at these thoughts—then wondered why she was puzzled.

One day when she bent over to drink from the pool of fresh water she saw her reflection and blinked with uncertainty at it. Held up her hands and spread her thumbs wide, looked at the mud caked there. Then plunged them into the pool, shattering her image and wondered yet again why this bothered her.

Each morning she would look out to sea and search for the uruketo. But it never returned. This upset her because it was a change from the rhythm of the days that she had grown so used to. Sleeping, eating, sleeping. Nothing else. She was no longer at peace and regretted this greatly. Why was she upset? What was bothering her? She knew—and put the memory from her. It was very peaceful on the beach.

RETURN TO EDEN   199

Then one day she awoke. She was standing on the
beach and one of her companions was before her, waist
deep in the sea. *Fish*, the fargi signed with a color change
of her hand. Then *fish* yet again.

"What fish?" Vaintè asked. "Fish where? More than
one fish? How big, how small, how many? Answer
commanded."

"*Fish*," the stupid, gap-jawed, bulge-eyed creature
signed yet again.

"Lump of worthlessness—rock of stupidity—mountain
of incoherence . . ." Vaintè stopped because the fargi had
dived in panic, swam away as fast as she could. Within a
moment all of the other fargi who had heard her outburst
were in the water. The beach emptied and her anger grew
and she spoke loudly, vehemently, writhing with the pas-
sion of her feelings.

"Insensate, stupid and mute creatures. Knowing nothing of the beauty of speaking, the flexibility of language,
the joys of coherence. You swim, you fish, you bask, you
sleep. You could be dead and there would be no difference. I could be dead . . ."

She was awake now, fully awake and fully rested, for
her sleep had been a long one. She did not know how
long, knew only that days and nights, many of them, had
passed. As the little waves broke and surged around her
legs she thought about what had happened and began to
understand a small amount of it. Deserted, deprived of
the world she knew, stripped of her city, her rank, her
power, she had been dumped on this beach to die.
Lanefenuu had wanted her dead, hoped for her death—
but that was not to be. She was not a witless fargi that
could be ordered to die, who would instantly obey.

But it had been very close. Yet her desire for survival
had been so great that she had retreated within herself,
lived a life that was a shadow of life. No more. The dark
days were behind her. But what lay ahead?

Vaintè was an eistaa, would always be one. Would lead
and others would follow. But not on this beach.

Surrounded by swamp on three sides, the ocean on the

other. It was nothing, no place to be, no place for her any more. When she had come here she had been ill. Now she was well. There was no reason to stay, nothing to remember, none to speak to in parting. Without a single backward glance she slipped into the sea, dived under and cleansed herself, surfaced and swam north. It was in this direction that the uruketo had gone, this was where the fargi had come from.

A rocky headland came into view ahead as she swam, and moved slowly behind her until it obscured sight of the beach where she had stayed so long. She did not turn to look for she had already forgotten it. There had to be a city somewhere up ahead. That was where she was going.

The great crescent of a bay appeared beyond the headland, golden sand rimming its shore. The swimming had tired her so she floated and let the waves carry her to the beach. The sand was smooth, unmarked by any footprint. She was alone now and greatly preferred that. Walking was easier than swimming: she covered a good deal of distance before dark.

In the morning she caught some fish, then went on. Each day was different and distinct now and she numbered them, thought about them while she was walking the beaches, swimming past cliffs or headlands.

On the first day she had reached the bay. It was so large that she had spent all of the second and most of the third day trudging along its shore. On the fourth the cliffs began, a mountain range that dropped directly into the sea. That night had been spent uncomfortably on a rocky ledge, spattered with spray from the breaking waves. On the sixth day she had passed the last of the cliffs and returned to the beach again.

On the thirty-fifth day she saw that her journey was coming to an end. At first the beach was like any other she had walked on—but suddenly became very different. In the calm water just offshore she saw the brief splashing of a school of fish—that were not fish. They surfaced and looked at her with tiny round eyes, dived instantly when she signed greeting. An immature efenburu, afraid of everything. They would eat—or be eaten—until one day the survivors would emerge from the ocean as fargi. Those with any intelligence would become yilanè and join in the life of the city.

If they were here in the ocean, then the birth beaches could not be too distant—nor were they. A natural bay had been deepened and reinforced. Dredged by eisekol, rimmed by soft sand. The guardians were in their appointed places, the males lolling in the ocean's edge. There was a hill above the beaches, obviously a favorite viewing place for well-trod paths marked it, leading away from the beaches and towards the tall trees of a city.

Vaintè paused. Until this moment she had not thought of what would happen after she had reached the city. Getting to this place, that is what had concerned her, the swimming, walking. She had known that a city must be north along the coast, knew that she must reach it. Now what?

What city was this? Who was the eistaa? She knew nothing, was as stupid as any fargi emerging from the sea. Looking back towards the ocean she saw an uruketo moving towards the harbor, small boats returning from fishing. A rich city, for all cities were rich. Fish and meat for the eating. Meat. She had not tasted it, not even thought about it during the timeless dark period that had passed. When she thought of it now she felt the taste of it in her mouth and wiped her tongue along her teeth. She would enter this city and eat. Then look at it, understand it, discover it. Just as any fargi would do. She would do the same. The paths all led to the city and she took the most direct one.

There were crowds of fargi ahead, then a file of them carrying bundles, two Yilanè walking behind, talking. Vaintè understood some of it as they passed and yearned to hear more. But first she must eat; she felt saliva on her lips as she thought of cool, jellied meat; she licked them dry. A group of fargi was coming towards her. She stopped in their path and they shuffled to a stop as well, gaped at her.

"Are you yilanè? Which of you speaks/understands?"

They moved aside, looking towards a larger fargi to the rear who signed small comprehension.

"Food. You understand food?"

"Eat food. Eat good."

They were all plump, all eating well—and now it was her turn.

"We eat. You go. We eat."

"Food, food," the other fargi muttered excitedly. They may have just eaten, it made no difference. They were animated at the thought.

"Food," the slightly yilanè fargi said, with a crude modifier of movement. They started off towards the city and Vaintè followed in their wake. Through the tree-arched streets, past the guarded hanalè, to the banks of a river. There was excitement and bustle here, silver fish and tubs of prepared meat. The fargi went to the fish, the only food they had known in their short lives, to be among their own. There were Yilanè near the meat, talking to each other, their conversation incomprehensible and confusing to the newcomers. Not so Vaintè. She walked to the vats, and every movement of her body signed strength and ability. The Yilanè of no rank moved aside for her and she reached in and ate. One of the Yilanè was looking at her, welcomed her and wished good eating. With her mouth full Vaintè could only sign appreciation and gratitude in return.

"What is this city?" she asked as she reached for more meat, her modifiers equal-to-equal.

"It is Yebeisk. The Eistaa of great authority is Saagakel."

"Yebeisk and Saagakel are known in all of the cities of Entoban∗."

"You are a Yilanè of wisdom. And which is your city?"

"I travel now and know many cities." This was an accurate statement. Vaintè took a bite of meat in order to avoid any amplification of detail. But she could not hide the overtones of strength and power that were associated with the cities she had visited and her listener was aware of this. When the other Yilanè spoke again it was as from someone slightly lower down to one a good deal higher up.

"The city welcomes the visitor."

"Well spoken. I would see the ambesed and look upon the Eistaa who sits there."

"Pleasure of guidance when eating finished. May honored visitor's name be known?"

"Vaintè. And yours?"

"Opsotesi."

The afternoon was warm so they took a shaded route through the streets and under the trees, wandered from the river to the foothills beyond, then back to the ambesed. By this time the midday heat was gone and the ambesed stirred with movement.

"Admirable," Vaintè said, with qualifiers of great appreciation. Opsotesi arched with pleasure.

The ambesed was an open glade with tall trees forming a backdrop behind it. Through the center a stream of fresh water flowed, its course turning back and forth in gentle arcs. The stream was spanned by shining metal arched bridges that were decorated with loops of wire and set with glinting stones.

Vaintè and her new companion were standing on the public side of the ambesed along with many other Yilanè. Some of these bent over and drank from the stream, others splashed it on their limbs to cool them. But on the far side of the water there were no crowds. The grass there was green and untrampled. Small groups talked together, while the largest group of all was around the Eistaa who sat in the place of honor.

"An ambesed reflects its eistaa," Vaintè said. "As I look at this my respect for your Eistaa grows."

"Twice I have spoken to her," Opsotesi said proudly. "I have skill at speaking and carry messages for many."

"Appreciation of talents. Tell me of these messages for they must have been of importance if the Eistaa would hear of them."

"Importance magnified. I stood on the dock when an

uruketo arrived and there were those of high rank aboard.
I took their names to great Saagakel."

"Yilanè of importance, Eistaa of greatness," Vaintè said,
repeating the titles to hide her growing boredom. Opsotesi
spoke well, but her only skill was in speaking; she would
never rise very high. Yet she knew the city. "And what
else did you speak of to the Eistaa?"

"Matter of darkness." Her body moved in unhappy
memory. "A stranger came to the city. I was told to bring
notice of this stranger . . ."

Her speaking stopped, rigid, and she signed doubt,
identification/clarity. Vaintè spoke strongly and curtly.

"Opsotesi, you address me with dark questions. What
is the reason?"

"Apologies! Doubts of stupidity. You are a stranger—
but you could not be as that stranger was. She was—"

Again she broke off, moving with fear. Vaintè signed
friendship and curiosity of identification. She already had
her suspicions. Opsotesi still could not speak so Vaintè
encouraged her.

"I know of those who are outcast. Though I am not of
them, despise them, I know of them. So speak—was it of a
Daughter of Life that you were informed?"

"It was! Apologies for fear. Vaintè is above me, ahead
of me in every way. That is the matter of which I spoke.
There was anger, we fled."

Vaintè calmed her, flattered her strength and speaking
ability. Then decided what she must do.

"I have come a long way, friend Opsotesi, and am
tired. But not so tired that I cannot do my duty and speak
my gratitude to your Eistaa for pleasures enjoyed of your
city."

Opsotesi was widemouthed now like a fargi. "You—
would do that? Just speak to her without being summoned?"

"She will speak to me if she wishes. I will simply make
my presence known."

Strength of purpose straightened Vaintè's back, fullness of knowledge glowed in her eyes. Opsotesi bid her
farewell, lowest to highest and she acknowledged this with

the slightest movement. When Vaintè now walked forward the Yilanè grew silent and made way for her. When she reached the shining bridge she stopped to admire it aloud, then went on. Those about the Eistaa saw her approach but did not move for they were proud of their positions and did not relinquish them easily. Vaintè made no protest, just sat back slowly onto her tail, beyond the circle, her arms formed into a sign of respectful attention.

Curiosity won in the end as they became aware of the stranger and her dignified presence. The nearest, a fat Yilanè with purple designs on her arms and down her chest, continuing onto the rolls of fat as well, looked at her with one cold eye. Then turned her head, wattles swinging and spoke a rude query.

"Explain presence, highest to lowest."

Vaintè gave her one disdainful glance, then looked back to the Eistaa. The fat one's crest flared because she was not used to being dismissed this rudely. Saagakel, who was indeed an Eistaa of intelligence, was aware of this exchange and enjoyed it. Watched but did not interrupt. Ostuku was fat and lazy and deserved a little reduction of status as well as of weight.

"Answer demanded stranger!" Ostuku ordered.

Vaintè looked at her coldly and spoke with minimum movements, rejection without insult. "I am commanded only by those of power: I speak only to those with grace."

Ostuku gasped, angered and confused. The sureness of the visitor was real, her presence imposing. She turned away from Vaintè, not willing to go on with the exchange.

"An accomplished Yilanè," Saagakel thought, and of course communicated this thought to those around her. Vaintè heard it as well and signed respectful gratitude, pleasure of presence. All of the others were watching now and Vaintè was suddenly the center of attention. She saw this, stood and spoke.

"Apologies, Saagakel Eistaa of power. I did not mean to impose myself on your presence, wishing just to experience the pleasures of your ambesed, the strength of your presence. I withdraw for I have caused an interruption."

"A welcome one, for events of the day are boring beyond belief. Come forward and tell us of yourself and of your visit to Yebeisk."

Vaintè did as she had been commanded, moving closer to the Eistaa. "I am Vaintè, she who was Eistaa of Alpèasak." When she spoke the city's name she added modifiers of darkness and termination. Saagakel responded with knowledge of circumstance.

"We have heard of your city and those who died there. Killer ustuzou, event of great unhappiness."

"Happiness restored. Ustuzou driven out, the city Yilanè once again—for Ikhalmenets has gone to Alpèasak."

Saagakel signed knowledge and memory. "I have heard of that great event from uruketo of Ikhalmenets that called here. I also heard of one who drove out the ustuzou. Coincidence of great importance, for that Yilanè also bore the name of Vaintè."

Vaintè lowered her eyes and tried to speak humbly, succeeded slightly.

"There is only one Yilanè of small importance who bears the name Vaintè."

Saagakel expressed great pleasure. "Doubly welcome to my city, Vaintè. You must tell me of this new land of Gendasi∗ across the ocean and of all the things that have happened there. Here, sit close to my right thumbs, and speak to us. Move, fat Ostuku, and make room for our new comrade."

TWENTY-TWO

Each day after that Vaintè would go the ambesed and join
the circle of confidantes that ringed the Eistaa. It was a
pleasure to watch the flow of a great city again, the problems being brought to Saagakel, her orders issued. She
delegated authority easily, but always in limited terms;
have these fields prepared, those animals moved, the fishing catch to be improved. Those who acted for her would
then be ignored—until they reported success of assign-
ment. It was always success because any Yilanè who did
not carry out the Eistaa's directions, precisely and completely, was never seen again in the ruling half of the
ambesed. Vaintè admired this, as well as the not too
obvious fact that none of the assistants were ever delegated power in more than one area—or for more than a
limited amount of time. Saagakel was the Eistaa and saw
to it that no other had the experience or opportunity to
aspire to that place.

When her day's work was finished, the Eistaa would
bathe in the pool of warm water hidden by the trees
behind her place of power. Once she was refreshed and

cleansed, meat would be brought to her and she would eat
with great pleasure. Then, on most days, she would sign
to Vaintè to tell them more about Gendasi∗ distant across
the sea, of Alpèasak the city that grew and was Yilanè, was
burnt and infected by ustuzou, was reclaimed again in the
end. There was so much to tell that Vaintè could choose
the content and manner of telling. Her listeners noticed
no gaps in her history for she told it in separate units and
each unit was complete. They were entertained, horrified,
fascinated and grateful. They, like Vaintè, wanted the
story to be long in the telling in order to extract the
maximum amount of diversion.

Vaintè for her part wanted to learn everything she
could about the city and the Eistaa. After the long, bleak
time of silence it was pleasure magnified to speak and to
listen. By avoiding those topics that caused her pain of
memory she healed herself. Yebeisk was a fine city to be
in. Like all other cities it was centered on the ambesed.
Around and above the ambesed there grew the city tree,
the complex web of life that nourished and formed the
city. To one side, there was the sea, as in all cities, always
ocean or river, where the birth beaches were. On all the
other flanks the fields and forests stretched away until
they reached the outermost rampart of the city. A living
wall of trees and poisonous plants—and great indestructi-
ble animals like nenitesk and onetsensast, living fossils of
bygone ages, that protected the city from the creatures of
the wild forests. The city ended at the wall. Beyond it
were the mountains, deserts and dry plains, unsuitable for
Yilanè, stretching into the unmeasurable distance, un-
charted and unmapped; although there were those few
who knew ways across them. Then, when the soil and the
climate became amenable again, there would be another
wall and another city. All across the great continent of
Entoban∗ the wild country stretched between the cities of
the Yilanè.

One day there appeared, out of the trackless forest, a
hunter of great skill by the name of Fafnepto. She was not
of Yebeisk, or of any city that anyone knew of, for she

moved from one to the other as it pleased her. Fafnepto had just arrived from one of these distant cities and all present listened to her with eagerness.

"You have returned, Fafnepto," Saagakel said, with modifiers of appreciation, rewards pending.

"I have, Eistaa, as I said I would." She touched the container on the grass next to her with one foot. Tall and strong, her skin scarred by her years beyond the cities, she reminded Vaintè of one who had been very close to her, one Stallan, once her staunchest ally and friend. A hunter as well; it was no chance resemblance. Although Fafnepto did bear a disfigurement that made her unique. Some creature, she never spoke of it and none dared ask, had lashed her across the head and rib cage, leaving an immense length of scar. This cut across her face and had removed her left eye. It was said that she saw better with the remaining eye than others did with two, which was undoubtedly true.

"I have brought that which you requested, Eistaa. The eggs lie safe in here."

Saagakel moved with gratitude and pleasure. "Fafnepto, first among Yilanè of strength and wisdom, do you speak of the eggs of the okhalakx?" She signed pleasure un- bounded at Fafnepto's affirmative answer. The listeners echoed the pleasure, all except for Vaintè.

"You are not familiar with the okhalakx?" Saagakel asked.

"Apologies for ignorance," Vaintè said.

"Lack of information, one day to be replaced by plea- sure. It is one of the older animals, found in very few cities. Solid of body, strong of skull—and most important— tasty of flesh. We had a small herd, they grow slowly, but they were destroyed by disease. A tragedy turned now to a happiness by Fafnepto, for whom the city's gratitude is boundless. Requests of any magnitude granted."

"One," Fafnepto said in a plain-spoken, rough but not impolite manner. She turned a penetrating eye on Vaintè. "I have been told that this visitor has great knowledge of Gendasi∗, land across the sea. And of the ustuzou and other animals there. I have questions about them I would ask."

"My knowledge is yours," Vaintè said, and Saagakel was gratified by her loyalty and clarity of speech. Fafnepto signed her away from the group and they walked by the stream.

"The ustuzou I know are small and covered with fur," Fafnepto said. "It is said that they are different in Gendasi∗."

"Some are just as you have said. But there are larger ones with branching horns that make the best eating. We kept them in the city for that. Then there are the others of some intelligence and much guile. Poisonous creatures, fit only to be destroyed. As they destroyed Alpèasak, though it grew again."

"Those are the ones of which I heard. Are they yilanè?"

"No. It has been said that they converse with each other, but none can understand it. There was one once who was yilanè, a creature of great destruction."

When she talked now of Kerrick Vaintè felt her body move with expressions of great loathing and hatred. So strong were these that she had to stop and force herself into silence to regain control. Fafnepto waited, patient and unmoving, until Vaintè could speak again.

"You have seen how I feel. That one ustuzou has destroyed everything that I have worked for."

"I will kill it for you if I can find it."

Vaintè felt a great warmth of feeling towards this stolid, scarred Yilanè and it shaped her speaking. "I believe you, strong Fafnepto, and thank you. I will tell you all that I know about the creatures and Inegban∗, for they are different in many ways."

Fafnepto was a good listener and asked only for amplification and clarification on points of particular interest. Vaintè spoke of things that she had not even thought about since returning to Gendasi∗. This calmed her and made the speaking all that more pleasant. When she had finished she hesitated and Fafnepto caught the suggestion of question unspoken.

"If Vaintè has need of something—tell me."

"Not need, curiosity that is more than curiosity. You, who are both of this city and of other cities, might speak to me of it. Yebeisk has made me welcome and I am privileged to talk often with the Eistaa. There is freedom of speaking—yet there is one thing that no one talks of. Something that if it is suggested to exist is rejected. Since this is a strong rejection I have not mentioned it here. May I speak of it to you?"

"Tell me what it is."

"The Daughters of Life."

The hunter signed for respectful silence even before Vaintè had finished speaking the name. She looked on all sides as she said it, saw that none were close enough to hear, then led Vaintè further away, to a sunny spot behind low hedges where the others were out of sight.

"We are here," Fafnepto said, "so no possible interpretation can be placed upon body movements. You were right to come to me for none other here would dare speak of what happened. Do you know much of the Daughters?"

"Far too much. Endless trouble/pain caused by them. I wish them all dead."

"As does the Eistaa. There were many here, imprisoned in a fruit grove to prevent their poison from spreading. Then more of the same arrived from outside the city and were also imprisoned. Their cause was taken up by one of science named Ambalasei. This is the one whose blood the Eistaa wishes to taste upon her teeth. Ambalasei freed them all and took them from here."

"Not easy to do."

"There was an uruketo. She ordered that without the Eistaa's knowledge, took it and all of the prisoners and has not been heard of since."

"Gone? But how?"

"That is beyond my knowledge. When no others were permitted to mention it, the Eistaa still spoke to me of the matter. In all the cities I visited I was to ask about the uruketo and its cargo. It has never reappeared. There is no trace."

Vaintè was still with internal thought for some time,

before turning to Fafnepto and speaking again. "I think
that you have deep reasons under your other reasons for
speaking with me. Is that true, Fafnepto?"

"It is."

"You asked about the ustuzou of Gendasi∗. And you
search for an uruketo. Is it your belief, do you think it
possible, that the uruketo has gone to Gendasi∗?"

"I have searched and spoken to many. Now I believe
that the uruketo has left Inegban∗. If it has—where could
it be?"

Vaintè thought carefully before she spoke again. "We
ask each other questions. We swim around an answer but
do not go near it. I will speak clearly. I think your uruketo
has crossed the ocean. The only question remaining is—do
you tell Saagakel of this? Or do I?"

"She has forbidden me to speak of the matter to her
ever again."

"Then the responsibility is mine for I have not been
forbidden. Were you in the city when all this happened?"

"No."

"I will need to know more of what occurred before I
dare mention it to the Eistaa. Who will talk to me about
it?"

"Talk to Ostuku. Behind the fat is a Yilanè of intelligence. She will aid you."

They parted in friendship, leaving Vaintè with much to
think about. She knew better than to hurry a matter as
delicate as this one. By putting it from her mind completely she let none of her new knowledge color any of her
speaking. But she was aware of Ostuku's movements and
one morning saw her opportunity. The Eistaa had been
speaking to her advisers. After the conference Ostuku
waddled from the ambesed. Vaintè left at the same time
and was her friendliest.

"Ostuku closest to Saagakel. May I walk with you—or
are you embarked on matters of great urgency?"

"Matters of importance but not urgency."

"Then request of wisdom from one of greatest wisdom.
With privacy of conversation."

Ostuku considered this closely before she spoke. "The pleasure will be mine. There exists a garden grove of sunshine and shade where I take much comfort."

"Gratitude magnified multifold."

They strolled in silence to the grove which was indeed as Ostuku had said. Sunwarmed, ornately carved boards were there for sitting or reclining. Green grass and flowers surrounded the trunks of tall trees. They sought cool comfort in the shadows for the sun was getting high. When they were seated Vaintè went right to the point.

"I am in need of advice. I spoke to Fafnepto of my need and she said that your counsel was the wisest in the city—after the Eistaa's of course. It is a matter of great delicacy. I understand that all have been forbidden to speak of it with the Eistaa in hearing. I have special knowledge I wish to report. May I talk to you?"

Ostuku had been listening in silence until this moment. She looked briefly around the empty grove, then back to Vaintè.

"Does it concern the Daughters of Life?"

"It does."

Ostuku signed great worry, great distaste. "The Eistaa will not have them spoken of in her presence. But you and I may talk of them—if you assure me it is of the greatest importance."

"It is. Fafnepto has information about them she wishes Saagakel to know. Since she has also been forbidden to talk of this matter I will speak for her. But there are some things I must know of first that will clarify what I must say. Will you help?"

"For the sake of the Eistaa I will help. It was a matter of greatest anger for us all."

"I know that one named Ambalasei aided the escape of the prisoners that you had here. In an uruketo."

"She did. I never suspected the old creature of such effrontery and trickery. Fooled me, fooled us all. The Eistaa will never forgive her."

"Now the question. There were among the prisoners those who had but recently come to the city."

"There were."

"I must ask, although it was long ago. Do you remember their names?"

"Just one. An intelligent and strong Yilanè who had the courage to argue with the Eistaa. Bold but foolhardy. Her name was Enge."

Vaintè writhed with anger and other strong emotions, so much so that Ostuku leaned away. Seeing this Vaintè apologized quickly.

"Lowest to highest, none of what I feel is directed at you. Rather do I know this Enge creature, know her far too well because we-were/ended-now efenselè. This, and what Fafnepto has told me, comes together to form a possible answer. Knowledge/probability where Ambalasei and the uruketo have gone."

Ostuku signed gratitude. "To Fafnepto for sending you to me, to you for speaking your thoughts clearly. If you have this knowledge then, despite the ban, you must tell Saagakel at once. You are the only one who can do it. Will you—although you risk the Eistaa's anger?"

"For the kindness she and her city have shown me I would risk death."

"Well said. Gratitude from all. This matter has troubled the Eistaa for too long. Gratitude magnified many times if you can aid her."

"It will be done, this day. Request if possible to locate one with skill in painting for I must have arms of greatest importance before I speak."

"I will send for one. It will be done this day."

Saagakel, having seen to all the pressing matters of the city, leaned back on the sunwarmed wood and felt tired. Responsibility was no easy thing. She was aware of motion as those about her drew away and she looked and saw Vaintè slowly approaching. Her arms were painted and her body stiffened in signs of some importance/privacy of talking needed. Saagakel found this of great interest because it was the triviality of city affairs that fatigued her. She stirred and rose to her feet.

"I go to the pool in the trees where none will disturb me. Come with me Vaintè and we shall talk."

When they were alone she took a slab of, cool meat from the container, that always rested there in case of sudden hunger, bit into it and made the signs of sharing to Vaintè. Vaintè took a token ceremonial piece, chewed it slowly and swallowed before she spoke.

"I who was Eistaa, speak to you as Eistaa. We have both been made to suffer from the same source. I will speak of painful matters, but speak only because I see future termination of past difficulties. I would speak of the Daughters of Life whom I call the Daughters of Death. Will you hear me?"

Saagakel's body writhed with anger, as did Vaintè's in instant sympathy. There was hatred as well, and there can be no greater bond than hatred shared.

"Speak," Saagakel commanded, "for I can see that we are as one in this. Tell me what you know—and what you can do. Rid me of the burden that possesses my days and you will clasp my right thumbs as highest in all things. Speak!"

Vaintè signed gratitude and submission. "I must tell you of things past that bear on things present. We are born into an efenburu. We do not choose it. I had an efenselè whom I now reject. I wish her dead. Her name is Enge and she leads others in the Daughters of Death."

"An Enge came to this city, was imprisoned by me for she talked sedition. She talked of it to a respected scientist of advanced years named Ambalasei. What she said turned her from the natural way. She freed all of those deadly creatures and took them from here in one of my uruketo. They have not been seen or found since that day."

"Strong hunter Fafnepto talked to me of this, asked for any intelligence on the matter that I might have. We talked and with our joint knowledge concluded that facts of importance should be presented to you. I do that now because all others have been forbidden to speak of the matter."

"With reason. Anger without object present destroys."

"I know—for I have felt that way."

"Tell me all that you know."

"The uruketo left here and has not been seen since. No city in Entoban∗ knows of it."

"Then they are dead?"

"I think not. This Enge has been to Gendasi∗ and survived the destruction of Alpèasak. If she were not a Daughter of Death she has the ability to rule as an eistaa. It is my thought that she has taken the uruketo beyond your reach. For now."

"To Entoban∗? Is this possible?"

"Possible and probable. No city in Gendasi∗ would accept their cargo of death—and no city has seen them. But Entoban∗ is large, most of it unknown to us, warm and filled with good meat. She has gone there, your uruketo has gone there, the traitor Ambalasei has gone there. I have not seen this, know none who have seen this. But I feel it so strongly through my body as I say it that it must have happened in just that way."

Saagakel could not be still; she walked the length of the clearing, then back. Her muscles knotted and moved, her jaw snapped so hard that her teeth clashed together, but she was unaware of it. "What can be done?" she called out loudly. "You have been thinking of this—what can be done?"

"A search must be made. I know the land of Entoban∗ well for I have tracked and pursued the killer-ustuzou there. And killed them. There are Yilanè of science present in Alpèasak who have ways of searching and finding. Until now they have only looked for ustuzou—but they can find Yilanè just as well."

Saagakel was calmer now, drained by her fury. "I must think about this and make decisions. I am glad we talked, Vaintè, for I can now do something about the anger that is sealed within me. Go now and speak to Ostuku. Tell her to tell the others that in the morning we will discuss matters no longer forbidden. It will be like cleansing a wound, purifying it. We will, together, take action on this and there will be deaths. I was too kind."

"I as well. I treated them as Yilanè once, not the danger they were. They merit only death."

Hoatil ham tina grunnan, sassi
peria malom skermom mallivo.

TANU SAYING

---

*Anyone can bear misery, few are
the better for good times.*

TWENTY-THREE

The hillside above the spring was steep, the grass slicked by the afternoon rain. Kerrick missed his footing, skidded and fell, slid helplessly down the slope into a tangle of berry bushes. The thorns clung to him as he used the butt of his spear to clamber to his feet, ripped his skin as he pulled himself free. His thoughts had been on Nadaske before he fell, thinking that he should visit him on his solitary island, thinking in Yilanè of course. It was far better than Marbak for expressing dissatisfaction so now he writhed and verbalized disgusting descriptions of the thorny growths as he tore at their restraint. It was a fitting end to a depressing day. Heavy rain had interrupted the hunt, driven the game to cover. The few creatures they did disturb had easily avoided his arrows—to be killed by others. Once free of the thorns he went carefully down to the spring, dropped his spear and bow onto the cool moss, knelt beside them and splashed water onto the scratches in his skin. There was a crackling in the brush and he seized up his spear.

"I am Tanu, not murgu," Hanath said when he saw the

pointed spear. "Spare my life, brave sammadar, and I will respond with great kindness."

Kerrick growled in answer and drank from his cupped hands. Normally he enjoyed Hanath's good spirits—but not this day. He watched as the hunter lowered the large clay pot into the water to fill it.

"Women carry water, hunters bring meat," he said, ill-temperedly.

"They do," Hanath said, rinsing out the pot, cheerfully immune to any insult. "And this hunter brought plenty of meat to little Malagen before she baked this pot. Only she can make them this big, this strong."

"A hunter has no need of pots."

"This hunter does. A good pot to this hunter is worth a herd of deer."

Kerrick's ill-humor was forgotten as he considered this novel thought. "Why?"

"Why? You who have drunk with the Sasku manduktos and have tasted their porro, you ask me why? Porro that tastes better than a young deer's liver, better than having a woman, is far better than eating deer liver while having a woman . . ."

"I remember—Herilak told me. You and Morgil had trouble with the manduktos in the valley. He said that you stole and drank their porro."

"Never!" Hanath drew himself up, slapped his chest a mighty blow. "We are not thieves in the night who steal from others. Yes, we tasted some of theirs, a very little bit. Then we watched, saw how they made it. It is a very small secret. After that we made our own, drank that."

"And were quite sick?"

"We were." Hanath sat down on the bank, bent and drank deep from the full water pot at the memory. "It is a small secret, making porro, but it holds a big secret to get the mixture just right. We are still learning that secret."

"Still? Is that what the pot is for? More porro?"

"It is and it isn't. The manduktos make their porro from tagaso, but all that we brought with us has been used up. So now we must try other ways of making it. This is a very difficult thing to do."

"It is even more difficult to understand what you are talking about."

"I will tell you. You drank porro, you know how good it is!" Hanath's enthusiasm died. He sighed. "It can be very bad, too, when you get the making wrong. So simple. We put the dried porro grains into water to soak, just like making mush, stir them around. Add the moss, cover the pot, keep it warm—and in a few days, porro! Sometimes." He sighed again.

"What does the moss do?"

"We don't know—but nothing happens if it is not stirred in. Without it there is just old sour mush. But with it the mixture seethes, makes noise as if it were alive, sends up bubbles just like a swamp—"

"That sounds terrible."

"No, it is something excellent. The bubbles in swamp water stink, but porro bubbles tickle the nose, are very good. But they were better with the tagaso. Some of the seeds we use made us very sick." His frown vanished as he seized the filled pot and rose. "But today there is a new one. I think it is ready. You must come and try it."

"Only after you do," Kerrick said wisely. He picked up his weapons and went with the other hunter whose enthusiasm had returned with the memory of their new mixture.

"Here is how we thought, what we did. The mush from tagaso, it looks like the mush we make from other seeds. A seed is a seed—isn't that right? This time we have cut the tops off the grass that women make mush from. Then winnowed the grain. We soaked it and covered it, used the right moss, kept it in the sun. This morning when I put my ear to the pot I could hear no more happy bubbling. That pot has rested in the shade all day, Morgil has poured water over it to cool it. Now we try it!"

Kerrick had not been here before, had not realized the great effort that the two hunters had put into their new enthusiasm. They had raised their tent in an open vale away from the other sammads, where they could have sun and shade as needed for their bubbling labors. Large pots sat in the sun, cooled in the shade, lay broken and discarded where pot or mixture had brought tragedy. Morgil lay on his side, his arms about a pot, his head pressed against it.

"Not a sound," he cried cheerfully, then tipped some more water over the still-damp clay. "Shall we try it now?"

"Kerrick is here to help."

"He is a brave hunter—he shall try it first."

"Not that brave," Kerrick said, stepping back. "You have captured the porro, you shall drink it first."

Morgil cut the braided reeds that held the leaf covers in place: Hanath tore the leaves off and cast them aside. He bent over the open mouth of the pot and sniffed, turned, smiled.

"It smells the best so far."

"It smelled good last time," Morgil said with gloomy practicality. "We were sick for two days."

At this reminder they took up the clay cups and dipped them hesitantly into the pot. Morgil had depressed himself thoroughly and did not drink, but watched while Hanath sniffed, sipped, swallowed. He grimaced in thought —then smiled broadly.

"The best we have ever made! As good as the mandukto make, better even." He downed the rest of the cup, sighed and belched happily. Morgil gurgled his down enthusiastically. Kerrick dipped and tasted hesitantly.

"As good as the Sasku make," he agreed. "Better than theirs—because this porro is here and not in that valley so far away."

The only answer they made was rapid swallowing.

After this third cup Kerrick found that he liked to hear Hanath make stupid jokes—nor were they as stupid as always. Really quite funny. He was laughing so hard that he spilled most of his fourth cup and had to refill it. Morgil, who had been drinking twice as fast as the others, lay down, closed his eyes and began to snore. Kerrick sipped some more, then put his cup aside. He was beginning to understand why the manduktos only drank this on special occasions. Hanath was muttering to himself, laughing loudly at his own wit, so much so that he never noticed when Kerrick rose shakily to his feet and left. It was raining again, but now it did not bother him.

He walked slowly between the scattered tents, took great pleasure in the bustle and activity. Gray plumes of smoke rose up from the smokeholes to merge with misty rain. A woman called to another and there was the sound of sudden laughter. Nearby was a small meadow where the ground had been turned over, the tussocks of grass pulled out and thrown aside. The women had done this alone, since this was not suitable labor for hunters, and had carefully planted the charadis seed that Malagen had brought from the valley of the Sasku. The women all liked the softness of the cloth woven from the charadis fiber and were more than willing to grow the plants. Since the hunting had been so good there was now more than enough food for all. Time could be spared for the labors needed to raise the charadis. Cloth and strong pots: it was good to see these Sasku secrets being used now by the Tanu. Herilak emerged from his tent as Kerrick passed and called out in greeting.

"Was the hunting good?" Herilak asked.

"You were not there?"

"I found the tracks of large murgu to the north, two of them. I followed them with the death-stick."

"It does not sicken?"

"I watch it, keep it where none can see it, it is well fed. I killed two murgu. The carrion eaters were on the bodies before I left."

"There was too much rain for hunting. I brought back nothing. Others did better. All of the death-sticks do well, I talked with the others."

The fear was always there now, had to be alleviated constantly. The death-sticks were their lives. Kerrick turned about too quickly and had to clutch a tree for support. Herilak frowned.

"You are ill?"

"No—but I have been drinking some new porro."

"Then I understand. I have drunk it as well. Those two will be dead soon if they do not stop."

"The new jar was very good."

A woman called their names and they turned to Merrith who approached with a leaf-wrapped bundle. She opened it to reveal the still-smoking tubers inside.

"Baked in the fire," she said. "I dug them yesterday."

They cracked open the black-burnt skins, blew on their fingers, ate the sweet soft insides. She nodded approval at their appreciative murmurs. Kerrick felt a warmth of pleasure at this, something the others took for granted. To them the sammad was normal, to him a novelty to be greatly appreciated. When the sammads were together like this there were good things to eat—and drink!—much talk, sharing. It was a life that he had never known in his loneliness, that was appreciated the more because of this.

He should see Nadaske soon: it had been a very long time since his last visit. The thought came unbidden, unappreciated. Why, when everything was so good, why think of his friend's unhappiness? Why not enjoy what he had for himself? He must be getting to be like old Fraken who seemed to get more enjoyment from his complaints than from his pleasures. No, it wasn't that. It was because he was bound to the Yilanè male, understood his loneliness far too well. He was as alone among strangers as Kerrick had been among the Yilanè. He must go visit him. Soon.

"Have another," Merrith said.

"Yes, of course." He ate hungrily, Nadaske forgotten at once. Life in the sammads was very good.

As long as the death-sticks stayed healthy. That small worry was always present, always there.

Herilak turned about when he heard his name called, wiping the burnt crumbs from his fingers. It was the boy-without-a-name, solemn as always.

"The alladjex is very ill, he breathes with great difficulty. I fear that he is dying."

He had learned to control his feelings very well. When Fraken died the boy would take his name, become the new alladjex. Undoubtedly this was what he most desired, the end to his training and servitude, yet none of this showed now.

"He will speak, we must listen," Merrith said in a hushed voice. She had no great love for Fraken, his poultices or his predictions. But everyone knew that a person's dying words were the most important he would ever utter. With death so close there could be no lies. There were things in death unknown in life and these the dying could many times see. The death-words were very important. When the boy turned away they hurried after him.

Others in the sammad were there before them, still more drifting up as word was spread. Furs and skins had been laid by the fire. Fraken coughed weakly when they came up, his face thin and gaunt. His eyes were closed so perhaps there would be no death-words after all. But the boy-without-a-name bent and whispered in his ear. Fraken muttered something then his eyes opened and he looked around at the silent watchers. He coughed again before he could speak and the boy wiped a trace of blood from his lips.

"You are here because I am dying. I have told you things before and you have not listened. Now I die and now you will listen. This boy who will be Fraken knows how to read the future from the owl pellets. Listen to him for I have taught him well. Listen to me now for I see clearly what I have never seen before . . ."

He broke off, coughed again and again and lay back until some little strength returned. "Lift me," he said, and there was blood on his chin now. The boy supported his head so he could see across the fire to the silent, watching circle. His eyes moved across Herilak, rested on Kerrick and his face twisted with feeble anger.

"We are here in the land of the murgu and that is wrong. We should be in the mountains, in the snow. That is where we should be. Far away from the murgu, far away from thoughts of murgu, acts of murgu, sight of murgu, those who act like murgu."

Some of the watchers looked at Kerrick, then quickly away. He kept his face motionless, expressionless. The old man had always hated him, he knew that. His were not words of truth at dying but simply bitter revenge. Die quickly, Kerrick thought. You will not be missed.

"If we live among murgu we become like murgu. We are Tanu. Return to the mountains, return to the old ways."

His eyes closed with pain as he coughed over and over. Nor did they open again, although he did not die at once. Kerrick waited with the others, though he hated the old man, but knew that he did not dare to show this now. It was growing dark and the boy-without-a-name built the fire higher. Smoke blew over Fraken, but he was through with coughing. Herilak bent down and touched the old man's neck, then opened one eye with his fingers, closed it again, then rose to his feet.

"He is dead. This one is now Fraken."

Kerrick left then and walked slowly back to his tent in the darkness. He was not disturbed by the old man's dying hatred; he was rid of him at last. Fraken had been a venomous creature, better off dead. He wanted them to return to the mountains and snow—yet he had been more than happy to come south for the warmth.

There was no game to hunt now in those distant mountains—and far too much snow. There could be no way back now for the sammads. They would have to stay where they were, here in the warm south where the hunting was good.

As long as the death-sticks kept the killer murgu at bay. It always came back to that.

**essekakhesi essawalenot,
essentonindedei uruketobele.**
YILANÈ APOTHEGM

---

*Where the ocean currents flow the
uruketo swim.*

TWENTY-FOUR

Enge heard the shouted sounds as she came out of the shaded walkway, but they were without meaning until she could see Ambalasei as well as hear her voice. The old scientist was leaning back on a resting board and calling out to her assistant.

"Poke it—but do not injure it. Get it to attack the stick."

There was a fearful hissing and screeching from the far end of the clearing. Enge looked in some astonishment at Setèssei who was prodding a bird with a length of wood. The creature flapped wildly, losing feathers, bit into the stick with its teeth. It could not be a bird, not with teeth. Four more of the creatures were tied up close by, fluttering and hissing with fear.

"Now—" Ambalasei called out. "Release it."

A binding-animal was secured about its legs. Setèssei poked at it with the stick until she touched the nerve ganglion that opened its mouth. As soon as it was freed the creature ran, screaming, towards the trees. Its wings were extended and flapping and it made little soaring hops into the air. With one last screech it vanished into the undergrowth.

"Excellent," Ambalasei said, gesturing success of endeavor with her right hand. This turned instantly to a modifier of distaste/ displeasure as sharp pain shot through her bandaged thumb.

"Pleasure of presence," Enge said. "Unhappiness at injury hopefully soon healed."

"A hope that I share. Infection from accidental cut by stringknife during dissection. Slowness of healing indication of advanced age of organism."

"Ambalasei is heavy with years of wisdom."

"Heavy with years of years as well, Enge. Signs of age cannot be denied. But can be forgotten in pleasures of research/discovery. Did you see that creature run?"

"I did. Though reasons for captive/release flight were unclear, the creature itself unclear. It has the feathers of bird, but also teeth, no beak."

Ambalasei signed appreciation of observation. "Abandon your pursuit of Ugunenapsa's invisible theorizing and I shall make you into a true scientist. No? I did not think so. Complete waste of intelligence. As you have observed the pertinent thing about the ninkulileb are its teeth, that is why it is so named. That creature is a living fossil. I have seen beasts like it in rock from ages long gone. Yet on this isolated continent, so far from Inegban*, its descendants still live. You saw the teeth and the feathers. It is a link between early sauria and the estekel* who fly so well. Though perhaps not. Parallel evolution I believe. These creatures are more closely related to modern birds. Wings and feathers, yet not capable of being truly airborne yet, you witnessed that. Still a fast runner, aided by the wings, to capture insects and to escape predators. This continent is a revelation, the flora and fauna worth lifetimes of study."

Ambalasei peeled the nefmakel from her hand as she talked, glared angrily at the healing wound, signed Setèssei for a fresh wrapping. While her assistant was fitting it into place Ambalasei indicated query of presence to Enge.

"Concern over injury, desire for assistance."

"The injury heals, but hurts. Assistance in aid of what?"

"Omal reports misfortune in containers. Meat rots."

"Failure of enzyme. Setèssei will take care of that as she always does. And why does Enge bear a message that Omal herself could bring? Or any yilanè fargi for that matter."

"Ambalasei always penetrates another's thoughts even before they are spoken. Although the matter is of no importance to you, I seek clarity of thinking for aspects of truth that escape me."

"There are times when I feel like the only yilanè among yiliebe fargi. Where would this world be without my intelligence?"

Although the question was rhetorical Enge answered with solemn reassurance. "I do not speak for the world but only for myself and my companions. We would be dead. In the fullness of time this will not be forgotten." She signed subservience, lowest to highest.

"Well spoken. Flattering yet completely true. Now what is the latest application needed for my mighty wisdom?"

"I have had queries from many, the same question expressed in different ways, yet the same query and the same worry from all."

"The lazy creatures should work harder, think less. Your new fargi called Daughters of Life, yet still fargi of immense unreasoning stupidity, do most of the labor in this city. Giving the rest too much time to talk and argue."

"Ambalasei is correct, as always. But the query is one that I feel within myself as well. A fear for the future that cannot be placated. The fear of the ending. The fear of the death of this city."

Ambalasei snorted in anger. "Abstract thought breeds abstract fears. You are all healthy, the city grows well, there are few dangers and a great sufficiency of food. A Yilanè of real intelligence would take pleasure from this and not seek distant pain. You are all young and at the very beginning of what could be long and productive lives.

Why concern yourselves now with the distant future?
Don't bother to answer that for I can easily answer for
you. You are all Daughters of Contentiousness and will
never find true wisdom or true pleasure. Your continuous
arguments about means to an end are a means in an end to
themselves."

"Yet the future will be here one day . . ."

"Well I won't. You have made your own problems.
Now you must seek your own solutions. I am nearing the
end of my work here and when it is done I will leave."

"I have never considered . . ."

"But I have. I have given you your lives and your city.
They are yours to enjoy. After I have gone. Study the
thoughts of Ugunenapsa, seek your answers from her and
not from me. Setèssei, stir up another one of the ninkulileb.
Their flying that is not flying is most revealing, as are their
feathers that are closer to scales than feathers. Records
must be made. Science goes forward steadily, although
your Daughters of Life are obviously unaware of that."

Saagakel looked around at her attentive circle of advisers,
signed for closest attention, spoke. "Daughters of Life. I
speak their name and, though it angers me, I do not feel
the destroying rage that once possessed me, possessed us
all. I speak that detested name now because there is new
knowledge brought to us by Fafnepto, brought to us by
Vaintè. We must now find a way to use this new knowledge, to take my vengeance on those who wronged this
city, wronged your Eistaa."

There were shouts of agreement when Saagakel spoke,
angry promises of vengeance, heated queries for elucida-
tion. It was all quite enjoyable. Vaintè sat in stern silence
at Saagakel's right hand, spoke only when the Eistaa signed
permission.

"Your Eistaa has spoken to me of what happened here
when those creatures were unjustly freed, then fled in a
proud uruketo of this city. This is a wrong that must be
righted. To right this great wrong two things must be
considered. Leading this uncivilized pack of animals was

one named Enge. I know much of Enge and will tell you
of that. The uruketo has gone and none knows where. But
strong Saagakel here has knowledge of that. She has knowledge that the uruketo has not been seen in any of the
cities of Entoban∗. When you hear that you may think
that they have escaped your Eistaa's justice. This is not so.
I believe that I have the knowledge that will lead us to
them."

There was an interested hum of surprise at this, and
pleasure at mysteries about to be unfolded. Across the stream
the distant watchers tried to understand what was happening on Eistaa's side of the ambesed, could not, stayed and
watched intently anyway. It was obvious that matters of
great import were being discussed. They moved aside at
shouts for attention as Gunugul pushed her way through,
two burdened fargi following her. Vaintè pointed to the
newcomer.

"You all know Gunugul, eldest and most senior commander of the uruketo that serve this city. She has brought
something of importance to show us. Reveal your charts,
wise Gunugul, and tell us of their meaning so we may
understand."

With sharp commands Gunugul had the containers
lowered and opened, a chart removed and rolled out upon
the grass. The fargi stood, one to each side, stolid and
unmoving, their claws hooked over the chart to hold it in
position. The onlookers stirred and pushed each other
aside to see it. Though of course they understood nothing.
Gunugul pointed to the shaded green area to one side.

"This is Entoban∗, where this great city lies. And
here, on the ocean's edge, is the city of Yebeisk itself."
There was a murmur of appreciation as they stared hard at
the fleck of gold. Gunugul moved her thumb from the city
across the blueness of the chart. "The ocean stretches
away from Yebeisk. We have had the privilege of hearing
Vaintè tell us how she has crossed it in an uruketo to the
land on the other side, to Entoban∗ and the city of Alpèasak.
Put this away, give me the other chart."

They watched in expectation as this chart was unrolled

in turn, presented for their inspection. As mysterious and indecipherable to them as the first, but perhaps more fascinating because of that. Gunugul pointed again.

"Entoban∗. A large and empty continent. Empty that is of Yilanè, though it crawls with ustuzou as Vaintè has said. I have now shown you what Vaintè asked me to."

Gunugul stepped back but left the chart displayed for their fascinated gaze. Most of them listened to Vaintè with only one eye, still staring at this map of distant mysteries.

"I have told you of the city of Alpèasak. What I have not told you, since the matter was of greatest distaste to your Eistaa, therefore not fit for public discussion, was that there were Daughters of Life in that city. Many of them died while the city was growing, though not enough. Still more died when the city was destroyed, for unlike true Yilanè they do not die at the correct predestined time, but instead live on like vermin. I will tell you no more of this, it is too disgusting, but I will tell you this much so you will know how one of them lived when many died. How one lived who should have died. How one lived to come to this city to flee it again. One named Enge."

The chart was forgotten now. Every eye on Vaintè. Every voice hushed so they could hear clearly everything that she might say.

"This was one known as Enge, a Daughter of Life, who has a great if perverted intelligence. She has knowledge of far Entoban∗. She has knowledge of crossing the ocean."

Vaintè looked around at their gaping attention. So unusual was all this that she could see none but the Eistaa knew what she was going to say, where this connected trail of knowledge would lead. They leaned forward in silence, the perfect audience, every curved line of their bodies begging for her to speak.

"You have heard that the uruketo that fled this city cannot be found. Gunugul, could this uruketo cross the ocean?"

"Where the ocean currents flow the uruketo swim."

"Could it have crossed to distant Entoban∗?"

"Other uruketo have done this. This uruketo could do this."

Vaintè leaned back, turned to the Eistaa, spoke.

"It is my belief, Saagakel, Eistaa of Yebeisk, that your uruketo has crossed the ocean and has gone to Entoban* Not to the city of Alpèasak, for the eistaa there has little love for the Daughters of Death. The uruketo is not at that city, but it must be somewhere there along the shore. There is no place else that it could possibly be."

"Gone!" a councillor wailed in anguish. "Gone!" Others took up the cry but the Eistaa signed for attention and the silence was instant.

"You are Yilanè of small intelligence, even less enterprise. Which is why I lead and why you follow. Why you do not even consider for a moment that we can indeed go after these creatures, take them, slay them, wreak vengeance, bring back our uruketo in triumph."

When the meaning of this struck home their silence turned to cries of pleasure and astonishment, gratitude to the Eistaa, and certainty of victory. The Eistaa accepted the applause, which was only her due, while Vaintè stayed modestly and motionlessly behind her. Vaintè wanted no acclaim. She wanted revenge.

Saagakel wanted this as well, but revenge tempered by reticence. She wanted to pursue the uruketo, track it to the ends of the world where it had fled. Seize it and kill that ancient Ambalasei who had caused her this great ill. This was what she wanted to do.

This was what she knew she dare not do. She was Eistaa and this was her city. If she went away another would act for her, rule for her, and would surely replace her. When she returned there would be a new Eistaa sitting in her place. Revenge or rule—it was a simple choice.

"All leave," she ordered, signing instant dismissal across the water. "Vaintè stay. Gunugul stay. Fafnepto stay."

She wanted no discussion and no advice, even from her most trusted advisers. She had made a decision and what she ordered would be done. Now she leaned back in silent thought while the crowd dispersed, waited until the last of them had crossed the bridges before she spoke.

"Gunugul, you have told us that your uruketo can cross the ocean. When can you leave?"

"When you command, Eistaa. It is well fed and fat, my crew is ready. We can load the preserved meat and water in the time between a sunrise and a sunset. Then we can leave. You have seen the charts, the course is clear."

"Good. You shall command your uruketo as you always have. You will find your way to distant Entoban∗. When you reach those shores Vaintè will lead the search. She will tell you of the land and ocean there and you will search where she tells you to search. Will you do that for me, Vaintè?"

"I will do as you command, Eistaa. It will be my greatest pleasure to do as you order, for I seek the same thing that you seek. And when we find the uruketo—what then? What will you have me do with those who stole it from you?"

Vaintè's enthusiasm was greatly diminished when Saagakel spoke again, but she hid it beneath her posture of firm attention.

"When the uruketo is found you will turn to Fafnepto for your orders. Though you are not of this city, Fafnepto, will you act for this city? Will you seek out those who have wounded me and bring my stern justice to them? You are a hunter—will you hunt now for me?"

Fafnepto shaped her stance in rough obedience. "I will do as you order. It will be my pleasure. I have hunted all kinds of creatures before this, but never another Yilanè. I think they will make good sport and will be excellent game to track down."

"Well spoken. Now stay, while the others leave, and hear my instructions."

Vaintè was overly careful to let none of her displeasure show. She signed gratitude and respect before she turned away, for she surely felt those things towards the Eistaa who was giving her this opportunity. Only when she had crossed the silver bridge did she move with some bitter-

ness. She should have been in command and the Eistaa
knew that.

Which was exactly why she was not. None would ever
rule in Saagakel's place as long as she lived. She would
make all of the decisions and others would obey. Gunugul
would cross the ocean, Vaintè would find their prey. And
then—what?

She turned and looked at the two distant figures. Saw
their limbs move, could make out nothing of their conversation. What were Fafnepto's orders? Vaintè possessed
nothing. But had she any possessions, power, position,
she would have given them all up to overhear that distant
conversation. But she could not. She turned away and
hurried after the uruketo commander.

In addition to food and water she must see to it that
hèsotsan were taken aboard.

TWENTY-FIVE

"I have been here before," Vaintè said. "It was a lifetime ago. Or perhaps it was in another lifetime. I stood just where I am standing now. Where you now stand, Fafnepto, was the commander of the uruketo. She has since died. Erafnaìs was her name. I have not thought of her in a very long time. Her uruketo died so she died as well."

It had been an easy crossing. Some rain, no real storms. Vaintè had not slept continually like the others but had been here, high on the fin, for most of the time. Her thumbs, now gripped tight to the scarred skin, could feel the writhing movement as the creature surged through the sea, the powerful tail muscles driving it forward. With each thrust moving closer to Entoban*—from which she had twice been driven. There would be no third time. Fafnepto had emerged from the dark interior and stood beside her in the warm sunlight. She did not speak much, but was a good listener. She wanted to learn all there was to know about this new continent and respected Vaintè's knowledge. Vaintè was happy to share it.

The pupils of Fafnepto's eyes were thin slits as she

237

looked into the bright sun, she shaded them even further with one hand as she pointed to the horizon. "I see something there, distant in the water. More than one. Are they islands?"

"They are. Yesterday, when you were below, we passed a large island. That is the first thing to be seen after crossing the ocean. Now we come to this island chain. Their name is their being. Alakas-aksehent, the succession of golden, tumbled stones. Their sands and the water about them are warm all the year round. The islands extend in a line until they reach the mainland. There you will find the city of Alpèasak. That is the one place we shall not go, the one place where the uruketo we seek would not have gone."

"These islands—could those we seek possibly be there?"

"I think not. I was told there is little vegetation, less water. Those who flee will look for a shore where there are animals to hunt and eat."

"I understand that. Do you understand that to hunt an animal you must think like that animal?"

"I have never heard that before, but now that you say it I believe it. And thank you. We hunt fleeing Yilanè, we must think as these Yilanè would."

"You must try to think as those you hunt would think. I have talked many times with the scientist whose name is Ambalasei. I understand the parts of her that think as I do, for she wishes to know of all living things. I have brought her specimens, answered her questions. What I cannot understand is why she should have freed the prisoners, aided their escape."

"That question I cannot answer. It is inconceivable to me that any Yilanè of wisdom would voluntarily aid the Daughters of Death. But I can tell you of Enge, who is their leader. She has impressive intelligence, although greatly misdirected now."

"If she leads—then where would she lead them?"

"That is the very important question that must be answered. Answer that and we have found our prey."

"Would she go to the large island you mentioned now, that we passed yesterday?"

"Maninlè? I know nothing of it, other than its name, she would know even less . . ."

Vaintè broke off in sudden silence, turned and looked back at the froth of wake behind the uruketo, looked beyond it into the distance. Turned back to Fafnepto and signed respect and gratitude.

"You are indeed a hunter, and you have spoken what is indeed an important thought. We must send for the commander. Because none that I know of have ever visited that island, that does not mean that no one ever will. We must search its coastline. If the uruketo is there it will be found."

Gunugul agreed at once. The enteesenat that accompanied and fed the uruketo came swimming back at great speed when it made a long, slow turn in the sea. They leapt clear of the water, splashed back down, swam ahead of it until darkness. During the night they drifted with the current, as did their immense charge, and in the morning they followed as it approached the island's sandy shore.

"Mountains and forest," Vaintè said. "Fresh water and good hunting. This could be a refuge. We must look at all of the shoreline."

"How long will it take you to circle the island?" Fafnepto asked.

Gunugul signed lack of knowledge/dependent upon size. "Some days at least."

"Then I will go ashore, there by that promontory," Fafnepto said. "I have been too long in the ocean, too long from the forest. It is my greatest wish to see the animals of this new side of the earth. I will be at this place when you come back."

"You will take food?" Gunugul asked.

"Only my hèsotsan. I will have fresh meat ready for your return."

The hunter, her weapon held high, slipped into the water and swam easily ashore. The uruketo continued along the coast, Vaintè and the commander on the fin

looking closely at the beaches and cliffs as they moved by.
It was too much to expect that they would find their prey
this easily, this quickly. Nevertheless the hunt had begun.
Vaintè no longer felt only a passenger, was now a participant.

There were bays and natural harbors; they probed
each one. When they rounded the island's tip two days
later the uruketo had to be forced out of the current that it
had been following.

"It is the warm water," Gunugul said, "flowing up
from the south. The creature likes the warmth. Look
there, you can see the edge of the stream, the different
color. It is like a river in the ocean. That is how we find
our way, by following the currents."

Vaintè was watching the shore, half heard the commander's comments.

"Are there other islands to the south of this one?"
Gunugul asked. "There are none marked on my chart.
Has that area been explored?"

"I have no knowledge of any more islands. Certainly I
saw none the other times I came this way."

"Perhaps we should search further to the south as
well," Gunugul said, looking out at the empty ocean.
Vaintè joined her, gazing out at the blue water, the bank
of white clouds on the horizon. Further south? There
might very well be more islands there. For a moment she
hesitated, then signed firmness of decision.

"There is nothing there. Enge, the one who leads
them, knows the shores to the north and it is in that
direction that they will have fled. But we must circle this
island first. If they are not here we will then continue
to the north. It is there that we will find those we
seek."

And those whom I seek. Her body was rigid, the thought
came unbidden. She was here at Saagakel's behest, to
search for Enge and the scientist, Ambalasei, and the
uruketo. She and the Eistaa were as one in this search.
But Kerrick was out there too, and she would find him. As
she hated the Daughters she hated him. Perhaps more

strongly, because twice he had succeeded in defeating her. Not a third time. When she found him, that would be the end.

The small plant-eating marag hung by one of its back legs from the tree, mouth gaping in death. Kerrick finished flaying it, then cut off the dangling rear leg. It was fleshily round and made very good eating. He wrapped it in a large leaf which he sealed shut with thorns. When this was done he wiped his flint knife clean on the grass, then took up the bloody fragments of skin and carried them to the pit behind the trees. Flies rose up in buzzing protest when he threw the skin in among the bones and other rubbish. He fanned them away from his face, then went and washed his hands clean in the nearby stream.

When he returned he saw that the tent was still empty, Armun had not returned yet with the baby: he was annoyed at himself for his feeling of relief. If he wanted to see Nadaske that was no concern of others. But of course it was. Armun no longer protested aloud at his visits, but her silences spoke louder than words. Louder and longer silences when he took Arnwheet with him. He had not done this for a very long time, perhaps because of what he knew would follow. He would take him today. The boy was very good with his bow; perhaps they would find some game. He would take the hèsotsan only for protection from predators and let Arnwheet do all the hunting. This was the boy's eighth summer: he would be getting a bigger bow soon.

As always there was the small thrust of fear when he took the hèsotsan from its nest of furs. Motionless and alive—or silent and dead? The tiny mouth opened when he prodded it, its teeth chewed slowly on the fragment of raw flesh. Seizing up the bundled meat he went looking for his son.

The young boys were always easy to find; you just listened for the shrill shouting. They were on the shore near the swamp now, crowing with victory. One of their snares had caught a good-sized bird. It could not escape

because the snare on its ankle was secured to a heavy log,
but could still hiss and snap at them, its wings beating
furiously. Two of the boys were sitting on the overturned
boat, nursing bloody fingers where the sharp serrated
edge of the creature's bill had cut them. Arnwheet called
out happily when Kerrick came up.

"We caught it, Atta, all by ourselves, when it came to
feed on the grass. Isn't it fat?"

"Very. But are you sure that it didn't catch you? It
seems very much alive."

"Kill it, sammadar," one of the boys shouted and the
others took up the cry. The bird looked at him with a
wicked red eye and hissed again. He half raised the
hèsotsan. But they were used only for killing invading
murgu now. He handed the weapon to Arnwheet who
took it proudly.

"Hold it as I showed you and do not touch the spot
there."

"I know, I know!"

He puffed his chest out and the other boys looked on
jealously until Kerrick took out his knife and warily circled
the bird. It turned to face him, bill gaping wide. One of the
boys threw a stone which thumped into its side. It turned
its head around and Kerrick seized its neck, cut its
throat with a quick slash. It kicked and slumped into a
huddle of gory feathers. The boys shrieked even more
loudly and rushed forward. Kerrick retrieved the hèsotsan
from his son.

"I am taking this meat to the island for Nadaske. You
will come with me?"

Arnwheet squirmed and looked away. They were having such a good time here. Kerrick looked past him to the
boys' boat. He pointed to it. "You have been out in that?"

"Just into the swamp. The sammadars told us we could
take it no further. Two boys did. They were beaten so
hard they howled."

"It is a very good thing that your father is a sammadar
and does not have to worry about a beating. Run and get

your bow and we will take the boat to the island. We will hunt."

There was no disagreement now. Kerrick placed the hèsotsan carefully in the grass, then seized the edge of the small boat and turned it over. It had a definitely irregular interior and sat in the water at an odd angle. Still, it floated. There were two small paddles, little more than flattened lengths of wood, but they would do. There were hollowed out gourds as well, for bailing, and they undoubtedly would be needed. It might be wisest if they stayed close to shore. He pushed it into deeper water, retrieved the hèsotsan and climbed gingerly in. It rocked viciously and he shifted carefully about until it floated fairly level.

"Isn't it a fine boat?" Arnwheet shouted as he ran up. He splashed into the water and almost overturned it as he climbed aboard. Kerrick made hasty corrections, then pointed to the gourds.

"I'm getting a wet bottom. Get rid of the water and let us try not to rock this thing too much."

He had to be very careful how he dug the paddle in because the little boat was fearfully unstable. Arnwheet sat proudly in the bow and called out unneeded advice as they splashed along the shore. He had an arrow nocked to his bow, but any game was gone long before they appeared. Kerrick paddled around the island and across the narrow waterway to the smaller island on the ocean. Arnwheet almost overturned them again jumping ashore and it was with a feeling of great relief that Kerrick slipped into the waist deep water, holding the hèsotsan above his head. They pulled the boat up on the sand.

"Isn't it a good boat?" Arnwheet said in Marbak. Kerrick answered in Yilanè.

"Excellently grown/strongest wood to ride the water."

"It wasn't grown. We hollowed it out with fire."

"I know. But there is no way to say that in Yilanè."

"I don't like to talk that way."

The boy was rebellious and Kerrick did not want to force him. It was important that he keep his strength of will. When this boy grew up he would give orders, not take them. Lead not follow.

"Yilanè is good to talk. You can talk to Nadaske now because he cannot talk Marbak at all."

"The boys laugh. They have seen me talk to you and say I shake like a frightened girl."

"Never listen to those who cannot do what you can do. What you speak they can never learn. It is important that you do not forget."

"Why?"

Why? Why indeed? How to answer this so simple question? Kerrick dropped to the sand, crossed his legs as he thought.

"Here, sit beside me. We will rest for a bit and I will tell you of many important things. Not important to you now, but of the greatest importance one day. Do you remember how cold you were when we were all in the snow with the Paramutan?"

"It is better to be warm."

"It is—and that is why we are here. We can no longer live in the north because of the snow that never melts. But here in the south there are the murgu. Murgu we can kill and eat, murgu we must kill before they eat us." Arnwheet scarcely noticed when Kerrick continued in Yilanè. "And then there are Yilanè like Nadaske. They are not efenselè like him but would kill us all if they could. Because of this we have to know about them, must be on our guard against them. Once I was the only Tanu who could talk to them. Now there are two of us. One day you will be sammadar and you will do what I do now. We must know them. We need their hèsotsan if we are to live here. This is a very important thing that you must do one day. And only you can do it."

Arnwheet wriggled uncomfortably and dug his toes into the sand. He could hear what his father was telling him, but could not understand the full import of the words. He was only a very small boy.

Kerrick climbed to his feet and brushed off his legs. "Now we see our friend Nadaske, bring him the meat and he will sing songs for us. And on the way strong hunter will keep his bow drawn and perhaps we can bring fresh-killed meat as well."

Arnwheet gave one whoop of delight as he seized up his bow and nocked the arrow to it. Then he slitted his eyes and crouched low, as all good hunters did on the trail, and slipped silently up the tussocked hill. Kerrick followed after, wondering if the boy had understood anything that he had said. If not now, he would one day. The time would come when Kerrick would be dead and Arnwheet would be a hunter, a sammadar. The responsibility would then be his.

Nadaske was on the shore staring out to sea, turned and signed pleasure when Kerrick called out attention to speaking. Then signed pleasure multiplied when Kerrick gave him the meat. He sniffed the bundle and added another modifier of greater amplitude.

"Small-wet who is no longer small nor wet, efenselè Kerrick, meat of great pleasure. It has been too long since we last talked."

"We are here now," Kerrick said, knowing it had been a long time, not wanting to discuss it. He turned and found a bush thick enough to have a dark shadow beneath it. The sand was still very warm and he brushed the surface layer away to uncover the cooler sand below, then placed the hèsotsan into the shallow pit. No one knew how the disease had spread from one of them to the other, or if it had indeed spread that way. They still took every precaution and never let another hunter touch their hèsotsan, never brought one of the weapons near another.

Arnwheet was telling Nadaske about their successful bird hunt and Nadaske showed great interest in the idea of a noose to trap creatures. Kerrick did not interrupt or try to help the boy when he got into difficulty trying to explain a noose's construction and operation in Yilanè. It was Nadaske who asked the right questions, helped him speak the correct answers. Kerrick watched in silent pleasure. Nadaske was truly interested in the snare, wanted to know how it was made.

"If I can understand its construction I can easily make it. It is a fact known to everyone that all females are brutal things. A fact as well that all the skill and Yilanè art are confined to the males. You have seen artful/glowing the wire/stone nenitesk."

"Can I see it now?"

"Another time. Now I will show you something more interesting/edible."

They followed Nadaske to the landward side of the island where he had dug a pit just at tide level. He moved aside the flat rock that covered it to reveal the seaweed lined interior. Mixed in with the wet seaweed were fresh shellfish. He selected large and juicy ones for his guests, put another in his mouth and clamped down hard to break the shell.

"Nadaske's teeth are strong/manifold," Kerrick said, using his flint knife to prize open the shellfish. "Ustuzou teeth suited for other things. So stone tooth must be used."

"Metal tooth too," Arnwheet said, slipping the thong over his head and using his skymetal knife to attack the shell.

"No," Kerrick said, "don't use that." Arnwheet looked up, startled at the forcefulness of his negative modifiers. Kerrick wondered himself at the strength of his feelings. He passed over his flint knife, took the metal one and rubbed it with his fingers. It was scratched and nicked, but had a good edge to it, and a sharp point, where Arnwheet had sharpened it on a stone. "This was mine," he said. "It hung always about my neck on a thong, then from this metal collar as this knife does now."

"One bigger, one smaller, very much the same." Nadaske said. "Explanation of existence/relationship."

"Cut from skymetal, Herilak told me. He was there when it fell, a burning rock from the sky that was not stone at all, but metal. Skymetal. He was with the hunters when they searched for it. The one who found it was a sammadar named Amahast. As you can see the skymetal is hard, but it can be sawn by notched sheets of stone. That is how these knives were made, a large and a small one. Amahast wore the large one and the smaller was worn by his son. Amahast was my father. Now my son wears mine, as I did."

"What is father what is son?" Nadaske asked, rubbing his thumb over the shining surface of the knife.

"That will be hard to explain to you."

"You think that I am a fargi of low intelligence without intellect to understand/appreciate?"

Kerrick signed apologies for misunderstandings. "No, it is just that it has to do with the way ustuzou are born. There are no eggs, no efenburu in the sea. A child is born from its mother therefore knows its father as well."

Nadaske signed confusion and disbelief. "Kerrick spoke correctly. There are some things that are beyond understanding about ustuzou."

"You should think of Arnwheet and I as being of the smallest efenburu. Closer than close."

"Understanding partial, acceptance complete. Eat more shellfish."

By late afternoon Arnwheet became bored with the talk and looked around restlessly. Kerrick saw this and realized that it was important that he not be troubled seeing Nadaske. It must always be interesting, something to look forward to.

"It is time to leave," Kerrick said. "Perhaps the birds are returning to the swamp and you can shoot one."

"Shortness of visit/shortness of life," Nadaske said in a gloomy attempt to keep them longer.

"Soon again—with fresh meat," Kerrick said, turning away. He took up the hèsotsan, brushed a few grains of sand from it.

Stopped suddenly, very still.

"You see something I do not see," Nadaske said, reading alarm into the curve of his body.

"I see nothing. Just some sand on this stupid hèsotsan." He brushed at it with his fingers, then brushed it again.

The small gray patch would not come off.

TWENTY-SIX

Kerrick did not want to speak of what he had seen, as
though in keeping silent the spot would vanish, might
have never existed. Arnwheet approved of his silence as
he stalked ahead. He shot his arrow at a basking lizard,
came very close as it scuttled away into the grass. Then he
sat in the bow of the boat all the way back, trailing his
fingers in the water. Kerrick started to warn him with
sudden memory of doing the same thing when he was a
boy, the horror of the marag surging up from the sea. But
that had happened a long time ago: there was nothing to
fear from these shallow inland waters. They beached the
boat, turned it over and Arnwheet ran ahead to the tent.
Kerrick looked again at the hèsotsan. The spot was still
there.

There was silence around their fire. Armun knew where
they had gone and her disapproval was obvious in her
every movement. This one time Kerrick did not attempt
to talk to her, to make her forget their visit to the island:
he was just as silent as she. Arnwheet, tired from the day,
was asleep even before the first stars appeared. Kerrick

kicked sand over the smoldering fire then went to the
stream to wash his hands and arms. He rubbed them
thoroughly, then did it all a second time. Though if he had
brought the disease to the hèsotsan it was far too late for
this. He shook them dry and went down the path to
Herilak's tent.

When he came into the clearing he saw that Merrith
had moved her tent until it was just beside that of the
sammadar. Darras sat now in the open flap of the tent
holding a doll woven of straw. She was still a silent little
girl, but she did smile at him even though she did not
speak. The flap of Herilak's tent was closed and he heard
laughter from inside. He was going to call out when he
realized that it was woman's laughter. He had not known
about this before. It was a good thing. He sat down on the
fur beside Darras.

"I never saw that doll before."

"My grandmother made it. I watched her do it. Isn't
she nice? Her name is Melde. That was my mother's name
too."

"It is a very nice doll."

He added some dry branches to the fire and stirred it
until the wood crackled and the flames grew higher. The
flaps of the other tent were opened and Merrith came
over and sat next to him.

"Darras was telling me about her new doll. She is very
happy with it."

Merrith smiled and nodded agreement. "She is not the
only one who is filled with pleasure."

Herilak called out greetings and Kerrick went to join
him. They sat in darkness before the tent looking at the
woman and the little girl in the flickering firelight. Herilak
seemed as happy as Merrith was. Kerrick was reluctant to
spoil all this; Herilak had been grim and unsmiling for far
too long. They talked of hunting, the other sammads, and
of the Sasku valley. They did this until Merrith took the
girl into the tent and the flap was closed.

"It may be very hot here in the summer," Herilak

said. "But it is never cold in the winter. This island is a
very good place for the sammads."

"Will we ever go back to the mountains? That was
what old Fraken talked of when dying."

"Old Fraken was an old fool. I have heard you say that
many times. There is still the winter that does not stop to
the north."

"I think that my death-stick has the sickness."

Herilak was very still for a long time. When he finally
spoke the grim unhappiness was back in his voice.

"It had to happen some day. We all knew that it
would. This time we must get new death-sticks before the
old ones die, keep them apart."

"You mean go to the city again? Steal more of them?
Kill more murgu?"

"Can you think of any different thing to do?"

Kerrick had no quick answer for this. He sat in silence,
his hands clasped before him, wringing his fingers together so hard that his knuckles cracked. The moon rose
above the trees and drenched the clearing with cool light.
An owl drifted silently above their heads: a night creature
called distantly in the forest.

"No," Kerrick said with great reluctance. "I can think
of nothing else. We know now where the death-sticks are.
But if we are seen again . . ."

"You need not go this time. I know where the pit is
now."

"I am not afraid of going there!"

"I did not say that you were. I meant only that others
can take the risk. You have done your part, and more,
many times over."

"That is also not important. What I fear most is our
dependency on the murgu and the city. We will go now
because we must, then one day we will have to go again.
But one time when we go it will happen. Once when we
are in the city we will be seen by the murgu. And what
then?"

"You worry too much. Life is to be taken one day at a
time."

"That is no longer true. When we lived in the mountains and followed the deer you could say that. No longer. We are in a trap and there is no way out."

"We will be a bigger hunting party this time. We will bring back many death-sticks."

"No. Impossible. The risk is too great. Two hunters at most. And we will leave our own death-sticks behind here. Then, when we are distant from the sammads, we must wash ourselves and the skins we wear, many times. If there is a sickness it must not spread to the death-sticks we bring back."

"I do not understand your talk of washing and sickness."

"Neither do I," Kerrick said with a twisted smile. "But I was told about it by one who knew. This was before we met and I had been very sick . . ."

"Then it was a marag who told you this?"

"Yes. And after the attack on the city, then the valley where they grew special plants just to kill us, you can see clearly how much they know of living things. This marag of great knowledge told me that disease, infections, are spread by small living things."

"I have seen grubs in wounds."

"Living creatures even smaller than that, so small that you cannot see them. I know it is hard to believe, but I am just telling you what I was told. So perhaps what is killing the death-sticks passes from one to the other. I don't know. But if we can stop it by washing ourselves then we must do it."

"Surely we must. And any hunter would smell better for a good washing. It will be you and I then. We will go."

"No," Kerrick said with sudden firmness. "You are a sammadar and I cannot tell you what to do. I will take one who will obey me, who will do as I order. We will go in silence and avoid the murgu. Avoid killing if we see any of them. If you were there, and that should happen, would you obey an order not to kill?"

"I would not. You speak the truth in that. But who would you take? Your sammad is small, the boy Harl the only hunter you have."

"He is skilled and silent in the forest. He will go with me. That is the way it must be."

"You are making a mistake—"

"I might be—but it is my mistake."

Herilak frowned angrily but could think of nothing more to say. The decision had been made. "When do you leave?"

"Very soon. This time we must go there and get the death-sticks, bring them back before the others that we have here die. They must be ready for us when we need them."

There was little to add after this and they parted in silence.

Kerrick was still awake the next morning at first light, had slept little during the night. He lay unmoving, listening to Armun's gentle breathing, until sunlight touched the wall of the tent. Only then did he slip out quietly and go to the shelter where he kept the hèsotsan, to unwrap it carefully and hold it up in the light. The dead area was there, bigger now, still there.

The flap of the hunters' tent had been thrown back and Ortnar sat in the morning sunlight. His dead leg was stretched out before him on the ground, his perpetual scowl etched with deep lines into his face.

"I want to talk with Harl," Kerrick said.

"I still slept when he left, well before light. He knows a place by the stream where deer come at dawn. He will be a good hunter one day."

"I will speak with him when he returns." There was nothing to add, Ortnar was never one for small talk. Kerrick turned away and went to his own tent. Armun was awake, stirring the fire to life.

"I saw you looking at the death-stick. You worry too much about it."

"It is more than a worry. It has the sickness."

"Not again!" The words were a cry of pain, wrenched from her.

"Again. I will have to go to the murgu city. Again."

"No, not you. There are others who can go."

"Others could surely go—but they would never return. Only a Tanu who is half marag can understand that murgu city. Now I will eat and rest. I slept little last night."

The sun was high in the sky when he awoke. The sky was bright and he blinked into its glare. Harl was sitting outside, waiting for him in patient silence. Seeing him like this, his mind still clouded with sleep, Kerrick looked at him as a stranger. No longer the small boy, but a hunter grown. As soon as he saw that Kerrick was awake he stood and came over to the tent.

"Ortnar said you came to find me, you would speak to me."

"He told me that you were hunting. The deer came?"

"Right beneath me. Two are dead. What is it you want?"

Like Ortnar, he had no time for small talk. He used words like arrows, sharp and swift.

"I want you. Will you go to the murgu city with me? My death-stick has the sickness."

"How many will go?"

"You and I alone."

Harl's eyes opened wide. "You went with the sammadar Herilak last time."

"I did. And he killed the murgu we met. This time I wish to rely on skill in woodcraft and not killing. I wish to see and not be seen. Will you go with me?"

Harl smiled and held out his clenched fists, one above the other. "I will go. We will bring back death-sticks?"

"Yes. But you must tell me one thing now. Will you do as I order you to? If we see the murgu of the city they must not be killed. Will you do that?"

"You are asking a difficult thing."

"I know. But if you do not do it, then another will. You are of my sammad. If you will do as I ask you, then there will be no other hunter. It is your choice."

"Then I choose to come with you. I will do as you order, sammadar. When will we leave?"

"In the morning. Spear and bow only. The death-sticks stay here."

"What do we do then if we meet a large marag that we cannot kill with spear or arrow?"

"We die. So it is your skill in the forest that will lead us away from them. Can you do that?"

"Yes. We will do as the sammadar says."

They left at dawn, and by the heat of the day they were well upon the track south. When they came to the ford across the narrow river they took turns to scrub themselves clean in the clear water, one washing while the other stood guard. Harl could not see the reason for this, still he did as he was told. He grumbled about getting his bow and quiver wet, spread his arrows on the grass to dry. Kerrick looked at their packs of dried meat and ekkotaz.

"You cannot wash the meat," Harl said. Kerrick smiled.

"True. But we can eat it. Before we enter the city we throw away what we haven't finished, the bags as well. The last time we went I cut up the leather to bind the death-sticks. The illness could have been passed on that way. This time we will use split saplings and vines to hold them. They must not get the sickness again."

On the second day Harl stopped them with a raised hand, listened to the forest ahead. There was something there, large. They made a long swing out through the trees to the shore, went along the sand for the rest of the day. Only when the coast became swampy and impassable did they return inland. There were no other disturbances after this and they made very good time. When they reached the now-familiar outer reaches of the city Kerrick called a stop.

"We will go back to the last stream we crossed. Get rid of the meat bags and wash again."

"We will eat all the meat we can first."

"Yes, of course. Then go on in the afternoon." Harl frowned at this, seemed displeased. "There is a good reason to wait. The murgu in the city do not move around at night. If they are near the death-stick pens they will leave in time to be well back inside the city by dark. If we reach there at dusk we can get the death-sticks and find our way out even if it is after nightfall. Can that be done?"

"If I see a track by day I can walk it by night. It shall be as you say, sammadar."

By midafternoon, their leather garments still wet and cool against their skin, they penetrated the outer wall of the city. Kerrick went first, cutting and pushing aside the poisonous plants and thorns. Once past this barrier he whispered instructions to Harl who now led the way. Slower and slower, crawling the last distance to the earthen wall of the pen. Harl went on himself, then waved Kerrick forward.

"There is no one here, no tracks since the last rain."

"I still want to stay out of sight until it is darker. We can use these vines to make nets to carry the death-sticks."

It was near dusk when Harl pulled himself up onto the earthen wall, looked around and beckoned Kerrick forward. The hèsotsan were thick in the shallow water below and on the sandy bank. Kerrick threw clods down to chase the active ones away, then jumped down into the pit. There were hèsotsan close by on the sand, feebly moving their legs and unable to escape.

"These are the ones we want," he said. "I'll hand them up to you."

He passed up as many as they could carry easily, then took Harl's hand and pulled himself out. The hèsotsan hissed weakly when they were bound and tried to snap at their fingers. It was quickly done. They slung the bundled creatures over their shoulders and seized up their weapons.

"We have done it!" Kerrick said, already feeling the tension drain away. "Now—let's get out of here."

Harl led the way in an easy lope, back along the track they had followed when they had entered the city.

As he came around the end of the embankment there was the sharp crack of a hèsotsan and he collapsed. Dead before he hit the ground.

TWENTY-SEVEN

Kerrick stopped, fell backward, huddled against the earthen wall. Harl lay crumpled just before him. His mouth hung open and his eyes stared sightlessly at the sky. The bundle of hèsotsan lay across his chest with the creatures writhing slowly against their bonds.

Harl was dead. Killed by a hèsotsan. A Yilanè, it had to be a Yilanè who was out there, lying in wait. It had been a neatly planned trap. There was no way out of it. If he moved or tried to retreat he would be exposed. He could not go forward—and there was no way back. The instant they saw him they would shoot: a marauding ustuzou would be killed on sight.

Then he had to be Yilanè again.

"Attention to speaking!" He called out. Then added, "Death . . . negative!" It did not make much sense, but he wanted those who were waiting out there to hesitate before they fired. He laid the bundle of hèsotsan aside, rose slowly to his feet—then stepped out of cover calling out loudly as he did, his arms and thumbs held in the form of submission.

"I am unarmed. Do not kill me," he said as firmly and clearly as he could. His skin quivered, expecting the dart that would bring instant death. The Yilanè stood just ahead of him in the dense shrubbery. She had emerged from the shelter of the trees. Her hèsotsan was aimed directly at him. She appeared to be alone. All he could do was stand rigidly still, signing submission.

Intèpelei looked at him, never moving her weapon. But she did not fire.

"You are the ustuzou who is yilanè. I know of you."

"I am Kerrick who is Yilanè."

"Then you must be the one who went to Ikhalmenets and killed the uruketo of our city. You are that one?"

Kerrick thought of lying; there was no point to it.

"I am."

Intèpelei signed pleasure of discovery—but still kept the hèsotsan aimed at his chest. "Then I must take you to Lanefenuu who has talked much of the ustuzou and her hatred for you. I think she wants to see you before you die. Did you kill the three Yilanè and put them into the pit with the hèsotsan?"

"I did not kill them."

"But your kind of ustuzou did?"

"Yes."

"It was my thought that this was the explanation of their deaths. No other agreed with me. I did what had to be done. I have had fargi hidden near this place ever since that day. Fargi instructed to come to me if any ustuzou pass. One came to me this day. Now we go to speak with Lanefenuu."

"It is almost dark."

"Then you will hurry. For if it grows dark before we reach the ambesed I will kill you. Move quickly."

Kerrick stepped reluctantly forward, searching for a way out, finding none. This Yilanè was a hunter, he could tell that, knew he would be killed instantly if he tried to attack. She signed with her top thumbs as she stepped forward. Then shivered and almost fell.

The arrow made a thunking sound as it struck deep into her back.

She raised the hèsotsan, her hands shaking, pointing it towards Kerrick. It cracked once, the dart missed. She raised it higher.

The second arrow took her in the neck and she fell. Herilak ran silently up the path, looked down at the two bodies.

"I did not see the marag until it killed the boy. I did not have a clear shot until it moved into the track."

"You followed us."

"I did. I did not bring a death-stick but I followed you. There was a danger just the two of you alone. We must get rid of the bodies. Into the pit . . ."

"No, no need," Kerrick said wearily. "I talked to that one before you killed her, you heard me. She had guards posted to watch this track. They told her that we were coming."

"We must leave quickly!"

"No, she is a hunter, she came here alone. It is too dark now for others to follow her. But the watchers who saw us come and told her, they are in the city. Others will be here in the morning. We cannot hide the fact that we were here. They know now. I didn't want any killing, I thought it would be better without you. But you followed anyway. We should bury Harl."

"Foolish, waste of time. His tharm is in the stars and he cares not for the meat left behind. I will cut out my arrows, we will take the death-sticks and leave. By morning when they come here we will be far down the track."

Kerrick felt a great weariness. He knelt beside the dead boy and removed the bundle of hèsotsan. Then straightened Harl's limbs and closed his eyes. He rose slowly to his feet.

"I killed him," he said, bitterly. "I brought him here."

"The marag killed him. We have new death-sticks. Leave him now—and leave all thought of him. He was young but he was a good hunter. I will take his spear and bow. Another boy who wishes to be a hunter will get great strength from them."

There was nothing more to say, nothing that could be said. They had the weapons. With the bundles slung across their shoulders they started north, were quickly out of sight. It grew dark under the trees and shadows stretched across the two bodies, so alien to each other, now united in the inescapable bond of death.

There were no large carrion eaters here within the city, so the corpses were undisturbed during the night. At dawn the crows found them. Landed hesitantly and hopped forward, very suspicious of the large and unexpected gift. They were beginning to tear at the flesh when loud shouts disturbed them and they flapped away. The first fargi, hèsotsan held hesitantly before them, approached down the path. They milled about, looked into the forest, searched further along the track. Only when Muruspe came up, she had been careful to lead them only from the rear, was any order restored. Anatempè stood beside her, signing shock and grief.

"What is the meaning of this? What happened?"

"It is very clear what happened," Muruspe said, displaying immense distaste. "Intèpelei received warning of intrusion, she came alone, she died for her valor. She must have killed one ustuzou, others killed her. You are a Yilanè of science who assists Ukhereb. Can you tell me when this happened?"

Anatempè squatted down and touched the skin on both bodies. Signed unclarity of conclusion. "Not this morning. Perhaps during the night, probably late yesterday."

"Probably. The fargi who hid here yesterday said that she saw two ustuzou. Now one is dead here, the other gone. What were they doing here? Why did they come?"

Anatempè turned to look at the wall of the hèsotsan pit; Muruspe followed her gaze. "Has it anything to do with the hèsotsan?"

"Alpèasak is a large city. Twice killer ustuzou have come to this city. Twice there have been deaths at the hèsotsan pit."

"And the ustuzou use the hèsotsan as well as we do."
Muruspe was silent with inner thought, then signed atten-
tion to orders. "We will bring the bodies to the ambesed.
This is a matter for the Eistaa."

There were expressions of pain and dismay when the
sad column moved through the city. The fargi pushed
away from it, frightened by death of a Yilanè, sight of a
dead ustuzou. The two bodies were laid upon the ground
while Muruspe went to inform the Eistaa.

Lanefenuu stared down at the corpses stretched out on
the grass before her, stared in silent thought. Silence
filled the ambesed as well, since none dared interrupt her.
The two scientists, Ukhereb and Akotolp, had already
examined the bodies and agreed on what had probably
happened.

The ustuzou had been killed by a dart from a hèsotsan,
undoubtedly Intèpelei's own weapon. The hunter then
killed in turn by ustuzou stone tooth; there were mortal
wounds in her neck and back.

"Why did this ustuzou come to my city?" Lanefenuu
finally said, looking about the circle of her advisers. "The
killing of ustuzou has been ended. I ended it. Vaintè is
gone. We stay within our city—but they do not stay
within theirs. You know these creatures, Akotolp. You
knew them when you first came to Alpèasak, before you
fled destruction, before you returned. Why are they here?"

"I can only guess."

"Then guess. Without knowledge that is all any of us
can do."

"I think that . . . they came for hèsotsan. They have
their own stone teeth to kill with, but they like to kill as
well with our hèsotsan. They came to steal them from us."

"That was also my own thought. We must find out
more of this matter. Three hunters vanished to the north,
three Yilanè killed inside my city. Now, Akotolp, you
were to search. What have you found?"

"Nothing. No evidence of ustuzou near the city—or
even as far north as the round lake. The birds fly and I
have images."

"Then have the birds fly further. Those filthy creatures are out there and I want to know where. Find them. Should I send hunters to search?"

"That is not wise because these ustuzou are more cunning than any beast in the wild. They trap and kill our hunters. There was another thing that we did when they hid from the birds. There are owls that can fly by night, carrying creatures that can see in the darkness."

"Do that as well. They must be found."

"Have you found the ones we search for?" Fafnepto said as she pulled herself up onto the uruketo's back. Sea water dripped from her as she carefully wiped the nostrils of her hèsotsan to be sure that it could breathe easily.

"They are not on the coast of this island," Vaintè said. "Though they might have come here: it is important that we looked for them. It is a rich and fertile place. It was wise to search."

"The hunting is very good as well. I found the small horned ustuzou you told me of, killed them. Their flesh is very sweet." She signed up to Gunugul who was listening to them from the summit of the fin. "There is fresh meat on the shore for you. Is there a way to bring it here?"

"Gratitude/pleasure of eating. It will be arranged."

Crewmembers swam ashore, towing empty bladders to support the stacked carcasses. Fafnepto had outdone herself and devastated the local animal population. While they were waiting for the meat to be brought aboard Gunugul took out her charts and put her thumb on their exact location.

"North of us is the continent of Gendasi∗. Here is the city of Alpèasak. It appears that this city is close to the tip of a great peninsula of land—is this true?"

Vaintè tilted her hand in agreement. "It is indeed as you describe. I have journeyed up the eastern coast, we landed and killed ustuzou there. But if you go far enough north it becomes cold and there is winter always."

"Should we go that way?"

"My first reaction is a negative one. As Fafnepto has

advised I try to think as those we pursue. To go north they first had to pass Alpèasak and risk discovery. After that the further they went, the colder it would get. I don't think they went to the east. However there is warm ocean and a warm continent to the west, here where the blankness is upon your charts. I have gone that way by uruketo, and on land as well, and it continues for a great while. There is a large river here up which we journeyed. And all along the coast there are bays, beyond them forests rich with animals. I feel sure that they went this way."

"Then so shall we," Gunugul said. "I will take pleasure in adding to these charts."

In this way they reached the coast of Gendasi∗, sailing between the golden isles until they reached the sandy shores. Alpèasak was out of sight to the east and they sailed west. The coast moved by, a summer storm lashing the trees with rain, hiding them then revealing them again. The enteesenat jumped high, pleased with the variety of fish they could catch in these warm and shallow waters. Gunugul marked her chart, the crewmembers gorged themselves on the fresh meat that Fafnepto had provided. Vaintè was alive, watching the shore with infinite patience, looking forward with great anticipation to the deaths of all those who had opposed her.

TWENTY-EIGHT

Arnwheet was squatting in the shade blowing fiercely on his whistle. It was one that the Paramutan had made for him, with a moving rod at the end just like one of their pumps. But instead of spitting out water this whistle pumped out shrill and quavering noise that sliced through the afternoon heat. It was midsummer and the days were longer and hotter. Little could be done during the torrid afternoon, little had to be done. There was meat and fruit and all of the green things that grew in the earth, fish and wildfowl as well. There had been three full moons since Kerrick and Herilak had returned from the city with the new death-sticks. They had moved quickly and had not been followed. Since then no murgu had come out of the city that they knew of. The trail from the south was watched carefully, but none came. That incident was over. While two of the older death-sticks had sickened and died, none of the new ones had been affected. The sammads were well fed and at peace. A peace that they had not known since the long winters had begun.

The shrill wavering sound hung in the hot air: Kerrick

marveled at the boy's application. The sides of the tent
were rolled up to let what little breeze there was move
through. The baby was asleep and Armun was working the
knots out of her hair with a comb carved from horn.
Kerrick watched her with great pleasure. The whistle cut
off abruptly, then started again even more harshly. Kerrick
rolled over and saw that two hunters had joined Arnwheet
under the tree and were examining the whistle. One of
them, it was Hanath, Kerrick saw, was trying to play it,
his cheeks growing red with the effort. He passed it over
to Morgil who blew and worked the stem and elicited the
sound of a dying mastodon from it. Armun laughed at
their efforts. Kerrick rose, stretched and yawned, walked
out blinking into the blistering sunshine. Morgil panted
and gasped and handed the whistle back to the boy when
Kerrick joined them.

"You have so little to do than to come to steal Arnwheet's
toy?" Kerrick said.

"Hanath . . . told me of it," Morgil panted. "It makes
an awful noise. And was it made by the Paramutan you
told us about?"

"It was. They are very clever and carve bone and
wood. They make another thing like this, only bigger that
they use to suck water out of their boats."

"And they live on the ice and hunt fish in the cold and
there is snow?" Hanath said with great interest. "You
must tell us more about them."

"You have heard the stories, you know as much now as
I do. But what do you care about the Paramutan? Does
not your brewing of porro keep you even too busy to
hunt?"

"Many others hunt. They trade all the meat we need
for porro."

"And we have drunk enough porro for a while," Morgil
said. "It is good when it is good, but terrible when it is
bad. I think the manduktos do the right thing, drink it
only when something special happens. You told us the
Paramutan come south to trade. Do they come this far?"

"No, they hate the heat, they would die here. At the end of the summer, those that want to trade go to the shore to the north where the great river meets the ocean. That is the only place where they go."

"What is it they want to trade?"

"They bring cured hides, furs sometimes, rich eating fat. What they want in return are flint knives, spearheads, even arrowheads. They make their own kind of bone fishhooks, certain kind of spearheads, but they need our knives."

"I have the feeling that I need some furs," Hanath said, wiping sweat from his forehead with forefinger.

"I too," agreed Morgil. "We think that the time for trading has come."

Kerrick looked at them both with astonishment. "I think that the last thing you will need here are furs." The whistle wailed shrilly as Arnwheet blew it for his attentive audience. Kerrick thought about what they had said and smiled. "I don't think that it is furs that you want, but maybe a long trek, some hunting, cold weather and frost."

Morgil clasped his hands together and rolled his eyes skyward. "The sammadar sees our secret thoughts. He should be alladjex, not Fraken who is young and stupid."

"I don't have to be an alladjex to see that you two have not been on the trail for a long time—and want the smell of the northern forest in your nostrils again."

"Yes!" they said it as one and Hanath obviously spoke for them both. "Tell us where this place is where the Paramutan wait. We will make lots of knives . . ."

"Others will make them, we will trade them for porro," Morgil said. "But will these Paramutan come again to trade? You told us that they have crossed the ocean and now hunt and fish on a distant shore."

"They will come, they told me so. Crossing the ocean is nothing for them. There are those things they need that they can only get by trading with the Tanu. They will come."

"And we will be there to meet them. Can you tell us of where we can find the furry-faced ones?"

"You must ask Armun. She knows the place because that is where she first met the Paramutan."

She came out of the tent when he called her, sat next to Arnwheet and brushed his tangled hair from his face. He whistled happily at his growing audience.

"It is very easy to find," she said when they had explained what they wanted. "You must know the trail that comes from the mountains to the sea."

Kerrick felt a sudden excitement as she talked, could almost smell the chill mist blowing in from the ocean, the cold pelting of driving snow. He had forgotten what it was like to be cold. Not that he wanted to freeze to death again, but to eat a mouthful of snow, to walk in the dark pine woods—that was something worth doing. Under eager questioning Armun talked more about the Paramutan and the way they lived on the ice, the many things they made, the rotten fish they liked to eat. The two hunters listened closely to her words, gasping in fascination at their strange ways. When she had finished Hanath slapped Morgil so enthusiastically on the shoulder that he knocked him over on his side.

"We will do it," he cried. "We will go, now is the time to leave. We will go north and trade with the furry ones."

"Perhaps I will go with you," Kerrick said. "To show you the way."

Armun's eyes widened with shock. Before she could speak her anger he seized her hands in his. "We will both go, why not, take a mastodon to carry the things we wish to trade."

"That will be too slow," she said. "And we will not go, nor do I even wish to talk of it. The children are here . . ."

"And the children are safe here. Ysel eats soft-chewed food now, Arnwheet has his friends, while the sammads and many hunters are on all sides."

"I want to go too!" Arnwheet called out and Armun shushed him.

"This is a thing that hunters wish to do. You are not quite the grown hunter yet. Some day, but not now."

She took the boy back to the tent with her, leaving the three hunters with their heads bent close, making plans. She was concerned, but not worried. But what should she do if Kerrick said that he wished to go with them? She must decide before he returned. He wanted very much to go, that was clear. Perhaps life on this island was too easy. Certainly it was too hot. She laughed out loud. She would very much like to do this thing as well. By the time Kerrick had returned her mind was made up.

"I think those two have had a good idea," he said. His fingers twisted at the skymetal knife as he talked. "Of course there is no real need for furs here, not in the summer at least. But the Paramutan have many other things."

"Like what, whistles?"

"Not only whistles," he said angrily, then saw that she was smiling.

"You want to make this trek, don't you?"

"Yes, of course."

"Well so do I. It is too quiet here now, too hot. Malagen, the Sasku woman, she likes to look after Ysel, she will do it willingly if I go with you. Arnwheet has his friends and will not even know that we have gone. I think that it will be a very good thing to go north for a while. We will find cold rain, perhaps snow, and when we return the worst heat will be over."

A shadow passed across the clearing before the tent, drifted back. Kerrick stepped out and looked into the burning blue bowl of the sky, shielded his eyes with his hand. It was a large bird, an eagle perhaps, soaring in slow circles, a black silhouette against the sky. It was too high to make out any details. It moved away and he went back into the shade. Was it a Yilanè bird sent to look for them? Not that it mattered: Lanefenuu would never forget those dead uruketo. The fighting was over.

*   *   *

Day followed burning day as the uruketo swam slowly west along the coast. When the waves broke on the sandy shore they moved steadily, with at least three Yilanè on the fin at all times watching the coast slip by. Only when there were large inlets and bays did their progress slow as they made a careful search of the indented coastline. It became even slower when they came to one large bay with islands, it appeared to be a river mouth, that had to be carefully searched. Fafnepto was on the fin, blinking in the sunlight as she looked at the cool darkness under the trees close by. When they turned by a rocky headland she pointed it out to Vaintè.

"Oddness of rock shape, memorable/unforgettable. I will go ashore there and hunt fresh meat."

"Appreciated by all. When we have finished the search we will return and meet you here. Good hunting."

"For me, it is always good hunting." She climbed down the fin and slipped into the water.

It took almost the entire day to search the bay. After that they started up the river through large, sweeping bends. For the first time Vaintè began to worry that their search would be in vain. She knew that Gendasi* was large, but had never truly appreciated the size of this new continent. Always before she had followed on the track of the ustuzou, going where they led. Now, on her own, she was beginning to realize that even something as large as an uruketo would be difficult to find—when she had no idea of where to look. The river was still wide and deep, moving inland in lazy loops. The other uruketo could have easily come this way. Should they search further? It was a great relief to discover that sandbars soon blocked the channel and they had to return. There was no need to follow the river any more. Those they searched for must still be somewhere along the ocean's shore.

It was late afternoon before they returned to the rocky headland. Fafnepto was nowhere to be seen.

"Is this the place where she landed?" Gunugul asked. Vaintè signed assuredness of location. "Then she is still hunting. We will all enjoy pleasure/satisfaction to have fresh meat. I will have bladders floated ashore so we may leave when she returns."

Vaintè watched the crewmembers bring up the bladders and slide into the river with them. The water looked cool, the forested shore inviting. She had been in the smell-filled confines of the uruketo too long. A moment later she was slipping down from the uruketo's back and swimming strongly towards the beach.

"Excitement of discovery," one of the crewmembers called out, pointing to the corpses of five large deer lying in the tall grass.

Vaintè admired them, then looked up as Fafnepto herself appeared from under the trees. She signed urgency of speaking as Vaintè began to compliment her on her kill.

"There is a thing I would have you see Vaintè. This way."

"Has it to do with those we seek?"

"No. But I think it is the ustuzou you told me of. They are beyond these trees."

"They can be dangerous!"

"Not now. All dead."

The skin tent was on the far side of the small meadow near the stream. Two large ustuzou were crumpled on the ground before it, a third smaller one was lying nearby.

"I killed them before they saw me," Fafnepto said. "You said they could be deadly."

"You searched the structure?"

"Yes. None there. Many hides—and a hèsotsan."

One of the ustuzou lay face upwards. Vaintè turned the other one over with her foot claws, hopefully, but it was not Kerrick. "You were right to kill them," she said.

"Is this the stone tooth of which you spoke?" Fafnepto asked, pointing to the spear in the dead hunter's hand.

"It is one kind. Another is sent through the air, very much like the dart from a hèsotsan. Not poisonous but a great deal heavier. They are very dangerous beasts."

"Then we can be sure that the uruketo you seek is not near here."

"A wise observation. The search will continue."

Vaintè walked back to the shore in enforced silence, her body rippling with the intensity of her thoughts. She knew that the search for the uruketo and the Daughters of Life, as well as the renegade scientist, would go on. She had told Saagakel that she would do this. And Fafnepto was here to aid her in that search. But it would not go on forever. Now that she thought about it she realized that she cared little if Enge and her accomplices lived or died. Not now, not after seeing the bodies in the clearing. The sight of those dead ustuzou drove the present search from her thoughts. It wasn't important. What was of primary importance, what she really needed to do, was to find Kerrick.

Find him and kill him.

"Message of urgency/import for the Eistaa," the fargi said, trembling with the effort to remember what she had been instructed to say, to be clear and comprehensible in her speaking.

Lanefenuu leaned back on her board, her mouth working hard on a large portion of jellied meat. Her advisers sat in a circle about her, their attitudes appreciative of her wonderful appetite. She threw the bone aside and gestured a truncated continuance of talking to the fargi. The creature gaped in ignorance.

Muruspe caught the fargi's attention. "You are ordered to speak. Finish telling what was told to be said." The fargi gasped with sudden comprehension when she understood the simplified commands, spoke quickly before she forgot everything.

"Ukhereb reports discoveries of relevancy. Requests presence of Eistaa for revelation."

Lanefenuu waved the fargi out of sight, heaved herself to her feet, signed for a water-fruit and used it to clean her hands. "A request for my presence signifies matters of importance," she said. "We go."

As they left the ambesed two of her advisers hurried ahead to be sure her way was clear, the rest trailed behind. Muruspe, who was her efenselè as well as first adviser, walked at her side.

"Do you know what it can be, Muruspe?" Lanefenuu asked.

"I know no more of it than you do, Eistaa. But my hope is that these Yilanè of science have uncovered some evidence of the ustuzou that kill."

"My hope as well. A matter of lesser importance would have brought Ukhereb to the ambesed herself."

Akotolp was waiting at the dilated opening in the wall to greet them, signing pleasure and joyful anticipation.

"Apologies of request-for-presence from Ukhereb. That which we wish to show you could not be brought easily/ quickly."

"Show me at once—anticipation becomes unbearable."

Akotolp led the way into the dusky interior, then through another partition into a chamber of darkness. Only when the entrance had been sealed was it possible to see by the weak red glow being emitted by a cage of insects. Ukhereb held up a damp sheet of some white substance with dark marks upon it.

"This image would vanish if exposed to daylight at this moment. I wished the Eistaa to see it at once."

"Explanation of significance, meaning unclear." She bent close, following Ukhereb's pointing thumb.

"Image obtained from high in the air. These are trees around a clearing. This and this are the structures made of animal skins that the killing ustuzou erect. Here a group of three ustuzou, here more. And here and here."

"I see them now! They are so ugly. They are the same kind as the one killed here in the city?"

"They are the same. See the light fur on the head, skins bound about below."

"Where are they now?"

"North of the city. Not close, but north of us on an island on the shore. I will have other images for you to look at soon, the processing is now going on. In one of them I believe there is a hèsotsan."

"One of our hèsotsan," Lanefenuu said angrily. "This must end. Twice they came here, killed Yilanè, took hèsotsan away with them. This shall not happen a third time."

TWENTY-NINE

Even though the air was stifling under the trees, the biting insects a torment when they passed through the swampy areas, it was still good to be moving on the trail again. As pleasurable as life had been on the island, it had become a little too much like the valley of the Sasku. The sammads were now in one place and it seemed as though they were going to stay there. In the past there had been winter hunting and summer hunting, the berries and mushrooms of the autumn, the fresh shoots and roots in the spring. All of this had changed. The game was always close by, fruit ripe the year round, more of everything than they could possibly ever eat. But the cycle of the year was in the Tanu blood and they grew restless when they were too long in the same place. Now they were moving, four of them, heading north. Hanath and Morgil scouted ahead, sometimes fell behind and stalked game, ran to catch up with them. For Kerrick and Armun the trek was the greatest pleasure. They were together—and that was enough. They had no regrets at leaving the children behind—since they were far safer in the midst of the sammads than they would have been here on the trail.

If Kerrick had one regret it was the perfunctory leavetaking he had had with Nadaske. He had kept putting it off, one day ran into the other, there was always so much to do. Then it was the day to leave. It would have been easy to just have gone, certainly that would have pleased Armun, but he found that he could not do it that way. Nor was Arnwheet there, he was away with the other boys. They were ready to go. The last of the smoked meat and ekkotaz was being packed in on top of the stone knives, there was even some of the charadis cloth that Armun wanted to bring. It was time to leave. When Kerrick realized this he had simply turned his back and started towards the shore. Ignoring their shouted queries; he was doing what he had to do.

"You go from here?" Nadaske said, signing instant death. "Farewell forever then. Sharp stone teeth will rend Nadaske as soon as you are out of sight."

"I will be back, very soon. We go north to trade, that is all."

"That is all? That is everything. Our efenburu grows smaller all of the time. Imehei is gone. I look about me now and I do not see young wet-soft. Now he will come no more, for you will be gone. There is only loneliness in this place."

"You are alive here—and you do not go to the beaches."

Nadaske did not grow angry at this, turned instead and looked out at the empty ocean, the unmarked sand along the shore, pointed to it. "Here are beaches of loneliness. Perhaps I should have gone to the beaches of death with the others from the hanalè."

Kerrick could say nothing, add nothing. The despair of his friend was resolute. They sat in silence awhile before Kerrick stood to leave. Nadaske watched him with one eye but did not answer him when he spoke. In the end Kerrick could only walk away and leave the solitary and lonely figure on the beach, staring out at the empty sea.

But that was behind him now, forgotten in the pleasures of the trail. They had been walking for some days, to the count of more than half the count of a hunter, when Hanath found the signs of others along the trail they were following.

"See—here and here, they have bent the twigs as a sign for those who came after them. And that could be a track."

"An animal track," Kerrick said.

"That too, but Tanu have come this way as well." Morgil was down on all fours and sniffing at the ground. "They have, they must have gone there by the water."

The trail here skirted a vast bay, then crossed a river. Instead of staying with the rutted track they went along the river until Morgil smelled the air.

"Smoke!" he shouted. "There are Tanu here."

It was dusk before they came to the other sammads, the same ones that had been left behind when Herilak and his sammad had gone south. They called out and the hunters came running, the sammadar Har-Havola in the lead.

"We searched, never found you," he said.

"You did not go far enough south," Kerrick said.

"We are far enough south here. There is no snow in the winter, the hunting and fishing are good."

"And your death-sticks—they live?"

"Of course. One was stepped on and died. The others are as they always were."

"Then we have much to tell you. Our death-sticks died, but we now have others."

Har-Havola was distressed. "You must speak to us of this. Come, we will eat, there will be a feast. There are many good things to eat here and you will try them all."

They stayed one day, then another with the sammads, until on the third day it was decided that they must leave. "The trail is long," Kerrick said. "And we must go to the north and return as well."

"When next we hunt we will go to the south," Har-Havola said. "We will find your sammads on the island you have spoken of, tell them we have seen you. But we

will keep our death-sticks from theirs as you have warned.
May your journey be short, may you return in safety."

They went on through the heat of summer. Yet the fall
of the year was coming closer every day, and every day
they were that much further north. It was cool before
dawn now, the dew lay thick upon their sleeping skins.
When the deep ruts of the track they were following led to
the shore, the ocean lay before them, slate gray under a
gray sky. They sniffed the salt spray blowing in from the
breaking waves and Armun laughed out loud.

"It is cold and damp—but I like it."

Hanath shouted with pleasure and hurled his spear in
a high arc, far down the beach where it stuck upright in
the sand. He dropped his pack and ran to get it, Morgil
shouting and running after him. They came back, panting
and happy.

"I'm glad we made this journey," Kerrick said. "Even
if the Paramutan aren't there, it was still worth coming."

"They will be there. Did not Kalaleq say they would
return, that no ocean was too wide to stop him?"

"Yes—and he also said if he had no boat he would
swim the ocean. The Paramutan are great braggarts."

"I hope that they come."

They followed the beach towards the north, building
their fire that night in the lee of the sand dunes. The rain
that began to fall after dark was cool and the fog that rolled
in from the sea was damper and even cooler. Autumn was
not too far away.

In the morning Kerrick stirred the fire and put the last
of the wood upon it. The salt-encrusted driftwood crackled
and burnt fiercely with yellow and blue flames. Armun
spread their skins before it to dry. The two hunters still
lay wrapped in theirs, reluctant to emerge. Kerrick poked
them with the butt of his spear and elicited only groans.

"Up!" he called out. "We need some more wood for
the fire. Beasts of great laziness—emerge!"

"You had better get it yourself," Armun said.

He nodded agreement and pulled the wet madraps
onto his feet, then trudged to the top of the dune. The

rain had stopped and the fog was burning off, clear rays of
sunlight touched color from the sea. There was fresh seaweed, shells and other debris at the high tide mark. Any
wood there would be too wet. But there was an entire
dead tree further along the beach. He would break some
branches from that. Kerrick sniffed the sea air and looked
out beyond the breakers and spray. Something dark rode
up on a wave, then was gone. He dropped to the sand—
was it an uruketo? What were Yilanè doing this far to the
north? He shielded his eyes and tried to find it again
among the whitecapped waves.

There it was—but not an uruketo at all.

"A sail!" he shouted. "A sail, out there—the Paramutan
are out there!"

Armun ran to join him, the two hunters finally aroused
stumbling up behind her.

"It is a sail," she said. "But they are going south. What
are they doing out there?"

"The seaweed," Kerrick shouted. "Hanath—run and
get some, wood too, even if it is wet. Build up the fire so
they can see the smoke!"

Kerrick stirred the fire until it burned fiercely as the
two hunters staggered back with their burdens. He spread
the seaweed out thinly on top, so that it crackled and
smouldered but did not extinguish the fire; white clouds of
smoke boiled skyward.

"They are still going south," Armun cried. "They haven't
seen it."

"Bring more!"

The fire roared and the column of smoke thickened
and climbed higher before Hanath shouted from the beach.

"They have stopped, they're turning, they've seen it
now."

They watched from the top of the dune as the ikkergak
wallowed in the water, sail flapping, then came about on
the other tack with the big sail billowing full. It came
racing towards the shore, rose up on the waves and was
carried forward with a rush, onto the sand in a flurry of
foam. Dark figures waved and shouted to them while one

of them hung tight to the bow. Let go and dropped into the sea, splashed ashore. The two hunters hesitated but Kerrick and Armun ran across the sand towards the ship.

A wave washed over the Paramutan and he stood up, dripping and spluttering and calling out with joy.

"Here, not believed, hair of sunshine, friends of years."

"Kalaleq!" Kerrick shouted as the Paramutan staggered, laughing, from the sea. He seized Kerrick's arms and shook them, turned to Armun and shouted with joy, put his arms around her as well, until she had to push him away as his strong fingers seized her bottom.

"Where were you sailing to?" she asked him.

"South—but too hot, see I wear nothing but my fur." When she looked down he let his tail drop to reveal his privates but she slapped his arm and he lifted it into place again. The Paramutan never changed.

"Why—south?" Kerrick asked, clumsily, trying to remember the complex language.

"To seek hunters. We waited on the beach to the north but none came. We have hides and many good things. Then we thought to look further south, look for hunters. Never thinking that friends would await us here."

Hanath and Morgil came close and there were mutually incomprehensible greetings. Other Paramutan soon joined them. Shouting with pleasure and bringing the inevitable gifts of raw and rotten fish. Morgil's eyes bulged and watered as he forced himself to swallow a vile mouthful. Then they all went to the fire to share the fresh meat there. Kerrick cut off pieces of raw meat from yesterday's kill and these were received with cries of intense pleasure. Kalaleq gobbled his down, smearing his face with blood, while he told Armun everything that had happened since they had parted.

"The kill is good, the ularuaq fill the sea so full you can walk across it on their backs. All the women have had babies, sometimes three and four at a time. We have found how to catch and kill the big birds. And how is it for you here? You must tell me so I can tell Angajorqaq for she will beat me savagely if I do not remember and tell her everything."

"We are all together, there is peace. There are babies—but not like the Paramutan for we do not lie as well as the Paramutan. But all is well."

When all of the meat was gone the Paramutan ran to the ikkergak, now beached by the receding tide, and rooted out the bundles of hides. Hanath and Morgil brought their knives and spearheads to the beach and, with much excitement and shouting, the trading began. Armun was in great demand for translation. Kerrick sat down on the dune away from all the turmoil and Kalaleq came over to join him. The language was coming back to Kerrick now and talking was easier.

"We were filled with fear when we found that all the hunters were gone," Kalaleq said.

"Gone from the north and the snows. We have a camp far south of here. The hunting is good and it is warm all the time."

"I would die! Even here the heat burns." Kerrick smiled at this, his skin garments closed tight against the chill wind from the ocean. "We have caught much fish, sought out certain plants we must have for the takkuuk, leaves and the inner bark of certain trees for brewing with water for drinking. But the need for knives is great and we wept with fear that we would have to return without them. Now we weep with joy to have found you—and spearheads too."

Armun came to join them, handed Kalaleq the folded square of woven charadis cloth. Kalaleq shook it out and held it to the sky.

"What is it, unbelievable! Soft as the fur on a baby's bottom. Smells good too."

"It is for Angajorqaq," Armun said. "It can be worn around the head like this, let me show you. It is woven from the fibers of a certain plant. It is something the Sesak do. They are hunters who live inland, far from the sea."

"Oh, what skills they have, even though they must weep daily not being able to see the ocean. There are so many marvels here, this charadis, your spears, your bows, your spearheads, your knives, the ekkotaz—I must eat more!"

"You have many marvels as well," she said, laughing and pushing his hands away. Food and sex, that was the Paramutan way. "Your ikkergak that you sail in, your harpoons for killing, small boats with sails, pumps and whistles."

"You are right—we are so good! We make so many things my mind goes around and around just thinking about it."

Kerrick was smiling at the bragging and all the artifacts they told each other about, all the things they made. Tanu, Paramutan—even Sasku. They were so different, yet they were the same. They made things. So very different from the Yilanè who could make nothing. Only the Yilanè males were creative. They were artistic, made sculptures of metal, the two who had escaped the hanalè had even learned to fish and hunt. But the females constructed nothing. Everything they had was grown. They were good enough at this, at least the scientists were. But they were still incapable of making something even as simple as a spear.

Then Kerrick grew very still as the thought gripped him. The realization that the world was not what he had always thought it was. He had been born Tanu but grew up as a Yilanè and too much of his thinking was still Yilanè.

But no more! He could see the future with a greater clarity now. He knew just what it was he had to do.

eistaapeleghè eistaaii,
yilanè'ninkuru yilanè gebgeleb.

YILANÈ APOTHEGM

A Yilanè with two eistaa?
Disgustedly impossible/inconceivable.

THIRTY

It was the largest river that Fafnepto had ever seen, larger
even than the ones she knew in Entoban∗. The soil that it
carried spread far out into sea, formed banks and islands
that clogged the river's mouth. It took them many days
just to find the main channels through the islands, before
they entered the river itself where it flowed between high
bluffs. They swam the uruketo upstream for an entire day
and the river was just as wide as ever. That night they
drifted in the backcurrents of the shallows and in the
morning were ready to go on. Fafnepto saw that Gunugul
and Vaintè were already on the fin, climbed up to join
them. They had to hold tight to the edge of the fin which
was rocking back and forth as the uruketo thrashed itself
free of the shallow water. When they were once more in
the deep channel Fafnepto signed for attention.

"This is a large river," she said. "The size of it, and the
many days we have spent on this search, force me to a
single conclusion. I have come to the realization that
Gendasi∗ is not Entoban∗ and things cannot be done the
same way here. This land is rich, but it is empty. Not

282

empty of life as we well know, but empty of Yilanè. It is still strange to me to see a rivermouth like this without a fine city upon its banks. Then I remember that there are still cities in Entoban* that grow cold as the winter comes close. When I return I will go to them and tell them not to fear. There is an empty world here for the filling. You know that, Vaintè, for did you not grow the first city on these shores?"

"Alpèasak. I did. You are correct in everything you say."

"That reassures me. Now you must follow my thoughts again. The Eistaa Saagakel has entrusted me with this mission. She has ordered me to find the uruketo that was taken from her, to find Ambalasei who ordered its taking. Is this not what I agreed to do?"

"It is," Vaintè said, wondering what this was all leading to. Fafnepto was as circuitous with her language and thought processes as she was direct and decisive in the forest. Perhaps it was the solitary life. Vaintè hid her impatience in a posture of rigid attention to listening.

"Then you will understand my concern now that I have come to believe that I am not fulfilling the Eistaa's trust, nor following her orders, if we proceed as we have been doing. I have come to believe that we will never find that which we seek by chance. We must have aid."

"And what do you propose?" Vaintè said, having a very good idea of what was coming next.

"We must return along the coast, to the city of Alpèasak, and talk with those there. They may have some knowledge of the uruketo we seek."

"And they may not," Gunugul said.

"Then we have lost nothing because our search will continue. But it is my conclusion now that we must seek them out. Vaintè, what are your thoughts?"

Vaintè looked out at the width of the river and signed equality of choice. "The decision must be yours, Fafnepto, for the final command is yours. There may be knowledge of those we seek in Alpèasak. But you must know one thing before we go. The Eistaa there is Lanefenuu, she

who was Eistaa of Ikhalmenets before it came to Alpèasak.
It was I, as you know, who freed Alpèasak of the ustuzou
so she could bring her own city there. In her name I
pursued and killed the ustuzou, and then in her name I
ceased the war upon them. I have not spoken of it before
but I will tell you now. We were joined in friendship
once; we are joined no longer. I served her once; she
rejects my presence now. Do you understand?

Fafnepto's thumbs flicked in understanding-amplified.

"I have served many eistaa in many cities and know
their ways. Because they rule they issue orders only and
do not listen closely. They hear what they want to hear,
say what they want to say. What is between you and
Lanefenuu will remain between you. I serve Saagakel and
go to this city as her missionary. It is my thought that we
leave this river and return to the ocean. Then proceed to
Alpèasak. Will you do that Fafnepto?"

"You speak for my Eistaa. We go now to Alpèasak."

The enteesenat had never liked the murky river water,
now leapt high with pleasure and smacked back in a
welter of foam when they turned and headed downstream.
Once out in the open ocean they proceeded east along the
coast. Although there were still lookouts always posted on
the fin, they went far more quickly than they had on the
outward voyage. They passed the bays and inlets they had
searched before, but now stayed in the deeper water.
Gunugul had charted the currents and when the uruketo
followed them away from shore she did not change the
course. Once they were out of sight of land for three days
as they swam in a deep-sea current. When they next saw
the shore it was ahead of them, green with tropical trees.
Fafnepto joined Vaintè on the fin and her palm colors
signed recognition.

"I know this coast. We first went north along here after
leaving the islands."

Vaintè expressed agreement. "I think you are right—
and if you are, we are very close to Alpèasak."

"Is the city on the ocean?"

"On the ocean and the river as well. The beaches are

large, the water warm, the game abundant. It may not be as old as other Yilanè cities but in its youthfulness it has a newgrowth/attraction that many cities do not have."

The crewmember on watch had been summoned below. None could hear them now when they spoke. There were matters that Fafnepto wanted to know about.

"I have never visited seagirt Ikhalmenets."

"Nor will you ever. The snow of winter is there, all are gone."

"And all in Alpèasak now. Lanefenuu is Eistaa there now, just as you were Eistaa there once." Vaintè signed agreement. "I will talk with Lanefenuu and she will know of your presence. Before that time I would like to have more knowledge of her, and of you and her, and what will happen when you meet again."

Vaintè signed understanding. "As to the last—I do not know. For my part I will do nothing, say nothing. But I am sure that she will have a great deal to say. You yourself have told me that an eistaa respects no rule other than her own. This Eistaa commanded me to clear the city of the ustuzou that infested it. I did that. I pursued and killed them as they fled. I had them all between my thumbs, was about to kill them all—when the Eistaa stopped me. I obeyed her orders but I was not pleased. And it would be correct to say that she was not pleased that I was not pleased."

"Delicacy of relationship understood. Relationship of an eistaa to an eistaa a difficult one. I will not speak of the matter again." She started to add something but a crewmember came up from below and their conversation was at an end. In the short time before they reached Alpèasak there was no opportunity to resume it.

Vaintè had no desire to see Alpèasak again: she had no choice. She stood on the fin as the familiar landscape moved slowly by. There was the sandy beach where the uruketo had come for them when she had fled the city's destruction by fire, the trees behind it freshly grown where the others had burned. This was where she had left Alpèasak, watched Stallan die. Watched her city die. There

was the river now—and the worn wood of the docks and
the dark forms of uruketo. She had left from here the
second time, never thought that she would return. Now
she had—though not of her own choosing. None of the
turmoil of her thoughts showed for she stood rigid and
still. Stayed that way when Fafnepto joined her, while
Gunugul directed them close. Until the uruketo bumped
the dock as the creature sought the food placed there for
it.

Fafnepto was without her hèsotsan for the first time,
for it was not right to go armed into another's city. Normally she went unadorned but now, as her eistaa's representative, her arms were painted with likenesses of the
metal bridges of Yebeisk.

"For the moment, Gunugul," she said, "I would like
you to stay with the uruketo." Gunugul signed obedience
to commands as Fafnepto turned one eye to look at Vaintè.
"Do you also remain here?"

Vaintè signed a rough negative. "I do not cower in the
darkness. I am without fear. I will go with you to the
ambesed for I am also a representative of Saagakel."

Fafnepto acknowledged and accepted. "Then you will
lead the way for I am certain that you know where to go."

They climbed down from the fin and stepped onto the
scarred wood of the dock. The commander of the next
uruketo was there as well, a Yilanè whom Vaintè had
sailed with. She showed shock and confusion at Vaintè's
presence and did not greet her. Vaintè turned away with
cold disdain and kept her arms shaped that way as she led
the way into the city. The gaping fargi pressed back to let
them pass, crowded after them and followed behind. Vaintè
saw Yilanè whom she recognized, but she gave no outward
sign of this. Nor did they, for all knew of her differences
with the Eistaa. Now Yilanè as well as fargi followed in
their wake.

The city was as she had known it, for cities do not
change. The guarded hanalè was there, beyond it the first
of the meat vats. And there the wide and sunny way that
ended in the ambesed. Here there was one change as

Lanefenuu strove to remind herself of now-abandoned Ikhalmenets. Two males, surrounded and protected by guards, were carving the thick bole of the city tree. The peak of the central mountain of the island they had left was already clearly visible. Lanefenuu herself was supervising the work and did not turn until they were very close. Until Fafnepto stopped and made the politest sound for attention to speaking.

"My greetings to a stranger," Lanefenuu said—then stopped when she recognized Vaintè at Fafnepto's side. A flush of crimson swept through her crest as her lips pulled back from her teeth into the position that signified prepared-for-eating.

"You come here, Vaintè—you dare enter my ambesed!"

"I come under the orders of Saagakel, Eistaa of Yebeisk. She commands me now."

"Then you have indeed forgotten that I commanded you once. I banished you from Gendasi* and from Alpèasak —and from my presence forever. And yet you return."

The color was gone from her crest, her jaw clamped tightly closed, cold anger in every arch of her body. Vaintè did not speak and it was Fafnepto who bravely broke the silence.

"I am Fafnepto, sent to Gendasi* on a mission from Saagakel, Eistaa of Yebeisk. I bear you her greetings."

Lanefenuu looked briefly at Fafnepto, then away. "I will greet you and speak with you presently, Fafnepto. As soon as I dispose of this one rejected/returned."

"I am not one who can be disposed of. I wanted my presence here known. Now I return to the uruketo of Yebeisk. I will wait for you there, Fafnepto."

There was moaning on all sides as the nearest fargi fled the cold voices and poisonous postures of the two antagonists. Vaintè first stood unmoving after she had finished speaking, radiating lack of fear/firmness of resolve, then slowly turned away. She saw those whom she knew among the gathered Yilanè, but she gave no sign. Expressing strength and hatred in equal parts she slowly paced the length of the ambesed and was gone.

Fafnepto stood rigidly during all of this, remained that way until Lanefenuu could control her seething anger. Before she could speak the Eistaa signed for a water-fruit, drained it and hurled it aside. Only then did she turn one eye towards her visitor—the other still fixed firmly on the exit from the ambesed.

"I greet you Fafnepto," she finally said, "and welcome you here in the name of Saagakel, Eistaa of Yebeisk. What mission from her brings you across the ocean to my city?"

"A matter of grave concern, of theft and treachery, and those who speak of life but are part of death."

Lanefenuu signed for courteous temporary silence. These were grave matters and not fit for every fargi to hear or even know about. Her thumb twitched in Muruspe's direction; when her efenselè stepped forward she issued quick commands.

"All but those highest dismissed," Muruspe ordered with sharp movements of urgency. "This ambesed to be empty." Only after the last frightened fargi had stumbled through the exit did Lanefenuu speak again.

"Are those you speak of, are they called Daughters of Life?"

"They are."

"Tell me of the matter then. But know also that there are none here, nor will any ever be permitted in my city."

"Nor will they ever be permitted to return to Yebeisk. They were there and they fled, and that is what I must speak to you of and ask your assistance."

Lanefenuu listened stolidly, still moved by hatred at Vaintè's presence, fascinated and shocked as well by what she was hearing. When Fafnepto had finished there was a horrified buzz of comment from all those who had listened to her, which died instantly as Lanefenuu signed for silence.

"What you tell me is terrible indeed. Doubly terrible to me for I commanded/still-command an uruketo and the loss of one of those great creatures is a loss of part of one's life. I will do what I can to aid you. What is it that your eistaa wishes of me?"

"Information, simply. Has any in this city knowledge

of this uruketo? Is it possible that any of your commanders of your uruketo may have seen it? We have searched but have found no trace of it."

"I have no knowledge of it, but enquiries shall be made. Muruspe, send for all of my commanders. Send also for Ukhereb who may have seen an image of this missing uruketo among all of the images her birds bring to her. While this is being done come, sit here Fafnepto, and tell me of matters in Entoban* and how the cities fare there, for yours is the first uruketo to call here in a very long time."

Akotolp stepped forward and signed matters of importance/requesting speech. Lanefenuu signed her closer.

"This is Akotolp, a Yilanè of science who is wise in many ways. You have information for us?"

"Negative for the moment. I have aided in the preparation of the images. The only uruketo images that appear are of uruketo of this city. This was my belief until now. I will go myself for those images, have them brought here at once so you may examine them for consideration of identity."

Lanefenuu signed enthusiastic agreement. "I will look at these images and decide, for to me every uruketo has features as familiar as one of my own efenselè."

"It shall be done, Eistaa. Permission requested first for questions to guest."

"Granted."

Akotolp turned to the hunter, her tension hidden by her fat wattles that swayed when she moved. "It is known that I was one of those who left this city as it was taken by the ustuzou. You say that those who fled your city had knowledge of Gendasi* and it is your opinion that the uruketo has crossed the ocean."

"I said that. I have also reason to believe the uruketo is no longer on the Entoban* side of the ocean."

"There is one who fled with us, who was a leader of the Daughters of Life, who was of intelligence and had knowledge. Her name was Enge. Do you know the name?"

"I do. She was with them. They were aided in their escape by one of science named Ambalasei."

Akotolp was shocked, could scarcely speak. "Ambalasei! She who was my teacher."

"Not only your teacher—but a recent visitor to my city!" Lanefenuu said grimly. "Nor did she speak of these matters when she was here. Go, Akotolp, get the images and bring them at once. And you, Fafnepto, you were correct to seek information here, correct in assuming that the missing uruketo was now in Gendasi∗. You have all of my aid for I am as anxious as your own eistaa to see that it is found and those creatures of death punished. This will be done."

THIRTY-ONE

Gunugul had sent for fresh jellied meat, for she tired of the boring diet of preserved meat that they had brought with them. Now she chewed a welcome delicious mouthful. Vaintè had come back aboard some time ago, her rigid body rejecting communication, and had gone at once into the uruketo's interior. As a courtesy Gunugul ordered a crewmember to bring some of the meat to her.

Vaintè, still rigid with rage, saw the movements in the dim light and realized someone was standing before her with fresh meat. She acknowledged presence and took it, bit into it—then sent the deer leg flying to thud into the uruketo's side. She could not eat, could scarcely breathe, wanted to kill, could not. The dark interior was choking her so she rose to her feet and climbed stiffly up to the top of the fin. She was thankfully alone, the commander busy with others upon the dock. Through the haze of anger Vaintè was only barely aware of the activity below, the supplies being piled there, the enteesenat being fed, the coming and going of fargi busy on the city's business.

When something did catch her attention it took long moments to realize what it was.

It was a newcomer, a Yilanè of some rank for she ordered laden fargi before her. In the direction of the uruketo. Why had this disturbed her, this fat Yilanè? Fat? Of course, it was one she knew well. The scientist Akotolp. Who looked up and saw her—and made no sign of recognition. Turned and issued brusque orders to be obeyed instantly.

This was a matter of great interest, Vaintè could tell that at once. Akotolp now served the Eistaa and the city— but she had also once sworn that Vaintè was her eistaa for as long as she had breath. Now Akotolp was here—and undoubtedly without Lanefenuu's permission!

Vaintè stood aside as the fargi toiled up the fin with their burdens, carried them below as Akotolp ordered. Emerged again and were sent back into the city. Only when they were out of sight among the crowds did Akotolp wheeze and puff her way up the fin, to stumble over its edge. She glanced around, took a last look at the dock— then signed a silent and imperative *descend*!

Safely out of sight in the interior she turned to Vaintè with great happiness of return/reunion of pleasure.

"It is I who have the pleasure, Akotolp." Vaintè touched her thumbs as she would to her efenselè. "She who is Eistaa, who I would kill were I able, has offended and angered me. So sight/presence fat and familiar loyal figure brings the greatest happiness."

"The pleasure is mine to serve you, Eistaa. I was there, behind the others, when you faced the Eistaa. It was cowardly/wisest not to intervene at that time. I felt I could serve you better in other ways. I know of matters that no one else knows of, have reached conclusions that others will never reach, will give you information that no one else has. I listened closely to the hunter named Fafnepto when she spoke of your mission. You share it with her?"

"I do."

"Then your search is at an end. I know where the uruketo is!"

"You have seen it?"

"No—but there is a logic to many events that inescapably points to it. I have all of the evidence here with me. And evidence of another kind, of equal or greater importance to you."

"As you know there is only one thing of importance to me. Discovery/death Kerrick ustuzou."

"Of course!" Akotolp's wattles shook as she moved with pleasure of discovery/enlightenment of importance. "I am of strong opinion that I also know where he is!"

Vaintè shook with emotion, clutched Akotolp's arms between her thumbs so hard that the scientist gasped in sudden pain. Released her with apologies, overflowing of joy, thankfulness to the one in the world who aided her.

"You are my efenselè, Akotolp, as no other is. You fill an empty life, bring pleasure where there has been only nullity. Tell me what you know, but first of the ustuzou."

"He is close, that I can assure you, but all must be told in the proper order for complete understanding."

"Then speak, I bid you!"

"Ambalasei was here. She arrived one day, by uruketo, left the same way a few days later with great abruptness. I questioned and discovered the uruketo came and went away with her at once. None here knew the beast nor its commander."

"Then is it the one I seek?"

"Undoubtedly. And other matters of greatest interest. Before Ambalasei went away something of strangeness happened here. A Yilanè was discovered and captured on the birth beaches. It appears that she was attempting to abduct a male fresh from the sea. A crime of major importance. None knew her, she would not speak, died before she could be questioned. Do you see a relevance?"

Vaintè signed positive recognition. "Of course. She must have come on the uruketo with Ambalasei. Which in turn means—she was a Daughter of Death!"

"That is true! I just realized it today when I heard Fafnepto speak. It is your mind of great attainment that enables you to see instantly what was hidden from me all of this time. Ambalasei came on the uruketo, left on it, returned to these Daughters of Evil whom she has joined. And I believe I know where they went."

Vaintè was warm with appreciation, signed request for more information, lowest to highest, a form she had never used before in her entire life. Akotolp, swollen with pleasurable self-esteem, pointed at the containers the fargi had carried aboard.

"They have gone south. Ambalasei revealed to us that she has discovered an entirely new continent there. Thinking of it now, it seems obvious that she must have landed the Daughters somewhere on its shores. She showed us records that she had made, gave us specimens of scientific delight, revealed her voyage of discovery on a gigantic river of that continent. It is my belief that she must be there now, on the shores of that river, or at the estuary where it meets the ocean. She had no other records of exploration of the continent."

"I believe you, you could not be wrong. But that is only half of what I want to hear."

"The other half then concerns the ustuzou who penetrate this city, kill Yilanè, steal hèsotsan. We have firm evidence of that. I have flown the birds and have images here of ustuzou north of this city, on an island near the coast. One of them could be the creature you seek."

"While there is still brightness of daylight—I must see those images."

Even as she spoke the light from the open fin darkened, as though a cloud had passed over the sky. Vaintè looked up and saw that Fafnepto was descending. Fafnepto began to speak—then stopped when she saw Akotolp, signed a query.

"This is Akotolp," Vaintè said. "She served me when I was Eistaa here. A scientist of great note who has information of even greater note."

"I have spoken with Akotolp earlier today. Also, this same Akotolp was mentioned by the scientist, Ukhereb, just recently in the ambesed. She said that you both had met with the one we seek, Ambalasei."

"That is true."

"Ukhereb also said that Ambalasei brought evidence of a continent to the south of this one, of a river there. Ukhereb believes that Ambalasei and the uruketo we seek are there now. Are you of the same opinion?"

Akotolp was put out, tried not to show it, had believed the theory was hers alone. She finally had to sign positive agreement. "I do agree, yes, and further believe that those you seek, as well as the uruketo, are on the banks of this great river of which she spoke to us in such detail."

Fafnepto expressed agreement amplified. "Everything you both have said leads me to the same conclusion. As a hunter I also feel that this is correct. I sense our quarry out there. The commander now loads fresh meat and water. In the morning I will speak again with the Eistaa and then we will leave. We will go south to this river."

Vaintè interrupted with signs of importance of speaking. "They will not escape. We will surely track them there. But before we leave there are ustuzou along the coast, close by, that must be found and killed. They came to this city, killed Yilanè here. We must kill them in return—"

"No. We go south."

"It will take only a short time. It is of importance to me—"

"But not to me. We go south."

"I will talk to Gunugul. I'm sure she will agree that we do this one small thing first."

"Whether she agrees or not is of no importance. I am Lanefenuu's representative. I am ordering Gunugul south. I will tell her that now so there will be no misunderstandings while I am in the city."

She said this almost calmly, as though it was of no importance, looking directly at Vaintè all the while. The way she would look at an animal before she killed it. Vaintè returned the gaze just as emotionlessly, knowing that it was Fafnepto's victory this time. Also knew there was nothing that would make her change her mind. Vaintè's moment of justified revenge would have to be postponed.

"You are in command, we will do as you order. Be informed also that Akotolp has offered to leave with us, to help guide us in our quest." As Vaintè spoke her outward calm matched that of her antagonist. Fafnepto accepted this, signed gratitude, turned and left. So she did not see the blaze of color on Vaintè's palms, the curve of hatred in her fingers. Akotolp did, stepped back, rocked by the strength of feeling. It passed quickly as Vaintè fought and controlled her emotions, spoke calmly to Akotolp.

"It would be pleasure magnified for me to see the images of the ustuzou. The image now will suffice. I have waited this long to find him—I can wait that bit longer. Nor will this be a wasted journey. Those Daughters of Death escaped me when we fled this city. Their existence has long troubled me. It will be my pleasure to search them out now. Gratitude expressed/amplified—the images!"

Vaintè went through the sheets slowly, her limbs moving in emotive response as she did. Hatred, pleasure, discovery. When she had seen them all, she carefully went through them a second time and found one that drew her attention. The others fell from her thumbs as she held this one in the light from the fin; Akotolp retrieved the discarded sheets.

"Look at this, Akotolp," Vaintè finally said. "You have the eyes and the brain of a scientist. Tell me what you see here. Look at this figure."

Akotolp turned it until the light fell clearly upon it, examined it closely. "It is one of the killer ustuzou, probably a male since the females have other organs here. It shields its eyes as it gazes upwards, so the face is not clearly seen. There is something, a design perhaps, painted upon its upper thorax."

"You see it too! Could it be a metal tooth like the one you sealed in the bladder long ago?"

"The possibility is there/detail unhappily unclear. But it could be an artifact of metal."

"It is almost too much to believe, that it is the one I seek, that he is out there."

"Strong belief/probability. And there is another thing

of great interest that I neglected to mention to the eistaa. Here, upon this other sheet, you will see a crude structure of some kind. With two figures standing before it."

Akotolp signed excitement and pride of discovery as she passed over the sheet, touched the correct spot with one thumb, watched Vaintè's movements of disbelief.

"This is inexplicable. One is a Yilanè—the other ustuzou. How is this?"

"We can only guess. Perhaps the Yilanè has been captured, held prisoner. Not injured, for she appears in other pictures. And this is very close to the place where the ustuzou lairs are located."

Vaintè trembled with excitement. "Then the creature we have seen *must* be Kerrick, the one I seek. Only he can communicate with a Yilanè. How close are they?"

"Less than a day in an uruketo."

"And we are in an uruketo . . ." Vaintè's body twisted as strong emotions gripped her again and it took her a moment to regain control. "But not at the present time. Now we go south. There is one called Enge whom I would see again."

"One came to me," Enge said, "bringing the message that you wished to see me, a matter of urgency."

"Urgency obviously relative with Daughters of Drowsiness," Ambalasei said disgustedly. "That message was sent earlier today in the hope it might reach you before we all were dead of advanced age."

"Does the matter have urgency?"

"Only to me. My researches are complete. There is an entire continent to be explored—but others can do that. I have records and specimens for them to marvel at. I have opened the path that others may follow. I return now to Entoban*."

"Suddenness of decision unexpected/unhappiness, unwelcome information!"

"Only to you, Enge. Everyone else here will be glad to see me leave. Just as pleased as I will be to turn my back upon them. All of my records have been sealed and loaded

aboard the uruketo. Setèssei will go with me, but assures
me that she has trained two Daughters in use of nefmakel,
sanitation and wound repair. So you all will not instantly
die when we are gone."

"The suddenness of this confuses/saddens me. I knew
the day must come. The pleasure in your presence pro-
found. Absence will produce emptiness."

"Fill it with thoughts of Ambalasei like everyone else
here."

"I will do that of course. And will feel pleasure that the
uruketo will now be restored to Yebeisk."

"That pleasure will have to wait, since I am staying far
from Yebeisk and the undoubtedly furious Eistaa. When I
have reached Entoban∗ the uruketo returns here and becomes your responsibility."

"Gratified acceptance of responsibility."

"There is another responsibility we must discuss. Ac-
company me."

Instead of boarding the uruketo Ambalasei led the way
to the boat which floated close by. It was better trained
now and responded to Ambalasei's thumbs on its nerve
endings by moving smoothly out into the river. She guided
it to the shore beyond the city, then secured it to a tree
with the binding sucker on its carapace.

"Do you know this place?" she asked.

"Unforgettable. We saw the first Sorogetso just there.
I came here many times when learning their speech. They
are gone now." There were overtones of sorrow, not a
little regret, to her meaning.

"They are—and a good thing too. Their independence
is assured, their unique culture undefiled by followers of
Ugunenapsa. Come this way."

The floating tree was permanently in place now, its
branches sunk deep into the mud. They crossed and pushed
their way along the once-smooth pathway, now rank with
high grass. When they came to the overgrown clearing,
Ambalasei indicated the sodden and collapsed shelters
that the Sorogetso had made.

"The Sorogetso had to be taken away from the interfer-

ence of your argumentative associates. Their culture was
in danger. They are on the borderline between material-
manipulation and life-manipulation. A wonderful opportunity for observation/knowledge for scientists. Not for me
though. I will instruct others, send them to the place on
this river where the Sorogetso now dwell. To complete my
work. Which brings me to my last contribution in the
service of Ugunenapsa. A solution to a problem that has
had some of my attention. An intriguing proposition.
Continuity."

"Understanding escapes me."

"It shouldn't. Put baldly—when you all die so do
Ugunenapsa's theories."

"That is entirely too true and it grieves me greatly."

"Then cease your grieving. A solution is to hand."

They emerged from the trees to stand on the empty
beach of the lakeshore. Ambalasei looked around, then
called out the simplest sounds for attention to speaking.
After this she settled back on her tail with a weary sigh.
Enge could only sign puzzlement and lack of understanding.

There was a stirring in the shrubbery as a small and
immature fargi stepped out.

"Together," Ambalasei signed with color changes of
her palms.

"Together," the fargi answered, then came forward
hesitantly at the sight of Enge, trembling and stopping.

"Be without fear," Ambalasei said slowly and clearly.
"Bring others."

Enge could only stare after the fargi, her body shaped
in confusion and wild hope.

"Fargi . . . here?" she said. "And so small. Can they
be Sorogetso?"

"Obviously. I removed all those that were mature and
yilanè as you well know. But I observed juvenile efenburu
in the lake and was deeply concerned. It was my fear that
they would emerge and find none to speak with, would
face only certain death. At first I thought I would bring
them to join the others, but this represented certain problems. There are other younger efenburu in the lake who

will emerge later to join with the older ones. This is a natural process I did not want to interfere with too much. Then I saw the single obvious answer to two problems at one time. Can you tell me what that is?"

Enge choked with emotion, could barely speak. "Salvation. We will be here when they emerge, they will learn to speak, join with us, and in turn speak to the others when they too come onto the beaches."

"That solves their problem. And the other?"

"You are the salvation of the Daughters of Life. You insure for eternity the continuity of the wisdom of Ugunenapsa."

"I am not sure about eternity, but for a while at least. You do realize that you cannot interbreed with them, don't you? Their metabolic birth changes are far too different from ours. When they reach maturity you must be absolutely certain that Sorogetso mate only with Sorogetso. Can you control the lust of your Daughters?"

"Our lust is for wisdom only—you need have no fear."

"Good. You must also realize that you will only have cultural continuity, not genetic? One day the last of the present crop of Daughters will die of old age. There will be only Sorogetso then."

"I understand your meaning—and assure you again that it is of no importance. The Eight Principles of Ugunenapsa will live on, that is all that matters."

"Good. Then it is time for me to go. My important labors are finished here. I return to the adulation of civilized cities, the respect of eistaa. And pleasure at forgetting completely the dreaded name of Ugunenapsa."

THIRTY-TWO

The trading took up the better part of the first day, then extended into the next day as well. The Paramutan enjoyed it too much to finish with it quickly. Hanath and Morgil were soon possessed of the same enthusiasm, regretted only that they had not brought more to trade. Then someone had suggested fresh meat. All activities were suspended while the two hunters seized up their bows and hurried into the forest. While the Paramutan were the best hunters in the ocean they lacked the Tanu skills ashore. The four freshly killed deer were greeted with high-pitched shouts of approval.

There was feasting—and the trade continued. Then more feasting to celebrate its satisfying end. Kerrick sat away from the others, on one of the dunes that faced out over the sea, deep in thought. Armun came to join him and he took her hand and seated her beside him.

"They are teaching each other songs now," she said. "Though they have no idea at all of what they mean."

"We should have made some porro—then there really would be a celebration."

"Don't even say it out loud!" She laughed at the two hunters who were now demonstrating how the Tanu wrestled. "Even the thought of the Paramutan drinking porro is enough to make me want to flee."

There were more shouts and a loud thud as Kalaleq showed them that, even for their size, the Paramutan were strong wrestlers as well.

"I have been thinking about many things since we came here," Kerrick said. "I have made some important decisions. The first decision is to make you happier."

She held to his arm and laughed. "I could not be happier, we are together."

"Not completely. I know that there is a thing that bothers you—so I tell you that this is now finished, over. Arnwheet has many friends, but I have forced him to come with me to talk to the one on the island. And you hate that."

Her smile was gone now. "I do. But you are a hunter and I cannot tell you to do one thing, not another. You do as you must."

"I have been wrong. When we return I will see that the boy stays far away from the one you call a marag. But the marag is my friend and I take pleasure in talking to him. But Arnwheet can do as he wishes. If he wishes to forget how the murgu talk—he will forget."

"But you have said many times how important it is that he knows these things."

"I do not think that way any .longer. They are of no importance. I have been blind to what the world is really like. I look Tanu, but I think like a murgu. No longer. The world has not changed. Just the way I see it has changed."

Armun listened in silence, not understanding, but knowing that what he was saying was terribly important to him. He smiled at her attentive, silent stare, touched his finger to her lips.

"I think that I am not saying this right. The idea is clear in my head, but does not come out in the correct way. Look there, look at the Paramutan, at the wonderful things they make. Their ikkergak, the sails that move it, the pump for water, their carving, everything."

"They are very good at making those things."

"They are—but so are we. Our flint knives, our bows, spears, the tents we sleep in, we make all of them. Then think too of the Sasku with their pots and looms, woven cloth, crops . . ."

"And porro—we must never forget that!"

They laughed together while the wrestling on the beach grew even wilder. Two of the Paramutan were so absorbed in the match that they were engulfed by a wave— which everyone thought very hilarious.

"What I have said about making things is important," Kerrick said. "Even the porro is important. Because this is what we do. We make these things with our hands. The artifacts that we construct cannot die—because they have never lived. A spear is as good in the snow as it is in the jungle."

"This is true. But is it important?"

"To me—it is the most important discovery. I have been thinking like a murgu too long. The murgu make nothing. Most of them do nothing either—other than live, eat, die. But there are those few of the knowledge of science and they can control living things. I don't know how they do it—I have the feeling that I will never know. But I have been so stupid in thinking only about the things that they grow. How they do it, why they do it. Everything that I have planned, everything that I have done, has been done in the murgu way. I have tried to think like them always. This was a mistake and I now turn my back on them. I am all Tanu, not half marag. When I say this I see the truth. Let the death-sticks die. They are of no importance. I have made them important and others have believed me. But no more."

She was frightened. "Don't say that. Without the death-sticks we die to the south—and there is only winter to the north. You cannot say this."

"Listen and understand. I am one hunter. I may be dead tomorrow, I could have died yesterday. Because of me we use the death-sticks. When I lived among the murgu I saw how they used them to kill anything that attacked them, no matter what the size. I saw this and realized that if we had death-sticks as well we could also be able to survive in the south. And we have done that—but our lives now depend upon the death-sticks—and that is not right. We must find a way to do without them, a way that is natural to us. If our lives depend upon them, why then we are half-marag—and all are like me. But no more. I and all others must be all Tanu. The answer is right before us."

"I do not see it," she said, bewildered.

"Do you not remember the murgu island? How you lit the fire and Kalaleq killed the ship-creatures in the sea?"

"Yes, that is what happened."

"Then he will show us how to kill murgu the same way. We will learn to make takkuuk. That is the black poison in the bladders that makes you sick if you smell just a little bit of it. But on the spears it kills the largest marag. Do you not see the difference? Things that we know how to make can never die—like the death-sticks which sicken and die. The knowledge of the making cannot die either because many have it. We will make the takkuuk and live where we wish."

"I think that I understand now—understand that this is a very important thing for you. But maybe we will not be able to make takkuuk. Then what?"

He pulled her to her feet beside him. "We will be able to understand how it is done. We will ask now. Because what one can make another can make. We are not murgu, remember. And we must not try to be like them. Perhaps some day we will have their knowledge of the way living things are. Some day. But we do not need this knowledge now. Let us ask Kalaleq."

The Paramutan was lying back on the sand, gasping as he chewed a bit of raw liver, blood on his hands and face. His stomach was distended with feasting—but he wasn't going to give up yet.

"Greatest eater among all the Paramutan!" Kerrick called out.

"It is true! You have said it. And I am the greatest hunter as well . . ."

"Then you can do anything?"

"Anything!"

"You know how to make takkuuk?"

"Kalaleq knows everything there is to know, makes takkuuk that kills the biggest ularuaq."

"Will furry Paramutan of wisdom then tell simple Tanu how it is done?"

"Never!" he shouted, then roared with laughter and fell feebly back onto the sand. Neither Kerrick nor Armun thought this was very funny. Only when the laughter had died away and he had finished chewing and swallowing the last of the liver, did he explain.

"It is important and very hard to do. My father taught me, I will show my son Kukujuk how to do it when he is older. You are old enough to learn now. But you must trade for this secret knowledge."

"That is fair. What do you want?"

"The price is high. It is—one knife of stone with sharpest blade."

Kerrick took his knife out and handed it over. Kalaleq ran his thumb along the edge and muttered with happiness. "Now I will tell you, then I will show you. For not only must you mix the blood and entrails of certain fish, bury them in a warm place to rot. Dig them up and seal them to rot some more, but you must then mix in the juice pressed from the roots of the tall flowers that blossom only on these shores. That is one of the reasons we return here to trade. Trade and dig these roots. They must be in the takkuuk, they always have been. They help it to kill. Will you also fish with the takkuuk?"

"We are hunters. We want it for our spearpoints when we meet the largest murgu in the forest."

"It will kill them easily, have no fear."

"We have had very much fear," Armun said, then smiled. "But no longer."

And she no longer had her own private fears. That Arnwheet would become more murgu than Tanu. That fear was gone now. Kerrick would go alone to see the marag on the island. He would talk to the creature as she talked to the Paramutan. That was all. And one day the thing would die and that would be the end of it. Now there could be an end to fear.

"You're afraid to go to the island," Dall said, spitting on the ground to show the strength of his feelings.

"I am not afraid," Arnwheet said. "I just don't want to go. You are the one that should be afraid, your father beat you when you went. I saw you crying."

"I did not cry!"

"I saw you too!" one of the other boys shouted and jumped back when Dall swung about and tried to punch him.

Arnwheet started to move away. He was smaller than Dall and knew he could not beat him in a fight. He hoped that he would forget the whole thing. But this was not to be. Dall chased the other boy, then returned, still glowering in anger, stabbed Arnwheet painfully in the chest with his finger.

"I saw you go to the island with your father. I hid and I saw you and him go right up to the marag."

"You don't talk about my father."

"Why not?" Dall was sneering with pleasure now and all of the others were on his side. "You want to stop me? Try to stop me. Your father is half a marag. I saw him go like this and shiver and shake."

He twisted and danced about waving his arms and all of the boys thought this was very funny.

"You shut up!" was all that Arnwheet could think to say.

"And I saw Arnwheet doing it too, just like this, shake, shake, shake!"

The demonstration was greatly appreciated and he turned in a circle so they could all get a better look. Arnwheet's anger flared and he pushed the large boy in

the back and knocked him down, then kicked him hard
before he could struggle to his feet again. Dall was shouting with fury: Arnwheet ran.

Arnwheet was fast and the screaming Dall could not
quite catch him. All of the other boys followed, shouting
as well. Between the tents they raced, Arnwheet dodging
around them, then jumping over a fire. But Dall was
ahead of him now, grabbed him by the arm and spun him
about. Knocked him to the ground and began pummeling
him. His fist caught Arnwheet on the nose and blood
spurted high—the onlookers cheered. Dall stood up and
started to kick the smaller boy. Then screamed as a hard
hand painfully boxed his ear.

"Beat a smaller boy! Kick a smaller boy!" Merrith
shouted angrily. "Why not kick me, would you like to try
that?" She caught him another whack before he could
dodge her and get away. "Anyone else want some?" she
said glowering at the boys who disappeared as quickly as
Dall had done. Arnwheet sat up, sobbing, tears mixing
with the blood from his nose.

"Boys," she muttered to herself, and sat him down and
wiped the tears away. She dipped a cloth in cold water
and cleaned him, held it to his nose until the bleeding and
the sobbing had stopped.

"Go to your tent, lie down and stay quiet, or the
bleeding will start again," she said. "And try to stay out of
trouble."

Arnwheet felt very put upon. He scuffled through the
dust and kicked a stick aside. The boys made fun of
him—and it was true. He did look like that when he spoke
Yilanè. He would never do it again. Or maybe he would.
He could talk it and they couldn't. They were all stupid.
And he could go to the island—and they couldn't. Which
meant that he was better than they were. He would go
there now and they couldn't follow.

The tent was empty, Malagen was away with his sister.
And so were his mother and father, gone away for such a
long time. Nobody cared about him, nobody. Maybe only
Nadaske. He took up his bow and quiver of arrows, then

saw the fish spear near the door. He would take that too, show Nadaske how to catch fish with it.

He saw no one when he crossed over the island. The day was hot, he was dusty and dirty. And it felt good to swim the channel to the smaller island by the sea. He sat on the bank and looked back carefully at the undergrowth, but he had not been followed. Then he went along the shore, and when he saw the shelter ahead called out loudly for attention to speaking. Nadaske poked his head out, then emerged and signed pleasure at seeing.

"Pleasure of eating too," Arnwheet said, holding up the fish spear. "For stabbing/catching fish. I will show you how."

"Small one has wisdom beyond my comprehension. We shall stab fish!"

anbefeneleiaa akotkurusat, anbegaas
efengaasat.

UGUNENAPSA SAID:

_____

If you accept the truth of
Efeneleiaa you accept life.

THIRTY-THREE

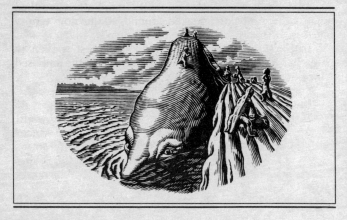

"Has all been loaded as ordered?" Ambalasei asked. Elem signed completeness.

"Everything that was brought to the dock has been put safely into the uruketo and secured. There is also a sufficiency of preserved eel, water enough for a long voyage, the creature itself has been well fed and rested. Doubts only as to destination."

"Entoban∗! You were informed. Is memory withering with age?"

"Memory is functioning. It is just that Entoban∗ is a vast continent, many ocean currents flow around it, specific city/ destination assures shortness of voyage."

"Perhaps it is longness of voyage that is needed. For the moment, for your information of determining course, Entoban∗ must suffice. There are many cities I must consider, comparisons shall be made. I am tired, Elem, in many ways, and this decision is an important one. I do not crave any more long voyages after this one, nor rough-life at the outer edge of knowledge-seeking. I want a city of comfort that will welcome me, where others can come to appreciate and study what I have learned. A life of physical and mental ease. With food a little more attractive than eel to eat." Ambalasei looked around at the now empty quarters, turned her back on it. "We leave."

"Instructions have been issued. A request spoken to me earlier, now made. For Ambalasei to attend the ambesed before departure."

"Suspicion of motives. Speeches and farewells?"

"I was not informed. Shall we go?"

Muttering complaints and disinterest, Ambalasei went. When they came close she heard the sound of many voices coming from the ambesed. They stilled as she entered.

"All talking of Ugunenapsa," she said disdainfully. "Great joy approaching me soonest to forget despised same and followers."

Despite her complaints she was pleased to see them all in attendance, moving aside respectfully as she approached. Enge stood beside the eistaa's resting place, and none complained now when Ambalasei seated herself there.

"No work being done today, obviously," she said.

"All are here. It is a collective wish."

"Is there a reason for this?"

"There is. There was discussion for many days . . ."

"That I certainly believe!"

". . . and many were the suggestions of the correct manner to express the gratitude that we feel, for what you have done for us. After lengthy consideration all were rejected as being insufficient in worth to be truly appreciative of what you have accomplished."

Ambalasei struggled to rise. "If all were rejected it is now possible for me to leave."

There was a hum of consternation at this and Enge stepped forward signing negative, remain, urgency, hurrying to make amends.

"You misunderstand, great Ambalasei, or it is my insufficiency in speaking. All other suggestions were rejected in favor of honoring you with that which is most precious to us. The Eight Principles of Ugunenapsa."

She paused then and there was absolute silence. "This

is what was decided. Henceforth and forever they shall be
called the Nine Principles of Ugunenapsa!"

It was upon Ambalasei's lips to ask when Ugunenapsa
had returned to dictate the ninth but felt that, even for
her, this would be a bit callous. She signed only fairly-
courteous attention.

"This is the ninth," Enge said, moving aside as Omal
and Satsat stepped forward. They chanted, in unison, and
what they said was echoed by all the listeners.

"The ninth principle of Ugunenapsa. The first Eight
Principles exist. They would not exist were it not for great
Ambalasei."

Ambalasei recognized this for what it was, the greatest
expression of gratitude that the Daughters of Life were
capable of. First for them always, came Ugunenapsa's
words. And now, forever linked with their existence, would
be the name of Ambalasei. These argumentative creatures
were actually capable of gratitude! For possibly the first
time in her long life she could not think of an insulting
remark. Could only sign the simplest gesture of acceptance and expression of her own gratitude.

Enge saw this, knew the old scientist far better than
Ambalasei would have believed possible. Understood her
reactions and appreciated her response. She turned and
spoke to the gathering.

"Ambalasei has thanked you all. It is time to leave her
in peace. Although she departs today—we now know that
she will never leave us. Ambalasei and Ugunenapsa, forever joined."

They filed out in silence until only Enge remained.
"May I walk with you to the uruketo? We have walked
together many times, and I have learned much from you
wise Ambalasei. Shall we go?"

Ambalasei struggled to rise, felt Enge's strong thumbs
helping her, stood and walked slowly from the ambesed
with her at her side. They went through the city in silence, until Ambalasei signed that she wished to rest in
the shade for the sun was very hot. When they stopped to
cool Enge signed request for information.

"Never refused, Enge, you know that. Without my continuing aid, yours and the entire Yilanè world, would be a poorer place."

"That is true. Which is the reason for my question. I am concerned. You speak always of your disbelief in Ugunenapsa and I find that both disconcerting and difficult to comprehend. You analyze our problems with great precision and aid us in understanding them better. But what of you yourself? What is your personal understanding? I hope that you will tell me. Is it your belief that Ugunenapsa's Nine Principles are correct?"

"No. Except for the ninth that is."

"Then—if you doubt that which is most important to us, why do you aid us?"

"A question I never thought you would ask. Are you asking it now because you have finally realized that I do not hold to your beliefs, never will?"

"Ambalasei is all-seeing, all-knowing. That is indeed the reason that I ask."

"The answer is a simple and obvious one—from my point of view. Like all Yilanè of science I care how life functions, relates, continues, changes, dies. This is the Yilanè way, has been, is now, will be. I am satisfied with it. But I am not closed-minded like all of the others. I wanted to study your group, and your Ugunenapsa, because she is the first thinker to ask a different question. Not how things work—but why? Most intriguing. Asking why has aided me in my own research and speculation, and I am grateful to you for that. If not for all the physical difficulties it entailed. When Ugunenapsa asked *why* for the first time something new came into our world. Asking why produced her principles, these in turn produced the Daughters of Life—who produced endless trouble by refusing to die in a normal Yilanè manner. It also produced an entirely new attitude to Yilanè ways. If the fact should be known, and I think it must be, I care nothing at all for Ugunenapsa or her theories. What I have really been interested in is studying you."

Enge was shaken, signed incomprehension, desire for explanation.

"I shall of course furnish that. Consider our ways, consider the Yilanè relationship, one to the other. The eistaa rules and all below obey. Or die. Fargi emerge from the ocean and are completely ignored. They are supplied with food, only because if they died that would be the end of all Yilanè, but given nothing else. If they persist, and have the will and the drive to learn, they become yilanè and may form part of the life of the city. Most don't. They wander off and, I presume, die. It must be said therefore, that all we Yilanè have offered one another is rejection and death. You however, Enge, offer compassion and hope. This is a very unusual and new thing."

"Hope signifies possibility of better tomorrow. I do not understand the other term."

"Nor could you be expected to since it is of my own construction, to describe a new concept. I mean an understanding of the unhappiness of others, linked with a desire to alleviate their miseries. This is why I have aided you. So stay here, stay safe in your city and study the *why* of life. I doubt if we shall speak again once I leave."

It was too abrupt, the parting had come too swiftly. And Ambalasei, with her usual stark frankness, had pointed out that they would undoubtedly never meet again. Enge's body moved as she searched for words and movements to express how she felt, could find nothing that was satisfactory.

Then they had reached the water's edge and Enge could still find nothing to say to express the depth of her feelings. In the end she simply touched Ambalasei's thumbs, as she would those of one of her efenselè and stepped away. Without a backward glance Ambalasei took Setèssei's waiting hand and was helped onto the uruketo. Elem looked down from the top of the fin, ready to issue the orders to leave, when the crewmember beside her signed for attention, pointed out into the river. She turned in the indicated direction, looked with rigid concentration.

"Urgency of listening," she called down to those below. "There is something distant in the river. Strong possibility of identification suggests—it is an uruketo."

"Impossibility," Ambalasei said, trying to peer into the distance. "Setèssei, with eyesight of raptor, what do you see?"

Setèssei climbed partway up the fin, did not speak until she was sure.

"It is as Elem has said. An uruketo coming in this direction."

"Impossibility of accidental discovery. If thin Ukhereb or fat Akotolp is aboard it signifies close attention to my notes. Undoubtedly a research voyage of their own. I still leave."

"Yilanè of science are always welcome," Enge said, looking out at the approaching uruketo. "We will learn from them—and they can possibly learn from us."

Ambalasei did not have Enge's placid acceptance of life. It had been her experience that most surprises turned out to be unwelcome ones. Despite this knowledge her curiosity won and she did not sign Elem to leave, but looked instead at the approaching creature with dark suspicion. There were Yilanè now visible on top of the uruketo's fin; identities still unknown. There was too great an element of chance to life. If she had left yesterday she would not have been present when this uruketo arrived. There was no point in even considering that now. Like the true scientist she waited stolidly for new evidence before she decided if the newcomer was welcome. Or not.

Setèssei spoke and decided that. "One on the fin is a hunter of your acquaintence from Yebeisk, the one known as Fafnepto."

"Unwelcome," Ambalasei said firmly. "Yesterday would have been a far better day to depart. We can expect nothing of benefit to arrive from Yebeisk. Do you know the others?"

"An uruketo commander, also from Yebeisk. The third is unfamiliar."

"Known to me," Enge said, with such dread and hatred in her speaking that Ambalasei was shocked, had never heard Enge like this before. "One known as Vaintè, once my efenselè, now rejected and despised. She was wise and led. Now death is her only follower."

Silence gripped them as they watched the dark form of the uruketo loom up and approach the dock, sending small waves slapping against the wood. Ambalasei considered boarding her own uruketo and leaving, realized it was too late when Fafnepto raised up a hèsotsan where it could be seen. There was no ignoring this message. This uruketo had brought a most unwelcome cargo.

Fafnepto jumped ashore and strode towards them, the hèsotsan firmly in her grip, with Vaintè, unarmed, only a pace behind. Ambalasei signed rejection and disgust.

"Is there a reason, Fafnepto, why you approach in such an insulting manner and draw negative attention to that weapon?"

"Good reason, Ambalasei. There is but a single hèsotsan present and I hold it. Therefore I issue the commands. I have been commissioned by Saagakel, Eistaa of Yebeisk, to follow and find you. To return there with this uruketo that you took without her permission."

"Wrong. It was mine to use with her permission."

"To use, yes, but Saagakel believes this use was not the one she originally intended."

"A matter of opinion. I assume that you wish to return the creature to Saagakel. Then take it."

"You as well, Ambalasei. The Eistaa would have you return as well. A refusal would not be accepted."

Ambalasei's body arched with scorn. "If I refuse—will you kill me, hunter?"

"Yes. And use your assistant's skill to preserve your body so that I can return with it, proving that my commission has been accomplished. Perhaps Saagakel will hang your tanned skin on the city's walls."

"Silence!" Enge commanded so strongly that Fafnepto recoiled, raising her weapon. "That a creature of such small worth should speak this way to a scientist of Ambalasei's standing is unacceptable/despicable. Silence and instant departure of uruketo ordered."

Fafnepto kept her weapon ready, looked coldly at Enge, ready for any attack. Vaintè stepped forward and signed threat/impossible.

"This one cannot commit violence," she said. "She is Enge who is a Daughter of Life/Death and can injure nothing."

Fafnepto lowered the hèsotsan and signed contempt. "Then she is the one of whom the Eistaa spoke. We have no need of her, she is of no concern to us. Just the uruketo and Ambalasei will return. These are my orders. I was also commanded to kill any who stood in my way."

Vaintè signed agreement. "A wise decision. These creatures spread only dissent. Killing them is an act of kindness. I am surprised that the eistaa of this city permits their presence."

"There is no eistaa here," Enge said with cold contempt. "Leave. You are not welcome. This is the city of Ugunenapsa and you are not welcome."

"Not welcome? To this fine city. Impossible to believe. I will speak with the eistaa."

"Do you not listen, creature of stupidity?" Ambalasei said. "There is no eistaa here. I grew this city, so I know whereof I speak."

A gasping and muffled sound of attention to speaking sounded loudly from the uruketo. Akotolp was clambering down from the fin, clumsily because of her fat and the container she carried.

"Teacher . . . Ambalasei," she said. "This is Vaintè whom I serve. You should listen to her because she is wise in every way. It was I who brought her your records, see they are here now, and she understood them and led us to this place."

"I think I have heard enough from you, Akotolp," Ambalasei said scornfully. "In the name of science I brought you my research and my findings. And to what use do you put them? You have led these repulsive creatures here. Now lead them away again."

"Enough empty talk," Fafnepto commanded. "These are my orders." She signed up at Elem. "You and all the

others aboard, you are commanded to instantly leave that
uruketo, for it will return to the city where it belongs. We
depart for Yebeisk at once—with both uruketo."

"And what of these creatures?" Vaintè asked, pointing
to Enge. "And what of their city?"

"It is of no concern of mine. We leave."

"I stay."

"That is your choice." Fafnepto turned to Elem who
still had not moved. "Were my orders not clear? Out of
the uruketo."

Akotolp had placed the container she carried on the
ground and opened it. Vaintè bent and reached inside.
Fafnepto was aware of the motion, turned to see what was
happening. Quickly raised her hèsotsan.

She was too late. The hèsotsan that Vaintè had removed from the container cracked once and the hunter
crumpled and fell. The spectators were rigid with shock.
All except Akotolp who had been expecting this. She
waddled over and took the hèsotsan from the corpse's
hand. Radiated smug satisfaction as she went to stand
beside Vaintè.

"Now," Vaintè said. "Now you will hear my commands."

THIRTY-FOUR

The murderous act had happened very quickly—had undoubtedly been planned to happen in just that way. All very obvious by hindsight, Ambalasei realized. Fafnepto had stood erectly before them, pride obvious in her hunting skill, her strength and her weapon. Not realizing that there were hunters in the cities that outdid any forest dweller in rapaciousness. Vaintè led, and this fat idiot Akotolp followed her instructions. She would have to be the one who had brought the hèsotsan, provided the material for this deadly ruse—had the effrontery to even use Ambalasei's own scientific records to conceal the presence of the weapon! Ambalasei turned to Akotolp, anger and detestation in every line of her body.

"Fat former student, now corpulent creature of deadly conspiracy. Return my scientific records at once for you are unfit to possess them."

Akotolp wavered before the storm of fury, the hèsotsan forgotten in her hands, trying to speak but unable to. Vaintè came to her rescue.

"Great Ambalasei, you are too angry with loyal Akotolp.

A long time ago she pledged to serve me, has done so faithfully ever since. She of course means no harm to you, her teacher. She and I both respect you and acknowledge your great wisdom. I am thankful also for your research into this new continent that permitted me to come here and complete the mission I had undertaken."

"You were commissioned to kill Fafnepto?!" Ambalasei said, her crest flaring with color.

"The death of Fafnepto was unfortunate but necessary. We both serve Saagakel and are here at her bidding. Unfortunately Fafnepto did not agree with me on matters of priority. Since a Yilanè of her type cannot be reasoned with she, unfortunately, had to suffer disproportionately for her opinions. Akotolp, let me have your hèsotsan before someone is killed by mistake. Do not shake so, you have done no wrong. You have done only your duty and have served me, your eistaa, for which I am grateful. And you will of course return Ambalasei's records to her?"

"If that is your wish, Vaintè."

"Not my wishes, but the desire of this great scientist whose orders we will obey."

Ambalasei signed disbelief as Akotolp brought the container to her side, then hurried away. "Do you obey all my wishes, Vaintè? What if I wish to remain here in this new city?"

Vaintè shaped her arms with regret. "Unfortunately, that is not possible. I was sent by Saagakel, Eistaa of Yebeisk, to return you to that city. That will be done. All of your records that Akotolp brought with us from Alpèasak are now in the uruketo and there they will remain. You will join them." She turned to Gunugul who descended from the fin and was standing as rigid as the others, numbed by the speed and shock of events. "There should be meat and water enough for a return to Yebeisk. Is there?"

"Yes, sufficient if many sleep during the journey."

"Excellent. You will return there at once with Ambalasei."

"What of this other uruketo? It was taken by Ambalasei, it must go back . . ."

"It has been recovered, unharmed, as you can see for yourself. Reassure great Saagakel that it will be returned one day to her city. But I will have use of it for a period of time. This use is all the reward I ask for my labors, for finding the uruketo, for finding and returning the one she sought."

"For killing Fafnepto," Ambalasei said with cold anger. "Enge spoke correctly—you are a poisonous and deadly creature, Vaintè. I have work, possessions, my assistant Setèssei in the stolen uruketo, now doubly stolen. What of them?"

"I offer all assistance. They return with you to Yebeisk of course. Transfer them now. And leave."

"And you will remain. What labors of magnified negativity do you plan to do here?"

"What I plan is no concern of yours, old one. Leave— and enjoy the attentions of the Eistaa."

Ambalasei signed disdain. "If you think the Eistaa will punish me, abandon that hope. She will present no problems to me. When I turn over the records of my discoveries to Saagakel she will forget all thoughts of revenge. Her city will be the center of the new learning and will welcome scientists from all Entoban*. Like any other eistaa she will take all of the credit. As for myself, one city is like any other city. It will suffice. Setèssei, supervise moving of my possessions. I now go and rest." She walked a few tired steps, then turned to Enge and signed departure immediate/final. "I am sorry to see these creatures of evil in your city, Enge."

"Do not concern yourself. The Principles of Ugunenapsa will survive."

"Good. I am particularly fond of the ninth."

She turned, climbed the uruketo's fin and vanished from sight.

Elem started to speak but Vaintè pointed the hèsotsan at her and signed silence on pain of death.

It was a long silence that continued as Ambalasei's containers were taken from one uruketo and loaded into

the other. Akotolp, her fear vanished with Ambalasei's
departure, took up Fafnepto's hèsotsan again and settled
back on her tail. Serving her eistaa. The commander,
Gunugul, was the last to board when the uruketo was
ready to leave. She turned and spoke coldly to Vaintè.

"The Eistaa shall hear exactly what happened here.
How Fafnepto died. Everything."

"Speak of it," Vaintè said, her contempt withering and
dismissive. "I did as I promised her, then did what I had
to do for myself. Now—depart."

She was silent again until the gap of water had opened
up between the uruketo and the dock. Only then did she
turn to Enge.

"That is done with. Now we look to the future. I
greatly admire this fine, fresh, new city that you have
here. You must tell me of it."

"I tell you nothing, will not speak with you, reject you
now as I have rejected you before. None here will acknowledge your existence."

"Do you realize how very difficult you are being? Can
you not understand that it is now I who will issue orders?
Your years of leadership are finished at last. It was power
that we have both always wanted, isn't it? You must admit
that to yourself—now that your days of power are ended.
You led these confused creatures and many died because
of your leadership. But, like me, you are very strong,
Enge. In the end your leadership carried them all across
the ocean and grew this city for them here. But these days
are over. I rule now. And there is absolutely nothing that
you can do about it. It is now I who will speak and be
obeyed." She raised and pointed the hèsotsan. "If I am
not obeyed then this shall speak for me. Do you believe
that?"

"I believe it. Of no one else, possibly. But of you I
believe it."

"Good. Then I shall tell you of this city, so obviously
new and freshly grown. For now that I look closely it is
obvious what happened here. You came to this place and

that wise scientist, Ambalasei, grew a city for you where none had been before. Since there is no eistaa here you must foolishly think of it as your city, as the city of the Daughters of Death. That is no longer the case. I am the eistaa now. And if this city ever had another name I do not want to hear it. Since I am Vaintè, the joy-hunter, I wish a *muru* of permanence to my city, a *tesi* to seize and catch that joy. This city is now named Muruvaintesi, the place where joy is hunted and caught forever. Is that not a very appropriate name?"

"It is so inappropriate that I instantly reject it—as will we all. Leave us."

"No! It is mine—and you will not resist me. Or perhaps you should. It would be easy enough for you to do that. This is your last chance, Enge. Fight back and regain control! Kill me Enge—and the city is yours again. But of course if you do that you have lost everything you profess to believe in! See, Enge, how well I know you. How I place you in an inescapable position. You either lose—or you lose."

Enge felt her temper flare, felt her thumbs open wide, felt the overwhelming desire to reach out and kill this despoiler who would destroy everything that she believed in, that she had devoted her life to.

Knew that if she gave in to these overwhelming desires she would destroy it herself.

The anger was still there, but she locked it deep within herself, let her arms drop to her side, turned away.

"You decide wisely," Vaintè said, arched with victory. "Now speak to your Daughters and tell them to keep this city functioning well while you are away. They have no choice, do they? They will work as they have always worked, but it shall be my city they work for, not theirs. Remind them that if they refuse and resist that they will die. I shall then bring fargi here to take their places. Go tell them this, then return here. We leave today for Gendasi* for I have one last task to perform before I remake this city. I very much want you to be there when I find and kill ustuzou Kerrick. You do want to be there, don't you?"

The anger and hatred had burned deep, showed now only in Enge's eyes. She let her gaze rest on Vaintè for a long moment, then turned and walked slowly away. Vaintè signed attention to the crewmembers of the uruketo.

"Who commands here?" she asked.

"I do," Elem said. "But I serve Ugunenapsa and not you. The uruketo remains here. You may now kill me."

"You do not escape that easily, commander. It is not you who will die—but your foolish companions. Every time you refuse my order I will kill one of them. Is that understood?"

Elem signed confusion and disbelief, impossibility of action.

"Possible enough," Vaintè said. "Akotolp, shoot one of these despicable creatures to show the survivors the strength of my resolution."

"No!" Elem shouted, stepping forward and standing before Akotolp's raised weapon. "The uruketo will leave as commanded, no more shall die." She looked at Fafnepto's corpse just beside her. "One is enough."

Enge walked stiffly into the city, the shock of Vaintè's arrival still not assimilated. This day she had gone from highest hopes to greatest despair. She met two Daughters on the path and they recoiled at the pain in her movements. She stopped and ordered her thoughts.

"Tell everyone, go to the ambesed now. Events of disastrous nature."

The word spread quickly and she walked slowly, deep in thought. They were gathering even before she arrived and when she spoke to them the silence was absolute. There were murmurs of pain when she told them what had happened, cries of despair when she described what more there was to come.

"I would like to tell you to have hope. At this moment I cannot."

"We shall leave the city," Satsat said. "I remember

this Vaintè—how could I ever forget her? As Ugunenapsa is the embodiment of life, she is that of death. We must leave the city. We die in either case."

Enge signed understanding. "You speak from fear. As terrible as she is, Vaintè is only a single Yilanè. We have not come this far to die at the slightest setback. This is our city. She will try to make it hers but we will resist with silence and work. When we speak it shall not be to her but to any fargi she may bring here. If they understand Ugunenapsa's words they will then become as we are— and we will have won. I ask you only to have faith in what we have done, and what we still have left to do. Stay here. Work hard. You may have to work even harder when we return. But we have no choice. If we truly follow Ugunenapsa's teachings we can do nothing else."

Satsat and Omal and Efen knew what lay in store for them. They knew Vaintè when she had been Eistaa of Alpèasak, before the city had been destroyed. They knew what she was capable of. They came and touched Enge's thumbs as efenselè and the others watched in silence. What they had all shared, how far they had come since first they had joined together to follow Ugunenapsa's will, steadied Enge and even gave her the strength to go ahead.

"I thank you for your aid. I thank you for the new thing I heard of this day called compassion. It is a term that wise Ambalasei used to describe something new that Ugunenapsa brought to the Yilanè. I will remember that and I will remember you when we leave here. Although there appears to be no hope—yet I still have hope. We may yet succeed."

With this she left them and went through the city to the river's shore. All of the others were within the uruketo save Vaintè who stood, waiting for her.

Enge had nothing to say, was scarcely aware of her. She climbed the fin and spoke to Elem who waited there.

"You may leave when you are ready. Do as you are

ordered to do, for these are creatures of great violence and death."

"It shall be as you say, Enge." Vaintè's shadow fell over them and Elem ignored it very much as Enge did. "Where we walk today is not important, as long as tomorrow and tomorrow's tomorrow we follow Ugunenapsa's path."

THIRTY-FIVE

It was a happy leavetaking because that was the Paramutan way. Everyone knew that if one showed unhappiness before a voyage it would only bring the worst kind of bad luck, blizzards, disaster. Hanath and Morgil were equally happy at the results of their trading, laughing and getting soaked alongside the Paramutan as they helped to push the ikkergak into the sea. The waves were large and broke over them before the craft was floating free. Kalaleq was the last to board, was pulled dripping from the water by strong hands on arms and tail.

"After the winter we will be here again. There will be much to trade. Come back!"

"We will," Armun called out, shouting to be heard above the crashing of the waves upon the beach. "We will be here."

"What did the furry one say?" Hanath asked with clattering teeth, blue with cold. He wrapped one of the new furs about him.

"They want us to trade here again."

"We will! Next time we will come early and make porro. They will like that."

"Don't even suggest it," Kerrick said. "Not until you have spent a winter snowbound with them. They are a very strange people."

"I like them," Morgil said. "They know how to enjoy themselves. Now you can tell us what that horrible black muck was that you buried. I can still smell it."

"That is what is going to keep us alive when these die," Kerrick said, picking up his hèsotsan. "The Paramutan make a powerful poison called takkuuk. It can kill the biggest creature in the sea. It will kill murgu too. Now we know how to make it. I don't know how but Armun remembers, she made it with Kalaleq. It seems very difficult."

"Not really," she said. "It is just entrails and blood made to rot in a special way, then certain roots are added. I know the plant, we were always told to never go near it or touch it. Now I know why."

"The stink will kill us before it kills a marag," Hanath said.

"I don't think so." Kerrick held up his spear. "When the poison is buried a second time it will be in small leather bags that will be wrapped around the spearpoints. We will bury the spears too, special spears only for killing murgu. Then, when we stab a marag, the spearpoint goes through the bag and into the flesh and the thing dies."

"We can certainly do that," Morgil said with great enthusiasm. "We will help you, Armun, make a lot of takkuuk spears. Then we can trade them to the other sammads. We can even trek to the valley of the Sasku, trade with them for cloth."

"You may never hunt again," Armun said. "You will trade anything now."

"Of course. We can hunt too, if we want to. But we like trading."

There were so many furs and rolls of hide that the two traders had to cut poles for a travois. It was heavy laden and they took turns dragging it when they started south. The nights were cold, the days crisp, the new furs and hides a pleasure to sleep in at night. The stars seemed

brighter here than they were on the island, Kerrick thought,
lying awake and watching them after Armun had gone to
sleep. Perhaps because they were the tharms of hunters,
therefore shone more brightly in the north, here where
the hunters had died. One day the snows might melt again
and they could go back to the mountains. Meanwhile they
lived, the sammads grew larger, the murgu would no
longer be a threat when the hèsotsan died. Tomorrow's
tomorrow was going to be good. This was a Yilanè phrase
that they used very often, and when he thought of this his
legs arched and his hands shaped the meaning. Armun
moaned in her sleep, disturbed by his movements, and he
lay still. Forget Yilanè, it was enough to be Tanu.

It was an easy trek south along the familiar path. Only
twice were they attacked by murgu large enough to need
killing with the death-sticks. And they ate well. Which-
ever of the two hunters was not pulling the travois would
slip into the forest. Catch up with them later with a
freshly killed marag or deer. They built a fire each night
and cooked the fresh meat, ate enough to last them through
the next day. In this way they moved steadily south.

When they came to the path that branched off to the
other sammads there was some discussion of the possibility of stopping. Hanath and Morgil wanted to trade. Kerrick
did not care either way, but Armun was firm.

"No. These sammads may have gone south. If they did
not you two can always come back to them. We return to
our own sammad. I have children there—and I want to
see them." She looked at Kerrick in a very accusing manner.

"I too, yes. We won't stop. We go directly to the
island."

The days were growing shorter, the distance that could
be traveled in daylight growing less as well. Armun was
troubled at their slow progress. She made them start out
on the trail before it was light, continue after dark.

"I grow tired," Hanath said one evening, looking up at
the darkening sky. "I think it would be better if we
stopped now."

"I am going on," she said firmly. "I am tired too—but

if we reach the camping place by the stream tonight, then we will be back on the island before dark tomorrow. I will go on by myself if you do not wish to. Give me one of the death-sticks."

"We go on, we go on," Hanath muttered leaning his weight against the straps.

It rained during the night but cleared before morning. Armun woke them, laughing at their complaints. But once on the trail they were all eager to return. They did not stop, but instead ate some of the cold meat as they walked. Not drinking anything since they were all able to go without water until dark. Kerrick did not notice the side trail until Morgil pointed it out, pushed newly grown branches aside to turn into it. Before they reached the river crossing they heard shouts ahead and met a hunting party. There were warm greetings and cries of appreciation at the fur and hides. The hunters were happy to help carry these new possessions and they went the faster.

Herilak called a loud greeting as they arrived among the sammads. Malagen came from their tent holding the baby. She laughed and called out to them and Armun seized up Ysel and held her high.

"The Paramutan were there and you traded well," Herilak said, feeling the softness of the furs.

"Better than you realize, sammadar," Kerrick said. "There is a thing they make called takkuuk, and we now know how to make it ourselves. It is going to be very important for all the Tanu."

"Where is Arnwheet?" Armun said, holding the baby tight to her as she looked around at the children who had run up. "Where is he?"

"He is not here—but I know where he is," one of the boys said. "He goes to the forbidden island by himself and wiggles like this with the marag there."

He shook back and forth, but his laughter turned to a cry of pain as Armun slapped out and sent him sprawling.

"You would not know that if you had not gone there yourself—and that is forbidden. He should not be there alone." She looked angrily at Kerrick when she said this.

"I will bring him back," he said, taking up his death-stick. "Walk with me, Herilak, for there are many things to tell you."

"I will," he said and went to get his bow and quiver.

"Have we reached the proper place?" Vaintè asked, holding the image sheet in the sunlight, then looking from it over to the nearby shore.

"We have," Akotolp said, touching it with her finger. "We are here. Close to these small islands on the coast. The one you see out there conceals the larger island inland, where the ustuzou lair is."

"Will the uruketo take us to it?"

"Unhappily, no. The water between the islands is too shallow."

"Understood. Now where is the place where the Yilanè is found?"

"There, on that island facing the sea."

"Then that is where we will land. We will speak with her. The ustuzou creatures are deadly. When we attack them it will be only to kill them. She will be able to help me, tell me if the one I seek is here, aid me in finding him. The others can live or die, it does not matter to me. It is his death that I must have." She signed brusque instructions to Elem. "Towards that island, go close. Order Enge up here."

They were just outside the breakers when Enge joined them on top of the fin.

"Swim to the shore," Vaintè commanded. "Akotolp will go with you. Do not forget that she brings her hèsotsan. I will join you with mine. If Elem has any thoughts of leaving once we are on the beach we will kill you. Is that understood?"

Enge signed understanding of filth, rejection of speaker, then climbed down to the uruketo's back. She was in the water and swimming towards shore long before the gasping Akotolp could follow. She made no attempt to escape knowing that Vaintè would kill those in the uruketo if she

did. Instead she waited on the beach until Akotolp arrived. Vaintè, swimming swiftly, was close behind her.

"I go first," she said. "Stay close behind me."

She climbed slowly up the dune, her sharp claws digging deep. Tough grass was rooted on the summit; she
stopped and parted it slowly to see what lay on the other
side. Halted, motionless, with only her hand behind her
signing sharp communication of silence. Looked down at
the two figures below her, listened as they talked.

"Try it again," Arnwheet said, holding the hardalt by
one tentacle, holding it before Nadaske.

"Grardal'," Nadaske said, holding his hand out at the
same time just as Arnwheet was doing.

"Not *grarrdle*," Arnwheet said. "Hardalt, just hardalt—
and don't hold your arm out like that."

"You did."

"Of course I did. But when you talk Marbak you do
not move, just make the sound."

"Stupid/ugly speech. Fit only for ustuzou." Nadaske
caught the movement from the bank above, looked with
one eye—dived forward towards the shelter.

"Instant cessation of motion," Vaintè ordered, striding
down the slope. "If you have a hèsotsan in there touch it
only if you wish to die. Emerge—empty of hand!"

Nadaske turned slowly, reluctantly, came into the sunlight again with his hands hanging limply at his sides.
Vaintè looked at him closely, leaned forward and sniffed
with delight.

"It is a male! One of a familiar aspect."

"We have met before, Vaintè. You would not remember. I do. You were Eistaa of Alpèasak when you sent me
to the birth beaches. I returned."

Vaintè expressed cold amusement at the obvious and
presumptuous anger of a mere male. Signed coarsely that
she would be happy to send him to the beaches again,
instantly if needed. But her attention was on Arnwheet
who stepped back, eyes wide with fear, looking from her
to the other murgu that came down the slope. The two of
them who held hèsotsan moved with harsh angularity, not

at all like Nadaske. He took another step backwards but stopped when the first one signed cessation of movement.

"I heard you speaking to this male. You are yilanè and that is unusual/impossible. But it has happened. Approach me, that is a command. Do you understand?"

Arnwheet shuffled forward, shivering with fear, signed understanding of meaning. Vaintè bent close, he could smell the foulness of her breath, reached out one thumb and touched the metal knife that hung around his neck.

"What does this artifact of metal signify? This one is smaller, but I have held another like this in my hand. And this smaller one, I have held it too, long ago. I was sent the larger one as a sign I should end the war that I was winning. It hung from the neck of the ustuzou of death, Kerrick. Explain instantly."

Arnwheet understood what this Yilanè was saying, although he did not understand the name she mentioned since the way Vaintè spoke Kerrick was incomprehensible. But the meaning was clear.

"There is only one other knife like this. It hangs about the neck of my . . . efenselè." This was the nearest he could get, could think of no term for father in Yilanè.

"Then you are efenselè of the one I seek. But where is he, why are you here alone? Inform me quickly of the meaning of this, male," she ordered, looking at Arnwheet with one eye, Nadaske with the other.

Nadaske did not bother to answer. Freedom was ended, life was ended. This was Vaintè, known for her cruelty. She would be immensely displeased at his escaping the hanalè and the death of the city, then living as free as any female. She would see that he suffered in many ways before he died on the beaches. All was ended. There was a movement in the shrubbery and he glanced that way. An animal of some kind, it did not matter, nothing mattered now.

Kerrick and Herilak had just reached the inlet when Dall burst from the bushes on the other side and hurled himself into the water, thrashed across it sobbing and gasping. Herilak pulled him from the water and shook him.

"You were beaten before for coming here. Now you will have a beating . . ."

"Murgu—out there! They come from the sea, murgu—"

Herilak took him by the jaw and pulled him close. "What kind of murgu? The kind that kill with death-sticks?"

"Yes," Dall said, then fell whimpering to the ground. Herilak spun about to follow Kerrick who had hurled himself into the water. Caught up with him on the other side, held him with a restraining hand.

"Slowly and silently, do not rush or you rush to your death." He fitted an arrow to his bow.

Kerrick pushed his hand away, ran on, not hearing his words. There were Yilanè here—and they had Arnwheet. He stumbled through the sand with Herilak close behind him. Ran along the shore and past the dune that shielded Nadaske's small campsite. Stopped with a cry of horror.

Herilak stopped as well, saw the four murgu, two of them armed, the boy there as well. He pulled the arrow to his chin, released it.

Kerrick pushed his arm aside and the arrow thudded into the dune.

"Don't! They'll kill him. Drop your bow. Do this for me, Herilak, do this thing for me."

He laid his own death-stick on the ground but Herilak stood firm, seeing only the ones he must kill. Seeing one of them aiming at Arnwheet. If this had been his son he would not have hesitated, although it would have meant the child's death, would have killed them all.

Arnwheet was Kerrick's son. Because of Herilak the boy had almost died once already. He could not be permitted to die now even if it meant Herilak's own death. Slowly, never taking his eyes off of them, he bent and placed the bow on the ground. The ugly marag behind Arnwheet grunted and quivered, its jaw opening to show the sharp, pointed teeth.

"You are correct in obedience," Vaintè said, her arms arched in triumph, her jaw agape to sign eating-of-victory.

"Let the small one go. I will stay in his place," Kerrick said.

"You value your efenselè ahead of your own life?"

"It could be a matter of great importance to this ustuzou," Akotolp said. "I have studied these animals. There is live birth without eggs, great attachment among small efenburu . . ." She grew silent at Vaintè's sharp command, her victorious speaking.

"It will end here, Kerrick. You have fought me too long, killed too many. This is my victory. I have my own city now. It will grow and prosper. You and these other two ustuzou now die. But die in the knowledge that your deaths are only the first. For I shall return with fargi and creatures of death grown by ever-loyal Akotolp. I will return and pursue your kind across all of Gendasi*. To seek out every stinking lair of your kind and kill every one of you. Think of that as you die. Think of it, slowly and carefully. I give you time so you will die with that knowledge uppermost in your thoughts."

Vaintè signed triumph in everything as she lifted her weapon. There was silence, the stillness of horror all about her. Enge could not move or act, gripped hard by the conflict of beliefs and affection. Arnwheet was terrified, Nadaske as unmoving as a statue. Only Akotolp signed understanding, perfection of action.

Nadaske shifted and Vaintè let one wary eye look at him, then back to Kerrick when she saw that the helpless male was turning away from her, unable to watch.

Nadaske faced the frightened boy, placed thumbs of sympathy and understanding on his shoulders.

Vaintè raised the hèsotsan, aimed at Herilak. "You shall be last, Kerrick. Watch your efenselè die first."

Nadaske lowered his hands, seized the metal knife where it hung on Arnwheet's neck, tore it free and turned swiftly about.

Thrust it hard into the side of Vaintè's neck.

Time stopped. Vaintè's eyes were wide with pain, she gasped, shuddered, her hands clamped so tight on the hèsotsan that it squirmed in her grip. Nadaske still held

the knife tight between strong thumbs. Blood spurted out
as he twisted it.

Vaintè crumpled, fell, turning and firing the weapon as
she went down. The sharp crack was muffled as Nadaske
dropped on top of her.

Akotolp, never a Yilanè of action, simply stared in
horror at the two bodies. Even before she thought to raise
her own hèsotsan she had it torn from her hands by Enge.

"The killing is over!" Enge cried out, holding the
weapon high over her head, throwing it strongly out into
the water.

"The killing is over," Kerrick echoed in Marbak, placing his hand gently on Herilak's arm as he grabbed up his
bow. "That one is my friend. She does not kill."

"Perhaps she doesn't—but what of the fat marag?"

"That one dies," Kerrick said, the cold of winter in his
voice. First in Marbak, then speaking in Yilanè. "You die,
don't you Akotolp? You should have died when Alpèasak
died, but I see that you have escaped. Now you are a
follower of Vaintè. But she is dead. Your city dead, your
eistaa dead. Why are you alive? There is no need to kill
you, for now you kill yourself. Follow her into death."

With a great surge of fear Akotolp knew that the ustuzou
spoke correctly. It was the end, the end . . .

Her eyes were glazed as she fell, sprawling hugely on
the sand. Still moving: soon dead.

Weeping fiercely Arnwheet ran to his father, grasped
him about the legs. Kerrick picked the boy up and held
him tightly.

"It is all over," he said with gentle weariness. "Our
friend Nadaske is dead, but he could not have died in a
better way. When you are older you will understand. He
will never have to go to the beaches. He will always be
remembered—for he killed this one who would have killed
us all." He looked at Enge. "Are there others?"

"No—just Daughters of Life. No others like these."

He looked down at Vaintè, dead at last. The creature
of death, dead beneath the one who had killed her. Bitter
bile rose in his throat and he felt a terrible sorrow.

"I do not want to hear of death again, think of it, see it." He turned to Herilak and gently pulled Arnwheet's hands free, gave him to the big hunter. "Take the boy to his mother. Dall will have raised the alarm. Stop the hunters, send them back, there is nothing for them here. Tell Armun what has happened, tell her I will be there soon."

Herilak took the boy, nodded agreement. "It shall be as you say, sammadar. I saw those two kill each other, saw that one just lie down and die. What has happened?"

"When I return I will tell you. For now it is enough to know that this one that lies there in her own blood, this was the one who led the murgu against us. With her death the war against us is ended. The battle is over."

"Then—we have won?"

"I cannot answer that. Can the battle we have fought ever be won or lost? Enough. It is over."

He watched as Herilak walked slowly away with his son. Then turned back to Enge who had been standing rigid in silence ever since she had disarmed Akotolp.

"I have just told my people that the battle between us is over. Is that true, teacher?"

Enge signed agreement and triumph. "Ended indeed, my student. Walk with me to the beach for I want to forget the violence here. My companions on the uruketo must know at once that their fear is ended as well. There is much I must tell you. When you were small I spoke to you of the Daughters of Life, but I do not think that you understood very much then. But you will understand now that there are many of us. We do not kill, we have a city of our own, and it is a city of peace."

"Perhaps all cities will be cities like that now. We want nothing from the Yilanè except to live in peace—as you do."

They came out on the top of the dune above the sea; an uruketo lay quietly in the ocean nearby, small waves running across its back. Enge signed attention and swim-this-way in the simplest of fargi language. She did it again, then again, until a Yilanè signed comprehension and climbed

down from the fin and slid into the sea. Only then did she
turn to Kerrick and express hope and doubt conjoined.

"I think that the Yilanè cities will leave your kind in
peace, since every eistaa now knows what fearful death
your fellow creatures bring. But will your kind leave the
cities in peace?"

"Of course. I will tell them what has happened, they
will stay away from Alpèasak."

"Forever? You will die one day, Kerrick. And what
will they do when you are gone and they see Alpèasak so
rich and so close? And so helpless against your kind."

"That day will never come."

"May you be correct in what you say. Though I see
peace now, in your lifetime and my lifetime, I think of
tomorrow's tomorrow. I see your kind, many of them,
coming to my city of peace and taking it from the Daughters of Life who will be there."

"It will not happen."

Kerrick watched as the Yilanè from the uruketo came
ashore, stood rigid with pleasure as Enge signed end of
conflict/end of killing. He realized that she had not answered him.

But, yes, he had to admit that there was the possibility. The Yilanè would never change, could not change.
But Tanu learned new things and changed all of the time.
If a conflict between the two ever came about—could
there be doubt about the final outcome?

"There are things I wish to tell you, but we must
leave," Enge said.

"Much to say, no time to say it in. Will we meet again,
Enge?"

"It is my hope that we can, my belief that we cannot."

"Mine as well. My friend Nadaske is dead. You are the
only other Yilanè I can call friend. I will remember that
friendship. But after today, seeing Vaintè dead at last, it is
my feeling that I want to forget all Yilanè. I was taken
among them by force, lived with violence, ended with
death. It is enough, Enge. I am Tanu. I remain Tanu."

Enge thought to speak to him of Ugunenapsa and of

the Spirit of Life that joined them, saw the coldness of his body, thought better of it.

"You are as you are. I am as I am."

She turned, slid into the water, swam away. He watched as the other joined her and the two of them clambered aboard the waiting uruketo. When it stood out to sea he turned and climbed the dune once again. The three dead Yilanè were as he had left them, although the flies had found them now. He bent and pulled the metal knife from Vaintè's neck, plunged it into the sand to clean it. The corpses must be buried. And this last embrace of death was not acceptable. He pulled Nadaske's body from atop Vaintè, closed his sightless eyes and straightened his body out upon the sand. As he turned to leave he remembered the nenitesk.

It was on a little ledge to the rear of Nadaske's shelter. The metal of the sculpture cool on his fingers, the polished stones gleaming in the sunlight when he held it up.

The sculpture in one hand, his son's knife in the other, he turned his back on the Yilanè and trudged off to join the Tanu.

ENVOY

These things happened and must be told. That is what the
alladjex always says when he speaks of things past. *Ashan
etcheran wariadith, aur skennast man eis*. That is the way
it is said in Marbak. I don't think I could say it any more
in Sesek. Armun could, she has always been very good
with other languages. In Paramutan it would be long and
stretched out, something like *Harvaqtangaq netsilikaktuvuk*.
We still see the Paramutan every year, to trade. The others
trade, I go just for the pleasure of being with those strange,
friendly people. Though we don't trade porro with them,
not since the first—and last—time. The broken arms and
legs mended. But a gouged-out eye can't grow back.

Armun talks about crossing the ocean with them once
again and I say why not? Our daughter, Ysel, has her own

hunter now and has gone off with him to the north. At
least Arnwheet is still here. He has grown to be a strong
and skillful hunter with his own sammad. Like many of
the other children who were raised on this island he does
not feel the need to trek every season, to follow the hunt
wherever it leads. I know that the women are the ones
who prefer this most of all. They don't want to leave their
charadis fields, their looms and ovens. They talk of how
they miss the snow and cold winters when the weather is
very hot here, but it is just talk. But many of the original
sammads have left, others have taken their place. Some
Tanu die. Ortnar, dragging his bad leg, still lives and
complains. But strong Herilak who survived a thousand
battles did not wake up one morning, was cold at Merrith's
side, dead during the night. Strange things happen. But
she has their son, Terin, to raise. He is growing large and
will be very much like his father.

These things happened and must be told. Easy enough
to say in Yilanè: *lulukhesnii igikurunkè, marikulugul
marikakotkuru*. With a tail lift that I never could do. I
must go to the city soon, to Alpèasak, talk to them there. I
wonder if Lanefenuu is still Eistaa? She certainly is if she
is still alive. It would not be easy to push her out. I must
talk to her. I have tried to talk to Arnwheet, but he says
that he does not speak Yilanè any more. Marbak is good
enough for him. I don't argue. I wonder if he still remembers his friend Nadaske, who killed Vaintè with his knife,
then was killed himself, right before our eyes. He used to
dream about it, wake up crying in the dark, he did that for
a long time. I think that I agree with him. There is no
reason now for him to remember how to speak Yilanè. He
wouldn't take the knife back, even after I scrubbed it
clean. But his son wears it now about his neck, and
Arnwheet wears mine. Father and son, the way it should be.

I miss its presence some times, cool against the skin of
my chest. But the shining metal ring is still there, will
always be there. Grown in place by Vaintè to keep me
prisoner. She is long dead—but it was never soon enough.
There is no counting the number dead because of her. I

must go to Alpèasak soon. Tell them they must be more
cautious, strengthen their wall, maybe move their birth
beaches. The young hunters brought the head to me so I
could tell them if this was the killing marag. It was not
very deadly, the eyes bulged, the jaw hung limp. Just a
fargi fresh from the sea. I said that it was, but they must
not kill any more of them. They laughed at that. They still
respect me, I think, but they do not obey.

What was it that Enge said before she left, that distant
day? That it would not always be a Yilanè world. I did not
believe her then. I think I do now. There seem to be
more and more Tanu about, more sammads than I could
ever count. Many have left this island. I can see a time,
not soon, not tomorrow, certainly not in my lifetime,
when there might be so many Tanu that would want to
hunt the land where Alpèasak now grows. Want to hunt
the herds there. I can see that happening.

I would like to see the valley of the Sasku again, but it
is a very long way away. Two hunters went there, came
back, they said everything there was the same. It will
probably always stay the same, that's the kind of people
they are. They said that Sanone was dead, he was very
old, otherwise everything was the same.

I think I will visit Alpèasak. Warn them to guard their
beaches better or more fargi will be slain. I see their
uruketo in the distance sometimes, so they will know what
is happening in the other cities of the Yilanè world. I
wonder if they will know of Enge and her new city far to
the south? Although she explained it, I could never understand the Daughters of Life. Enge and Vaintè, as different
as night and day. Well, Tanu can be like that so why not
Yilanè? It is a strange world we live in.

Strange. I heard someone talk about the alladjex and
they called him old Fraken. He is going bald, perhaps that
is it. But I remember when he was just the boy-without-a-
name. Things change I guess.

It is going to rain, I know. My hip always hurts when it
is going to rain. I think I will go hunting today. Though
we have enough meat. Or perhaps I will go to the island

where Nadaske used to live. Poor, lonely creature. Though I shouldn't say that. He left the hanalè, lived on his own, learned to hunt and fish. Learned to kill doing it, something that the Yilanè males never do. It was well learned, a blow well struck. I will never forget him.

Others have of course. Everyone has. I haven't. Ermanpadar never had a braver tharm in his belt of stars. Though I suppose that Yilanè don't have tharms. I wouldn't know about anything like that.

I was born Tanu, lived Yilanè, and am Tanu once again.

Or both really. I don't mind. Although I feel a strange loneliness at times. I have Armun, so it is not that kind of loneliness.

I must go to Alpèasak and talk to the eistaa, others there. I should have done it years ago. So perhaps it is too late. I am afraid that it is. Too late.

Nevertheless these things happened and they must be told.

The telling is over now.

THE WORLD
WEST OF EDEN

YILANÈ	346
History of the World	346
Physiology	351
Diet	352
Reproduction	353
Science	356
Culture	359
The Eight Principles of Ugunenapsa	361
Language	370
TANU	376
Language	379
PARAMUTAN	380
Environment	381
Language	382
DICTIONARIES	386
Yilanè–English	386
Marbak–English	390
Sesek–English	393
Angurpiaq–English	394
ZOOLOGY	397

YILANÈ

HISTORY OF THE WORLD

It must be pointed out at the very beginning of this
particular history that it differs from many "histories" currently popular. It differs in *kind,* a fact that the judicious
reader must always take into consideration. For far too
long Yilanè history has been the province of the fabulist
and the dreamer. Whereas the intelligent Yilanè would be
offended at any guesswork or wild speculation in a physics
or a biological text, the same reader will allow any sort of
imaginary excess in a work of history. A perfect example of
fiction purporting to be fact is the currently popular *history*
of this world that describes how a giant meteor struck the
Earth 75* million years ago and wiped out 85% of the species
then alive. It goes on to explain in great detail the manner in which warm-blooded creatures developed and
became the dominant life forms on this planet. This sort of

---

*For those readers not acquainted with large mathematical terms, see
page 359 for a complete description.

thing is what the present authors deplore; wild speculation instead of accurate historical research. No meteor of that size ever struck the Earth. The world as we see it is the world as it always has been, always will be, world without end. It is necessary therefore, in the light of other works of this nature, that we define the term *history* before we can proceed.

History, as it is known today, is far too often a very inexact science, so inexact that it is more fiction than fact, more speculation than presentation. This is due to intrinsic aspects of the Yilanè nature. We care little where we have been—but we know exactly where we are going. We are happy with changes of a short duration while at the same time we demand that the future shall be as the present, changeless and unchangeable. Since this need for long-term continuity is essential to our very nature we tend to feel unhappy about the past because it might have contained long-term changes that we would find offensive. Therefore we refer vaguely to "the egg of time" and assume in doing so that this was when the world was born, whole and new—and changeless ever since.

Which is of course nonsense. The moment has now arrived in Yilanè history to declare that history as we have known it is worthless. We could have referred to this present work as new-history, but refrain since this gives an element of credence to the "old-history." We therefore reject all other works of history to this date and declare that there is now only one history. This one.

In creating this history we are grateful for the very few Yilanè with an interest in the sciences of geology and paleontology. We wish to honor these sciences and declare them true ones, just as true as physics or chemistry, and not the subjects of sly laughter as they have been up to now. The past existed, no matter how much we might like to ignore this unpleasant fact. We feel that it is intellectually more courageous to admit it and accept this fact, to admit that the Yilanè did not appear suddenly when the egg of time cracked open. This is the true history and a far more exciting and fulfilling one.

Permit us one more slight divergence before this history begins. We do not intend to go back to the absolute beginning and the birth of prokaryotic life. That story has been unfolded in far greater detail in other works. Our history begins about 270 million years BP (before the present) when the reptiles were already well established in their dominant role on Earth.

At that time there were four main groups of socket-toothed reptiles that are referred to as thecodonts. These primitive creatures were equipped for a life of hunting for their prey in the water. They swam easily by moving their sizeable tails. Some of these thecodonts left the sea and went to the land where their manner of walking proved superior to many other creatures like the proterosuchians, the ancestors of the present-day crocodiles. You have seen the clumsy way that crocodiles walk, with their feet wide-spread, waddling along with their body actually hanging between their legs. Not so the superior thecodonts who thrust their entire limbs down and back with an upright stride.

Since the history of those days is written only in rocks, in the fossils preserved there, we find many gaps. While the details to fill these gaps may not be present, the overall record is still amazingly clear. Our remote ancestors were creatures called mososaurs, marine lizards of a very successful nature. They were specialized for their life in the sea with a tail fin, while their limbs had modified into flippers. One particular form of mososaur was *Tylosaurus*, a large and handsome creature. Large, in that the *Tylosaurus* were greater in length than six Yilanè. Handsome in that they resembled the Yilanè in many ways. The reason for this is that they were our direct ancestors.

If we place a representation of the skeleton of a modern Yilanè beside the skeleton of a *Tylosaurus* the relationship is immediately obvious. The digits of the limbs, hidden by the superficial flesh of the fins, reveal four fingers and four toes. So now we have two fingers on each hand and two opposed thumbs. The tail is our tail, suitably shortened. The resemblance is also clear in the rib

cage, a flowing wave of ribs from clavicle to pelvic girdle.
Look at these two similar skeletons and you see past and
present, side by side. There we are, developed and modified to dwell on land. There is our true history, not some
vague statement about appearing from the egg of time.
We are the descendants of these noble creatures who
some 40 million years ago became the Yilanè.

THE EARLY YEARS

Much of what follows is of necessity guesswork. But it is
appropriate guesswork that fits the facts of the fossil records, not airy-fairy flights of fancy such as imaginary giant
meteors. The record in the rocks is there to be read. We
simply assemble the parts and fit them together, just as
you might reassemble the broken pieces of an eggshell.

If you wish to assemble all of the pieces yourself, then
consult the relevant geological and paleontological texts.
In them you will discover the origin of species, how earlier species are modified to become later ones, you will
find revealed the history of the various ice ages, the phe-
nomenon of continental drift, even the record sealed in
rock that the magnetic pole was not always to the south,
the way it is now, but has varied between north and south
through the geological ages. You could do all of this for
yourself—or you can be satisfied with our description in
abbreviated form.

See then the world as it must have been 40 million
years BP when the first simple and happy Yilanè roamed
the Earth. It was a wetter and warmer world, with all the
food they needed there for the taking. Then, as now, the
Yilanè were carnivores, feasting on the flesh of the creatures that filled the land and the sea. The young, then as
now, gathered in efenburu in the sea and worked together
and ate well. What happened when they emerged on land
is not clear in the geological record and we can only guess.

Having learned cooperation in the sea, the Yilanè certainly would not lose it when they emerged from the

ocean and walked on solid ground. Then, as now, the
males were surely the same simple, kindly creatures and
would have needed protection. Then, as now, the beaches
would have been guarded while the males were torpid,
the eggs growing. Food was plentiful, life was good. Surely
this was the true egg of time, not the imaginary one, when
life was simple and serene.

In that early existence can be found the seeds of Yilanè
science as we know it today. It can be seen in the Wall of
Thorns here in this city. To defend the males, large crustacea
were seized and brandished at predators, their claws a
powerful defense. The bigger the claws, the more powerful the defense, so the largest would have been selected.
At the same time the strongest and most offensive corals
would have been chosen to defend the beaches from the
seaward side. The first, crude steps along the road to the
advanced biological science we now know would have
been mastered.

But this simple existence was doomed to end. As successful Yilanè grew strong and filled the Earth they would
have outgrown that first city on the edge of that ancient
sea. Another city would have grown, another and another.
When food shortages threatened the logical thing would
have been to wall in fields and raise food animals and
guard them from predators.

In doing this the Yilanè proved their superiority to the
inferior life forms. Look at Tyrannosaurus, a carnivore just
as we are carnivores. Yet these giant, stupid creatures can
only pursue with violence, tear down their prey, waste
most of the good meat on its carcass. They think never of
tomorrow, they neither tend herds nor do they cull. They
are witless destroyers. The superior Yilanè are intelligent
preservers. To a scientist all life forms are equal. To
destroy a species is to destroy our own species. Our respect for life can be seen in the manifold beasts in our
fields, species that would have vanished millennia ago had
it not been for our efforts. We are builders, not destroyers, preservers not consumers. It is obvious when these

facts are considered why we are the dominant species on this planet. It is no accident, it is only the logical end product of circumstance.

PHYSIOLOGY

In order to understand our own physiology we must first consider the physiology of other animals. Simple creatures, like most insects, are poikilothermic. That is they are at one with their environment, their body temperatures the same as the ambient air temperature. While this suffices on a small scale, more complex organisms require regularization of body temperature. These animals are homeothermic, that is they have a body temperature that is relatively constant and mostly independent of the temperature of the environment. The Yilanè belong to the kind of animals that are warm blooded and exothermic. All of the important animals in the world are exothermic since this way of controlling body temperature is far superior to that used by the ustuzou who must expend energy continually in order to maintain the same body temperature at all times.

We are one with our environment, utilizing the natural temperature differences to maintain the consistency of our own body temperatures. After a cool night we seek the sun; if we grow too warm we face into the breeze, expose less of our bodies to the sun, erect our crests or even seek the shade. We do this so automatically that we are no more aware of regulating our internal temperature than we are of breathing.

There are many other ways that our physiology is superior to that of the endothermic ustuzou. Not for us their endless search for food to feed the ravening cells. Our metabolism changes to suit the circumstance. As an example, on long voyages by uruketo we can simply slow down our bodily processes. Subjective time then passes quickly, while each individual will require less food.

An even more striking example of physiological superiority, unique to the Yilanè, is the inseparable relationship
of our metabolism to our culture; we are our city, our city
is us. One cannot live without the other. This is proven
by the irreversible physiological change that takes place, in
the very rare instances, when an individual transgresses the
rule of law, does that which is inadmissible by Yilanè
propriety. No external physical violence is needed to pe-
nalize the errant individual. Justice is there within her
body. The Eistaa, the embodiment of the city, our culture
and our rule of law, has only to order the errant individual
to leave the city while also depriving this same individual of her name. Thus rightly rejected the errant individual
suffers the irreversible physiological change that ends only
with her death.

The mechanism is hormonal, using prolactin which
normally regulates our metabolism and our sexual behavior. However when an errant individual is forcefully reminded of transgression her hypothalamus overloads and
she enters a continuous but unbalanced physiological state.
In our ancestors this was a survival factor that caused
hibernation. However, in our present evolved state, the
reaction is inevitably fatal.

DIET

It has been said that if you look into a creature's mouth
you will know what she eats. Dentition denotes diet. A
nenitesk has flat-topped, square teeth for grinding up the
immense amounts of vegetable matter it must eat, with
sharper-edged teeth in the front for cutting and tearing its
food loose. The neat, attractive rows of cone-shaped teeth
in our jaws denote our healthy and carnivorous fish-eating
diet. The thickness and strength of our jaws indicate that
molluscs once played a large part in our ancestors' diet for
we did—and still can—crush the shells of these tasty
creatures with our teeth.

REPRODUCTION

There are certain things that Yilanè do not talk about, and this is right and proper in a well-ordered society. When we are young and in the sea life is endless pleasure. This pleasure continues when we are fargi; our simple thoughts should not be burdened with subjects too complex to understand.

As Yilanè we not only can consider and discuss any matter, but we must do this if we are to understand the world we live in. The life-cycle of the Yilanè is perfect in its symmetry and we begin our observation of this circle of life at the time it begins, when the young emerge from father's protection and enter the sea.

This is the beginning of conscious life. Though all of the earliest activities are inborn reflexes—breathing, swimming, gathering in groups—intelligence is already developing. Communication begins, observation, cogitation and conclusion are initiated. Members of the young efenburu learn by observing the older ones.

This is where language begins. There are two main schools of thought about the origin of language among those who make a study of languages. Leaving out the detailed arguments, and phrasing them in a popular way, they might be called the swim-swim and the ping-ping theories. The swim-swim theory postulates that our first attempts at communication are brought about by imitations of other creatures in the sea: that is a movement of the hand and arm in imitation of the swimming movement of a fish would indicate the idea of a fish. On the other hand the ping-ping supporters say that sound came first, the sounds that fish make being imitated. We cannot know, we may never know which of these theories is true. But we can and have watched the young learning to communicate in the open sea.

The elements they use are all of the ones that they will use later, but simplified to a great degree. Basic movements of the limbs, colored indications with the palms, simple sound groupings. These suffice to join the members of each efenburu together, to build the strong bonds that will last through life, to teach the importance of mutual aid and cooperation.

Only when they emerge from the sea do the fargi discover that the world can be a difficult place. We may speculate that in distant times, when our race was young, the competition was not as severe. Only when communication in an advanced society became of utmost importance did the individual begin to suffer.

It is a law of nature that the weak fall by the way. The slow fish is eaten by the fast fish and does not breed. The faster fish survive to pass on their genes for swift-swimming. So it is with the Yilanè, for many of the fargi never learn to speak well enough to join the happy intercourse of the city. They are fed, for no Yilanè refuses food to another. But they feel insecure, unwanted, unsure of themselves as they watch others of their efenburu succeed in speaking to join in the busy life of the city. Dispirited they fish for their own food in the sea, wander away, are seen no more. We can feel for them, but we cannot help them. It is a law of nature that the weak shall fall by the way.

It goes without saying that of course these self-chosen rejects are all female. As we know all of the males are sought out and cherished the moment that they emerge from the ocean. Doomed would be the culture that allowed these simple, sweet, unthinking creatures to perish! Wet from the ocean they are brought to the hanalè to lead the life of comfort and ease which is their due. Fed and protected they live happy lives, looking forward only to the day when they can perform the ultimate service of preserving their race.

WARNING

What follows may be too explicit for some to absorb. Details may offend those of too delicate sensibilities. Since the authors of this study wish only to inform, anyone who feels they would not be happy with material of this sort should read only the following paragraph, then skip ahead to the section labeled Science.

There is a process within *reproduction* whereby a small portion of male tissue, called a sperm, is united with a small portion of female tissue, called an ovum. This ovum becomes an egg, and the male carries the egg in a special sac. When carrying the egg, and keeping it warm and comfy, the male gets very fat and happy and sleepy. One day the egg hatches and a lovely youngster goes into the sea, and that is all there is to it.

DETAILS OF A POSSIBLY OFFENSIVE NATURE

The union of the sperm and the ovum takes place during a process with the technical term *intercourse*. There follows a description of this event.

A male is brought to a state of excitement by the stimulations of a female. When this happens one or both of the male reproductive organs becomes engorged and emerges from the penis sac at the base of the tail. As soon as this occurs the female mounts the male and receives the penis into her cloaca. At this point mutual stimulation, which need not be described, causes the male to expel a large number of sperm. These specialized organisms find and unite with ova inside the female body to produce fertilized eggs.

With the sperm is also released a prostaglandin that produces a reaction within the female body that produces rigidity in the limbs, among other things, that prolongs the sexual union for a lengthy time, a good portion of the day. (Intercourse without production of the hormone is technically named a *perversion* and will not be discussed here.) During this period the fertilized eggs quickly develop and grow, until they are extruded into the male's pouch.

The female's part is now finished, her vital role fulfilled, and responsibility for the continuation of the Yilanè race now becomes that of the male. The fertilized egg now contains the genes of both male and female. The implanted eggs now grow placentas and increase in size as they draw sustenance; for this to occur major changes happen in the male body. There is first the urge to return to the sea, the warm sea, and this is done within two days, since a stable temperature is needed for the maturing eggs. Once on the beach and in the sea the male enjoys a physiological change, growing torpid and slow, sleeping most of the time. This state remains until the eggs hatch and the young are born and enter the sea.

It should be mentioned, though it has no bearing upon the continuation of our species, that a few males die on the beaches each year as their bodies resist the metabolic change back to their normal condition. But since this only affects males it is of no importance.

Thus the life-cycle of the Yilanè begins anew.

SCIENCE

There are many sciences, each a specialized system of study, too detailed to go into in this brief history. Those interested can consult specialized works that deal with Chromosome Surgery, Chemistry, Geology, Physics, Astronomy, etc. Note will only be taken here of Genetic Engineering and Mathematics.

Like all else in Yilanè history the true history of our biological development is lost in the mists of time. We can, however, make some logical assumptions that explain the facts as we know them now. With patience enough—and time enough—any biological problem can be solved. In the beginning it can be assumed that crude breeding was the only technique that was used. As time passed, and greater interest evolved in how reproduction actually took place, research into gene structure would have begun. The first real breakthrough would have been when the researchers succeeded in crystallizing the genome, that is bringing about evolutionary stasis. Only when we can stop evolution can we begin to understand it.

At this point the uninformed reader may be puzzled and might be inclined to ask—how does one stop evolution and make genetic changes? The answer is not a simple one and in order to answer it we must begin at the beginning.

In order to understand Genetic Engineering some knowledge of the biological makeup of life on this planet must be considered. Organisms exist as two grades. The simplest are the prokaryotes, ordinary bacteria, blue-green bacteria, blue-green algae, viruses and so on. The other larger and more complex life forms, the eukaryotes, will be considered in a moment. First let us look at the prokaryotes.

All of these have their genetic material as rings of DNA, or RNA in some viruses. These tiny organisms seem to be economizing on their genetic material because many of these coding regions overlap. They possess special DNA sequences between genes for at least two purposes. Firstly, there is the control of gene function, such as the turning off of gene transcription by the products of the coded enzyme in operons, and for providing sequences recognized by transcription or replication enzymes. Secondly, there are DNA sequences that incorporate the DNA between them into other strands of DNA. (Examples would be into a host bacterium, for a plasmid or a bacteriophage, or a host eukaryote cell for a virus.) There are bacteria that produce a few enzymes which actually snip or join DNA by recognizing specific sequences for snipping or joining between two nucleotides. By using these enzymes it is possible to determine the sequence of DNA lengths. This is done by digesting them sequentially with enzymes which recognize the different sequences. Then each mixture of shorter resultant sequences is analyzed with other enzymes.

This is a lengthy process requiring millions of tries. But then Yilanè patience is infinite and we have had millions of years to develop the process. In order to recognize particular sequences radioactive DNA or RNA messengers are attached specifically with base complementation along their length. Afterwards special enzymes are used to remove a specific length and insert it into another organism's DNA ring.

This is the way that bacterial DNA rings are modified. Firstly by the use of plasmids, natural bacterial 'sex' sequences. Secondly by phages, viruses that naturally attack bacteria. And thirdly by using cosmids, artificial DNA circles with special joining sequences, any of which can be tailored to include new or modified genes, so that the modified bacteria can make new proteins.

So it can be seen that it is relatively easy to change the protein chemistry of bacteria, simple eukaryotes such as yeast, and to reprogram other eukaryotic cells in a similar simple manner.

It is much more complicated to produce desired changes in the larger eukaryotic animals. In these creatures the egg itself is programmed in the mother's ovary, where it builds upon itself in the foundation of the embryo's development. Only after completion of this embryonic structure does each cell produce proteins that change the cell itself, as well as other nearby cells, in a process that finally results in the juvenile organism. How this process has been mastered and altered is too complex to go into in this curtailed discussion. There are other facets of Yilanè science that have to be considered.

Mathematics must be discussed since many Yilanè have heard of this, and since all of the sciences employ it, though they will not have run across it at other times. The following explanation, although brief, is accurate.

The science of Mathematics is based upon numbers. If you wish to understand numbers spread your hands out before you, palms down, and inner thumbs touching. Wriggle your outside thumb on the right. That is called number one. Now moving one finger at a time from right to left, the adjacent finger is two, the next finger three, the inner thumb four. Left inside thumb five, fingers six and seven, and finally the outside thumb on the left is ten. Ten is also called base, a technical term that we will not go into here. It is enough to know that numbering starts over again after the base is reached, ten-and-one, ten-and-two, right up to two-times-ten. There is no limit to the number of multiples of ten that you can have. That is why numbers are so important in the sciences where things are weighed, measured, recorded, counted, etc. Mathematics itself is very simple, just a recording of things that are bigger than things, smaller than other things, equal or not equal to other things.

The origin of mathematics is lost in time. Although mathematicians themselves believe that the base ten was chosen because we have ten fingers. They say that any number may be chosen as a base, though this seems highly unlikely. If we took two for a base then 2 would be 10, $3 = 11$, then on with $4 = 100$, $5 = 101$, $6 = 110$ and so on. Very clumsy and impractical and of no real use. It has even been suggested that if ustuzou could count, a singularly wild idea in any case, that their base 10 would be our 12. All our numbers would change as well; the 40 million years of Yilanè existence would shrink to a mere 32 million years. You can see where such unwise speculation might lead so it is best we abandon such unhealthy theorizing.

CULTURE

We have had to introduce a number of new terms in this history, and *culture* is another one. It might be defined as the sum total of the way we live as it is transmitted down through the ages. We can assume that our culture had historical beginnings, though we cannot possibly imagine what they might have been. All we can do is describe our existence now.

Every Yilanè has her city, for Yilanè life revolves around the city. When we emerge from the sea we can only look on in speechless awe at the beauty and symmetry of our city. We go there as fargi and are taken in and fed. We listen and learn from others. We watch and learn. When we can speak we offer our services and are treated kindly. We see all the manifold life of the city and are drawn to one part or another. Some of us serve humbly and well with the herds and in the slaughterhouses. All Yilanè who read this should remember that service is not only in the sciences and the studies that you do; it is in service and all Yilanè are equal in that.

As a city is built in rings, with fields and animals outermost, the living city next, the birth beaches and the ambesed at the heart of it, so also is our culture built. The large circle of fargi outermost. Within them the assistants and the trained laborers in the various specialities. They in turn circle about the scientists, the supervisors, the builders—all those at the peak of their learned skills. They in turn look to the city leaders, and all look to the Eistaa who rules. It is logical, simple, complete, the only possible culture to have.

This is the world of the Yilanè. It has been this way since the egg of time, and will go on forever. Where there are Yilanè there is Yilanè rule and law and all are happy.

At the two poles of our globe there is great cold and discomfort and Yilanè are too wise to penetrate these places. But only recently it has been discovered that there are comfortable places in this world where there are no Yilanè. We owe it to ourselves and to the world to fill these empty spaces. Some of these places contain ustuzou, unpleasant ustuzou. In the interests of science we must examine these creatures. Most readers will close this volume now since they have no interest in such matters. Therefore what follows in the section beginning on this page is for those with specialized interests.

When discussing unpleasant matters it must be mentioned that monolithic as the Yilanè culture may seem, it must of course encompass minor variations. And, it must be said, schisms as well. For the student who wishes to know all of the details of the world and existence, no matter how repugnant, there follows a description of a belief based upon the thoughts of a Yilanè named Ugunenapsa, also called Farneskei for obvious reasons. It is advised that these thoughts should not be seen by the young and the impressionable.

It must also be emphasized quite strongly that the publication of these writings is in no way an endorsement of them.

THE EIGHT PRINCIPLES OF UGUNENAPSA

ONE
We exist between the Thumbs of the Spirit of Life which is named Efeneleiaa.

All principles spring from this singular and most significant insight: Yilanè and all other living creatures live between the Thumbs of the Spirit of Life. This insight came to me as a revelation, that is it was something that was always there, existing since the Egg of Time, that once seen was evident and obviously true. But the study that led to the insight, that was a revelation, took many years of study, much stern thought, even more extensive questioning and seeking of answers. During these years my quest took me through all of the principles of all of our fields of knowledge. In doing this my mind was stretched to its limits before attaining success. Until what has always existed was seen at last.

First I saw that the Spirit of Life must be within me, for I was alive. If it was within me, therefore it must be within all other Yilanè as well. With this comprehension came the final and complete understanding that all other living creatures also exist as well between the Thumbs of the Spirit. Most creatures do not have the capacity to comprehend the reality of their own existence; most Yilanè as well. They will not search out this knowledge. Only those Seekers for Understanding do begin to understand, and when they do they become Daughters of Life. In all of existence they are the only ones who are willing to realize or recognize this truth.

From this basic principle, this truth, many implications follow. Only some of these have I been able to consider and understand. Of these I include only the most general here. It will be seen that all of the other insights I have labored to comprehend and to teach and share with others, all of them follow from this single revealed foundation, this root source, this well of truth from which all that follows draws strength. I liken this truth to the cherished seed from which springs the tree that will be the city. My seed of truth, like the city's seed, grows a great taproot into the earth, then a mighty trunk into the sky. From which grow many branches that are insights that encompass the world of living things. This image constructs and embodies my second principle.

TWO
We all dwell in the City of Life.

When this has been stated there instantly appears the implication that this principle may be a threat to our traditional Yilanè way of life. This implication can only be explored when we understand completely an earlier, older, greater tradition; that we are all citizens of one great world-encompassing city; the City of Life.

Consider this. As full citizens of this greater City we are equally members of the City, so if equally members we are then equal in value, equal in worth. Rank and rule are now seen as being different from our traditional order of ruler and ruled. Equality becomes based upon our mutual citizenship in Life and not upon political, social or linguistic skills that normally determine our daily order. The eistaa of a city and the fargi still wet from the sea are both equal citizens in this larger City of Life. They will each be equally sustained, valued, enriched in direct proportion to the degree of realization and acceptance each achieves of this true order of life.

The basic truth of this observation may be seen in, and explained by, the Yilanè respect for all other species, our unstinting efforts to aid species that are threatened and to preserve the continuity of all species. We do this although we are unaware of the underlying principle upon which all of our actions and inclinations are based. It must be mentioned that even our greatest scientists, those who have manipulated life forms, changing and adapting them for our comfort and pragmatic benefits, even they have not seen the permeating principle of this shared citizenship in the great City of Life.

It has also, unfortunately, remained hidden from even our best and most powerful eistaa. Although they have the power of ordering and control, life and death, they still have not seen the underlying principle from which their own power flows. It may also be unhappily said that many a strong eistaa by placing herself above this greater power has demanded an allegiance to herself that contradicts the greater citizenship that we all share. Although this may be caused by selfishness and the urge for absolute control, it is basically an unknowing lack of knowledge of the hidden truth.

THREE

The Spirit of Life, Efeneleiaa, is the supreme Eistaa of the City of Life and we are citizens and beings in this city.

Efeneleiaa's benevolence sustains our lives and the provenance of living. This rich luminescence enlightens us. To understand and know this Spirit of Life is to find meaning of self, through allegiance to Life and through kinship with all living things. Her qualities of sedate affirmation of life enable us to endure when death strikes those around us who do not know of her and her Way. We who know then come to see ourselves differently, apart from the unknowing, and see our lives and the lives of others in a totally different manner.

FOUR

*When we know the Greater Truth we are possessed
of a new strength, for we then have a greater and
higher center of identity and loyalty.*

Knowing this truth bestows upon us a power and focus
of life that others do not possess. The knowledge that we
are Citizens of Life provides the causality for us to join
together as Daughters of Life. Although we live as other
Yilanè do in cities, and acknowledge the rule of the eistaa
just as others do, we live there in the knowledge that our
ultimate allegiance is pledged to the Spirit of Life. We are
then embued with a greater sense of allegiance to a greater
eistaa that goes far beyond the realm of the eistaa of our
city. We serve the eistaa of the lesser city and are loyal to
her. But only as long as she does not command us to
violate the Principles of Life. If this should happen then
we must reject her commands and obey the greater commands of Efeneleiaa.

This higher allegiance to a superior center of loyalty by
one who truly understands the meaning of Efeneleiaa
enables the believer to continue affirming life, by living,
when the eistaa's wrath is turned upon her. This is a
positive and not a negative act, for dying is the negation of
living. It is the eistaa who orders death who has violated
the Principles of Life. So what the eistaa sees as a defiance
of authority is in reality an obedience to a higher authority.
The opposite is also true: if we violate Efeneleiaa's principles
we die—even though an eistaa orders us to live on.

FIVE

*The power to know The Truth requires a new
vision of the mind. This vision enables the viewer
to look at those things seen by all living beings,
but to look beyond the surface to the unseen but
present true order of existence.*

Conscious awareness of the True Order of things enables us to identify with and give our allegiance to the

Spirit of Life. This new vision, however, cannot be acquired without a major effort. It calls for a strict discipline of the mind, a conscious developing of the powers of the mind until the ability is realized to see in all things a pattern of a higher order. To be aware of this order in which all living things exist and become fulfilled.

There may be other paths that lead to the truth. If they exist I have not found them yet. But I have set my feet upon this path that has carried me through the barrier of seeing in the same manner as all others see. Now I behold reality in a different and enlightened way. I found this path by asking questions about the seemingly normal and obvious. But these were questions that Yilanè do not normally ask. I wanted to know why we are as we are. I wanted to know why we live as we do, follow the rules of existence as we do, relate one to the other as we do. I wanted to know why the eistaa is above and the fargi below. I wanted to know why we continually follow ways that are familiar and comfortable. Through our knowledge of all the sciences we modify all of the existing life-forms to meet our short-term needs. Yet we never consider modifying ourselves. For Yilanè want only stability and order for Yilanè. Tomorrow's tomorrow will be as yesterday's yesterday. We accept this way unquestioningly, so much so that even asking about it is seen as a threat.

Therefore I sought the fundamental facts of our existence and questioned them. But when I did I received only pragmatic answers. Answers such as when this certain thing is done that certain thing will result. But this is an observation and not a reason. The most basic and most important questions about our lives were never asked. Not only were they not asked, they were never even considered. Although all of life is taken under observation and shown to be mutable, our own existence as Yilanè was considered to be an exception. Yet this is impossible since we are one with all other life.

Seeing this and understanding this I took the process

of asking questions, then seeking the true answers, as my model of mental discipline and mind development. My first consideration was the most important consideration of all: life and death. Yilanè live and die as all creatures live and die. With a single major exception. A Yilanè abolished from her city by her eistaa will fall and die without a blow being struck. Yet this same Yilanè when obeying a benevolent order by her eistaa to leave the city, and then return, will not die. Why? What is the special control over life and death that the eistaa have? What could it be?

It could not be physical, for only communication is exchanged. But it had to be something shared by all Yilanè. Could it be that there is a higher or more basic force, invisible, unseen, yet universal? If so, what must this force be like? Is it unique to Yilanè or is it a force that unites all forms of life, even though we have never sought for it or attempted to examine it before? Is there a unity of some kind on which all depends, something that all forms of life have in common that is much more significant than our apparent differences? If one could know such a source, become consciously aware of it, would one not then become better able to affirm life and the strength of life, and thus be better able to understand the reality behind or within the various appearances of everyday life, existence and struggle?

SIX

There is an Order of Interdependence within and sustaining all living things, an Order that is more than those living things themselves, but also an Order in which all living things participate, knowingly or unknowingly—an Order that has existed since the Egg of Time.

With the new vision of mind, we see the Order of Interdependence of all things. When seen in its entirety and observed to be functioning correctly, this Order is a coordinated totality of parts functioning in harmonious relativity.

In this harmonious relationship within the Order, competition occurs only as the result of ignorance of the complexity of interrelationships, as well as from seeing only a part of the totality and one's self as a distinct, separate part—as if one were the whole and independent of others and other parts. In all truth, in this interdependent order, one's own worth is achieved and realized by helping others to realize their own worth.

The worth of self must be understood and realized in relation to the whole. This provides for and fosters self-affirmation as the appropriate good, but a self-affirmation of Life wherein one affirms self as part of the whole, which is the Way of Life. This is quite different from, and moves well beyond, the egoism of an eistaa and the pragmatism of Yilanè cities. It is more like the warm relationship of efenselè within the seaborne efenburu, where such peaceful cooperation and harmony seem natural. But it is natural and without conscious consideration. Though unremarked until now this Order has existed since the Egg of Time.

We can know this Order and understand it because there is a correlation of rational order between the workings of the developed mind and the order of all things in the domain of the Spirit of Life. The laws of our nature are part of the pervasive order of the Way of Life. It is an illusion to think of personal uniqueness in the sense of individual isolation. Each individual is equal in being part of the whole. Individuality is real, but individuality only within the equality in belonging to the City of Life, being part of that city as a Yilanè is part of a physical city, not as separated entities. Our minds are limited instances of the Spirit of Life as expressed through thought; our bodies are instances of the Spirit of Life as expressed through extension; our lives are instances of the Spirit of Life as expressed through affirmation of life.

Insofar as we understand these interrelationships of minds to minds, of bodies to bodies, of lives to lives, our

minds are enlarged and in this way lose their limitations
and the restrictions manifested when we tend to consider
them uniquely ours. By knowing and understanding this
Order and living in accord with it, we become affirmers of
that Order and of life.

SEVEN

*Daughters of Life are enabled and obligated, by
the recognition and understanding of that Order
and in loyalty to the Spirit of Life, to live for
peace and affirmation of life.*

Once seen, known and understood, the newness,
strangeness and beauty of this Way and Order of Life and
of Efeneleiaa may tempt us to suspend our activities and
reside only in meditation or ecstatic enthrallment of the
vision. Thus did I live until I became aware of the dangers
of this isolation. For to do this only would be to overlook
and ignore the way that each of us can benefit self and
others and fulfill self and whole. This may be accomplished by working peacefully with others in cooperative
harmony to affirm Life.

Since the whole operates better when all parts consciously operate together for the affirmation of the whole
which is the reaffirmation of the parts, all Daughters of
Life—we who know and understand the Way and Order—
by the very fact of our awareness, also have an obligation
to spread this knowledge of Life and the Spirit of Life to
others. Efeneleiaa's way is the way of harmony, the way of
peace and cooperation among all citizens of her City.

EIGHT

*Daughters of Life bear the responsibility to help
all others to know the Spirit of Life and the Truth
of the Way of Life.*

We who know the Way must help others to learn and
understand, to consciously follow the Spirit of Life. How-

ever when this truth is stated two immensely important questions arise. Firstly, how can we do this in the face of those who will our deaths? Secondly, how can we maintain the peace and harmony that affirms while we continue to live by causing death? Must we cease to eat to avoid killing that which nourishes us?

Firstly, just as every day has two parts, a dark side and a bright side, so do we have two opposed forces dwelling within us. The darkness of the will to death and the brightness of the will to life. So even those who hate us the most have within them the will of life as well, and this is in accord with Efeneleiaa. Our affirmation of life will change those who live in affirmation of death, just as this knowledge changed us.

The answer to the second is that if we do not eat we will die. We sit at the summit of a great vine of interrelated life that begins with insensate plants, continues up through more complex forms of plants to the herbivores to the carnivores, to us. It appears ordained that each cell in this vine of life must exist to nourish the cell above that culminates in Yilanè, then in us, the only part of the vine to understand the totality of it. Therefore there is no act of killing or of death but only the act of nourishing. Taking the life of an animal or fish for food is not the negation of life but a form of the affirmation of life. That life contributes to sustaining another life and thus becomes a way of strengthening life. So it is and so it has been with all life forms in the sea, on land and in the air since the Egg of Time.

Yet to take life needlessly, or to kill for reasons other than the need for food, is the negation of life, the violation of the Way of Life and an offense to the Spirit of Life. It is to avoid such violation and negation that the Daughters of the City of Life must follow this Way and teach others to follow the Way of harmony and peace and the affirmation of Life—for Peace is the Way of Life that reigns in the domain of the Spirit of Life.

Translator's Note
Here the translation from the Yilanè ends. For some understanding of the complex—and fascinating—problems that face the translator working with this unusual language please see the following section.

LANGUAGE

Slow development, for millions of years, has created a rich and complex language. So complex in fact that many never manage to master it and never become Yilanè. This cultural handicap separates the race into two subgroups, one of which, barred from the life in the cities, remains in a feral state, living off the life in the sea for the most part. Not breeding because of their inability to protect the torpid males from predators. Their loss means that the gene pool of the species is slowly being altered, but the process is a glacially slow one.

The Yilanè speak in a linked chain of gestalts, with each gestalt containing one to four concepts. Each gestalt also has a control sign which is indicated by a stylized body posture or movement that has some relationship to the overall meaning. These gestalts are rarely the same because they have so many possible combinations, approximately 125,000,000,000.

Any attempts to transcribe Yilanè in English presents formidable problems. Firstly the control signs, the stylized body positions, have to be considered. An incomplete listing, with stylized transcription symbols, follows:

Hunch	↑	Star	*	Whirl	+
Cower	↗	Climb	ꓒ	Sway	↓
Stoop	ꓩ	Fall	↗	Shake	ꓕ
Stretch	Y	Lift	ꓭ	Reach[1]	ꓸ

Diamond	φ	Leap	⊣	Reach[2]	⫤
Squat	h	Rise	�	Sit	⟨
Lie	⊢⊣	Push	⅄	Neutral	⊥
Embrace	⅄	Swim	∼	Tailsweep (clockwise)	⟫
Bask	×	Plunge	⟨	Tailsweep (anticlock)	⟨

The sounds of Yilanè approximate those of humans, but for a basic understanding it is not necessary to consider all the differences. However, in English transcriptions zh is the sound in rouge, x the ch in loch. Th and dh are rarely used. There are four extra sigils denoting sounds particular to Yilanè. They are ' (glottal stop), < (tock), ! (click), and * (smack of lips).

The richness of the language and the difficulty of accurate transcription can be seen in the translation of the following expression:

> To leave father's love and enter the embrace of the sea is the first pain of life—the first joy is the comrades who join you there.

First the kernel string of gestalts, each one with a separate controller, numbered C1 to C12 for ease of reference:

C1 (×) enge

C2 (⊢⊣) han.natè. ihei

C3 (⅄) aga.ptè

C4 (⟨) embo.[1] *kè.[2] ka<

C5 (⟨) igi. rubu. shei[3]

C6 (∼) kakh.shei. sèsè

C7 (⌐) *hè. awa. ihei*
//[4]

C8 (✦) *hè. vai<. ihei*

C9 (∼) *kakh. shei. intè*

C10 (Y) *end. pelei. uu*

C11 (∼) *asak. hen*

C12 (⌐) *enge*

(1) At this point Circumambience is also suggested by rotation of the tail tip.
(2) Warmth also suggested by movement of jaw muscles as if to gape.
(3) Note that units 4 and 5 are linked by controllers, 3 and 5 by paired opposite concepts at the start.
(4) The Yilanè pauses here and repeats gestalts in reverse order to form a deliberate balance or chiasmus.

A literal translation of this, with the definition of the control signs in brackets, reads as follows:

C1	(Bask)	Love
C2	(Lie)	Maleness. Friend. Senses of Touch/Smell/Feel
C3	(Push)	Departure. Self
C4	(Fall)	Pressure. Stickiness. Cessation
C5	(Fall)	Entry. Weightlessness. Cold
C6	(Swim)	Salt. Cold. Motion
C7	(Cower)	Numeral 1. Pain. Senses of Touch/Smell/Feel
C8	(Star)	Numeral 1. Joy. Senses of Touch/Smell/Feel
C9	(Swim)	Salt. Cold. Hunt
C10	(Stretch)	Vision. Discovery. Increase
C11	(Swim)	Beach. Male/Female
C12	(Reach)	Love.

A broad transcription of this would be:

> *Enge hantèhei, agatè embokèka iirubushei kak-
> sheisè, hèawahei; hèvai'ihei, kaksheintè, enpeleiuu
> asahen enge.*

The most accurate translation into English would be in
verse, but barring that this is an approximate translation:

> *The love of your father, to be expelled from it and
> go into the cold unloving sea, that is the first pain
> of life: the first joy of life (in that cold hunting
> ground) is to come upon your friends and feel
> their love close round you.*

The basic differences between human language and
Yilanè are so great as to be almost insurmountable for
someone attempting to learn Yilanè. Human beings, talking to each other in different languages, start by picking
things up and naming them. Rock . . . wood . . . leaf.
After some understanding they go on to actions: "Throw
the rock, pick up the leaf."

This just cannot happen with the Yilanè. They do not
name things but describe them. Instead of the noun "chair"
they would say "Small wood to sit on." Where we would
use a single noun, "door," the Yilanè would have different
constructions. "Entry to a warm place." From the other
side it might be "Exit to a cold place."

You will find an example of this in volume one of the
West of Eden trilogy. Enge attempts to teach the young
Tanu girl, Ysel, to speak in the correct Yilanè manner.
The basic concepts always elude her. She manages to
memorize a few words and has some slight idea of the use
of controllers. When Vaintè attempts to talk to her the
exchange goes like this:

Vaintè says: (✱) esekapen (↑) yidshepen (Y)
yileibesat (Y) efenduuruu (↑) yilsatuu (✱) yilsatefen

Which can be translated as: (Star) top-demand (Hunch)
this-one-speaking-demand (Stretch) speech-difficulty-equality

(Stretch) life-continuation-increase (Hunch) speech-equality-increase (Star) speech-equality-life

"I personally demand it most urgently! Speak, please, as well as one of the Yileibe. This way you will keep on living and growing. Speech means growth—please! Speech means life—understand!"

The best that Ysel can do is say, "has leibe ènè uu." She thinks that she is saying "I find it hard to talk, please." What comes out, however, fatally for her, is more like "female—age/entropy—suppleness—increase." The mistakes she has made are:

(1) *has* does not mean "I," but "female." The confusion was caused by Enge pointing to herself when she said it.

(2) *leibe* does indeed signify "difficult"—if it is said with a controller that implies some degree of constraint, for instance "Hunch," "Stoop," or "Squat." Without this the meaning edges towards *age*, that is the process of something running down, not only Yilanè.

(3) *ènè* does not mean *talk* at all, but indicates suppleness since the Yilanè associate these ideas very often.

(4) *uu* is a common termination used by Enge in her lessons for encouragement. But it signifies concepts like "growth, go on, try." It does not mean *please*.

Since Ysel has no tail she cannot make the cower gesture correctly. In addition she makes the fatal mistake of imitating Vaintè's last posture, the Star, that of threatening dominance. So Vaintè thinks that Ysel was saying something like "The old female grows adroit," or possibly even "Growing supple puts years on females." This is nonsense and Vaintè rightly loses her temper, her anger fed by the fact that she was polite to this animal, she may not have cowered but she did hunch as well as star. Ysel's fate is sealed.

By contrast Kerrick comes out with: (⟩) esekakurud (⫶) esekyilshan (Ɪ) elel (Ɪ) leibeleibe

That is he communicates (Cower) top-disgust-cessation
(Lift) top-speech-volition (Neutral) longlong (Neutral)
hardhard

Which Vaintè understands as "I very much don't want
to die. I want very much to talk. (Giving up). Very long,
very hard." At first Vaintè doesn't notice the "cower" for he
has no tail. But she does recognize the "lift" and slowly
realizes what he is trying to say.

TANU

The history of the Earth is written in its stones. While there are still unanswered questions, the overall history of our planet from the Paleozoic Era up to today is recorded in fossil remains. This was the age of ancient life, 605 million years ago, when the only creatures in the warm and shallow seas were worms, jellyfish and other back-boneless animals. The continents then were still joined together in a single large landmass that has been named Pangea.

Even then some of the sea creatures were using lime to build shells for protection and support. The development of internal skeletons came later, with the first fish. Later fish had lungs and lobe-like fins that could be used to support them when they emerged from the sea and ventured onto the land. From these the amphibians developed about 290 million years ago, the ancestors of the first reptiles.

The first dinosaurs appeared on Earth just over 205 million years ago. By the time the first sea-filled cracks were appearing in Pangea 200 million years ago, the dinosaurs had spread all over the world, to every part of the first giant continent that would later separate into the smaller continents we know today. This was their world, where they filled every ecological niche, and their rule was absolute for 135 million years.

It took a worldwide disaster to disturb their dominance. A ten-kilometer-wide meteor that struck the ocean and hurled millions of tons of dust and water high into the atmosphere. The dinosaurs died. Seventy percent of all species then living died. The way was open for the tiny, shrew-like mammals—the ancestors of all mammalian life today—to develop and populate the globe.

It was galactic chance, the dice-game of eternity, that this great piece of rock hit at that time, in that manner, and caused the global disturbance that it did.

But what if it had missed? What if the laws of chance had ruled otherwise and this bomb from space had not hit the Earth? What would the world be like today?

The first and most obvious difference would be the absence of Iceland, for these volcanic islands mark the place where the meteor struck and penetrated to the mantle below.

The second greatest difference would be in the history of global climate, still not completely understood. We know that different ice ages came and went—but we do not know why. We know that the polarity of the Earth has changed in the past, with the north magnetic pole where the south is now—but we do not know why. It seems a certainty that if the meteor had not hit and the incredible atmospheric change had not occurred, that the same progression of ice ages and accompanying continent building would not have occurred in precisely the same manner.

Look at our world as it might have been.

The rule of the dinosaurs is unbroken. The world is theirs and they are dominant on every continent—and the Yilanè rise above them all.

Except in the western hemisphere. Although South America is dominated by reptiles this is not completely true to the north. The land bridge of Central America, that connects North and South America, has been sunk beneath the ocean at different geological times. At one crucial time the break coincided with the spread of the vast sea that covered most of North America. The ice sheet of the glaciers that next came south stretched almost to the edge of this inland sea so that for millions of years the climate was northern, barely temperate in midsummer. The cold-blooded species died out and the warm-blooded species became dominant. They expanded and developed and became the dominant life forms of this landmass.

In time, as the ice sheets withdrew, the mammals expanded north. By the time the land bridge of Central America rose from the sea again the warm-blooded creatures ruled the continent between the oceans. Yet they could not stand against the slow return of the reptiles. There is no defense, other than retreat, from armored creatures weighing 80 tons or more.

Only in the north, in the foothills and the mountains, could the mammals survive. Among them were the New World primates, from whom the Tanu are descended.

There are no Old World mammals here because the Old World is saurian. There are no bears or canines. But the New World deer abound, from small species to immense ones as large as a moose. The mastodons are here as are many marsupials including saber-toothed tigers. Mammalia in rich diversity live in the fertile band south of the ice and north of the cold-blooded saurians.

Most of the Tanu, imprisoned by a harsh environment, have never developed beyond the hunter-gatherer stage. But at this they are immensely successful. There are some exceptions, like the Sasku, who have moved on to a stable existence of neolithic farming. They have developed the settled skills of pottery and weaving, as well as a more complex and stratified society. But this does not mean that they are superior in any way to the hunting Tanu who have a rich language, simple art forms, many survival skills and a basic family group relationship.

The same might be said of the Paramutan who occupy a perilous ecological niche in the subarctic. Their skills are manifold, their culture small and communal. They are completely dependent upon the hunt and upon the single marine creature, the ularuaq, for their material existence.

LANGUAGE

Marbak is the language spoken by the sammads. Like the other languages spoken by the Tanu, it is a modern dialect of the lost parent language that has been named Eastern Coastal. In Marbak "man" is *hannas*, the plural *hannasan*. Variations are *hennas* in Wedaman, *hnas* in Levrewasan, *neses* in Lebnaroi, etc.

All of the names of these small tribal groups are descriptive, e.g., Wedaman means "the island ones," Levrewasan "tent-black-ones," that is the people of the black tents. Like man, *hannas*, woman *linga*, plural *lingai*, has widespread similarity. A person, sex not specified, is *ter*, while the plural tanu is generally accepted as referring to all other people.

The most common masculine noun declension is:

	SINGULAR	PLURAL
Nominative	hannas	hannasan
Accusative	hannas	hannasan
Genitive	hannasa	hannasanna
Dative	hannasi	hannasanni
Locative	hannasi	hannasanni
Instrumental	hannasom	hannasom

PARAMUTAN

Like the Tanu, the Paramutan are descended from the New World primates. Although fossil evidence is lacking, gene analysis reveals that Tanu and Paramutan are genealogically quite close and only their great physical separation has prevented inbreeding up until this time. Although superficial resemblance does not seem to bear this out, i.e. the fur-covered Paramutan and the relatively hairless Tanu, it should be noted that both groups have approximately the same number of hair follicles. Many Tanu are born with rudimentary tails, merely an external projection of the coccyx, which contain exactly the same number of bones as the Paramutan tail.

Therefore the obvious physical differences between the groups are of little importance; what is relevant are the social and cultural factors. The Paramutan migrated further north than any of the other primates. We may postulate population pressure from behind or relevant technology that made subarctic existence first a possibility, then a necessity. Their dependence upon a single major source for food, raw materials, existence itself (the ularuaq) allows no other possibility. Their use of north-temperate materials (wood for their boats, oak-tanning of hides) is still important—but the ularuaq is irreplaceable to their existence as their culture is constituted now.

It must be pointed out that Paramutan is a misnomer since this is a Marbak word that means "raw-meat-eaters." The correct term, in their own language, is *Angurpiaq*, meaning "real people," for this is how they see them-

selves. In their solitary existence in the northern wastes
they feel, with some good reason, that they are the
real people, the only people. This is why they call
the Tanu *Erqigdlit*, the fantasy people. Strangers who
come from an unreal world who therefore must be unreal
themselves.

ENVIRONMENT

The Paramutan live in the subarctic because of the abundant food to be found in the ocean. There are many more
living creatures in the sea than on the land—and many
more kinds. Life began in the sea and all of the major
animal groups have many representatives still living there.
The basis of all open ocean productivity is the floating
unicellular algae. These microscopic plants live only in the
top few meters of water where they can obtain energy
from the sun. There are about 600 common kinds of algae
which form the basis of the food chain. They are first eaten
by tiny planktonic animals, the most common of which is
the copepod crustacea of the genus *Calanus*. (The com-
monest animal on Earth—both by numbers and weight.)
These are eaten in turn by larger, shrimp-like crustacea
as well as many other animals including jellyfish, arrow-
worms, baby fish, many larvae of molluscs and squid, as
well as even larger benthic crustacea such as crabs and
lobsters.

The product of all this activity is a slow rain of corpses
and excreta that sinks down to the bacteria on the ocean
bed. The essential nutrients, particularly nitrogen and
potassium produced by the bacteria, are carried away
by the deep-sea currents. This is the primary source of
the abundant life in the polar oceans. Despite the low
temperature and lack of light their productivity is high
and virtually continuous. For the cold is indeed the
source of the ingredients that nourish life. The temperature
of the surface water is a chill four degrees centigrade—

while the warm currents from the south range from five to eight degrees. The warmer water rises through the colder, denser water to feed the abundant life on the surface.

An unusual feature of the ice shelf is the qunguleq that fills an ecological niche that is empty in the world as we know it. The cold eco-system of the qunguleq is unlike any other in the ocean. Rooted in the ice, the great skirt of green tendrils spreads out through the sea, taking nourishment from the water and energy from the sun. This northern meadow is grazed by the ularuaq, the largest living creatures in the world. They tear at the strands with their thick, muscular lips, taking food and life from the qunguleq. They are utterly dependent upon this single food source. With the southerly movement of the arctic ice cap the ocean currents have been changed and emerge further to the west. The ularuaq follow the qunguleq and the Paramutan in turn must follow the ularuaq. Every link in the food chain is dependent upon the link before it.

LANGUAGE

Any student of the Angurpiaq language will quickly discover how few terminal sounds there are. Because of this it may appear superficially simple at first, but greater study will reveal its richness and complexities.

The difficulty for Marbak speakers is that the *k* sound must be distinguished from the *q* sound. The latter is made with the tongue much further back than the *k*. The closest approximation that a non-native speaker might make would be *-rk*.

There are also two distinct forms of *l*, one voiced, the other unvoiced. The unvoiced form is transcribed here as *-dl* or *-tl* to note this important difference.

Linguistic difficulty is not a one-way street. The Angurpiaq have problems with some of the Marbak sounds,

finding them virtually unsayable. For example Armun
emerges as "Arramun" and Harl as "Harral" and so forth.

One of the most interesting things about the structure
of this language is that it consists only of nouns and verbs.
One of these begins every word. However this root term
is open to scores of affixes which then can combine with
even more affixes. In this way sentence-long words are
built up. For example:

> *qingik* a house
> *qingirssuak* a large house
> *qingiliorpoq* he builds a house
> *qingirssualiorpoq* he builds a large house
> *qingirssualiorfilik* a man can build a large house,
>   and so on, apparently without end.

It is very important that the right-branching nature of
this be noted. We are all used to left-branching constructions, such as:

house

a house

a large house

Once one system is used by a native speaker it becomes
"natural" to speak that way and organize language in
this manner, making learning a new order particularly
difficult.

In addition to affixes, nouns and verbs also have suf-
fixes. These are used to mark case, person or mood. Verbs
can be in the Indicative mood, or Interrogative, Subjunc-
tive, Optative, Conjunctive, Infinitive. As an example of
how this functions let us take "like" which in the infinitive
is *alutora*.

> *alutoroq* he likes
> *alutorut* she likes
> *alutorauk* does he like?
> *alutorassuk* do they like?

>*alutorliuk* may he like (Optative)
>*alutorlissuk* may they like
>*alutorpagit* he may like (Subjunctive)
>*alutorpatigik* they may like

Although Marbak and Angurpiaq are not linguistically
related they are structurally related, even if in a mirror-
image fashion. If Armun, for instance, was to use *alutora*
for "like," then point to herself and then to some object
that she likes it would be comprehensible. The Angurpiaq
might consider her stupid for getting the ending wrong,
but they would understand what she was trying to say.
This as opposed to Yilanè where nothing would be understood at all that wasn't expressed within specific and pre-
cise narrow bounds.

One thing that is very imprecise in Angurpiaq is the
sense of time, for they are indifferent time-keepers at the
best. There is a vague form of future tense, but it is rarely
used. The term most often heard is *tamnagok* which can
mean once upon a time, or it can also mean then or
now—or even in a bit. The only other time-related term is
eetchuk which signifies a long *long* time ago. This is so
unspecific that it could mean forty or even two thousand
years.

As is to be expected their language reflects their
physical existence. They mark many distinctions that
do not exist in Marbak, yet completely ignore others.
For obvious reasons there are a number of terms for
snow. They refer to packed snow, powder snow, frozen
snow, wet snow, snow that you can cut blocks from
and even snow that balls underfoot. Yet on the other
hand green and blue are not distinguished as separate
colors. And while red can be told from yellow there is
no separate designation for orange. Since the terms for
these colors are only affixes, never used as words of
their own, there is really no clear sense of their exact
meaning.

It has been theorized that their strong feeling for affixes and innumerable connections and cross-connections may have some relationship with the Angurpiaq deftness and ability to see how mechanical parts fit together. Though it is certainly true that their assembled and tied boat frameworks, their navigational charts, reflect this it must be emphasized that this is a theory only.

DICTIONARIES

YILANÈ–ENGLISH

(Note: this list includes both single elements and some commonly repeated gestalts.)

aa	in
aga	departure
aglè	passage
aka	disgust
akas	growing land
akel	goodness
akse	stone
alak	succession
Alakas-aksehent	Florida Keys
alè	cage
alpè	beauty
ambei	height
ambesed	central meeting place
anat	bodily extremity
ankanaal	land-surrounded ocean
ankè	presence
apen	demand
asak	beach
ast	tooth
asto	movement
awa	pain
ban*	home
buru	circumambience

dee	this
ee	out
eede	that
eesen	flatness
efen	life
efenburu	group formed in childhood
efenselè	member of an efenburu
eisek	mud
eisekol	dredging animal
eiset	responsibility
eistaa	city leader
eksei	caution
elin	small
elinou	small saurian carnivore
embo	pressure
empè	commendation
end	vision
enet	lake
ènè	suppleness
enge	love
enteesenat	plesiosaur
ento	each single
Entoban*<	Africa
erek	speed
esek	top
esekasak	birth-beach guardian
esik	south
espei	posture
estekel*	pterodactyl
eto<	shoot
fafn	catch
far<	inquiry
fargi	one learning to speak
gen	new
Genaglè	Straits of Gibraltar

Gendasi*	North America
gul	hearing
gulawatsan	scream creature
hais	mind
han	maleness
hanalè	male residence
has	female
has	yellowness
hè	numeral 1
hen	male/female
hent	revolution
hèsotsan	dart-firing creature
hornsopa	genetic shape
huruksast	monoclonius
igi	entry
ihei	sense of smell/touch/feel
ineg	old
inlè	large size
intè	hunt
ipol	rub, buff
Isegnet	Mediterranean
isek	north
ka<	cessation
kain	line of sight
kakh	salt
kal	poison
kalkasi	thornbush
kasei	thorn
kem	light
khets	convexity
kiyis	east
kru	short

NB. These two concepts
are always distinguished
by choice of controller.

lan<	copulation
leibe	difficulty
lek	badness
mal	absence of worry
man<	last
Maninlè	Cuba
masinduu	optical projector
melik	dark
melikkasei	poison-thorn vines
natè	friend
nefmakel	bandage-creature
neni	skull
nenitesk	triceratops
nin	absence
ninsè	the unresponsive
nu*	adequacy
okhalakx	herbivore
okol	gut
onetsensast	stegosaurus
pelei	discovery
rubu	weightlessness
ruud	cessation
ruutsa	ankylosaurus
sanduu	microscope
sas<	speed
sat	equality
selè	bondage

sèsè	motion
sete	purpose-orientated group
shak	change
shan	volition
shei	cold
sokèi	cleared land
son*	element
stal	prey
takh	clean
tarakast	mount for riding
tesk	concavity
top	run
tsan	animal
tso	excrement
trumal	a joint attack
tuup	fat, torpid
ugunkshaa	recording creature
umnun	treated meat
unut	crawl
unutakh	hair-eating slug
uruketo	mutated ichthyosaur
uruktop	eight-legged beast of burden
urukub	brontosaurus
ustu	blood
uu	increase
ustuzou	mammalia
yil	speech
yiliebe	incapable of speech

MARBAK–ENGLISH

allas	path
alladjex	shaman
amaratan	immortal ones (divine creatures)
arnwheet	hawk

as	how
atta	father (dim.)
bana	son (dim.)
beka	to knot
benseel	sphagnum moss
bleit	cold
dalas	soup
dalasstar	strong soup
dia	to be
drija	bleed
eghoman	the vowed ones
ekkotaz	nuts & berry paste
elka	to light
erman	sky
Ermanpadar	sky-father, a spirit
es	if
ey	always
fa	to look
falla	to wait
faldar	fire
gentinaz	leader
grunnan	misery
ham, hammar	to be able to (sing., pl.)
hannas	man
hannasan	men
hans	war party
hardalt	squid
harian	joyful ones
hault	twenty (count of a man)
himin	mountain
hoatil	everyone
istak	path

Kargu   mountain people
katisk   cheerful
kell   wedge
kurmar   river
kurro   boss

las   down
levrelag   camping ground
Levrewasan   the black tent people
ley   (burnt) clearing
linga   woman
lingai   women
lissa   to know

madrap   moccasin
mal   good
man   must
margalus   murgu counsellor
mar   hair
marag   cold-blooded animal
marin   star
markiz   winter
marsk   ichthyosaur
mensa   to arrange
modia   maybe
mo trig   my child
murgu   plural of marag

nat   killer
naudinz   hunter
nenitesk   triceratops
nep   long

parad   ford
Paramutan   raw-meat-eaters, northern people

rath   hot

sammad	mixed male/female band
sammadar	elected head of the sammad
sassi	few
sia	to go
skerm	period of time
so	as, that, who
stakkiz	summer
stessi	beach
tais	grain
tanu	people
tarril	brother
ter	person
terred	group of people on a mission
terredar	leader of a terred
tharm	spirit or soul
tina	to bear
to	at
torsk	ichthyosaur
torskan	ichthyosaurs
torskanat	ichthyosaur's bone
ulfadan	long-beards
veigil	heavy, important
wedam	island

SESEK–ENGLISH

bansemnilla	marsupial carnivore
charadis	flax
Deifoben	place of the golden beaches
Kadair	sky god
Karognis	god of evil

mandukto	priest
porro	beer
tagaso	maize-corn
waliskis	mastodon

ANGURPIAQ–ENGLISH

NOUNS

angurpiaq	real people
erqigdlit	fantasy people
etat	forest
ikkergak	large boat
imaq	open sea
inge	vulva
munga	small fish, codling
nangeq	destination
paukarut	tent
qingik	house, shelter
qivio	path
qunguleq	arctic seaweed
takkuuk	poison
ularuaq	large aquatic mammal

VERBS

alutora	like
ardlerpa	hunt

ikagput	be many
liorpa	build
misugpa	eat
muluva	be absent
nagsoqipa	be equal, make no distinction
nakoyoark	be excellent
siagpai	be important
takugu	see
tingava	intercourse

AFFIXES

-adluinar	completely
-eetchuk	long ago
-guaq	inferior
-kaq	small
-luarpoq	too much
-qaq	quick
-taq	new-caught
-tamnagok	then, now, soon

ZOOLOGY

BANSEMNILLA
(Metatheria: Didelphys dimidiata)

A reddish-gray marsupial with three deep black bands down its back. It has a prehensile tail and opposable toes on its hind feet. It is carnivorous, favoring rats and mice, and is bred by the Sasku to eliminate these vermin from their corncribs.

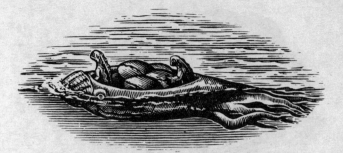

BOAT

(Cephalopoda: Archeololigo olcostephanus mutatus)

Yilanè surface water transport. Propulsion is obtained by a strong jet of water expelled to the stern. The creatures have only rudimentary intelligence like their ancestral squids, but can be trained to follow certain simple commands.

CLOAK
(Selachii: Elasmobranchus kappe mutatus)

Used by the Yilanè for warmth during the night or inclement weather. These creatures have absolutely no intelligence, but if they are well fed they will maintain a body temperature of approximately 102 degrees F.

D E E R
(Eutheria: Cervus mazama mazama)

A small deer with antlers as unbranched spikes. It is found in great numbers in the North Temperate Zone. The Tanu value these creatures both for their meat and their skins. The hides are tanned to make clothing and small leather articles (e.g. moccasins [*madrap*] and bags).

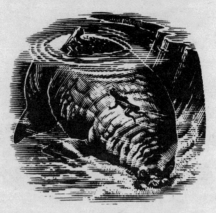

EISEKOL
(Eutheria: Trichecbus latirostris mutatus)

An herbivorous aquatic mammal which dredges for underwater plants in its original unaltered state. Gene manipulation has greatly increased the animal's size so that it can be utilized for underwater channel clearing, as well as dredging.

ELINOU

(Saurischia: Coelurosaurus compsognathus)

A small and agile dinosaur, much appreciated by the Yilanè for its pursuit and destruction of small mammalian vermin. Because of its colorful markings and complaisant nature it is often given the status of a pet.

ENTEESENAT
(Sauropterygia: Elasmosaurus plesiosaurus)

A predaceous marine reptile well adapted to pelagic life and relatively unchanged since the Cretaceous period. They have small short heads and long snake-like necks. The paddle-like flippers are similar to those of the marine turtle. Newer varieties have been developed with greater cranial capacity that enable them to be trained to supply food for the larger uruketo *(Ichthyosaurus monstrosus mutatus)*.

E P E T R U K
(Saurischia: Tyrannosaurus rex)

The largest and most powerfully armed of the great carnosaurs. Over forty feet long, the males weigh up to seven tons. The forearms are small but strong. Because of its great weight it is quite slow, therefore attacks only the largest animals. A large amount of its diet is obtained by driving smaller carnivores from their kill.

ESTEKEL*
(Pterosauria: Pterodactylus Quetzalcoatlus)

The largest of the flying reptiles with a wingspan of over thirty feet. The bones are very light and strong, while the weight of the immense toothed beak is balanced by the bony outcrop on the back of the skull. They are found solely at the mouths of large rivers since they can only become airborne in locations such as this where large waves run counter to the prevailing winds.

GREATDEER
(Eutheria: Alces machlis gigas)

The largest of all the deer. It is distinguished from other members of the *Cervidae* by the spread of the impressive antlers of the males. Hunted by the Tanu, not only for its meat, but for its hide which is preferred for use in covering their tents.

GULAWATSAN
(Ranidae: Dimorphognathus mutatus)

The application of gene-splitting for controlled mutation can be appreciated when the gulawatsan is examined closely. This was formerly a toothed frog, but the present form appears to have little resemblance to its forebears. Their powerful croaking, heard in tropical jungles during the mating season, has been enhanced and increased until the sound emitted is deafening in close proximity.

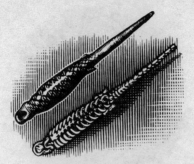

HÈSOTSAN
(Squamiata: Paravaranus comensualis mutatus)

This species of monitor lizard has been so modified that it now bears little resemblance to the original. Steam generating glands from *Brachinus* beetles violently project a dart which is poisoned when it passes over the sex organs of a commensal *Tetradontid* fish. This poison, the most deadly known, produces paralysis and death when as little as 500 molecules are present.

ISEKUL*
(Columbae: Columba palumbus)

This gentle bird presents an ideal example of Yilanè science at its most practical. Like many other species, this one uses magnetized iron particles in its forebrain to detect the Earth's magnetic field as an aid in navigation. Through selective breeding the isekul* will now point its head in any selected direction for long periods of time, until distracted by thirst or hunger.

LONGTOOTH
(Metatheria: Machaerodus neogeus)

Long-tusked member of the marsupial tiger family. A large and ferocious carnivore that uses its greatly extended upper canine teeth to bring down its prey. Some Kargu hunters have a commensal relationship with these beasts to aid them in hunting.

MASINDUU
(Anuva: Rana catesbiana mutatus mutatus)

The sanduu is an accepted laboratory creature for magnifying images up to 200 times. However it lacks versatility in that only one observer at a time can utilize it. The masinduu is a variation that permits the image to be projected onto any white surface to be viewed by two or more researchers.

MASTODON
(Eutheria: Mastodon americanus)

A large mammal noted for its long upper tusks. It has a prehensile trunk reaching to the ground. Its domestication by the Tanu permits them to cover great distances when hunting and foraging, using the mastodons to pull large travois.

NAEBAK
(Psittacosauria: Psittacosaurus)

One of the family of small "parrot lizards," so called because of their narrow, hornless head and sharp parrot-like beak used for biting through tough leaves and woody stems. They browse on all fours, but can run as well using only their strong back legs.

NENITESK
(Ornithischia: Triceratops elatus)

Herbivorous quadruped characterized by the possession of three horns set in a bony protective shield, unchanged since the Cretaceous period. They reproduce by laying eggs. Their brain capacity is small and their intelligence even smaller. Since they are slow growing they are of little use for meat supply, but are extremely decorative.

NESKHAK
(Gadus macrocephalus)

A mutated warm-water fish, adapted for varying conditions and altered so that the ambient water temperature can be measured by noting the color changes on the creature's sides.

NINKULILEB
(Archaeopteryx compsoghathus)

An intermediate form of development somewhere between birds and dinosaurs. Simple feathers, fingers at the wing tips, and a slim, toothed jaw make this creature distinctly different from both ancestors and possible descendants.

OKHALAKX
(Plateosauridia: Plateosaurus edibilus)

One of the largest of the "flat lizards," so called because of their solid bodies and strong skulls. Although these creatures normally walk on all fours they rear up on their hind legs to graze the tops of trees. Its flesh is considered particularly tasty and is much sought after.

ONETSENSAST
(Ornithischia: Stegosaurus variatus)

The largest of the plated dinosaurs. These immense herbivorous creatures are protected from attack by two rows of plates down the neck and back, as well as heavy spikes on the tail. They first developed in the late Jurassic period and only careful preservation by the Yilanè has prevented the destruction of this living fossil.

RUUTSA
(Ankylosauria: Euoplocephalus)

This giant creature is perhaps the most dramatic of the "living fossils" so carefully preserved by the Yilanè. Covered with great plates of armor, studded with spines, and protecting itself by the great ball at the end of its tail, it is hard to believe that it is a vegetarian and completely harmless, except in self-defense. This species has not changed in over one hundred million years.

SANDUU
(Anuva: Rana catesbiana mutatus)

Extensive gene manipulation has altered this animal in almost every way; only its outer skin reveals its origins. Magnification of up to 200 power is available by proper use of sunlight directed through the different organic lenses of its head.

SPIKE-BACK
(Nodosaurid anklyosaurus: Hylaeosaurus)

With small teeth and weak jaws, these harmless creatures graze on low-growing plants. Their only protection from predators is their flexible armor of bony slabs, plates and spikes, set in tough skin and sheathed with horn.

TARAKAST

(Ornithischia: Segnosaurus shiungisaurus mutatus)

A sharp-beaked carnivorous dinosaur, the largest examples being over thirteen feet in length. They are difficult to train and require great strength to manage, but when properly broken make a desirable Yilanè mount.

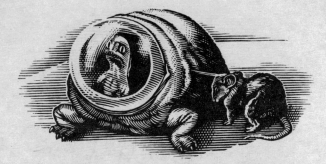

UGUNKSHAA

(Squamata: Phrynosoma fiernsyna mutatus)

Since the Yilanè language is dependent upon skin color and body movements, as well as sound, keeping written records is impossible; therefore writing has never developed. Historically knowledge was passed on verbally, and the recording of this information only became possible when an organic liquid crystal display was developed for visual accompaniment of the auditory memory records.

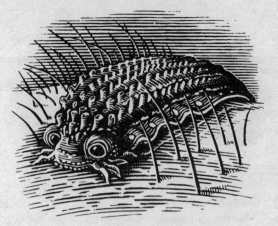

UNUTAKH

(Cephalopoda: Deroceras agreste mutatus)

One of the highly modified animals used in Yilanè technology. This cephalopod digests protein matter, especially hair and modified epidermal plates with ease.

URUKETO
(Ichthyopterygia: Ichthyosaurus monstrosus mutatus)

This is the largest of the "fish-lizards," a family of immense aquatic dinosaurs. Millennia of gene surgery and breeding have developed a strain of ichthyosaurs very different from the parent stock. There is a large chamber situated above the spine and centered on the dorsal fin that is used for both crew and cargo.

URUKTOP

(Chelonia: Psittacosaurus montanoceratops mutatus)

One of the most extensively modified of the Yilanè animals. Used for land transportation, it can carry heavy loads for great distances since after gene-doubling it has eight legs.

ACKNOWLEDGMENTS

In writing this novel I have sought the advice of experts in various fields. The biology of the Yilanè is the work of Dr. Jack Cohen. The Yilanè, Sasku, Paramutan and Tanu languages are the work of Prof. T.A. Shippey. The philosophy of the Daughters of Life was developed with the active collaboration of Dr. Robert E. Myers. This would have been a far different and lesser book without their help and advice. My gratitude to them is infinite.

About the Author

HARRY HARRISON is one of the most successful and respected authors of speculative fiction writing today. In a career that spans over three decades, Harry Harrison has written such novels as *Deathworld, To The Stars, Skyfall, Make Room! Make Room!* and bestsellers such as *West of Eden* and the *Stainless Steel Rat* series. Harrison worked as a commercial artist, art director and editor before turning to writing full time. A past president of the World Science Fiction Association, he is also a noted anthologist, editing the acclaimed Nova series and co-editing the highly praised *Decade* and *Year's Best SF* volumes with British author Brian Aldiss. Harry Harrison was born in Stamford, Connecticut, has made his home in Mexico and in several European countries over the years, and now lives in Ireland. He is presently at work on a new novel.

Special Offer
Buy a Bantam Book
for only 50¢.

Now you can have Bantam's catalog filled with hundreds of titles plus take advantage of our unique and exciting bonus book offer. A special offer which gives you the opportunity to purchase a Bantam book for only 50¢. Here's how!

By ordering any five books at the regular price per order, you can also choose any other single book listed (up to a $5.95 value) for just 50¢. Some restrictions do apply, but for further details why not send for Bantam's catalog of titles today!

Just send us your name and address and we will send you a catalog!